T. E Bridgett, Thomas Francis Knox

The true story of the Catholic hierarchy deposed by Queen Elizabeth

With fuller memoirs of its last two survivors

T. E Bridgett, Thomas Francis Knox

The true story of the Catholic hierarchy deposed by Queen Elizabeth
With fuller memoirs of its last two survivors

ISBN/EAN: 9783741189753

Manufactured in Europe, USA, Canada, Australia, Japa

Cover: Foto ©Andreas Hilbeck / pixelio.de

Manufactured and distributed by brebook publishing software
(www.brebook.com)

T. E Bridgett, Thomas Francis Knox

The true story of the Catholic hierarchy deposed by Queen Elizabeth

TABLE OF CONTENTS.

———⟨∞⟩———

PREFACE.

WHEN the violent and uncontrolled passions of Henry VIII. rose up against the unity of God's Church, only one member of the English Hierarchy was found faithful to his trust. Blessed John Fisher stood alone in his refusal to incur the guilt of schism. His blood, however, was not shed in vain; for when the policy of Henry's illegitimate daughter Elizabeth led her to break again with the Holy See, the divinely created centre of unity, and to involve the country once more in schism and heresy, of the whole Hierarchy only one member proved faithless. The rest imitated the constancy of Fisher, if not to martyrdom, yet to the endurance of deprivation, poverty, and imprisonment.

In a former book I have tried to state the authentic facts regarding the Martyr Bishop of Henry VIII.[1] I have here done the same for the Confessor Bishops of Elizabeth. The two books thus illustrate one subject—the glad obedience paid by the true guardians of God's Church to the civil power when acting within its divinely appointed sphere, and their resistance, at any cost to them-

[1] *Life of Blessed John Fisher* (Burns & Oates, 1888).

selves, to its encroachments and usurpations. The books, however, were not composed on a preconceived plan.

In 1876, I edited a volume of *Sermons on the Sacraments*, by Dr. Watson, last Catholic Bishop of Lincoln. In collecting the materials for a short memoir of the author, I was much struck by the strange misstatements regarding him and the other deprived bishops in almost all the books I examined, both Catholic and Protestant. Not one gave accurately the facts that I had made sure of from unpublished but authentic documents; and there had been a studious desire on the part of a long series of writers to deny, or conceal, or underrate the amount of suffering and persecution endured by the unflinching Catholic prelates.

Just at the same time the late Father Thomas F. Knox, of the London Oratory, published in *The Month* an interesting biography of another of the deprived bishops, Thomas Goldwell of St. Asaph's. Watson and Goldwell were the last survivors of the ancient Hierarchy, and their histories were in many respects a contrast. Watson's life was spent altogether in England, Goldwell's for the most part on the Continent. Watson was involved in Henry's schism, whereas Goldwell had passed his early manhood in communion with the Church. But while Watson proved the sincerity of his return by twenty-five years of imprisonment for the faith, Goldwell again managed to escape to Italy, and manifested his zeal in active labours and the observances of regular discipline as a Theatine. It

occurred to both Fr. Knox and myself that the
two lives, if reprinted together, would add interest
one to the other, especially if accompanied by some
general account of the sufferings and constancy of
the other members of the Hierarchy. We left the
matter for a future day, as we were both engaged in
other work, and since then the death of Fr. Knox
has thrown the duty of preparing this account upon
me. It has involved not only the examination of a
great number of printed books, but still more of
original manuscripts. The examination of printed
books has disclosed that very few of them could be
trusted. The contradictions and mistakes, not to
say misrepresentations, were gross and almost in-
numerable. But the Calendars of State Papers and
the Catalogues of MSS. in the British Museum
indicated many sources of authentic information,
of which I have availed myself. I have found, not
without some regret, that my narrative must necessarily be of a contentious character. It would have
been much more pleasant to have given the simple
facts of my story, leaving aside all controversy ; but
such a course would have been unavailing against
widespread mistakes and accepted historical myths.
It is easy to erect a house on open ground in the
country, but not so to build in an ancient city. The
ground has to be cleared, old buildings pulled down
and carted away, old foundations dug up, and old
sewers filled.

In thus finding fault with others I am, of course,
claiming accuracy and challenging verification myself. I cannot have escaped some minor incidental

mistakes, but as regards the substance of the following notes—the extent of the imprisonments of these victims of Queen Elizabeth's supremacy—I have no fear of refutation. Most of the documents quoted have been copied from the original MSS.; and even when they had been printed by Strype or others I have generally taken the precaution to verify their accuracy. Strype was laborious, but is by no means to be implicitly trusted. I have shown elsewhere the credulity of Strype in accepting certain gross forgeries, and, at the same time, his unfairness in seeking to accredit them by reference to documents he had never seen, and which, in fact, never existed.[1]

I have been able to supply several links of evidence, not merely from papers in the Public Record Office and the British Museum, but by extracts from the *Privy Council Registers*. For these last, as well as for much other help, my thanks are due to the kindness and indefatigable zeal of Miss Lambert, eldest daughter of the Right Hon. Sir John Lambert, K.C.B., member of Her Majesty's Privy Council, as well as to the courtesy of C. Lennox Peel, Esq., C.B., Secretary of the Council. I have also to thank R. T. Gunton, Esq., Private Secretary to the Marquis of Salisbury, for transcripts of the valuable and pathetic letter of Bishop Watson, and that of Horn, given at pp. 184-7. To the Rev. Joseph Stevenson, S.J., and the Rev. J. Morris I am indebted for the use of a transcript of Sanders' Report to Cardinal Morone of the things done in England at the acces-

---

[1] Letters in *The Tablet*, beginning 13th April, 1889.

sion of Elizabeth. This valuable document, still unprinted, and hitherto, I believe, unused, is in the *Secret Archives of the Vatican*, lxiv. 7-28, ff. 252-273. The report was written in the third year of Elizabeth, 1561.[1] Sanders tells what he had himself seen, and what he had ascertained from the relation of others. There are a few inaccuracies in his narrative, as there will always be if a man tries to write down from memory, and without the assistance of any documents, the public events of which he has been an eye-witness, or in which he has been an actor. He will not always observe the exact order of events, or may attribute to one a speech made by another. To anyone who shall write a full history of the Reformation this authentic report of Sanders will be indispensable.

Thus far as to the sources of my book. As regards its character it is purely historical. I do not discuss the deprivation of the bishops theologically or canonically. The righteousness of their cause I here presuppose. Their names have been long in oblivion, and their constancy but partially known even to the few. But God, who counts every hair on the heads of His martyrs, and every weary hour in the endurance of His confessors, to bestow a full and everlasting reward, has also in His providence preserved for our days the documents which, if properly known and weighed, should make them illustrious on earth.

But if the reader must not look here for a theological or a controversial treatise, neither must he

---

[1] " I will run over such things as have happened to us in the last two and a half years " (fol. 52).

expect to find a series of interesting biographies.
He will find the authentic records of a brave and
multiform endurance. Though the names of fifteen
confessors of the faith are here commemorated, of
two only have complete lives been even attempted.
Of the remainder, not the achievements but the
disappointments are recorded; not the labours of
their youth and manhood, but the privations and
sufferings of their maturity and old age. They were
zealously engaged in reorganising and re-establishing
the Catholic Church in England, when, by the death
of Queen Mary and the accession of the daughter
of Anne Boleyn, their labours were cut short and
exchanged for sufferings.

> " Alas !
> Vain earth ! false world ! Foundations must be laid
> In heaven, for 'mid the wreck of Is and Was,
> Things incomplete and purposes betrayed,
> Make sadder transit o'er truth's mystic glass,
> Than noblest objects utterly decayed."[1]

I have tried to put before the reader the story of
men who *had* laid the foundation of their work in
heaven, and, if I mistake not, their broken croziers
and empty thrones show more grandly in the glass
of truth than would their recumbent effigies, had
they been laid to rest with solemn rites in the aisles
of their cathedral churches. Their work was not
incomplete, because they preached their faith by
sufferings rather than by words; nor were their pur-
poses betrayed when they refused to betray the trust
which God and the Church had committed to them.

[1] Wordsworth, " Sonnet on Malham Cove ".

It is a sad history indeed, that of the overthrow of the re-erected Church in England, yet it is in some respects a bright and glorious one, as is the history of many a wreck, in which the officers perish heroically in their efforts to save the vessel and the crew.

I am aware that there are not biographical details sufficient to leave distinct impressions connected with each name that will be recorded; yet my purpose will be the more evident on that account. I have not chosen out of many centuries a number of the more illustrious English prelates, but have related the trial which at the same moment fell on a whole hierarchy, and how it was encountered. The lesson of their faith and charity will not be obscure, even though the reader may fail to keep distinct in his memory the special heroism of each. Among the "great cloud of witnesses" mentioned by St. Paul there were several of whom no inspired biography had been written. One heroic deed accomplished, one cruel death accepted for God, was in many instances all that the name recalled; yet the words of the Apostle ring in our ears: "They recovered from their infirmity, and became valiant in war . . . they had trial of mockeries and stripes, moreover also of bonds and prisons . . . they were approved by the testimony of faith ".[1]

T. E. BRIDGETT.

[1] *Heb.* xi.

CATHOLIC HIERARCHY.

CHAPTER I.

MISREPRESENTATION AND IGNORANCE.

THE deposition of a whole Hierarchy by the civil power, as it is one of the most important acts in English history, ought to be most fully and accurately recorded by historians. Yet there is probably no great event to which so little attention has been given, or with regard to which so many errors are current. One after another our historians, both Protestant and Catholic, have been satisfied to reproduce almost the very words of Camden and Lord Burghley, without an attempt to test or verify their assertions. Yet those writers were both mere partisans of Elizabeth, and on this subject, at least, they practised deliberate suppression of the truth, while half their statements are not only inaccurate, but false, as may be proved by unimpeachable documents. The object of this sketch is to correct these misrepresentations by an accurate narrative of facts. I shall in this chapter reproduce the accounts which have been considered authoritative, merely noting falsehoods and omissions, but reserving the proofs.

Lord Burghley comes first, both in time and in importance. He also wrote more cautiously, as being nearer to those who were well informed. His book, called *Execution*

I

of Justice in England, written in reply to Allen's *Apology, or Defence of the Jesuits and Seminarists,* appeared in 1583, and was published in several languages. Its purpose was to convince the world that the English martyrs had been put to death for treason, not for religion. One of his arguments is that the deposed bishops, who professed the same religion, were neither put to death nor persecuted.

"Though there are many subjects known in the realm, that differ in some opinions of religion from the Church of England, and that do also not forbear to profess the same, yet in that they do also profess loyalty and obedience to Her Majesty, and offer readily in Her Majesty's defence to impugn and resist any foreign force, though it should come or be procured from the Pope himself, none of these sort are for their contrary opinions in religion prosecuted or charged with any crimes or pains of treason, nor yet willingly searched in their consciences for their contrary opinions, that savour not of treason. And of these sorts there have been and are a number of persons, not of such base and vulgar note as those were which of late have been executed, as, in particular, some by name are well known, and not unfit to be remembered. The first and chiefest by office was D. Heath, that was Archbishop of York and Lord Chancellor of England in Queen Mary's time, who, at the first coming of Her Majesty to the crown, showing himself a faithful and quiet subject, continued in both the said offices, though in religion then manifestly differing, and yet was he not restrained of his liberty, nor deprived of his proper lands and goods, but leaving willingly both his offices, lived in his own house very discreetly, and enjoyed all his purchased lands during all his natural life, until by very age he departed this world, and then left his house and living to his friends—an example of gentleness never matched in Queen Mary's time. The like did one D. Pool, that had been Bishop of Peterborough, an ancient, grave person, and a very quiet subject. There were also others that had been bishops, and in great estimation, as D. Tunstall, Bishop of Durham, a person of great reputation, and also whilst he lived of very quiet behaviour. There were also others—D. White and D. Oglethorpe, one of Winchester, the other of Carlisle, Bishops, persons of courteous natures; and he of Carlisle so inclined to dutifulness to the Queen's Majesty, as he did the office at the consecration and coronation of Her Majesty in the Church of Westminster; and D. Thurleby and D. Watson, yet living, one of Ely, the other of Lincoln, Bishops—the one of nature affable, the other altogether sour, and yet living. Whereto may be added the Bishop (then) of Exeter, Turberville, an honest gentleman, but a simple Bishop, who lived at his own liberty to the end of his life, and none of all these pressed with any capital pain, though they maintained the Pope's authority against the laws of the realm; and some abbots, as M. Feckenam, yet living, a person also of quiet and courteous behaviour for a great time. Some also were deans, as D. Boxall, Dean of Windsor, a person of great modesty, learning, and knowledge; D. Cole, Dean of Paul's, a person more earnest than discreet; D. Reynolds, Dean of Exeter, not unlearned; and many such others having borne office and dignities in the Church, and that had made profession against the Pope, which they only began in Queen Mary's time to change; yet were these never to this day burdened with capital pains, nor yet deprived of any of their goods or proper livelihoods, but only removed from their ecclesiastical offices, which they would not exercise according to the laws. And most of them, and many others of their sort, for a great time were retained in bishops' houses in very civil and courteous manner, without charge to themselves or their friends, until the time that the Pope began, by his bulls and messages, to offer trouble to the realm, by stirring of rebellion; about which time only some of these aforenamed, being found busier in matters of State, tending to stir troubles, than was meet for the common quiet of the realm, were removed, to other more private places, where such other wanderers as were men known to move sedition might be restrained from common resorting to them to increase trouble, as the Pope's bull gave manifest occasion to doubt; and yet without charging them in their consciences or otherwise by any inquisition to bring them into danger of any capital law, so as no one was called to any capital or bloody question upon matters of religion, but have all enjoyed their life as the course of nature would; and such of them as yet remain may, if they will not be authors or instruments of rebellion or sedition, enjoy the time that God and nature shall yield them without danger of life or member."[1]

The main assertion here of Lord Burghley—that the deposed bishops were neither slaughtered nor maimed—is doubtless true;[2] but the assertion that because they were peaceable subjects they were allowed to live quiet and peaceable lives is altogether false. He does not in so many words deny their imprisonment; yet, by allowing that there was just so far an exception to their perfect freedom—that they were at one period the quasi-guests of Elizabeth's hospitable bishops, and by the declaration that they "all *enjoyed* their life as the course of nature would"—he utterly excludes the notion of real imprisonment. Who could possibly have guessed from his words that Watson of Lincoln had already spent four-and-twenty years in confinement; Thirlby of Ely nearly eleven; Bonner of London ten; Bourne of Bath and Wells, Turberville of Exeter,

---

[1] From Reprint in Somers' *Tracts*, vol. i., p. 192. (Ed. 1809.)

[2] Watson's loss of sight and sciatica through imprisonment come, however, very near to maiming.

Scott of Chester, Pate of Worcester, and Heath of York—
more than three? Who could have gathered that the
"courteous" White of Winchester was kept in the Tower
till he contracted a deadly sickness, and was then sent to
his brother's house to die?—that Tunstall of Durham, notwithstanding his "high reputation and quiet behaviour," was
confined in Parker's house till his death?—and that the
liberty of Poole of Peterborough consisted in ranging
within three miles of London? Yet these things are facts
that I shall presently prove. They were known to be facts
by Lord Burghley, since he was the chief author of them.

Camden, the royal historiographer, wrote thirty years later,[1]
yet he could have told the truth if he would. All document—even the records of the Privy Council—were acces-
sible to him. Besides several positive mis-statements, he has
adopted, like Lord Burghley, the two forms of deceit—
suppression of the truth, and suggestion of what is false.
He makes a general eulogy of the old bishops, as if to
display his candour, and then lets the reader conclude that
if such men were, for necessary reasons of State, deprived of
office, they were at all events treated with eminent courtesy.

"As many as refused to swear," he writes, "were turned
out of their livings, dignities, and bishoprics . . . and
fourteen bishops, being all which then sat, saving only
Anthony, Bishop of Llandaff, to the calamity of his see,
namely, *Nicholas Heath*, Archbishop of York, who of late
had voluntarily given over his office of Chancellor, and
lived securely many years, serving God and following his
studies in his manor of Cobham, in Surrey, being in such
great grace with the Queen that she visited him many times
with marvellous kindness.

"*Edmund Bonner*, Bishop of London, one that had been
employed in embassies to the Emperor, the Bishop of

[1] The first part of the *Annals* appeared in 1615.

Rome, and the French King, but with his authority had joined such a sourness of nature that amongst all men he underwent the note of cruelty, and was kept in prison a great part of his life." He was, as Camden well knew, kept in prison from his deposition till his life's end, and surely "sourness of nature" is no just ground for imprisonment, nor is "note of cruelty," unless maladministration of law were brought home as a legal offence, which it never was. Camden continues his enumeration : " *Cuthbert Tunstall*, Bishop of Durham, a man passing well seen in all kind of more polished literature, having run through many degrees of honour at home, and worthily performed embassies abroad, who, being a young man, sharply impugned the Pope's primacy in a long epistle to Cardinal Pole, and, being an old man, died at Lambeth in free custody ".

Free custody (*libera custodia*) is a happy expression, like clean dirtiness or cold warmth : whether it was a happy state we will consider later on.

"At Lambeth, also," continues Camden, " *Thirlby*, Bishop of Ely, let his life, having gotten great commendation of wisdom by an embassy to Rome, about tendering obedience to the See of Rome, and by the treaty of Cambray ". For his wisdom, instead of "commendation," he received at the hands of Elizabeth nearly four years' imprisonment in the Tower, and seven with Matthew Parker. It was more convenient for Camden to slur this over. He also passes in silence the three years' prison of " *Gilbert Bourne*, Bishop of Bath and Wells," merely saying, "who had deserved well of his see". Next come "*John Christopherson*, Bishop of Chichester, who, being a very learned Grecian, most faithfully translated much of Eusebius and Philo for the use of Christendom ; *John White*, Bishop of Winchester, meanly[1]

---

[1] "Meanly" seems to be equivalent to "fairly well "—in orig., *vulgariter doctus*.

learned and a tolerable poet, as those times afforded; *Thomas Watson*, Bishop of Lincoln, learned in deep divinity, but surly with an austere gravity". This is very unfair of Camden. The only surliness in Watson was his patient endurance, for conscience' sake, of twenty-five years' hardship in prison. He goes on: "*Ralph Bayne*, Bishop of Coventry and Lichfield, who was a second restorer of the Hebrew tongue, and the King's professor thereof at Paris, when good letters reflourished under Francis the First; *Owen Ogelthorpe*, Bishop of Carlisle; *James Turberville*, Bishop of Exeter; *David Pole*, Bishop of Peterborough—these men were first sent to prison, but most of them were shortly after committed to the custody of their friends or of bishops, save two that were more perverse, namely, Lincoln and Winchester, who threatened to excommunicate the Queen. But three—namely, *Cuthbert Scott* of Chester, *Richard Pate* of Worcester, *Thomas Goldwell* of St. Asaph—voluntarily departed the land."[1] In this passage Camden says the number was fourteen, and then goes on to name fifteen. Even so he is wrong, for he puts in the list Christopherson, who was dead, and omits Bishop Morgan, of St. David's. He next distinguishes between those sent to prison and others who left England. Goldwell alone escaped to the Continent without imprisonment. He says that *shortly after* they were delivered from prison. Now Tunstall, Bayne, White, Ogelthorpe, and Morgan died within a few months. All the rest, except Poole, endured not months but years of imprisonment in jails, before the modified restraint afterwards conceded to some.

These words, "shortly after," have been constantly interpreted to mean "after a few days or weeks," and were no doubt intended thus to be understood. Burnet, Speed,

[1] Camden's *Annals*, transl. by R. N. (*i.e.*, Norton), p. 17. London, 1635.

Heylin, Fuller, Strype, Collier, repeat what Burghley and
Camden had told them, each endeavouring to soften the lot
of the deposed bishops more and more. It is not necessary
here to transcribe their general account. Any special misstatement shall be noticed in its place. From these the
tradition has come down to our own day. The following is
the account given by the late Dean Hook: "It reflects
great credit upon the Primate," he writes, in his life of
Parker, "and upon Elizabeth's government in general, that,
notwithstanding their dissent, the deprived prelates were
treated with the greatest consideration and kindness. Parker
was very lenient in pressing the oath of supremacy. Heath,
the Archbishop of York, being a man of fortune, lived at
his own private house at Chobham, within four miles of
Windsor, and at his residence he frequently received visits
from the Queen. Bishop Thirlby lived with Parker, both at
Lambeth and at Bekesbourne, the archiepiscopal residence
near Canterbury. He did not die till 26th August, 1570,
and, according to Bishop Godwin, he found more happiness
—though nominally under restraint—during this period of
his life than he had done heretofore in the midst of the
fullest stream of his highest honours.[1] On his death, the
Archbishop had him decently buried within the chancel of
the parish church of Lambeth, where a fair stone was laid
upon his grave. Dr. Tunstall, the ex-Bishop of Durham,
and Parker had long been friends, and the friendship was
not disturbed by differences of opinion.

"The plan adopted with the recusant bishops was to
quarter them upon one of the conforming prelates; and, as
was the case with Parker, the prelate upon whom this duty
was imposed permitted his prisoner, if he was to be so
accounted, to live as one of the family. The custodian was

[1] Godwin's assertion is an empty flourish of a man who knew
nothing on the subject.

only responsible for the prelate under his care, that he should not leave the country. 'These prelates,' says Fuller, 'had sweet chambers, soft beds, warm fires, plentiful and whole-some diet, each bishop faring like an archbishop, differing nothing from their former living, saving *that* was on their own charges, and *this* at the cost of another.'[1] Something must have depended, of course, upon the temper of the host, and something also on that of the compulsory guest. . . . Bishop Bonner was a low, coarse, vulgar man. He was at first quartered on the Bishop of Lincoln, but made himself so disagreeable that, at last,[2] he was placed within the rules of the Marshalsea prison; that is, he was permitted to occupy within a prescribed circuit a house of his own, being restrained from passing beyond certain boundaries. The bishops thus accommodated conformed more or less to the new order of things, but to this Dr. White and Dr. Watson could not conscientiously submit. Watson was at first committed to the custody of Grindal, Bishop of London, and afterwards to that of Cox, Bishop of Ely. Instead, however, of meeting courteous treatment with courtesy, Watson was found 'preaching against the State,'[3] and it was deemed necessary to place him under closer restraint. Wisbeach Castle was assigned to him for a resi-dence, and there, in 1584, he died."[4]

Later on Dr. Hook writes: "The consideration, kind-ness, and marked humanity evinced by Parker in all his dealings with these distinguished and unfortunate person-ages may be fairly produced as telling in his favour, and as

[1] What could Fuller know about their beds and diet ?

[2] He was never quartered on the Bishop of Lincoln. His making making himself disagreeable is, therefore, an amiable fancy of the Dean's.

[3] This has not a shadow of foundation.

[4] *Life of Parker*, p. 259.

proving him to be—what he really was—a kind-hearted
man.   And the praise which is due to him must be shared
by Elizabeth and her government, and the more so when
we call to mind the rude and heartless manner in which the
laws against heresy were enforced by such coarse-minded
men as Bonner, in the reign of Queen Mary." [1]   As regards
these last words of Dean Hook, I am at a loss as to their
meaning.   Where is the basis of comparison between two
things altogether different?   The treatment of heretics may
have been severe or heartless in the reign of Mary, but
what has that to do with the treatment of bishops, who were
neither guilty of heresy nor accused of it, nor punished for
heartlessness towards heretics, nor deposed for any canonical
cause, nor accused of any crime but that of fidelity to what
had been honoured in England for a thousand years?   Yet
another modern writer, Canon Perry, in his sketch of the
Reformation in England, begins his account of the treatment of the deposed bishops by the triumphant boast:
"There were no retaliatory burnings".[2]   There is little
excuse for the gross ignorance of Dean Hook on a
subject he was bound to investigate carefully, after having
undertaken to write, in the fullest detail, the lives of the
Archbishops of Canterbury.   Since his main contention is to
prove that those who preceded and those who followed the
Reformation form one unbroken series, it belonged essen-
tially to his subject to discover and record accurately the
resistance made by the ancient hierarchy to the new
doctrines and discipline, and the treatment of the bishops

---

[1] *Life of Parker*, p. 541.

[2] This author has managed to compress into a few paragraphs every
error of his predecessors, and I could hardly draw up a better list of
statements to be examined and refuted than by transcribing this page
of a handbook, provided under high sanction, for the correct and
scientific teaching of history, in 1886.

after their deposition. Yet he seems to have consulted no original documents, and with the exception of the limits placed upon Bonner's movements, and the last transfer of Watson to Wisbeach, he knows nothing of imprisonments.

A still more surprising instance of ignorance on this subject is to be found in some words of Dr. Jessopp. "Of the deprived bishops all, except Scott, Bishop of Chichester, and Goldwell, of St. Asaph, who slipped away across the Channel, were suffered to remain unmolested, though under surveillance, and, as far I know, absolutely unprovided for." [1] Dr. Jessopp is treating of later matters, and was not bound by his subject to make any special research into the fate of the bishops. Yet this statement of a writer so well informed in history, and who delights, above all things, in accuracy, serves to gauge the general ignorance on this matter. Yet Dr. Jessopp, even when writing a rapid review, should not call Scott Bishop of Chichester, instead of Chester, nor omit the name of Pate of Worcester, if he mentions those who left England. He might, too, have known something of the prisons of Watson and Bonner, even if he had never heard of the shorter confinements of so many others, which I shall presently notice.

Even Catholic writers came to acquiesce in the accuracy of the Protestant tradition regarding Elizabeth's gentle courtesy. The early writers knew better, though they had no means of examining records; but when Strype was bold enough to "doubt whether any of the bishops were imprisoned after deprivation," and accused "Protestants of taking on credit what Popish authors wrote," [2] Catholics became afraid lest there had been some exaggeration, and, having no means of learning the truth, thought it better to follow their Protestant teachers. Charles Butler, one of the best informed

---

[1] *One Generation of a Norfolk House*, p. 72.

[2] *Annals*, vol. i., part i., p. 206.

men of his day in Catholic affairs, summed up his knowledge
of the fate of the bishops in the following short paragraph.
After stating that *sixteen* bishops refused the oath of
supremacy and were displaced and imprisoned, he adds :
" But the imprisonment was gently managed, and the greater
part of them were left prisoners at large.   Some were permitted to cross the seas and died abroad.   In consequence
of some real or alleged imprudence, Watson of Lincoln was
placed in strict confinement in Wisbeach Castle ; he appears
to have been the only prelate against whom the Government proceeded with severity." [1]   Every word in this
paragraph is incorrect.   No one was *permitted* to cross the
sea, though three escaped, two of whom had previously
endured years of imprisonment in the Tower.   But I need
not anticipate.   I have shown cause for reopening this
subject.   My purpose, however, is not to re-write such parts
of this history as have been accurately related, but to fill up
some omissions and correct some mis-statements.   After a
general account of the action of the bishops on the accession
of Elizabeth, and of their deprivation and heroic constancy
under persecution, I shall trace the history of each in the
chronological order of their deaths.

[1] *Historical Memoirs of the English Catholics*, vol. iii., 142. —
Lingard was not so easily misled.   He says that the bishops " were
objects of persecution, with perhaps one exception, as long as they
lived ".   I will not give the whole passage, because it contains some
errors, but it merely *under*states the amount of the persecution.

NOTE TO CHAPTER I.

Perhaps the worst offender of all is Mr. S. Hubert Burke, since he has in the third volume of his *Historical Portraits* a chapter on the Marian Bishops, and makes profession of a special study of his subject. Among the deposed bishops of 1559, he places Dr. Day of Chichester, who died in August, 1556; he tells us that the Bishops of Winchester and Lincoln were committed to the Tower at the close of the Westminster Conference for not taking the oath of supremacy, though the Act of Supremacy was not then passed; that Dr. Watson of Lincoln was confined in Wisbeach Castle for twenty-four years, whereas his imprisonment there was only of four years' duration; that Queen Elizabeth sent Bishop Thirlby of Ely as her ambassador into Scotland, which is of course quite untrue; that Bishop Kitchin of Llandaff supported the Bill of Uniformity in Parliament, and was one of the four consecrators of Parker, two assertions which the slightest reference to books would have shown him to be false. These and many other fables he affirms, on the authority of writers, of whom all that can be said is that their MSS. and their names were known only to himself. He interprets the well-known clause "benefit of clergy" to mean the right to be assisted by the clergy before execution, and to receive the sacraments, and complains that the bishops were treated like murderers and outlaws, being denied the benefit of clergy and "the rights of all religious consolation at the hour of death," and this too though not one of them was executed! I have not cared to examine Mr. Burke's volumes beyond this chapter.

CHAPTER II.

QUEEN MARY died 17th November, 1558, at St. James's, and on the same day, at Lambeth, died her relative and faithful friend, Cardinal Reginald Pole, Archbishop of Canterbury. A few days later, his friend and executor, Monsignor Luigi Priuli, wrote to his brother in Venice : " On the 17th instant, seven hours after midnight, the Queen passed from this life, and my Most Reverend Lord followed her at seven o'clock on the evening of the same day ".[1] On 10th December, the same day on which Queen Mary's funeral began in Westminster, the Cardinal's body was carried towards Canterbury. Bishops Pate of Worcester and Goldwell of St. Asaph's, by desire of Priuli and consent of the Queen, attended the funeral. Thus the Hierarchy was deprived of its leader and head.

---

[1] For Priuli's letter see *Report upon the Documents in the Archives of Venice*, by T. D. Hardy (1866), p. 59 ; or *Calendar of Venetian State Papers*, vi., part iii., n. 1287-1292. Priuli, as an eye-witness, is of course correct, and Sanders, in his letter to Cardinal Morone, writes that the Queen and Cardinal were removed in one day. It is curious, however, how many variations there are regarding the date of Pole's death. Machyn in his *Diary* says that he died " the 19th, between 5 and 6 in the morning " (p. 178). Philipps and Strype, Lemon, Spencer Hall, and Kennett, all put his death on the 18th ; and Cecil, who was in or about London at the time, enters his death on the 18th in his *Memoria Mortuorum*, and also in his notes on Elizabeth's reign (Murdin, *State Papers*, 745, 747). As Pole died in the evening of the 17th, no doubt the news only got out on the 18th.

The dioceses of Oxford, Salisbury, Bangor, Gloucester, and Hereford were vacant by the recent deaths of their occupants. Dr. Maurice Clenock had been nominated to Bangor, Dr. Thomas Reynolds to Hereford, Dr. Francis Mallett to Salisbury, and Dr. Thomas Wood to St. Asaph's, in place of Dr. Goldwell, translated to Oxford. Some of these appointments had not been confirmed by the Pope, and all were set aside by Elizabeth. These men, by their subsequent sufferings in English prisons, or labours in exile, showed themselves worthy of the choice that had been made of them ; but as they were not in possession of their sees, I do not here undertake their history.

Before the end of the year 1558 four more dioceses became vacant. Maurice Griffin of Rochester died 20th November, John Hopton of Norwich, John Christopherson of Chichester, and John Holyman of Bristol in December. Of these it is not necessary to say anything here. They died in communion with the Catholic Church, and in possession of their sees. Thus, then, at the opening of the year 1559, of the whole English Hierarchy[1] only sixteen bishops survived.[2] No one of the bishops had made any opposition whatever to the accession of Elizabeth. All who were in London hastened to meet her and kiss her hand. Yet Elizabeth and some of her friends had made up their minds to an " alteration in religion ". A document of Sir

---

[1] There is a mystery about the date of the death of the Bishop of Man (lately united to the Province of York) which I have been unable to clear up. Mr. Lea has carefully discussed the matter in his *Succession of Spiritual Jurisdiction in the Church of England*, yet he has not solved all the difficulties.

[2] There were also in the country several suffragan bishops, with whose subsequent history I am not here concerned. One of them at least lived and died a staunch Catholic, Robert Pursglove, about whom there is much to tell. But I confine my notes to the Hierarchy.

William Cecil or Sir Thomas Smith is still in existence, in which the full scheme is drawn out in detail.[1]   Until things were ripe, the Holy Mass was to continue, and no innovation to be allowed.   "As for Her Highness' conscience till then, if there be some other devout sort of prayer or memory and the seldomer Mass."   The plotter anticipated that "bishops and all the clergy will see their own ruin.   In confession and preaching they will persuade the people from it.   They will conspire with whosoever will attempt, and pretend to do God a sacrifice in letting the alteration, though it be with murder of Christian men and treason."   To counteract these supposed dangers it was proposed that "the bishops and clergy, being all made and chosen such as were thought the stoutest and mightiest champions of the Pope's Church . . . these Her Majesty, being inclined to use much clemency, yet must seek, as well by Parliament as by the just laws of England, in the *præmunire* and other such penal laws, to bring again in order ; and being found in the default, not to pardon, till they confess their fault, put themselves wholly to Her Highness' mercy, abjure the Pope of Rome, and conform themselves to the new alteration.   And by these means well handled, Her Majesty's necessity of money may be somewhat relieved."

The change that was thus sketched soon came to be suspected, partly from Elizabeth's well-known opinions, partly from the men with whom she was seen in consultation, and partly from some of her own acts and words. The imprisonment of the Bishop of Chichester in the Tower for his sermon, and the confinement of the Bishop of Winchester in his own house for his funeral sermon on

[1] It is printed in Strype, and in Tierney's *Dodd*, vol. ii., Appendix 33 ; and more correctly in Mr. Pocock's edition of *Burnet*, vol. v., p. 327.

Queen Mary,[1] were no doubt intended as warnings. An eye-witness thus describes what happened on Christmas Day, 1558 : " This night I came home late from London, and for news you shall understand that yesterday, being Christmas Day, the Queen's Majesty repaired to her great closet, with her nobles and ladies, as hath been accustomed at such high feasts, and she perceived a bishop preparing himself to Mass, all in the old form, she tarried there until the Gospel was done ; and when all the people looked for her to have offered, according to the old fashion, she, with her nobles, returned again from the closet and the Mass unto her privy chamber, which was strange unto divers ".[2] Two days afterwards came out a proclamation forbidding all preaching and all alteration in ceremonies " until consultation might be had in Parliament by Her Majesty and her three estates of the realm ".

Knowing then what was coming, the bishops all refused to perform the ceremony of the coronation. Cardinal Allen, writing twenty-four years later of their conduct at this period, says : " Whose courage and resistance for quarrel of God's religion was such in them, and specially in the said Archbishop" [Heath of York], "that he worthily, as became his excellency, refused to anoint or crown the Queen's Majesty that now is . . . and so did all the rest of the bishops refuse the same, until with much ado they obtained the Bishop of Carlisle, the inferior almost of all the rest, to do that function. . . . The cause why they durst not then, nor could be adduced by any human fear or authority to invest her was, that they had evident probabilities and arguments to doubt that she meant either not to take the oath, or not to keep the same, which all Christian kings (and

[1] This will be mentioned later on, in the particular account of that bishop.

[2] Sir William Fitzwilliam, *apud* Ellis *Orig. Lett.*, ii. 262.

specially ours in England) do make in the coronation, for maintenance of Holy Church's laws, honours, peace, and privileges, and other duties due to every state, as in the time and grant of King Edward the Confessor. They doubted also lest she should refuse, in the very time of her sacre, the solemn divine ceremony of unction." [1]

Sanders, in his letter to Cardinal Morone, written in 1561, thus relates the matter: "The Archbishop refused the function, having understood that, in some respects, it was intended to perform the ceremony in a schismatical manner. Many other of the bishops also refused, but at length the Bishop of Carlisle undertook it, not as a favourer of heresy, but lest the Queen should be angry if no one would anoint her, and so have a better excuse for overthrowing religion. Nor at this time were things so desperate, but that some hoped it might still be possible to turn her from her purpose. The rest of the bishops assisted at the anointing." [2] This presence of several bishops at the ceremony is confirmed by Machyn in his *Diary*, [3] and by the detailed account in Nichol's *Royal Progresses*. The Queen found it easy, on this occasion, to take the required oath, and to conform with, or at least to endure, all the Catholic ceremonial, including the Unction, the Pontifical Mass, and the Communion.

In execution of her secret plan, the Queen soon began to remove Catholics from places of trust. Archbishop Heath had voluntarily resigned the Chancellorship as soon as he could after her accession; and, in February, 1559, Bishop Bourne, of Bath and Wells, was deprived of the Presidency of Wales. [4] She had promised, in her proclamation of 27th

---

[1] Allen's *Answer to English Justice*, p. 60.

[2] Vatican MS., f. 258, trans. from Latin.

[3] Machyn, p. 187.

[4] See later, under their names.

December, to consult her three estates, but she had no intention whatever of listening to the estate of the clergy,[1] whether in Parliament or Convocation. It will not be necessary here to enter at any length into the history of Elizabeth's first Parliament. I do not wish to re-write what may be found accurately stated in ordinary histories, and on this subject there was no room for mistake, since both in the Journal of the House of Lords and in the collection of D'Ewes, the presence and action of each bishop is stated. It is enough to make a brief summary.

The Parliament began on Wednesday, 25th January, 1559, and was dissolved on Monday, 8th May, following. The Bishops of Durham (Tunstall), Peterborough (Poole), Bath and Wells (Bourne), and St. David's (Morgan), were not present. All of them appointed the Archbishop of York (Heath) as proxy, with others, in case of his absence. The Bishop of Lincoln (Watson) was also absent through sickness.[2] The Bishop of Ely (Thirlby) was on an embassy in France, but took his place in Parliament on his return in April. He also had appointed the Archbishop to be his proxy. The Bishop of St. Asaph's (Goldwell) had not received his writ.[3] Sir Nicolas Bacon, the Lord Keeper, in his opening speech, declared that "the good King Hezekiah had no greater desire to amend what was amiss in his time, nor the noble Queen Hester a better heart to overthrow the mighty enemies of God's elect, than our Sovereign Lady and Mistress hath to do that " [*i.e.*, what]

---

[1] The three estates are, of course, the Clergy, the Peers, and the Commons. See Stubbs, *Const. History*, vol. ii., ch. xv., who remarks that "a pious courtesy gave the first place to the clergy" (p. 168).

[2] I find no mention of his proxy. He probably expected his illness to abate, so as to allow of his presence.

[3] He had asked for leave of absence; but mentions that he had received no writ (*Domestic Eliz.*, i. 52).

"may be just and acceptable in God's sight". This was ambiguous ; but there was no ambiguity in the bills brought into Parliament. They are well known—a bill for the restitution and annexation of first fruits to the Crown, one for the supremacy of the Crown and abolition of all foreign jurisdiction, one for conformity of common prayer and administration of sacraments, certain bills detrimental to the temporal interests of the Church, and one for restoring the Queen in blood. To this last no opposition was offered by any bishop.[1] To all the others they made a united and vigorous resistance, but without effect.

The Bishop of Llandaff, who afterwards weakly yielded by taking the oath of supremacy, opposed the imposition of the oath in all the stages of the Bill and in the final division on 29th April.

In opposing the Supremacy Bill, the Archbishop of York said : " If by this relinquishing of the See of Rome there were none other matter than a withdrawing of our obedience from the Pope's person, Paul, the fourth of that name, which hath declared himself to be a very austere, stern father to us, ever since his first entrance into Peter's chair, then the cause were not of such great importance, as it is in very deed, when, by the relinquishing and forsaking of the See of Rome, we must forsake and flee from these four things : 1st, all general councils ; 2nd, all canonical and ecclesiastical laws of the Church of Christ ; 3rd, the judgment of all other Christian princes ; and 4th, we must forsake and flee the unity of the Christian Church, and by leaping out of St. Peter's ship, hazard ourselves to be overwhelmed and drowned in the waters of schism, sects, and divisions".

----

[1] " Billa communi omnium procerum assensu conclusa est," says the Lords' Journal.

He then goes on to prove these four points, and afterwards considers the nature of the supremacy, and that it neither belonged to Parliament to give, nor could a king, much less a queen, receive it.[1]

The speech of the Bishop of Chester (Cuthbert Scott) has also been preserved. He develops the necessity of unity, using the ordinary texts and arguments in defence of the supremacy of St. Peter and his successors, the bishops of Rome. He mentions that there were already " thirty-four sundry sects in Christendom ". He replies to certain objections :. " There is alleged," he says, " a provincial council or assembly of the bishops and clergy of this realm of England " [the convocation of 1534] " by which the authority of the Bishop of Rome was abolished and disallowed. But, first, a particular or provincial council can make no determination against the universal Church of Christ. Secondly, of the learned men that were the doers there, so many as be dead, before they died, were penitent, and cried God mercy for their act ; and those that do live, as all your lordships do know, hath openly revoked the same, acknowledging their error."

He then objects that such waverers cannot be trusted. He replies : " He which once has run so hastily or rashly that he hath overthrown himself and fallen and broken his brow or his shin, will after that take heed to walk more warily, as we have seen by the Apostles of Our Saviour Christ, which did all forsake Him and run away when He was apprehended by the Jews, and specially by St. Peter, which did thrice deny Him. And yet after, as well Peter as all the rest of the Apostles, did return again to their Master,

[1] This speech is clearly genuine. It was probably written out by Heath. Strype has printed it from Fox's MS. and Parker's *Synodalia*, C.C.C.C.; *Annals*, vol. i., part ii., p. 399. Also vol. i., part i., p. 107, where he defends its genuineness against Burnet.

Christ, and never would after, for neither persecution nor
death, forsake or deny Him any more." In these last
words, Scott answers beforehand the sneer of Burnet and
others, who make much of the unworthy yielding of some
of these bishops under Henry VIII., and explain their
constancy under Elizabeth, either as mere obstinacy, caused
by shame, or temporising in the hope of a change.[1]

The same Bishop Scott made another speech against the
new liturgy, which has also been preserved. One of the
preceding speakers had lamented the blindness of his
Popish forefathers. Scott replied, that if those forefathers could appear, they would say—" Nolite flere super
me sed super vos et filios vestros " (Weep not for me, but for
yourselves and for your children). He warned them of
the frightful account they would render to God if they not
only erred themselves, but caused a whole realm to err, and
that, in their ignorance of Divine things, they were in the
greatest danger of thus doing.[2]

I must now turn from Parliament to Convocation. It is
not necessary, however, to recite here at length what will be
found in every history—the five articles of a profession of
faith, drawn up by the Lower House, and presented by
them on the 17th February, 1559, to the bishops. The
first three regard the Blessed Sacrament of the altar, the
last the exclusive right of the pastors of the Church to
determine matters of faith and of ecclesiastical discipline.
The fourth was as follows: " The supreme power of
feeding and governing the militant Church of Christ, and
of confirming his brethren, was given to St. Peter, the
Apostle, and to his legitimate successors in the Apostolic

---

[1] Mr. Froude attributes their " fierce doggedness " to their hopes
of being reinstated by Philip (*History*, i. 91). Yet when all possible
hope was gone, they were just as " fierce," or firm.

[2] Strype, *Annals*, i. 448.

See, as Vicars of Christ". On the 28th February, the bishops promised to present these articles to the Upper House of Parliament the very next day (1st March). On the 10th March, the Bishop of London informed the Convocation that a copy of these articles had been forwarded to each of the Universities, and that all the articles, except the last, had been subscribed by those bodies. The Bishop of London, as President of Convocation, presented the articles to the Lord Keeper (Bacon), who received them graciously, but made no reply. No attention was given in Parliament or by the Queen to this unanimous action of the clergy.

A short digression may be allowed here regarding a strange statement recently put forward by Mr. Gladstone.[1] He says that " it is plain that while the lower clergy framed a document which, if a little ambiguous, was clearly hostile" [to the Royal Supremacy], "the bishops took no part. It is not," he adds, "too much to say, that they carefully and steadily avoided taking a part. There were, indeed, but four of them present."[2] This is really an amazing statement. If few bishops attended Convocation, it was because all who were in London were engaged day after day in Parliament, in fighting the very battle in behalf of the supremacy of the Sovereign Pontiff, which the Lower House of Convocation declared to be a Divine law of the Church. But, says Mr. Gladstone, the Convocation of both Houses, that is to say, the English Church, had denied this supremacy in 1534, and that act had never been retracted *by the Church*, though it had by the State. Hence the mere declaration of the Lower House in 1559 and the individual action of the bishops were incapable of establishing an ecclesiastical law or definition of faith. "The

[1] Article in *The Nineteenth Century* (July, 1888), on " The Elizabethan Settlement of Religion ".

[2] *Ibid.*, p. 12.

oath," he says, " which was legally tendered to the bishops,"
and refused by them, "asserted, on behalf of the crown,
less than was contained in the unrepealed and, therefore,
still effective declarations of the Anglican Convocations." [1]

But is it true that Convocation had never retracted its
own proceedings in 1534? We have just listened to Bishop
Scott's declaration in Parliament that "those that do live,
as all your lordships do know, hath openly revoked the same,
acknowledging their error". Nor had this been a mere
private or individual act. In the petition of both Houses of
Convocation to Philip and Mary, with regard to the
secularisation of ecclesiastical property, made on 7th
December, 1554, they speak of this secularisation as in itself
invalid, having been made "during the mischievous time of
schism "—*in pernicioso hujus regni præterito schismate*—but
because of the trouble it would cause to revoke it, they ask
that Cardinal Pole should obtain a dispensation from the
Holy See to allow it.[2] The Lower House had also petitioned
the Upper "that the statute of the submission of the clergy
(made *anno* 25, Henry VIII.), and all other statutes made
during the time of the late schism, in derogation of the
liberties and jurisdiction of the Church, from the first year
of King Henry VIII., may be repealed, and the Church
restored *in integrum*," [3] and this had been done in Parliament. Mr. Gladstone does not find a dogmatic decree,
drawn up by the Convocation in the time of Queen Mary,
reversing in so many words the article to which the Convocation of 1534 had assented, under the pressure of Henry
VIII. He writes: "It is most remarkable that, although
the actual bishops and clergy had, through expulsions and
burnings, become sufficiently conformable, there was no

[1] Article in *The Nineteenth Century*, p. 12.
[2] Cardwell's *Synodalia*, vol. ii., p. 430.
[3] *Ibid.*, p. 436.

doctrinal and no legislative action of the Convocations ". What need·of doctrinal action ? It was notorious to every one that Convocation in 1534 had not been free. Therefore, in 1554, all the acts of that and the following Convocations were simply put aside as null and void, as done in the time of schism, and the only desire was that Parliament also should revoke its acts.[1] To return, then, to the conduct of the bishops in 1559. Instead of paying attention to the declaration of the Lower House of Convocation which had been presented to Parliament, Elizabeth, by the advice of her crafty counsellors, arranged for a public conference on certain matters of religion at Westminster. A detailed history of this conference may be found in Collier,[2] and in

---

[1] Since I wrote the above, Mr. Gladstone's article has been admirably answered in an article in the *Dublin Review* for October, 1888, by Rev. J. Morris, S.J., and by Mr. St. George Mivart, in the *Tablet* of 15th December, 1888. Mr. Mivart says: " The Act of Convocation " [under Henry] " was one *ultra vires*, and one necessarily null and void, *ipso facto*, in the eyes of all those who adhered to the old system, although in the eyes of non-papal statesmen it was accepted as a valid surrender of the spirituality to the temporality. . . . When the Government " [under Mary] " chose to restore papal supremacy, the Parliament by itself *alone* could do, and did do, all that was necessary in the eyes either of Catholics or Protestants to effect that end, apart from the action of the Pope himself. The State would have no need of the co-operation of Convocation, which had already effaced itself. . . . In the eyes of the anti-papal party Convocation could not of its own will and power take back that which it had ceded to the Crown ; and in the eyes of the papal party it was not less·impotent to restore that which never had been, and never could be, abolished. Nevertheless, the National Church did all it need have done in the eyes of either party. Its bishops knelt with the lords temporal, the commons, and their Queen, to receive papal absolution. . . . On Elizabeth's accession, the National Church, already in full communion with Rome . . . had nothing to do (from the papal point of view) save to defend as much as it could the then existing state of things."

[2] Vol. vi., p. 207.

my memoir of Bishop Watson I have treated of it sufficiently for my purpose. I shall, therefore, here pass . it by, and merely mention its results.

The conference was held in the last days of March, 1559, and on Monday, 3rd April, 1559, White (Bishop of Winchester) and Watson (of Lincoln) were sent to the Tower. The other Catholic disputants—Baynes (of Lichfield), Scott (of Chester), and Ogelthorpe (of Carlisle), and Henry Cole, John Harpsfield, and William Chedsey, Archdeacons of Lewes, Canterbury, and Middlesex—were commanded by the Council to give bonds to make their appearance before the Lords of the Council as often as they sat, and not to depart from the cities of London and Westminster, and to pay such fines as should be imposed on them for their contempt of the Queen's order. The Bishop of Lichfield was bound in 2000 marks, the Bishop of Chester in £1000, and the Bishop of Carlisle in 500 marks. They waited personally on the Council every day till 12th May, and on the 11th they were fined as follows: Lichfield, £333 6s. 8d.; Carlisle, £250; and Chester, 200 marks (or £133 6s. 8d.). After relating this, Strype remarks: "Thus gently did these bishops feel the displeasure of the Lords of the Council".[1] Probably a more appropriate reflection would be: Thus did Elizabeth's Councillors begin to carry out their scheme of relieving the emptiness of the Exchequer, by seizing every opportunity of fining the prelates.

It is worthy of admiration that the names of these three bishops, then under the daily threats of the Court, appear, nevertheless, in every division in Parliament during that time as opponents to the Government measures.[2] So far

---

[1] Strype, *Annals*, i. 140.

[2] For proof of this, I refer to the Journal of the Lords, or to that of Sir Symonds D'Ewes.

were they from being intimidated or seeking to avoid the
threatened fine, by either voting against their conscience or
absence from Parliament.

Parliament having been dissolved on 8th May, the bishops
had to await the operation of the new laws that had been
passed for "the alteration of religion". Hitherto they had
acted with absolute unanimity, with the single exception of
the consent of the Bishop of Carlisle to perform the coronation service. The Queen, speaking to the Spanish ambassador De Feria, on 19th March, 1559, had called the bishops
"a set of lazy scamps"; and the ambassador had replied
that the scamps were the preachers to whom she had been
listening—that the bishops, if necessary, were ready to die
for the truth. This De Feria related to Philip, adding:
"Your Majesty would admire the courage they are
showing".[1]

[1] See Froude, i. 67.

CHAPTER III.

WE have seen the energy and unanimity with which the bishops sought to avert the threatened catastrophe, or at least to clear their souls of all responsibility for what they were unable to prevent. Hitherto we have walked on a fairly well-beaten track, but in future the ground is full of pitfalls. We must tread cautiously. We have to consider not the law only but the facts, what could be done legally, and what actually was done.

The Act of Supremacy (as it is commonly called), or " Act to restore to the Crown the ancient Jurisdiction over the Estate Ecclesiastical or Spiritual, and abolish all Foreign Powers repugnant to the same " (as it was legally designated), revived most of the ecclesiastical legislation of Henry VIII. and Edward VI., that had been abolished by Queen Mary. It decreed that no foreign prince or prelate, spiritual or temporal, should at any time exercise any manner of jurisdiction or authority within this realm ; and that all such jurisdictions, pre-eminences, spiritual and ecclesiastical, as by any spiritual or ecclesiastical power had heretofore been, or might lawfully be exercised, for the visitation of the ecclesiastical state or persons, and for reformation of the same, and of errors, heresies, schisms, abuses, &c., should for ever be annexed to the Imperial Crown. And to enforce this, it was enacted that every bishop or other ecclesiastical officer, every temporal judge or justice, and every other person receiving the wages of the Crown, should " make, take, and receive a corporal oath upon the evangelist" to this purpose. The form of oath was prescribed. In case of refusal of the oath, the person refusing was to forfeit all promotion, benefit, and office, and be disabled from receiving any other office.

The Act further decreed that if any person, after the end of thirty days from the close of the session, should, by writing, or express words, deed, or act, advisedly, maliciously, and directly affirm or defend the authority or jurisdiction of any foreign prelate heretofore claimed, used, or usurped within this realm, such person, being thereof lawfully convicted, for his first offence should forfeit all his goods and chattels, as well real as personal ; for a second offence, should incur the dangers and penalties of *præmunire ;* and for a third offence be judged guilty of high treason, and suffer the pains of death.

It is to be noted that there is no mention of any penalty of imprisonment for refusing the oath. The imprisonments of which I am going to speak were altogether arbitrary and illegal.[1]

Commissioners were at once[2] appointed to require and receive the oath, and before the end of the year 1559 it had been offered to all the bishops. But the Commissioners proceeded slowly and cautiously. They waited many months for some, in the hopes of conformity. They delayed also in the vain endeavour to persuade some of the

---

[1] The penalties were, however, increased in the second Parliament of 1563, as well as the classes of persons liable to take the oath. The first refusal of the oath became *præmunire*, the second high treason. The oath could be tendered a second time to all who had held ecclesiastical office in the reigns of Henry, Edward, or Mary. The penalties for defending the power of the Sovereign Pontiff were also increased. The first offence was *præmunire*, the second high treason.

[2] The Lord Keeper and seventeen others. Letters in Rymer, dated 23rd May, 1559.

existing Hierarchy to consecrate Parker and other well-known heretics, in order to fill up the vacant sees. The exact date of deposition will be given under the name of each bishop. It is enough to say here that Bonner of London was deposed in May; the Bishops of Lichfield, Chester, Carlisle, Lincoln, Winchester, and Worcester, in June; those of York, St. Asaph, Ely, in July; the Bishop of Durham in September; those of Bath and Wells and of Peterborough in October, and of Exeter in November. The date of the deposition of St. David's I have not been able to ascertain with certainty.

A few words will be sufficient about the Bishop of Llandaff, Anthony Kitchin (*alias* Dunstan). Machyn mentions him as having been deprived, with four others, on 21st June.[1] But though he made some difficulty at taking the oath, he asked time to deliberate, and was lost. Whether he ever actually swore is uncertain, but he did what was equivalent. On the 18th July he gave a written promise that, "with all his power, cunning, and ability, he would set forth in his own person, and cause all others under his jurisdiction to accept and obey the whole course of religion now approved, and would require the oath from others receiving office".[2]

He only lived till October, 1563, to enjoy the dignity and ease to which he sacrificed his conscience, and bears as little reputation among Protestants as with Catholics. Camden calls him the "calamity of his see," apparently for his alienation of its estates. Heylin says, that "having formerly submitted to every change, he resolved to show himself no changeling in not conforming to the higher

---

[1] *Diary*, pp. 200, 201.
[2] MS., C.C.C.C., n. 114, p. 155. Also printed in Canon Estcourt's *Question of Angl. Ordin.*, p. 93.

powers". Godwin is more vehement, and calls him "the shame and reproach of his see".

Before the deposition of the Bishops of Durham, Bath, and Peterborough, a commission, dated 9th September, was issued to them, together with Kitchin, Barlow, and Scory, commanding them to consecrate Parker to be Archbishop of Canterbury. "It is difficult," writes Canon Estcourt, "to understand how anyone could expect that a commission would be executed which bore so gross an insult in the face of it. Not merely to require them to consecrate a married priest, notoriously suspected of heresy, but to join with them two suspended, excommunicated, ecclesiastics, calling themselves bishops, relapsed heretics, and apostate religious, was sufficient of itself to prevent the execution of the mandate. There is no record whether they were ever formally cited, nor in what manner their refusal was given."[1] Even Kitchin in this matter seems to have had a conscience, and courage to obey it.

Sanders' remarks on this man are curious : "Of Llandaff, it is doubtful if he ought to be considered a bishop, because, after the reconciliation of the kingdom unto Mary, he alone is said not to have sought confirmation from the Apostolic See. It is, therefore, not to be wondered at that he yielded to the schism and consecrated bishops outside the Church. Nor is that holy band of bishops contaminated by his defection, who never was a lawful bishop."[2]

---

[1] *Question of Angl. Ordin.*, p. 85.

[2] Vatican MS., f. 266 (b). This clause is very strange. No author, Catholic or Protestant, now asserts that Kitchin took part in the consecration of Parker or of any other member of Elizabeth's hierarchy. Yet the rumour had reached Sanders that he had done so. The well-known story of the Nag's Head consecration, derived from the prisoners at Wisbeach, has two parts—(1) that Kitchin was about to consecrate, when deterred by the threats of Bonner ; (2) that Scory thereupon carried out some mock consecration. Sanders' assertion in the text certainly lends some support to the first half of the story.

Thus, then, by the end of the year 1559, fifteen bishops had been deprived of their sees by the civil power, and many dioceses were vacant by death; one only of the ancient hierarchy remained in possession of his episcopal throne, though by an act which forfeited it canonically. It is somewhat curious that as early as 1583 confusion prevailed in the minds of the Catholic exiles as to these transactions. In that year Dr. Gregory Martin, in a letter addressed to his sister, and afterwards published under the title of *The Love of the Soul*, writes of "twenty-three bishops all deprived of their livings these twenty years, and now but two of them alive". Another Catholic writer, Dr. Champney, in his book called *Vocation of Bishops*, written in 1616, says: "At the Nag's Head, in Cheapside, by accorded appointment, met all those that were nominated to bishopricks, vacant either by death, *as was that of Canterbury only*, or by unjust deposition, as were all the rest".

Rishton ought to have been accurate, since he introduces his list, written in 1585, as follows: "To preserve the names of these illustrious confessors from oblivion, I give them here". Yet he names only twelve, omitting Bishop Morgan of St. David's, Bishop Pate of Worcester, and, most strangely, Bishop Watson of Lincoln.[1]

These authors had some excuse for their errors, as they were living in exile, without documents. But it was mere carelessness made Stow speak of those deposed as thirteen or fourteen, and Strype, with his followers, put them at fourteen. Heylin also makes up a list of fourteen, by omitting the Bishops of Worcester and St. Asaph, and inserting the Bishop of Chichester, who was dead. Even Wharton, the learned and accurate, in the book written expressly to correct the errors of Burnet, states that "in all,

---

[1] In his additions, or fourth book of Sanders, p. 260 (Ed. Lewis).

fourteen bishops were deprived," though he only gives the names of thirteen, omitting the Bishop of Bath and Wells and the Bishop of St. David's.[1]

Has any other important fact of history been treated after this fashion by so large a number of writers ? The frequency of error will be my excuse for stating once more that the oath of supremacy was tendered to sixteen bishops, of whom fifteen refused it and were deprived.

Far worse are the mistakes and false reports regarding the numbers imprisoned, and the length and severity of their imprisonment. Some specimens have been given in the first chapter of this sketch ; I shall notice others when dealing with the bishops singly. I confine myself in this chapter to imprisonment in the strictest sense of the word, confinement in buildings set apart for restraint on liberty.

The first question that arises is : Who had authority to imprison, and for what cause, or by what law, could imprisonment be inflicted? The writer on ecclesiastical affairs in Knight's *Pictorial History of England* says : " Although the deprived prelates were also at first sent to prison, in conformity with one of the provisions of the statute, only Bonner, White, and Watson were retained in confinement ".[2] It would be difficult to compress more errors into the same number of words. There is in the statute no provision whatever imposing the penalty of imprisonment for refusal of the oath. In the second place, not one bishop was imprisoned consequently on his refusal, nor until after an interval of several months. Thirdly, when the imprisonment was inflicted, no less than eight bishops were " retained in confinement " for years ; yet one of the three mentioned by this writer was not among the number,

[1] *Specimen of Some Errors*, p. 151.
[2] *Pictorial History of England*, book vi., ch. ii., p. 738.

3

for he was dead. I refer to Bishop White, whose imprisonment preceded his deposition, and was inflicted, not by the
Ecclesiastical Commissioners, but by the Council, for his
supposed contumacy at the Westminster Conference, and
before the Bill of Supremacy had passed the Parliament.

Another modern writer, the poet and historian Southey,
in his *Book of the Church*, has given a different explanation
of the imprisonments. He seems to have noticed that there
was a considerable interval between the deposition and the
committal to prison, and writes as follows : "When it
appeared that some of these bishops preached against the
new order of things, and encouraged a seditious spirit in
those who flocked to them (White and Watson venturing
even to threaten the Queen with excommunication), it was
found necessary to place them under some degree of
restraint ".[1] Everything in this passage is pure fiction or
mere conjecture. The imprisonments by the Commissioners
began in May, 1560. White was then dead. Watson had
been released at the conclusion of his first term of imprisonment for contumacy. It is not pretended by anyone
except Southey that he provoked a second imprisonment by
threat of excommunication. That charge in Camden, its
first author, regards his committal to the Tower during the
session of Parliament, fourteen months before. The other
reasons mentioned by Southey, the preaching sedition and
the flocking of disaffected people to the deposed prelates,
are not grounded on any state paper or contemporary
chronicler.

The truth then appears to be, that when the Commissioners, in virtue of the new law, had required the oath, and
punished its refusal by privation, they were embarrassed at
the presence of so many illustrious men remaining at liberty
in the country. The only legal offence they could lay to

[1] *Book of the Church*, ch. xv., p. 392.

their charge was their absence from the new worship, and this especially at Easter in 1560. They, therefore, procured the excommunication of three at least—Archbishop Heath of York, Bishop Bonner of London, and Bishop Thirlby of Ely[1]—probably of the rest. Moreover, as regards imprisonment, in the days of the Tudors no legal charge or trial was considered essential before punishment. The Privy Council possessed or assumed judicial powers of a very vague and extended nature. They had the general superintendence of the Commonwealth, and supplied for the weakness or deficiency of the law. "They pretended," writes Mr. Dicey, in his essay on the Privy Council,[2] "not merely collectively as the Council, but individually as councillors, to possess the privilege of arresting their fellow-citizens." This power the Queen and Council could delegate to a commission, as is well known from the history of the Star Chamber.

We need not then look for any violated statute, or any special charge made against the bishops. Their existence at liberty in England was judged to be injurious to the new order of things. Policy required their incarceration or

---

[1] Strype (*Annals,* i. 212) gives the date of Bonner's excommunication as 28th July, 1560, and of the others as Feb., 1560. This is 1561 (N.S.). Strpye copied from Machyn, who mentions the excommunication of Heath and Thirlby in Feb., 1561, and that they were then in the Tower.

[2] *Arnold Prize Essay,* 1860 ; reprint in 1887, p. 116. The growth, decay, and variations of the functions of the Privy Council are the key of English history. "Anyone who examines the most certain facts of history," says Mr. Dicey, "will be convinced that from the accession of Henry VII. till the meeting of the Long Parliament the Council interfered in all matters, small as well as great" (p. 105). Towards the end of Elizabeth's reign the judges petitioned "that Her Majesty's subjects be not committed or detained in prison, by the command of any nobleman or councillor, against the laws of the realm, to the grievous charge and oppression of Her Majesty's subjects" (p. 119).

restriction to certain places. The discretion given to
the Commissioners seems to have been very wide. In a
return made by them in 1561, we find that, while some recusants were sent for an indefinite period to the Tower, the
Marshalsea, the Fleet, or other prisons, others were confined
to certain counties, others to a limited range about the
place assigned for their dwelling, others were left free as to
all England, with the exception of the localities where they
were known, or liable to influence or be influenced. Thus,
e.g., John Rastall, William Giblett, and other "late
scholars of Oxford," are simply "restrained from the
Universities"; Alexander Beesar, who is described as "old,
wealthy, and stubborn," is confined to two miles round
Hanbury; John Dale, late of Cambridge, not altogether
unlearned, but very perverse, "is restricted within ten miles
of Newmarket, save towards London or Cambridge";
Henry Cumberford, late of Lichfield, is confined to county
Suffolk, "with liberty to travel, twice every year, into
Staffordshire, allowing six weeks each time"—he is said to
be "learned but wilful, and meet to be considered";
"Purseglove, late suffragan of Hull," is said to be "very
wealthy, stiff in papistry, and of estimation in the country"
—his range is fixed "within twelve miles of Ugthorpe,
county York". These are a few of a long list of such
restraints, the schedule being signed by Edmund (Grindall),
Bishop of London; Richard (Cox) of Ely; William (Down-
ham) of Chester, and three other Commissioners.[1] They
return also lists of those who have "fled over the seas";
those who are "prisoners by order of us" in the Fleet, the
Marshalsea, the King's Bench, and the two counties; and
lastly, of "evil-disposed persons, who lurk so secretly that
process cannot be served on them ".

[1] *P. R. O., Dom. Eliz.*, Addenda, xi. 45.

From all this it is apparent that if some of the bishops were locked up in the Tower, the Marshalsea, and the Fleet, it was not because they were guilty of any offence against any statute, but that the Commissioners did not judge their public appearance desirable, while they considered that the imprisonment of men so conspicuous, and so "stout in papistry," might serve as a salutary example to all inclined to be obstinate. The period of confinement was not limited, but perpetual or indefinite, at the will of the Queen or Council.

For these reasons then, in the summer of 1560, the Commissioners issued arrests against eight of the deposed bishops—that is to say, against all then alive in England, with the single exception of Dr. Poole of Peterborough; for though fifteen had been deposed, one had since left the country, and five had died within a few months of their deposition. Dr. Bonner, the Bishop of London, was thrown into the Marshalsea on 20th April, there to remain until his death, nearly ten years later. As there is no controversy as regards the length of his imprisonment, I will leave the details to be discussed under his own name.

Dr. Scott of Chester was imprisoned in the Fleet on May 13, 1560, and was liberated four years later, to be placed under a milder restraint. The proofs and details of his case I will also reserve.

Six other bishops were committed to the Tower. On this fact, and on the length of their imprisonment, I must dwell with some detail, since it has been persistently ignored by one writer after another. Southey, affecting to give a full account of the treatment of the deprived bishops, has not a word about it, except that he says that "Heath, after a short imprisonment, was allowed to reside upon his own lordship of Chobham". Now the *short* imprisonment of Heath lasted for three years and a half, and was (I repeat) shared

by five other bishops. Strype " doubts much whether any
of the bishops were imprisoned after their deprivation,"
adding that Protestant writers have taken on credit what
popish authors write.[1] If he had said *immediately* after
their deprivation he need not have written with hesitation.
But Strype has himself been the principal false guide on this
road.   His words have been taken to deny any imprisonment of the recusants as recusants, with a few later and trivial
exceptions, which he attempts to explain.   He is wholly
silent on the long and general imprisonment.   The only
hint at it is the following : "Some of the bishops were
under some confinement for *some time in the year following*,
viz., 1560, for then I find six of them, together with an
abbot and a dean, in the Tower. . . . These were now permitted to come together to their meals . . . but *after a
little time* they were all committed to easier restraints, and
some restored to their perfect liberty."[2]   This is all—a few
months community or collegiate life in the Tower in 1560!
In his particular account of each bishop even this is
omitted.   Thus he writes of Bishop Thirlby of Ely that
"he had his liberty till he began to preach against the
Reformation, but being pardoned afterwards, was in the
custody of the Archbishop".   Now Bishop Thirlby was one
of the six bishops mentioned above as shut up in the Tower
in 1560, and as he remained there, shut up *in close confinement*, until September, 1563, at which period he was transferred direct from the Tower to the custody of Parker, it is
quite evident that he had no opportunity of "preaching
against the Reformation," except, indeed, by the example of
his patient endurance.
    Let us turn, then, from these misleading annalists to the
State Papers.   There exists a return, made by Sir Edward

Annals, i., part i., p. 206.   [2] *Ibid.*, i. 211.

Warner, Lieutenant of the Tower, on 26th May, 1561, of all the prisoners in the Tower. It runs as follows: "Dr. Heath, late Bishop of York, committed 10th June, 1560; Dr. Thirlby, late Bishop of Ely, committed 3rd June, 1560; Dr. Watson, late of Lincoln, Dr. Pate, late of Worcester (and Dr. Feckenham, late Abbot of Westminster), committed on 20th May, 1560; Dr. Turberville of Exeter,. Dr. Bourne of Bath, and Dr. Boxall (Dean of Peterborough and Windsor), committed on 18th June, 1560. The causes of these eight foresaid persons is known to your Lordships, and needeth no further rehearsall."[1] These dates are confirmed from Machyn's *Diary*, but on the 20th May he enters by mistake the name of Dr. Cole, Dean of St. Paul's, for that of Dr. Pate. Cole, as he rightly says a little later, was sent to the Fleet.

Another return, made on the 3rd July, 1561, gives the same list, with the same days of commital.[2]

Thus, then, at the time of this document they had already been more than a year in confinement. They had been committed by the Archbishop of Canterbury and other Commissioners; and a letter from the Council to the Archbishop, of 4th September, 1560, is quoted by Strype, allowing them to dine together at two tables, *should he approve of it.* But it is quite untrue that after a little while this was exchanged for liberty, or even for easier restraint.

On the 14th June, 1562, the Lieutenant writes to the Lords of the Council as follows: "First he putteth your Lordships in remembrance that the late bishops, with Mr. Feckenham and Mr. Boxall, being all eight in number, be *close and severally* kept, for the which they continually call upon him to make in their names humble suit to have more liberty; informing your Lordships therewith how

---

[1] *P. R. O., Dom. Eliz.*, xvii. 13. [2] *Ibid.*, xviii. 3.

troublesome it is to serve so many persons severally so long together ".[1]

We have no evidence that the proposal of the Council of permitting the bishops to meet at meal-time was ever carried out. It was left to the discretion of Dr. Parker. But the above letter of the Lieutenant is evidence that, if the permission was ever granted, it was soon withdrawn, for he complains that it had been a great trouble to him to serve them separately *so long*. This must be well noted, since prison discipline was by no means uniform in those days. Sometimes prisoners were allowed or could purchase great liberty, and boarded themselves ; sometimes they dined at a common table, paying as at a modern *table d'hôte ;* while some lived in a most wretched fashion on the proceeds of the alms box.[2] The six bishops in the Tower had not been allowed to range freely within their enclosure, nor to meet and converse even for an hour. They were shut up in separate cells even at their meals, and, though waited on by their own servants, both masters and servants had to board themselves, and that too at exorbitant prices.

The same six bishops are still found in a list of prisoners dated the 5th September, 1562,[3] and they all continued until the following September, 1563, as will be seen presently in the account of their deliverance.

Allusions to the imprisoned bishops occur in the writings of the Protestant reformers. Thus Jewell, in a letter to Peter Martyr, 7th February, 1562, says : " The Marian bishops are still confined in the Tower, and are going on in their old way " ; and again to Bullinger, 9th February : " Some few of the bishops who were furious in the late

---

[1] *P. R. O., Dom. Eliz.*, xxiii. 40.

[2] See Dr. Jessopp's interesting Introduction to the *Economy of the Fleet* (Camd. Soc., 1879).

[3] *P. R. O., Dom. Eliz.*, xxiv. 39, i.

Marian times cannot as yet, in so short a time, for very shame, return to their senses.   They are therefore confined in the Tower, lest their contagion should infect others." This last clause indicates that they were imprisoned, not for violation of any law, but as a measure of State policy.   Cox of Ely writes, 5th August, 1562 : " The heads of our Popish clergy are still kept in confinement.   They are treated indeed with kindness, but relax nothing of their Popery.   Others are living at large, scattered about in different parts of the kingdom, but without any function, unless, perhaps, where they may be sowing the seeds of impiety in secret." [1]

These things are told in a few lines, but how much they contain !   Let us try to realise what is meant by three years' imprisonment in the Tower, the Fleet, and the Marshalsea, in the first years of Elizabeth.   Several writers talk of it as a pleasant, easy life, without dignity, indeed, but without cares.   " Even the murderous Bonner," writes Mr. Froude, " had no worse fate to fear than some ' room befitting his condition,' in the Tower or the Marshalsea, with the garden walls for the limit of his exercise—such a fate as for 1200 years the religious orders throughout Christendom had voluntarily chosen for themselves, in retiring from a world with which intercourse imperilled their souls." [2]   One hardly knows whether this is intended as mockery of the bishops, or a sneer at the religious orders ; perhaps the two are mingled.   But even Mr. Froude would probably admit that monastic seclusion would be intolerable to monks without the monastic life, without choir, without Mass, without Communion, and without occupation, manual or mental.

Very inconsistently with the above words, but with far

---

[1] *Zurich Letters,* i. 43, 44, 49.   [2] *History of Eliz.,* i. 89.

more truth, Mr. Froude, in describing the death of Cardinal
Pole, writes, that he "was taken away in mercy, to escape a
second exile, or *the living death of the Tower*".[1] It would
be to no purpose, even if it could be proved that the prison
diet was wholesome and abundant, and that garden exercise
was not denied.   Educated, learned, distinguished men were
deprived of their liberty, of social intercourse, of correspondence, of books, and of all the external consolations of religion, and in the vigour of their life condemned to drag out
weary, purposeless days and nights for years, and that for no
crime, by no law, at the caprice of a woman whom they had
helped to place on the throne.   But they had not that limited
freedom or " free custody " which historians seem to think
so delightful.   They were kept " close and severally," *i.e.*, in
separate cells, and without even solitary exercise.

Not only were they not allowed Catholic worship, they were
threatened, on one occasion, that if they persisted in refusing
to receive the Protestant Communion at Easter in the same
form as the Queen, their heads should fall on the scaffold.
They refused to a man.   So, at least, runs the report of the
Spanish Ambassador.[2]   This was in 1562.   A similar threat
was held out in 1563, if they continued to refuse the oath of
supremacy ;[3] and this, at least, was no idle threat, for the
Parliament that met early in that year had given authority
to propose the oath a second time, and made a second
refusal high treason, with penalty of death.   Either the
clemency or the fears of the Queen kept back the hands of
the Ecclesiastical Commissioners, as we learn from a letter
of Dr. Parker ;[4] but, as this reluctance was unknown, it did

---

[1] *History of Eliz.*, i. 5.

[2] *Documents of Simancas* (Ed. 1865), p. 80.   The document is
placed by the editor at the end of 1562.

[3] *Ibid.*, p. 85.

[4] I will give this in the account of Dr. Bonner.

not prevent the penalty of death being held *in terrorem* over the bishops and other deprived ecclesiastics.

There were some, indeed, outside clamouring for the blood of the bishops. Nowell, the new Protestant Dean of St. Paul's, preached in Westminster, and Day, Provost of Eton, preached in St. Paul's at the opening of Parliament and Convocation on 12th January, 1563. The subject of both was the propriety of " killing the caged wolves ".[1]

These things were reported to the Emperor Ferdinand, and he bestirred himself in their behalf. From a letter written on 24th September, 1563, a few days after the release of the bishops from the Tower, but before the news could have reached the Emperor, we find that already, some months previously, he had interceded in favour of the imprisoned bishops.[2] In the translation made at the time, he says :—
" We were right glad for to understand that your Grace did accept, in very good part, the letters which we sent unto your Grace certain months afore this. In the which we did heartily require your Grace that you would not execute any rigorous languor upon the bishops in prison, and the subjects of your realm which profess the Catholic religion."[3]
The Queen replied, 3rd November, that it was a matter of great moment for her to act so gently with those who had so insolently acted against her laws and the quiet of her subjects, amongst whom the chief were those who, during the reign of her father and brother, offered the doctrine to others which they now so obstinately reject. These men she had spared at his request, but not without offending her own people.[4]

---

[1] See Froude, *Hist.*, vii. 479, 541.

[2] See MS., *Cotton Vesp.*, f. 3 (in B. Mus.), p. 487.

[3] *P. R. O., Dom. Eliz.*, Addenda, vol. xxviii., n. 58 v.

[4] *P. R. O., Foreign*, 1361, p. 581. The Emperor also asked for liberty of worship. This the Queen altogether refuses. Camden *(Annals*, p. 20, Eng. tr.) gives this wrongly in 1559. The letters are also in Strype, *Annals*, i., part ii., p. 572.

The release of the six bishops from the Tower took place in the middle of September, 1563. Dr. Heath of York and Dr. Turberville of Exeter were thenceforth merely restricted to certain localities. Dr. Pate of Worcester escaped to the Continent. The remaining three were transferred to another kind of prison, the custody of the Protestant Prelates: Bishop Thirlby to that of Dr. Parker of Canterbury, Bishop Bourne to that of Dr. Bullingham of Lincoln, the Bishop of Lincoln to that of Dr. Cox of Ely. Bishop Scott of Chester still remained for a time in the Fleet, and Bishop Bonner of London in the Marshalsea. Stow thus relates the matter in some notes which he did not venture to publish: "Anno, 1563. In September, the old bishops and divers doctors was removed out of the Tower into the new bishops' houses, there to remain prisoners under their custody. The plague being in the city was thought to be the cause. But their deliverance, or rather change of prison, did so much offend the people that the preachers at Paul's Cross, and on other places, both of the city and country, preached, as it is thought of many wise men, very seditiously, as Baldwin at Paul's Cross, wishing a gallows set up in Smithfield, and the old bishops and other papists to be hanged thereon. Himself died of the plague the next week after." [1]

The Emperor Ferdinand still continued his care. Among the instructions to Don Diego Guzman de Silva, in January, 1564, one was that "he was to intercede pressingly in behalf of the bishops, and to convince the Queen that it was opposed even to the spirit of the reformed religion to compel men to renounce the faith they held". Consequently, De Silva sought private interviews with the Queen,

---

[1] *Three Fifteenth Century Chronicles and Contemporary Notes of Occurrences in the Reign of Queen Elizabeth*, by John Stow (Ed. by James Gairdner; Camd. Soc., 1880), p. 126.

and explained to her that, although his instructions forbade
him to meddle with religious questions, he yet felt that it
was his duty relative to the bishops and other principal
men, and assured her the adherents of the old faith were
more dutifully inclined to her than those of the new.   This
she admitted, and gave orders to mitigate the confinement
of the Bishop of London, and assured De Silva she did not
read German books, but St. Jerome and St. Augustine." [1]

Having given in this chapter some account of the united
action and constancy of the bishops, with their first imprisonments, I shall in the next trace out the heroism of each one
of them in greater detail, and carry on the story to their
deaths.   This general review may be appropriately concluded by recording the impression made by their constancy
on their Catholic and Protestant contemporaries.

Laurence Vaux was the last warden of the collegiate
church of Manchester.[2]   He had refused the oath, and been
deprived, and bound over to remain in the county of
Worcester.[3]   In 1561 he escaped to Louvain.   In 1566 Dr.
Harding and Dr. Sanders received a commission from St.
Pius V. to promulgate in England the decision made by the
Fathers of the Council of Trent in 1562, and confirmed by
St. Pius himself in 1566, that the English committed mortal
sin, and were guilty of schism or heresy, if they attended the
places of worship of the Establishment, under the circumstances that then existed.   Lawrence Vaux was one of those
who were appointed to enter England and publish the papal
decision, with special faculties to absolve and to reconcile.
On 2nd November, 1566, he wrote a long letter to one of
his friends in Lancashire, which fell into the hands of the

[1] *Simancas Documents*, pp. 88, 93.

[2] Now the Protestant cathedral, but commonly called by the people
" the old church ".

[3] *P. R. O., Dom. Eliz.*, Addenda, xi. 45.

Government.[1] In this letter he uses, among others, the
following argument : "There is not one of the old bishops
or godly priests of God that will be present at the schismatical service or damnable communion now used, for the
which cause they have lost their livings—some be in
corporal prison, some in exile, and, like good pastors, be
ready to suffer death in that cause, as it is the duty and
office of bishops to go before their flock, and to be their
leaders in matters of faith and religion. So the clergy and
laity are bounden to follow their example, if they intend to
be partakers, with the bishops, of the joys of heaven. And,
thanks be to God, a number not only of the clergy, but as
well of the temporality, both of them that be worshipful and
inferiors to them, do follow their bishops constantly, and
will in no wise come to the schismatical service. And such
as frequenteth the schismatical service now used in the
Church in England must either contemn them as fond,
foolish men, that refuse to be present at service, or else
their own consciences will accuse them that they do naughty,
in that they do contrary to the example given them of the
bishops."

Even had no proofs come to us, we might have been sure
that language like this among Catholics would have exasperated the intruded Protestant bishops beyond endurance.
Their feelings, however, have been left on record. In 1563
a short paper or tract had been cast abroad by an anonymous
Catholic regarding the great fire that had burnt down the
steeple of St. Paul's, London. In this the writer had mentioned the constancy of the Catholic bishops. Pilkington,
whom Elizabeth had placed at Durham, was transported
into one of his paroxysms of ribald fury : "I think the holy
bishops he cracks so much of have their calling of the

---

[1] *P. R. O., Dom. Eliz.*, xli. 1. It is printed at length by Mr.
Simpson in *The Rambler* for December, 1857.

Dutch name that signifies *bitesheep*, rather than of the Greek that teaches to save sheep by his painful diligence ".[1]

The Catholic writer had said that they were "ready to suffer death afore they will consent to any part of this religion ". Pilkington replied: " If they were opposed as they opposed other, I doubt not but they would as soon eat the faggot as feel it burn them. . . . And when he cracks much that they have lost their livings, and be in prison, and banished, let the world judge whether they ever lived more merrily, quietly, fared better, lay easilier, had more plenty of all things, than they have now. They are as pale in prison as a butcher's boll, they are lean as a fat hog, they lie at ease unto their bones ache with rising early. . . . They would fain be counted to suffer for religion, if any man would believe it. The poor Protestant, which has his liberty, lives in more misery, need, debt, reproach, and contempt than these Pope's prisoners, who, he says, have lost all. It is better in the world to be Pope's prisoner than Christ's preacher. God amend all."[2] The real cause of this tirade was that Queen Mary had assisted the Catholic bishops to recover estates alienated under Henry and Edward; whereas Queen Elizabeth, before any of her bishops were consecrated, had exchanged some of their fairest estates for pretended equivalents in benefices. This generosity of the Catholic Queen, and rapacity of the Protestant Queen, were thus interpreted by Pilkington: " The world gives to the Papist honours, castles, towers, and all that it has. To the Protestant, if he give anything, it is thought too much; and of those things that it gives, it gives the worst that can be picked out, and yet thinks it too good."[3]

[1] *Burning of St. Paul's*, p. 495 (Pilkington's *Works*, Parker Soc.).
[2] *Ibid.*, p. 622.
[3] *Ibid.*, p. 594.

The language he used of his venerable predecessor (Dr. Tunstall) was as follows: " In Durham, I grant, the bishop that now is, and his predecessor, were not of one religion in divers points, nor made bishops after one fashion. This has neither cruche " [*i.e.*, crosier] " nor mitre, never sware against his Prince his allegiance to the Pope; this has neither power to christen bells, nor hallow chalices and superaltars as the other had, and with gladness praises God that keeps him from such filthiness."[1] As his predecessor not only submitted to imprisonment, under Elizabeth, for allegiance to the Pope, but also under King Edward for resisting the division and spoliation of the bishopric of which Pilkington was now in enjoyment, one might have expected, if not gratitude, at least decency towards his memory.

Time did not soften this man's hatred. At his death, in 1575, he left a writing unfinished, in which he thus alludes to the one Catholic bishop then surviving—Dr. Watson of Lincoln, who had been his fellow-student at St. John's, Cambridge: " The Lord suffereth some of His enemies to live in shame, who in so long time cannot repent, but are given up to their own lusts and hardened hearts, so far as man can judge; besides many other young whelps of their teaching, which can bark in corners and make themselves merry with railing and scoffing at the Holy Scriptures of God, the ministers and professors of it. Yea, some become so shameless that they would call their dogs by the names of the first writers and professors of it."[2] As Pilkington generally spoke of the Catholic bishops as "the Pope's horned cattle," in allusion to their mitres, called Cardinal Pole "Carnal Fool," and Pope Hildebrand "Hellbrand," he should not have thought the Catholic gentlemen so

[1] *Burning of St. Paul's*, p. 586.   [2] *Expos. upon Nehemiah*, p. 401.

shameless for calling a bull-dog by the name of Luther, a snappish cur by that of Calvin, or a fawning spaniel by that of Cranmer. These were innocent jokes, and a pardonable retaliation for the fines and imprisonments that were wearing them out.

One other paper will complete this chapter, by telling what was thought of the confessors in Rome. It is among the letters of Cardinal Morone, *de rebus Angliæ*. It bears no date, but was certainly written between July, 1560, and September, 1563, while the six bishops were in the Tower, and under the hope that Elizabeth might yet be reconciled with the Church. It is a proposal for filling up the vacant sees. It was proposed to translate the Archbishop of York to Canterbury, and Dr. Watson, Bishop of Lincoln, to York; Dr. Scott, Bishop of Chester, to Durham. The other surviving bishops were to retain their sees, ·and names were proposed for filling up those that were vacant. There are a few omissions and mistakes in this document that show the writer could not have been then in England.[1] The bishops were to prove themselves not unworthy of the high esteem with which they were regarded. We will now pursue their histories individually.

[1] Published from the original in the Vatican by Dr. M. Brady, in his *Episcopal Succession*, vol. ii. 322.

APPENDIX TO CHAPTER III.

SOME APOCRYPHAL STORIES.

In the preceding sketch I have purposely omitted certain incidents that are put forward conspicuously by some modern writers. These incidents are four in number: 1. The discovery by the Council, after the death of Queen Mary, of treasonable correspondence compromising to some of the bishops, and the generous forbearance of Elizabeth and her

Council thereupon. 2. The verbal protest addressed to the Queen by the bishops, on 15th May, 1559, and the Queen's defiant reply. 3. The remonstrance written by five bishops to the Queen, in December, 1559, and her letter to them. 4. Their threatening letter to Parker, in 1560, and his retort. I have said nothing of these things in relating the history of the bishops, because I believe them all to be mere fables and forgeries.

Not one of these incidents is mentioned by any author whose work appeared within a hundred and twenty years from the dates assigned; yet, had they taken place, they could not have failed to be known and recorded. No trace will be found of them in the writers and chroniclers of the sixteenth century—such as Burghley, Hayward, Fox, Stow, Holinshed; nor in any Catholic writer of the same period—such as Sander, Allen, Harding, Rishton, &c. Nor, again, is there any allusion to them in the historians of the seventeenth century—such as Camden, Fuller, or Heylin. They are derived from a small book published in Dublin in 1683, called *The Hunting of the Romish Fox*, &c., by Robert Ware. This book is often quoted as the production of Sir James Ware, the well-known Irish antiquary, since it is professedly drawn from his *Historical Collections*. It is really a farrago of forgeries by Sir James Ware's second son, Robert, who, after his father's death, in 1666, first wrote his own mischievous concoctions among his father's papers, and then drew them out and printed them in books and pamphlets. I have laid bare the history of these forgeries in a series of papers in the *Tablet* newspaper, beginning 13th April, 1889. I do not think it necessary to repeat their refutation here. I will merely say that they were adopted by Strype, who, while giving marginal references to Ware's book, states either in note or text that the original authority is Sir William Cecil, or Sir Henry Sidney, whose "memorials" came through Archbishop Usher into the papers of Sir James Ware. The strength of a chain is that of its weakest link, and here the weak link is Robert Ware. The "memorials" never existed; and the supposed events are both intrinsically improbable and historically impossible. Yet from Strype they were adopted by Collier, and are found in most modern historians.

CHAPTER IV.

BISHOPS TUNSTALL, BAYNE, MORGAN, OGELTHORPE, AND WHITE.

I HAVE no thought of writing a series of biographies of the Catholic bishops who survived Queen Mary. Notices of them may be found in many books, and the diligence of Anthony à Wood and his editor, Mr. Bliss, as well as that of Mr. Cooper, has collected almost everything that can now be learnt about their early life.[1] All that I shall attempt to do is to set down succinctly those facts of their later life which prove their invincible constancy and the extent of their sufferings for Catholic faith and unity. This will necessitate some slight repetition of things already said, but the whole matter will gain in clearness, and help to prevent a repetition of the mistakes hitherto current. I shall arrange these notes in the chronological order of the bishops' deaths, and thus the two complete lives to which this sketch is an introduction will fall naturally into their places. . It has been already said that the number of bishops deposed by Queen Elizabeth was fifteen.

CUTHBERT TUNSTALL (of Durham),
Deposed 28th September, 1559; died 15th November, 1559.

At the time of his deprivation, Tunstall was eighty-five years old. His name had long been famous, not only in

[1] See *Athenæ Oxonienses* (Ed. Wood, Bliss), and Cooper's *Athenæ Cantabrigienses.*

England but throughout Europe. Erasmus had written of him in 1516, that he was a man of the most exquisite judgment, both in Greek and Latin literature, beyond any of his countrymen, but at the same time of incredible modesty, and of sweet and joyful manners. Sir Thomas More, who had been associated with him in an embassy, wished to commemorate his friend's virtues even in his own epitaph : *Quo viro vix habet orbis hodie quicquam eruditius, prudentius, melius.* Yet when Sir Thomas and he were tried in the furnace in 1534, Tunstall showed that there was dross mixed with the gold. In his studies at Oxford and Cambridge, or more probably in his legal studies at Padua, he had imbibed what have been called Gallican principles in their extremest form.

Dr. Knight has written of him : " It may be remarked of this man, that though he was so inflexible in the latter part of his life, and so stiff in his Popish principles, yet in the reign of Henry VIII. he was a strenuous assertor of the King's supremacy, and wrote a very severe letter to Cardinal Pole, then abroad, upon this head, and bid fair—as it was then thought—to be a zealous Protestant, but stopped short and became immovably attached to Popery ".[1] This is a mistaken estimate. Of Protestantism, in the ordinary sense of the word, he had no taint whatever at any period of his life. But he had at first a false estimate of the supremacy of the Holy See, which he lived to correct; and his exaggerated view of royal authority in the Church had been reduced to absurdity by the logic of facts in the reigns of Henry and Edward. When Pole, not long after the martyrdom of More and Fisher, sent his MS. treatise[2] to the King of England, in refutation of his claim of supremacy and in re-

---

[1] Knight's *Life of Erasmus.*

[2] Published many years afterwards with the title *De Unitate Ecclesiæ.*

proach of his tyranny and cruelty, Henry put the treatise into the hands of Tunstall, who in the spring of 1536 wrote a letter to Pole. In this he says : " Ye presuppose for a ground the King's Grace to be swerved from the unity of Christ's Church, and that in taking upon him the title of Supreme Head of the Church of England he intendeth to separate his Church of England from the unity of the whole body of Christendom, taking upon him the office belonging to spiritual men—grounded in the Scripture—of immediate cure of souls, and attribute to himself that [which] belongeth to priesthood, as to preach and teach the Word of God and to minister the sacraments, and that he doth not know what longeth to a king's office and what unto priesthood. Wherein, surely both you and all other so thinking of him do err too far . . . for his first purpose and intent is to see the laws of Almighty God purely and sincerely preached and taught, and Christ's faith, without blot, kept and obeyed in his realm, and not to separate himself or his realm anywise from the unity of Christ's Catholic Church, but immovably, at all time, to keep and observe the same, and to reduce his Church of England out of all captivity of foreign powers heretofore usurped therein, into the pristine estate that all churches of all realms were in at the beginning ; and to abolish and clearly put away such usurpation as heretofore in this realm the Bishops of Rome have [exercised] to their great advantage, and impoverishing of the realm and the King's subjects of the same."[1] This was his theory of royal supremacy, based entirely on the presumption that the Catholic faith and discipline could remain integral and intact by their own coherence, and that England's kings would always be Catholic, and act as zealous Defenders of the Faith and promoters of discipline. No wonder that after witnessing the vacillations of him who was to keep the Church "immovable at all times,"

---

[1] Cotton MS., in Br. Mus., " Cleopatra," E. vi., p. 389.

and the entire revolution in religious matters during the reign of Edward, he reconsidered his theory and rejected it.

In the same letter to Pole he had written as follows : " And where ye do find a fault with me, in that I fainted in my heart and would not die for the Bishop of Rome's authority, when the matter was first purposed unto me, surely it was not fainting that made me agreeable thereunto, for I never saw the day—since I knew the progress and continuance of Christendom from the beginning, and read such histories ecclesiastical and ordinances, from age to age, as do manifestly declare the same—that ever I thought to shed one drop of my blood therefor. For sure I am none of them that heretofore had advantage, by that authority, would have lost one penny thereof to have saved my life, nor will not do to save yours if it should be in such necessity."

To these last words, so unworthy of a Catholic bishop, Pole answered as follows : " Good my Lord tell me,—my Lord of Rochester or Master More, did they hope of such succour ? Did they think the Pope would send a host to deliver them from death ? What words be these in so great a matter, for the gravity of such a man as you ever have been esteemed ! . . . It is Christ's cause, my Lord, and for His sake died these great men, your great friends, whom you may not think of so little spirit, nor of so vile mind, that they saw not wherefore they died, or that they died for any respect, advantage, or thing to be looked for in this world.

" But you say : ' There be now as great learned men in Divinity in this realm as be in other countries '. But how much more greater than my Lord of Rochester or Master More, or other holy, learned men that died for this cause ? I can say no more, but God send you a livelier spirit than you show now to His honour." [1]

---

[1] Letter dated 1st August, 1536. It is printed in full by Strype, *Memorials*, vol. i., part ii., n. 83, p. 306.

Tunstall did indeed show a livelier spirit at the accession of Elizabeth than he had done five-and-twenty years before. Strype says, most falsely and calumniously: "Before his death, by the Archbishop's (Parker's) means, he was brought off from papistical fancies".[1] This is contradicted by both acts and words. Tunstall was in Durham at Queen Mary's death. On account of his great age he was specially exempted by Elizabeth from being present either at her coronation or in Parliament.[2] But after the passing of the Act of Supremacy, and the appointment of the Commission to require the oaths of the clergy, it was necessary for him to come to London. On the 14th of July, 1559, he was at Doncaster, "onward of his journey to Court . . . taking small journeys, though they were great to him, carrying his old carcass with him," as he wrote to the Earl of Shrewsbury.[3] Machyn writes in his *Diary*: "The 20th day of July, the good old Bishop of Durham came riding to London with threescore horse, and so to Southwark, unto Master Dolman's house, a tallow chandler, and there he lies [*i.e.*, resides] against the chaingate".[4]

He found all things in London undergoing change. The new Anglican Prayer Book was to have become obligatory on the Feast of St. John Baptist (24th June), but in the Chapel Royal and many other places the Protestants had not waited so long. On 11th June the Blessed Sacrament had been removed from St. Paul's;[5] images were being pulled down and altars destroyed. Ten bishops and many priests had been deprived. The Grey Friars of Greenwich,

[1] Strype's *Parker*, book i., cap. x., p. 94.

[2] *P. R. O., Dom. Eliz.*, i. 37.

[3] Strype, *Annals*, i., pt. i., p. 30.

[4] *Diary*, p. 204.

[5] *Documents from Simancas.* p. 26 ; also, Strype, *Annals*, i. 254, 260, 287.

the Black Friars of Smithfield, the priests and nuns of Syon and the Charterhouse, the Abbot and monks of Westminster, had been deposed or had left ;[1] furious sermons were being preached at St. Paul's Cross. A visitation was being made of the diocese of London by Horn and others, and great bonfires were burning in the streets, fed with roods and sacred images.[2]

De Quadra, the new Spanish ambassador, informs Philip that the old Bishop of Durham had reminded the Queen that her father had enjoined in his will the maintenance of the Catholic religion, at which remonstrance the Council had laughed.[3] By a letter still extant, written on 19th August, to Sir William Cecil, we find how eager the bishop was to see the Queen, though he should have to travel to Hampton Court or Windsor or elsewhere. He then adds : " And where I do understand out of my diocese [4] of a warning for a visitation to be had there, this shall be to advertise your Mastership, that albeit I would be as glad to serve the Queen's Highness, and to set forward all her affairs to her contentation as any subject in her realm, yet if the same visitation shall proceed to such end in my diocese of Durham, as I do plainly see to be set forth here in London, as pulling down of altars, defacing of churches by taking away of the crucifixes, I cannot in my conscience consent to it, being pastor there. Because I cannot myself agree to be a 'sacramentary,'[5] nor to have any new doctrine taught in my diocese. Whereof I thought meet to advertise your Mastership, humbly beseeching the same not to think me

---

[1] Machyn, p. 204.

[2] *Ibid.*, p. 207.

[3] *Simancas*, p. 64.

[4] *I.e.*, whereas I have received news from my diocese.

[5] The name given to the disciples of Calvin and Zuingli, who made light of the sacraments.

thereunto moved either for any forwardness, malice, or contempt, but only because my conscience will not suffer me to receive and allow any doctrine in my diocese other than Catholic, as knoweth Almighty Jesu, who ever preserve your Mastership to His pleasure and yours.

"From London, the 19th of August, 1559.

"Your Mastership's humble most assured loving friend,

"CUTHBERT, DURHAM."[1]

Notwithstanding this protest, on 9th September he was placed in the Commission for the consecration of Parker,[2] but in this he declined to act. Nothing, therefore, remained but to exact from him the oath of supremacy. On what day this was done is not ascertained; but on 27th September the Privy Council write from Hampton Court to Parker to lodge the Bishop of Durham in his own house at Lambeth, to confer with him on matters of religion, to let him have one man to attend on him, to let him have meat and drink and all things necessary as to him appertain, but to have a vigilant eye that none have access to him but those whom Parker shall appoint.[3]

Probably, before this letter was received his deposition had taken place. Machyn writes: "The 28th day of September was Michaelmas eve, was the old Bishop of Durham, Dr. Tunstall, deposed of his bishopric, because he should not receive the rents for that quarter".[4] But as Parker hastened to send the Council good hopes of the pliability of his prisoner, the following answer was returned on the 2nd October:

[1] *P. R. O., Dom. Eliz.*, vi. 22. A similar letter is addressed to Sir Thomas Parry.

[2] *Ibid.*, n. 41.

[3] *Parker Corresp.*, p. 77 (Parker Soc.) This is what Camden calls "free custody".

[4] *Diary*, p. 214.

"My good Lord, the contents of your yesterday's letter I have imparted to Her Majesty and others of Her Majesty's Council. It is much liked the comfort that ye give of the Bishop of Durham's towardness, wherein I pray God ye be not deceived. It is meant, if he will conform himself, that both he shall remain bishop and in good favour and credit ; otherwise, he must needs receive the common order of those which refuse to obey laws. Good my Lord, travail herein as ye may with speed.—2nd October [1559].

"Yours assuredly,

"W. CECIL." [1]

Parker had been too hasty, and had mistaken courtesy for submission or vacillation. Three days later Cecil wrote again : "My good Lord, the Queen's Majesty is very sorry that ye can prevail no more with Mr. Tunstall, and so am I, I assure you ; for the recovery of such a man would have furthered the common affairs of this realm very much. Her Majesty would that he should have liberty to send to Durham for discharge of his household. And further, ye may say to him that I trust Her Majesty will be pleased to appoint him some convenient pension, in consideration of his reverend age, which shall also be the larger as his conformity shall give occasion.

"From Westminster, the 5th October, 1559,

"W. CECIL." [2]

Of the last six weeks of the venerable confessor's life on earth we have no record. He died on the 15th November, 1559. From the following letter it seems that his death was sudden :

"My Lord of Durham hath one of his executors here,

[1] *Parker Corresp.*, p. 77.
[2] *Ibid.*, p. 78.

the other is in the north, where also is his testament.   This
executor saith that his mind was to be homely and plainly
buried.   Consider you whether it were not best to prescribe
some homest manner of his interring, lest it might else be
evil judged that the order of his funeral were at the Council's
appointment, not known abroad that the handling of it were
only at his executors' liberality.   I have sealed up two small
caskets, wherein I think no great substance, either of money
or of writings.   There is one roll of books which he purposed to deliver to the Queen, which is nothing else but
King Henry's Testament, and a book, *Contra communica-
tionem utriusque speciei*, and such matter.   The body, by
reason of his sudden departure, cannot be long kept.   Thus
Jesus preserve you.   This 18th of November [1559].

" Your beadman,

" M. EL. C." [1]

The funeral took place the next day, and he was buried
in the church at Lambeth.[2]   Holinshed writes that Alexander Nowell, soon after Dean of St. Paul's, preached his
funeral sermon, and gave him great commendation.

It is not with a wish to deprive Parker of the credit of an
act of kindliness, but for the sake of truth, that I remark
that authors have stated wrongly that the expenses of
Tunstall's funeral were defrayed by the Archbishop-elect.
It is evident from the letter just given that Tunstall left
some money, and the funeral was paid for by the executors.
That such a man as Nowell should have been called in to
preach at his funeral was either the doing of Parker or of the
Council.   It is equally incorrect to say, as Southey does,
that Tunstall " lived at Parker's table, and was treated by
him as an honourable guest ".   He was ordered by the
Council to receive convenient diet, but whether he shared

[1] *Parker Corresp.*, p. 106.   Machyn, p. 218.

the table of Dr. and Mrs. Parker we do not know. We should like to think that he was spared the indignity. But even should a prisoner be summoned to dine with his jailor, he is no guest, but a prisoner still.

An epitaph on a brass plate was placed under the communion table. It was the composition of Walter Haddon, an elegant Latin writer, but has no great merit.[1]

An interesting notice of the Tunstall family may be found in the Rev. T. Gibson's *History of Lydiate*.[2] The family remained Catholic. They removed from the village of Tunstall, in North Lancashire, to Wickliffe, in Yorkshire. Cuthbert Tunstall, in 1718, took the name of Constable. Sir F. T. Constable, Bart. of Burton Constable and Wickliffe, is lineal descendant of the Tunstalls.

RALPH BAYNE (of Lichfield and Coventry),

Deposed 21st June, 1559 ; died 18th November, 1559.

This bishop had never been involved in schism. An alumnus of the College of St. John's at Cambridge, he had profited by the foundation of Blessed John Fisher, and followed in his footsteps. He was resident in France during the troubles of Henry VIII. and Edward VI., having been appointed Professor of Hebrew in the University of Paris. He published two works on Hebrew Grammar and an exegetical treatise, *In Proverbia Salamonis*.

He was a staunch opponent of all the Anti-Catholic measures in Elizabeth's first Parliament. As one of the

---

[1] Mr. J. G. Nichols, in his *Notes on Machyn*, says that Tunstall died on 15th November. If Ducarel, in his *History of Lambeth*, has rightly copied the epitaph, he died on the 18th.

Mr. Cave-Brown, the most recent historian of the Palace, makes the prodigious blunder that Tunstall lived at Lambeth with Parker, "the large-hearted and the tolerant," for above ten years" (p. 227).

[2] P. 202.

champions of the Catholic side in the Westminster Conference, he was condemned to appear personally each day on
which the Council sat for six weeks, and at last to pay a
fine of £333 6s. 8d.[1] On his refusal to take the oath of
supremacy, he was deposed 21st June, 1559.[2]

Sanders, in his letter to Cardinal Morone, gives the following interesting account of him : " He was of such constancy
of mind in this persecution that he always went with joy to
any questioning, and returned still happier. But having
been deposed and sent away on bail, he was sitting, both
sick and sorrowful, in his chair, when he heard a voice saying to him : ' Be of good courage, for thou shalt suffer
martyrdom '. He is said, by persons worthy of all credit,
to have related this occurrence, but without saying what
kind of martyrdom he would endure. But it was thus. He
suffered such excruciating torment from the stone for six
days, that to the bystanders, among whom were the Bishop
of Chester and the Dean of St. Paul's, the pain seemed
quite unbearable : yet he did not complain, but lifting his
eyes at one time to heaven, and at another resting them on
a crucifix, he invoked the Name of Jesus to the last moment
of his life." [3]

His death took place at Islington, 18th November, 1559,
and on the 24th he was buried in the Church of St. Dun-
stan-in-the-West, in Fleet Street, as appears by the parish
register.[4] It is a mistake of Wharton to say that he was
buried in Islington, and an error of Dodd to say that his
illness was increased by imprisonment.[5]

[1] *Council Register*, p. 286.

[2] Machyn, p. 200.

[3] Vatican MS., f. 261.

[4] Mr. Nichols, note to Machyn, p. 378.

[5] Wharton (*Anglia Sacra*), p. 458, who quotes W. Whitlock;
Dodd, *Church History* (Biographical Part).

HENRY MORGAN (of St. David's),

Deposed 21st June (?), 1559 ; died 23rd December, 1559.

The Bishop of Menevia or St. David's was excused from attendance in the first Parliament of Elizabeth. He gave his proxy to Archbishop Heath. It is certain that he was deposed, since, at the licence for the election of a successor, the see is declared vacant *per legitimam deprivationem Henrici Morgan.*[1] Of the day I can find no certain record. Machyn, however, states that five bishops were deprived 21st June, 1559. He mentions the Bishops of Lichfield, Carlisle, Chester, and Llandaff (who at first seems to have refused the oath), and the Bishop of ——, leaving the name blank. As all other dates of deprivation are known, this can only be the Bishop of St. David's or the Bishop of Worcester.

His health was, probably, failing, and he was left at liberty, and died 23rd December, the same year, 1559.[2]

Dodd says that, after his deprivation, he lived with his relations near Oxford, especially with Mr. Owen of Godstow, leaving behind him a very great character for his innocent life and charity towards the poor. By his last will he ordered that his body should be buried in Woolvercote Church. He left £4 yearly to be paid to two Masters of Arts at Oxford, to pray for his soul during the term of five years." Masses, of course, were now illegal, and this was the only form in which such a legacy could be made.[3]

OWEN OGELTHORPE (of Carlisle),

Deposed 21st June, 1559 ; died (end of) December, 1559.

The name of Bishop Ogelthorpe appears rather con-

[1] Rymer, *Fœdera*, xv. 561.

[2] Stubbs, *Reg. Sacr.*

[3] Fox has a story that he died a horrible death, which Anthony à Wood refutes.

spicuously in the records of the early days of Elizabeth. He was present in the Parliament January to May, 1559, and, together with the other bishops, gave all the opposition he could to the revolutionary measures of the Government. I have already[1] given the account of an eye-witness of the Christmas Mass of 1558. "The Queen," he says, "left the Chapel immediately after the Gospel". Other authors tell us that the celebrant, on this occasion, was the Bishop of Carlisle. Cardinal Allen, who was in England at the time, and may be considered well informed, has left the following account. He is explaining why the bishops distrusted Queen Elizabeth, and expected her to refuse the unction at the Convocation : "They doubted," he says, "because they saw, not long before, Her Highness, at her first entrance to that high estate, command a certain bishop, even the same Carlisle now named, standing ready to say Mass before her, not to elevate the holy consecrated Host, but to omit that ceremony, because she liked it not. Which the said bishop, to his great honour, constantly refused to obey,—a thing that in one of us poor men now, perchance, would be accompted high treason and disloyalty towards our Sovereign. And of this his courage in God's cause it never repented him ; but for doing the other office at the coronation, when he saw the issue of the matter, and the Church's holy law and faith, against the condition of her consecration and acceptation into that Royal room, violated . . . he sore repented him all the days of his life, which were for that special cause both short and wearisome afterwards unto him."[2]

He was one of those chosen to maintain the Catholic side in the Conference of Westminster in March, 1559, and I have already related that, on account of what the Council

---

[1] See p. 17.   [2] *True and Modest Defence*, p. 51.

were pleased to consider contempt of Her Majesty's orders, after the daily humiliation of reporting himself to the Council for six weeks, he was fined in the sum of £133 6s. 8d.[1] Such was the gratitude of the Queen for his conciliatory spirit in performing the coronation service. Lord Burghley says not a word of the fine when he praises the bishop's " courteous nature and inclination to dutifulness ".[2]

He was cited to take the oath of supremacy, and on his refusal was deprived, 21st June, 1559.[3] He died in London (of apoplexy, according to Heylin) towards the end of December. He was buried in St. Dunstan's-in-the-West, 4th January, 1560, as the worthy undertaker, Machyn, remarks, " with alff a doseñ skochyons of armes,"[4] but, of course, without dirge or requiem.

As the refusal of the Bishop of Carlisle to omit the elevation at the bidding of the Queen has been called in question, I will add two contemporary accounts to those already given. The Spanish ambassador, De Feria, distinctly names him, and adds that, when the Queen sent word to him not to elevate, the bishop replied that she should be mistress of his goods and life, but not of his conscience, whereupon she left the Chapel after the Gospel.[5]

Sanders, in his letter to Cardinal Morone, writes : " It having been customary that, at the Feast of the Nativity,

---

[1] *Council Register*, p. 286.

[2] See *supra*, p. 3.

[3] Machyn, p. 200.

[4] *Diary*, p. 221. " Scocheons," says Mr Nichols, " were the lowest description of heraldic ensign allotted for funerals. Mere gentlemen had no penon, but as many scocheons as were desired. But the funerals of the higher ranks were also provided with scocheons, in addition to their other insignia. They were made of metal, silk, buckram, or paper. They bore the arms of the family, the bishopric or the society to which the deceased belonged."

[5] *Simancas Documents*, p. 48.

one of the bishops should say Mass in the Royal Chapel, the Bishop of Carlisle, being vested, stood at the altar, when two messengers of the Queen forbade him to elevate the Sacred Host. He was astounded at this novelty, but boldly replied : 'Whether he should say Mass at that altar or not was as the Queen pleased ; but with what rite and with what ceremonies it should be said, he, being a bishop, knew quite well, nor would he make any change'. When the messengers departed, he began the celebration, and proceeded in all things according to the ancient rite. But the Queen, not enduring to pay adoration to so great a Sacrament, left after the reading of the Gospel, satisfied (as I think) with a Mass of the catechumens, though she was not worthy of that rank."[1] This was written about two years after the event.

Sanders adds that, after his deprivation, he was cast into prison, and that his grief for having crowned Elizabeth hastened, as many thought, his death. Of this imprisonment I have seen no other mention. But Sanders was in England at the time.

In addition to the above testimonies, we have the sworn evidence of Edmund Daniel, Dean of Hereford, made in Rome in 1570. " I was present," he says, " when the Queen Elizabeth in her chapel,[2] when the Bishop of Carlisle was celebrating Mass, while the choir was singing the Gloria, sent her secretary to him, bidding him not to elevate. But the bishop, as I have heard, replied that he should elevate the Host according to the custom of the Catholic Church. The Queen, therefore, left before the Gospel, and her secretary told me she left not to witness the elevation. And the dean [of the chapel] commanded

[1] Vatican MS., 64, 7, 28, f. 260.
[2] He says *sub anno* 1559. The date was Christmas, 1558.

me to celebrate on St. Stephen's Day, without elevating. This I refused to do. Therefore she sent her own chaplain, named Minter, who celebrated without elevation, and I saw the Queen assisting at his Mass." [1]

JOHN WHITE (of Winchester),
Deposed 26th June, 1559; died 12th Jan., 1560.

John White, a native of Farnham, in Surrey, had been educated at Winchester and New College, Oxford, and had been Warden of Winchester. He had refused to conform to Protestant innovations under Edward VI., and under Mary had been promoted to the See of Lincoln, and thence translated to Winchester. He was a good Latin poet, as well as a learned controversialist.

After Elizabeth's accession, he had preached at the funeral of the Bishop of Rochester, in the Church of St. Magnus, in London, on the 30th November, 1558,[2] and at the funeral of Queen Mary, in Westminster Abbey, on the 14th December. This sermon has been preserved.[3] The eulogy of Queen Mary was supposed to reflect on the known opinions and anticipated conduct of her sister, and gave so much offence that the bishop received orders from the Council to consider himself a prisoner within his house in Southwark. This, however, was not of long duration. He was admonished and set at liberty on 19th January;[4] was probably present at the coronation, as he certainly was at the Parliament. He was one of the eight Catholic disputants in the Conference in Westminster Abbey.[5] On

[1] Ladercius, iii. 204, quoted by Lewis in note to Rishton's additions to Sanders.

[2] Machyn, p. 180.

[3] Strype, *Memorials*, App. iii.; Tierney's *Dodd*, ii., App. xxxii.

[4] *Council Register.*

[5] For this, see the *Life of Watson.*

Monday, the 3rd April, the Conference having been broken up, the Bishops of Winchester and Lincoln were sent prisoners to the Tower.[1] The Council ordered them to be kept in sure and separate wards, suffering them to have attendance by their own servants, and to provide their own bedding and furniture. They were to be appointed "some convenient lodging meet for persons of their sort, using them also otherwise well".

The Council also at once sent Sir Ambrose Cave and Sir Richard Sackville, two of their number, to the bishops' London houses, "to peruse their studies and writings, and to take order with their officers for the surety of their goods".[2]

Two entries in the *Council Register* show the nature of this imprisonment. On the 9th May a letter was written to the Lieutenant of the Tower, "to suffer the Bishop of Winchester's cook from time to time to attend upon him for the dressing of his meat, so as he speak only with him in his [the Lieutenant's] presence, or such as he shall appoint. And, in like sort, to suffer the Lady White, his sister,[3] to repair unto him at such times as he [the Lieutenant] shall think meet, so as *ut supra*"—*i.e.*, the interview not to be a private one.

Again, on the 11th, certain officers to repair to the Bishop of Winchester for the understanding of his reckonings and accounts; but they must only speak with him in the Lieutenant's presence.

On the 26th June the Bishop of Winchester was brought

---

[1] Machyn, p. 192.

[2] *Council Reg.*, vol. i.

[3] This may mean his sister-in-law. Both his sister and his sister-in-law were named Lady White. His brother was Sir John White, his brother-in-law Sir Thomas White. See note of Mr. Nichols in Machyn's *Diary*, p. 378.

from the Tower to the Sheriff's house in Mincing Lane, where the oath was proposed to him by the Commissioners, and by him refused. He was at once re-conveyed to the Tower.[1]

Machyn tells us that, on the 7th July, my good Lord of Winchester, Dr. White, came out of the Tower, with the Lieutenant, Sir Edward Warner, by six in the morning, and so to my Lord Keeper of the Broad Seal [Sir Nicolas Bacon], and from thence unto Master Whyte, alderman, and there he lies.[2]   He had thus been in strict, solitary confinement for rather more than three months, and during that time deprived of all opportunity of public worship or reception of the holy Sacraments.

His brother-in-law, Sir Thomas White, alderman, had a house at South Warnborough, in Hampshire.[3]   Thither he retired ; but his health had been seriously affected in the unhealthy prison, and he suffered for the next six months from an ague, which carried him off on the 12th January, 1560.   He left large legacies to his servants, says Machyn.[4] He desired by his will to be buried in his own cathedral, and this was not refused him.   The funeral took place on 15th January.

Strype has said : "White died in liberty. Although he had liberty to walk abroad, he would not be quiet, but he would needs preach, which he did seditiously in his Romish pontifical vestments ; but, upon his acknowledgment of his misdemeanour, he was set free."   I cannot tell the source from which this is derived, nor have I sufficient trust in Strype's accuracy to accept it simply on his word.   If, how-

[1] Machyn, p. 201.

[2] *Diary*, p. 203.   The Lord Keeper was one of the Ecclesiastical Commissioners.

[3] Milner's *Winchester*, i. 282 ; 3rd ed.

[4] *Diary*, p. 223.

ever, it is true, it is all the more honourable to the zeal of the good bishop.

His reason for wishing to be buried in his cathedral, as expressed in his will, was : *Ut in novissima die resurgam cum patribus et filiis quorum fidem teneo.*[1] He had, when warden of Winchester College, prepared his burial-place, and written his epitaph there.

[1] Wood, *Athen. Ox.*

APPENDIX TO CHAPTER IV.

Though my purpose in this sketch is to correct historical misstatements, I should weary my readers if I noticed all the blunders in Miss Strickland's account of the first years of Elizabeth. Every sentence teems with inaccuracies. In one place[1] she says : " There were but *five or six* Catholic bishops surviving the pestilence, and these all obstinately refused to perform the ceremony " of coronation. A few pages later : " *Thirteen* prelates, in consequence of refusing to take the oath declaring the Queen's supremacy, were ejected by this Parliament from their sees ".[2]

In her account of the coronation, Miss Strickland writes : " The Queen's perplexity regarding the prelate who was to crown her must have continued till the last moment, because had Dr. Oglethorpe, the Bishop of Carlisle, been earlier prevailed on to perform the ceremony, it is certain proper vestments could have been prepared for him, instead of borrowing them from Bonner, which was actually done on the spur of the moment ". Now, nothing whatever was done on the spur of the moment. The coronation took place on Sunday, 15th January, 1559. Long before, the part of each bishop had been assigned, for several took part in the ceremony, though the Bishop of Carlisle was the officiant and the celebrant. He was not the preacher. As regards the vestments, there were some of special magnificence, reserved for such regal ceremonies, and these were naturally in the custody of the Bishop of London. The order of the Council for their delivery at Westminster was issued four days before the ceremony. The following is the entry in the *Council Register:* " 11th

[1] Vol. iv., p. 144; ed. 1851.   [2] *Ibid.*, p. 157.

January.   A letter to the Bishop of London to lend to the Bishop of
Carleol, who is appointed to execute the solemnity of the Queen's
Majesty's coronation *universum apparatum Pontificium quo uti
solent Episcopi in hujusmodi magnificis illustrissimorum regum in-
augurationibus.*"

Again, Miss Strickland writes: " Elizabeth attended in person at
her sister's interment, and listened attentively to her funeral sermon,
preached by Dr. White, Bishop of Winchester, which was in Latin.
. . . Had Dr. White preached in English his sermon might have
done her much mischief. . . . In conclusion, he observed that Queen
Mary had left a sister, a lady of great worth also, whom they were
bound to obey; ' for,' said he, ' *melior est canis vivus leone mortuo* '.
Elizabeth was too good a Latinist not to fire at this elegant simile.
. . . As the bishop descended the pulpit stairs, Elizabeth ordered
him under arrest. He defied her, and threatened her with excommunication, for which she cared not a rush. He was a prelate of
austere but irreproachable manners, exceedingly desirous of testifying
his opinions by a public martyrdom. Elizabeth was too wise to
indulge him with that distinction."

Everything in this passage is incorrect. The sermon was preached
in English, not in Latin, though texts of Scripture are quoted in
Latin, according to the custom.[1]   Queen Elizabeth does not seem to
have been present, but the bishop spoke in every way honourably of
her : " Let us comfort ourselves in the other sister whom God hath
left, wishing her a prosperous reign, in peace and tranquillity, with
the blessing which the prophet speaketh of, if it be God's will *ut
videat filios filiorum et pacem super Israel*, ever confessing that,
though God hath mercifully provided for them both, yet *Maria
optimum partem elegit*; because it is still a conclusion : *laudavi
mortuos magis quam viventes*".   The words about the live dog and
dead lion occur in a different part of the sermon, and a meaning is
given them that could by no possibility reflect on the Queen. " One
living dog," says White, " one vigilant minister in the Church barking
against sin and heresy, is better than ten dreaming dead lions, or
great ecclesiastics who let things take their course." It is not clear
what gave offence, not so much to the Queen as to her Council.
Probably it was the praise given to Mary for not calling herself Head
of the Church, and the saying that if a woman could be Head the
Church would have a dumb head, since it is forbidden to a woman to

[1] It is printed fully by Strype in his *Memorials*, App. iii.

speak in the Church. But it had been resolved to seize every opportunity to find fault with and humble the bishops.

Miss Strickland's description of the bishop threatening the Queen there and then with excommunication is an application of her own to this occasion of what Camden wrote regarding the Westminster Conference, four months later, though it is equally untrue of either. Bishop White's manners were in no way austere; on the contrary, he was of a courteous nature, according to Lord Burghley. His wish and efforts to provoke martyrdom have no grounds either in history or historians.

CHAPTER V

CUTHBERT SCOTT (of Chester),
Deposed 21st June, 1559; died 1565.

THERE is no one of the bishops about whom so many mistakes are made as about the Bishop of Chester. Mr. Bruce, in his notes to Hayward, whom he edited for the Camden Society, writes as follows: " All the lists of the deposed bishops differ ; the following I believe to be a correct one ". He has gathered it from Rymer's authentic documents, and it is correct, with one exception ; for he has omitted from his list Cuthbert Scott, Bishop of Chester, though with regard to his deprivation there was neither doubt nor obscurity. His name, however, had not been mentioned by Lord Burghley nor by Andrewes. Camden had merely said that "he voluntarily departed the land ". Heylin mentioned his deposition, but told nothing of his subsequent history. Collier writes: " As for Cuthbert Scott, Bishop of Chester, Richard Pate of Worcester, and Thomas Goldwell of St. Asaph's, they had the liberty of retiring beyond the sea, which they made their choice". Yet this is probably the very last kind of liberty the Queen would have granted them ; and it was not till after long imprisonment that two of them contrived to escape. Southey is content with the single phrase: " Three of the ex-bishops withdrew to the Continent ". Even Lingard does not seem to be aware of the imprisonments of Scott and Pate, for he classes them with Goldwell: "Scott of Chester, Goldwell of St. Asaph, and Pate of Worcester found the means of retiring to the Continent"; which is quite true, but inadequate and misleading. Lastly, Charles Butler says: "Some were permitted to cross the seas, and died abroad".

I have spoken sufficiently in a former chapter of Scott's zeal in Elizabeth's first Parliament, and given some extracts from his speeches: I have also mentioned his treatment by the Council, and the fine imposed on him after the Conference of Westminster. He was deposed for refusing the oath of supremacy on 21st June, 1559.[1]

A document, apparently in the handwriting of the principal jailor of the Fleet prison, runs as follows: "This yis the names off all the bysshopes doctors and pristes that were prisoners in the flytte for Religion synse the fyrste yere of the raygne of quene Elizabethe an. dom. 1558". Amongst them is: "A byshoppe Mr. Cutberte Skotte was commyttyd on ye 13 of May 1561". In the same list are Dr. Nicolas Harpsfield, committed 20th August, 1559; his brother, Dr. John Harpsfield, committed 9th July, 1561; Mr. Thomas Wood, "priste and electyd a bisshope," committed the 20th November, 1561, and several more.[2] But the writer must have made an error in the year as regards Dr. Scott, since in a return made on 3rd July, 1561, to the Council, the warden of the Fleet says: "Cutberd Scott som tyme byschopp of Chester was committied presoner to the fflete the xiii of maij an. dom. 1560 by the Quenis Majesties commyssioners. And his cause ys to me unknown."[3]

---

[1] Machyn (p. 201), who calls him the Bishop of Westchester.
[2] Harl. MS., "Pluto," L. E. 360-7.
[3] *P. R. O., Dom. Eliz.*, xviii. 5.

Of the nature of Dr. Scott's imprisonment, in addition to what has been said in a former chapter, some special conjecture may be made from a document still preserved among the Petyt MSS. in the Inner Temple. In the first year of the bishop's imprisonment some constitutions were made for the government of the Fleet prison. The 12th article runs as follows : " That the Warden shall take of every man or woman that shall sit at the parlour-commons 2s. 4d. weekly for his bed and chamber, and of every man or woman that shall sit at the hall-commons 14d. for his bed and chamber, lying like prisoners two in a bed together ". In addition to this 2s. 4d. for the privilege of sleeping alone, the bishop had to pay 18s. 6d. a week for his board. This we know by a document signed by him : " We, the prisoners undernamed, having deliberately consulted thereupon, do now agree, with the assent of the Warden, that every person of the degrees hereunder written, for their weekly commons and wine, over and besides the rate for their bed and chamber, shall weekly pay—a knight, a doctor of divinity, and other having 200 marks a year living, 18s. 6d. An esquire, a gentleman, or other person at parlour-commons shall pay for their weekly commons and wine 10s."[1] Thus, then, for board and lodging in the Fleet, the unfortunate prisoners who wished to maintain some decency paid more than £1 a week, or about £10 a week in modern value.

After *four years'* confinement in this jail, the bishop was released, on his bond that he would remain within twenty miles distance from Finchingfield in Essex, and make his personal appearance before the Ecclesiastical Commissioners

---

[1] The document is printed in the *Eleventh Report of the Historical Manuscripts Commission*, App., part vii., p. 247 (1888). The names of Cuthbert Scott, Henry Cole, and Nicholas Harpsfield are signed to it, with those of several laymen.

when duly summoned.[1] This was a penal obligation, and not a *parole d'honneur;* and the bishop did not consider himself bound by it, but managed to escape into Belgium. His flight acted unfavourably on some other prisoners ; for when Dr. Boxall, Dean of Windsor, who had been several years confined in the Tower, and in September, 1563, had been transferred to the custody of Dr. Parker, petitioned for his release, the answer sent to him by the Council was as follows, on 23rd June, 1564: "Forasmuch as one Dr. Scott, sometime Bishop of Chester, receiving favour upon his own bond and the bond of his friends, hath withdrawn himself without regard had either of his own bond or the danger of his friends, and therein hath committed the act of contempt of the Queen's Majesty, a matter much noted and many ways evil reported unto us, we cannot therefore conveniently accord Mr. Boxall's suit, seeing the former lenity and gentleness used to others in this case hath so freshly wrought a lack of consideration in the person of the said Scott, which Mr. Boxall, being a wise man, can consider".[2] Probably Dr. Boxall, being a wise man, made some other reflections than on the "lenity and gentleness" of the Council. He reflected that he, as well as Dr. Scott, was enduring prison for no offence, and by no law.

I have been fortunate enough to discover one other notice of Dr. Scott. In a Latin life of Blessed John Fisher, written in Paris early in the next century, the writer says : "In this same college"—Christ's College, Cambridge —"was brought up that Bishop of Chester, Cuthbert Scott, who, being in Louvain at the time when that sacred war was beginning to be waged by Dr. Harding and his companions with so much success, by his authority and his money gave

---

[1] *P. R. O., Dom. Eliz.,* xxxv. 38.

[2] MS. in C. C. C. C., n. 114; printed in Strype's *Parker,* p. 218.

no little help ".[1]   He alludes to the controversy with Jewell.
Dr. Scott died some time in 1565, but I have not been able
to discover the exact date.   His epitaph was written by
Richard Shacklock, a lawyer and scholar, who was living as
an exile for his faith in Belgium.[2]

RICHARD PATE (of Worcester),

Deprived June, 1559 ; died 23rd November, 1565.

The Bishop of Worcester has the distinction of having
been one of the two bishops who represented the English
Church in the Council of Trent.[3] Having been sent by
Henry on an embassy in 1540, he refused to return to
England, and was attainted. He was appointed to the
bishopric of Worcester by the Pope on 8th July, 1541,
and was probably consecrated in Italy, but he did not
receive the temporalities of his see till the reign of Queen
Mary.

He was present in the Council of Trent on 29th
December, 1546,[4] as well as in 1552. He returned to
England in 1554.

Throughout the first Parliament of Elizabeth he voted
with the rest of the bishops against every anti-Catholic
measure of the Government. The exact date of his
deprivation is not ascertained, but as the spiritualities of

[1] " In eodem collegio enutritus erat Episcopus Cestrensis, Cuth-
bertus Scott, qui tunc Lovanii agens, quando sacrum illud bellum a
D. Hardingo et sociis feliciter inchoatum erat, auctoritate sua et
opibus sine dubio haud mediocriter juvit."—Harl. MS., 7030.

[2] See *Extracts from the Registers of the Stationers' Company*, by
J. Payne Collier, p. 121. A counter epitaph or epigram seems to have
been written and printed by Thomas Drant, 1565-6.

[3] The other was Thomas Goldwell, of St. Asaph's. There was of
course another, and a very illustrious, Englishman, but Cardinal Pole
was not a bishop, nor even a priest, when president of the Council.

[4] Pallavicini's *History of the Council*, book viii., ch. xvii.

the vacant see were seized on 30th June, 1559,[1] it is probable that he was deposed about the 24th or 25th June.

Cardinal Bellarmine, under the name of Tortus, had complained of the imprisonment of so many bishops. The Protestant.Andrewes replied to him in a work called *Tortura Torti.* He writes of Pate and Goldwell as follows : " I grant that Pate of Worcester and Goldwell of St. Asaph's left the country, but neither of them by any sentence of the law, but by their own free will ".[2] It is curious that this is literally true, while conveying an utterly false meaning. Andrewes implies that the law left them free to go, whereas they had to escape the vigilance of the Government. He implies also that neither of them was imprisoned. I have already given the documents which prove that Bishop Pate was committed to the Tower on 20th May, 1560, and was not delivered until September, 1563.[3]

He is said by Dodd to have been present at the close of the Council of Trent on 3rd December, 1563, and subscribed in the name of the Catholic Church in England ; but of this I can find no confirmation. His death is thus entered in a list of obits written on an old Psalterium now in Exeter College, Oxford: "Nov. 23 Obitus venerabilis Richardi Pates episcopi Wigornensis 1565 ".[4]

His will, drawn up by him on 12th February, 1561, while in the Tower, is still preserved in the English College, Rome. I give the most interesting parts.[5] " In

---

[1] *Reg. Cant. apud* Harmer (*i.e.*, Wharton), *Specimen*, p. 151.

[2] " De Pato Wigornensi, de Goldwello ibidem Asaphensi et illos excessisse regno fatemur, neutrum tamen ex legis sententia aliqua, tantum quia ipsi voluerunt " (p. 147).

[3] See p. 39.

[4] See letter to the *Academy*, by Mr. C. W. Boase, 15th April, 1876.

[5] It is printed at length by Dr. Maziere Brady in his *Episcopal Succession*, vol. ii., 283.

Dei nomine. Amen. I Richard Pate, the late Bushop of Worcester, being at this present in competent bodyly helth and of perfyte memorye, for the uncertainty of my calling oute of this transitorie lyfe by syckness or otherwyse, as almyghty God shall despose, have thought it good and expedient without further delai to make now my last will and testament in manner and forme following : First I doe commend my sowle into the merciful hands of almyghty God, my creator, trusting to have hir saved by the merits of Jesus Christ his only begotten Son my redeemer : and the sam by the intercession of our blessed lady his mother the Virgin Marye, and of all holly saynts of his Catholyke Church, as well triumphant in heaven as yet militant in earth : And my body to be decently buried in that parish churche where it shall fortune me to die, or otherwhere, at the appoyntment of myne executors." He then bequeaths certain sums invested in Rome at the *monte de la fede* and the *monte della farina* to the " Right Rev. Father in God Thomas Goldwell, my Lord Assaphen, and my dear friend Mr. Henry Pinynges " to dispense as directed. They were at once to make an instrument conveying these monies " to my See and the Cathedral Church of Worcester ". " During the tyme this scisme goes in the realme, my wyll ys that no penny of the sayd annuities, nor yet any knowledge thereof, shold come unto the mencyoned Cathedral Church, but the disposycyon of the same, duryng the said scisme, shalbe hollye at your discretions and at the discretyon of the longest lyving of you bothe, to be bestowed in almes upon our poore country men and women, as well religiouse as secular, which at this present for conscience sake are fled into those partyes, and have not wherewith to susteyne themselves.

" When it shall please God to send the return of our realme to the unite of Christes Churche, then I wold have you convey the instrument before made by you of my donacyon thereof, unto my Cathedral Church ; and then the sayd annuities to be employed upon an obit once in the year for my sowle, my father and mother, John and Elinor Pate, and Mr Seth Hollaindes, the late dean of the same, and the ministers of the Church to have 20 nobles for theyr payns, and to the poore people of Worcester on the same day to be distributed in almes 20 marks, and other 20 marks yearly to be given in exhibycion to the helpe and furthirance of 4 scholars and students in Gloceter College, in the Universitie of Oxford," &c.[1]

" And whereas my sayd testament unto you mayd ys not so formally as the lawe paraventure requirethe, the same not being confirmed by any notaryes seale, I must request you, and those unto whom the approbacyon thereof shall appertayne, to consyder myne estate at the makyng thereof, and how I was at that present a cloose prisoner for my faythe and defence of the unite of Christ's Church in the Tower of London, and could have none other better mean to expresse my mynde unto you."

Mass, says Dr. Brady, is still said for Richard Pate in the Church of the English College, Rome, on the 5th of October, annually ; but, if we may trust the entry in the *Calendar* given above, Dr. Brady is wrong in considering the 5th October the day of his death.[2]

---

[1] A noble was 6s. 8d., a mark 13s. 4d.

[2] Le Plat, in his list of bishops present in the Council of Trent, wrongly puts Bishop Pate's death in 1559. Ricardus Patus, Anglus Episcopus Vigornensis, El., 1534 ; Ob. 1559. It is curious also that the writ *Significavit* for the confirmation of Edwin Sands (18th Dec., 1559) speaks of the See of Worcester as vacant by the death of the last bishop (unnamed) ; but the writ for the restitution of the temporalities mentions the " deprivation of Richard Pate. the late bishop " (Rymer, xv. 550, 553).

DAVID POOLE (of Peterborough),
Deposed November, 1559; died June, 1568.

Not much can be told about Dr. Poole, or Pole.[1] There
exists a letter of his to Sir William Cecil, dated 28th
December, 1558, thanking him for a gift he had sent him of
a buck and a doe. In the same letter he begs the Queen
to accept a small gift of twenty marks, and that she will
excuse his attendance in Parliament.[2] From this it would
appear that there was some friendship between him and the
new Secretary. And, writing twenty years later, Cecil
speaks of him as " an ancient, grave person and very quiet
subject ".[3]

His history is one on which the various Protestant
historians dwell with emphasis. " Pole of Peterborough,"
writes Andrewes, "was treated with the greatest courtesy,
by the kindness of the Queen enjoyed continuous freedom,
till he at last died at a good old age in his own estate."[4]
What could Bellarmine or the English Catholics on the
Continent have to say against such a splendid proof of
tolerance and liberality? There is, however, another view of
things ; and though Dr. Poole did not share the Tower or
the Marshalsea with his brother bishops, he had opportunities of proving his constancy and of acquiring the merit
of a confessor. He refused to consecrate Parker when his
name was placed on the Commission ; and when the oath

[1] Burnet calls him a brother of Cardinal Pole, but is refuted by
Harmer (*i.e.*, Wharton).—*Specimen*, p. 145.

[2] *P. R. O., Dom. Elis.*, i. 48.

[3] See *supra*, p. 3.

[4] "Polus Petriburgensis summa comitate habitus, liber semper
principis beneficio, et in agro suo matura ætate discessit " (*Tortura
Torti*, p. 146). Heylin repeats this word for word, except that he
translates *in agro suo* " on one of his farms," to give the reader
a vision of large possessions quietly enjoyed.

of supremacy was tendered, he endured the penalty of deprivation rather than take it. The spiritualities of his see were seized on the 11th November, 1559. His deposition must have preceded by a few days.[1]

In a return of " recusants which are abroad and bound to certain places," placed by Mrs. Green in the *Calendar* in 1561, there is the following entry : " David Poole, late Bishop of Peterborough, to remain in the city of London and suburbs, or within three miles compass about the same ". And opposite his name the following character is given : " A man known and reported to live quietly, and therefore hitherto tolerated ".[2]

If he continued to be tolerated it was not owing to the tolerant spirit of the new bishops. Among the MSS. of the Marquis of Salisbury is a letter of Thomas Bentham, Bishop of Lichfield and Coventry, to the Council, dated 10th November, 1564, in which he complains that "whereas the country is too much hindered in all good things pertaining to religion, yet the abiding of Doctor Poole, late Bishop of Peterborough, with Bryan Fowler, Esq., causeth many people to think worse of the regiment and religion than else they would do, because divers lewd priests have resort thither". The bishop therefore suggests that his removal would do much good to the country.[3]

Bishop Willis says : " In his will, which I have seen, dated 17th May, and proved 6th July, 1568, he names no place of burial, but leaves it to his executors, who were his

---

[1] Harmer's *Specimen*, p. 151. Willis, in his *Survey of Cathedrals* (iii. 505), says he was deposed about June. This is clearly wrong, since his name was in the Commission for Parker's consecration on 9th September.

[2] *P. R. O., Dom. Eliz.*, Addenda, xi. 45.

[3] " Calendar of MSS. of Marquis of Salisbury," part i. 309, in the App. of *Historical MSS. Commission*, 1883.

own Archdeacon Dr. Binnesley, and one Wilkinson. However, as his death seems to have happened in London in June, 1568, I presume he was interred in St. Paul's Cathedral in that city, though I find no memorial for him there or anywhere else. In his said will he bequeathed his books at London and Peterborough, of Divinity and Law, to All-Souls' College Library (Oxford)." [1]

It is pleasant to think that, resident in a Catholic house, Bishop Poole may from time to time have been able to celebrate the Divine Mysteries, and perhaps received the last sacraments at the hands of one of those " lewd priests," as Bentham calls them, who resorted to him, a privilege shared by few of his episcopal brethren.

EDMUND BONNER (of London),

Deposed 29th May, 1559; died 5th September, 1569.

From the *Council Register* we find that a letter was sent to the Bishop of London by the Council, on 3rd January, 1559, " that he should come the next day to the Vice-Chamberlain, and bring with him all such commissions as were made to him and others for the examination and ordering of heresies and other misorders in the Church in the time of the late Queen ". And a few days previously (18th December, 1558) a return had been asked of the official of the Arches of the persons who had been called before the Bishop of London by commission, and of the judgment and fines.[2] These measures show that it was the hope of Sir William Cecil and Elizabeth's other Protestant advisers that proof might be found that Bishop Bonner had gone beyond his commission, or exceeded the limits of the law. As no such charge was brought against him, it may be presumed that no such proofs were found.

[1] *Survey of Cathedrals*, iii. 505.

[2] *Council Reg., Eliz.*, vol. i. (MS.).

There is a curious entry in the *Council Register*, on 18th December, 1558, which shows that even Elizabeth's Council imposed unpleasant judicial tasks upon him : " A letter to the Bishop of London, with certain examinations taken of men that practised conjuring in the city of London, sent unto him by Mr. Attorney, wherein he is willed to proceed by such severe punishment against them that should be proved culpable herein, according to the order of ecclesiastical laws, as he shall think meet ". Yet, according to Miss Strickland and the authorities she quotes, Elizabeth's confidential maid, Blanche Parry, was an adept in the art of conjuring, and the Queen would not be crowned until Dr. Dee, the conjuror, had chosen for her a lucky day.

The Bishop of London, the See of Canterbury being vacant, was asked by the Dean and Chapter of Canterbury to preside in Convocation. But his duties were merely formal, and his action was confined to presenting the petition of the lower House of Convocation to the House of Peers in Parliament in favour of the Catholic doctrine. He was active in Parliament, and voted with the other bishops. He was the first among the bishops to whom the oath was offered, and he has therefore the credit of being the first to have refused the oath and incurred the penalties. He was deprived on 29th May, 1559.

It has been asserted by many writers that Bonner was confined in prison for his own security. Andrewes was, I believe, the originator of this myth. " It was not safe for him to go out, lest he should have been stoned."[1] The myth was developed by Fuller : " Bonner was imprisoned in the Marshalsea, a jail being conceived the safest place to secure him from the people's fury, every hand itching to

---

[1] " Ut nec tutum esset ei prodire in publicum, ne saxis obrueretur " (*Tortura Torti*, p. 147).

give a good squeeze to that sponge of blood ". Southey goes one step farther : " Though Bonner was allowed to go abroad, he dared not, because of the hatred of the people. He never betrayed the slightest shame or compunction for the cruelties which he had committed, but maintained to the last the same coarse and insolent temper ; indeed, it was rumoured and believed that he looked for no life but the present, and therefore had no. hope or fear beyond it."[1] Thus our historians write according to the fancy of the moment. If the bishop is known to have been active in Parliament, he is painted by Mr. Froude as " standing out with unshaken daring to brave the execrations that were heaped upon his name ". If he is known to have been shut up in prison, he is painted by Mr. Southey as not daring to show himself. Now the simple fact is this. After his deprivation, on 29th May, 1559, he remained at liberty in London for nearly a year, not flying before the infuriated people, nor, as far as we know, molested by them ; and his committal to prison was neither for his own safeguard nor in punishment for present or past offences, but by a measure in which he shared the fate of Heath and Bourne and Turberville, who are acknowledged to have been men in great esteem and every way popular.[2]

A return of prisoners in the Marshalsea, made on 2nd July, 1561, gives : " Dr. Bonner, sent in the 20th April, 1560, upon the commandment of the Lord Archbishop of Canterbury and others, the Queen's Majesty's Commissioners—viz., for matter of religion ".[3]

[1] *Book of Church*, ch. xv. Surely Bonner's most malignant enemy never accused him of passing judgment of heresy on such grounds as those on which Southey passes judgment of atheism.

[2] Sanders, however, in his letter to Cardinal Morone, admits that he was so hated by the London populace that he could scarcely venture abroad. He tells this to his honour.

[3] *P. R. O., Dom. Eliz.*, xviii. 2.

Our imaginative historians are equally positive as to the mildness with which the bishop's imprisonment was conducted. As they could not deny that it lasted till his death, that is to say, for nine and a half years, they were determined it should be only a pleasant retirement. Andrewes seems again to have the credit of the invention. "It is true," he says to Bellarmine, "he grew old in prison, but if you had seen where, you would not have said that he was worn out with hunger. He lived luxuriously; there were gardens and orchards if he wished to walk; in fact, with the exception that his range was limited, there was nothing whatever like a prison." This has been repeated by succeeding writers as if the testimony of Andrewes had been that of an eye-witness, though he wrote about forty years after Bonner's death. I do not pretend to know the exact treatment of Bonner; but if Heath and Watson, Pate and Turberville, were condemned to "close and several" confinement in the Tower,[1] there is no likelihood that greater indulgence was granted to Bonner in the Marshalsea. We know, too, that at the intercession of De Silva, the Spanish ambassador, in 1564, the Queen "gave orders to mitigate the confinement of the Bishop of London"[2]—an expression which proves the severity exercised till then, whatever it may imply as to the future.

The Marshalsea prison was in Southwark, and thus in the diocese of Winchester. The Parliament of 1563 had authorised the Protestant bishops to require the oath of supremacy from any who had held office in the last three reigns, and had made the penalty of the first refusal perpetual imprisonment, and of the second death. But in April, 1564, Archbishop Parker, in consequence of a conversation with Cecil, drew up a form of circular to the bishops,

[1] See *ante*, p. 39.   [2] *Documents of Simancas*, p. 93.

which Cecil corrected and completed.[1] In this they were instructed not to tender the oath to anyone a second time, without first referring the matter to himself. They were to keep this instruction secret to themselves, but Parker kept secret from them that he did this by the Queen's wish, since, as he says, he had found them to be very leaky—*pleni rimarum*—and it would have "discouraged the honest Protestants and rejoiced the (Popish) adversaries" too much had the Queen's leniency become known.[2]

An exception, however, was made as regards Bishop Bonner. It was agreed between Archbishop Parker of Canterbury, Bishop Grindal of London, and Bishop Horn of Winchester, to readminister the oath and entangle him in the penalties of refusal. This we learn from the following letter of Grindal to Sir W. Cecil: "For Dr. Bonner's oath I did of purpose not trouble you with it aforehand, that if any misliked the matter ye might *liquido jurare* ye were not privy of it. Notwithstanding I had my Lord of Canterbury's approbation by letters, and I used good advice of the learned in the laws. I could wish that the judges were moved that expedition may be used before them. A thing obtained with such difficulty would not the better lie without all execution, and no more meet man to begin withal than that person. God keep you. Yours in Christ, Edm. London. 2nd May, 1564."

Grindal had miscalculated. He and his brother intruders were eager to execute the new law, "obtained with such difficulty," against those whose places they filled; but Bonner was not the man to begin with. He was skilled in civil no less than in canon law, and he thoroughly baffled them.[3] He pleaded before the judges that he could not be

---

[1] *Parker Corresp.*, p. 174.   [2] *Ibid.*, p. 173.

[3] He was allowed the help of Plowden and Wray to defend his cause.

indicted for violation of the law of 1563, since, though it empowered bishops to exact the oath, Horn was not lawful Bishop of Winchester. "That the said Mr. Robert Horn not being lawful Bishop of Winchester, but an usurper, intruder, and unlawful possessioner thereof, for that according to the laws of the Catholic Church, and the statutes and ordinances of this realm, the said Mr. Robert Horn was not elected, consecrated, or provided," &c.[1] The judges allowed the plea, but the cause never came to trial. The plea caused great alarm. Randolph wrote from Edinburgh to Cecil, 30th March, 1565 : " The tale is, that Bonner in his defence at his arraignment said that there was never a lawful bishop in England, which so astonished a great number of the best learned that yet they know not what answer to give him ; and when it was determined he should have suffered, he is remitted to the place from whence he came, and no more said unto him ".[2] It is well known that an Act of Parliament was made in eighth Elizabeth to heal all legal informalities in the consecration of the first Anglican bishops. In her thirty-ninth year another law was made that all sentences of deprivation made against bishops and deans up to 10th November in her fourth year should be taken for good and sufficient.

In the meantime Bonner had written a long Latin letter to the Queen protesting his allegiance to her, notwithstanding his refusal of the oath of supremacy, which he justifies on the plea of conscience.[3] There are some stories of his repartee, which show good humour rather than sense of dignity. On his way to prison, on return from this trial, or on his first

---

[1] See Strype, *Annals*, i., part i., pp. 5, 6.

[2] *P. R. O., Scotland*, x. 66.

[3] The original is in the Petyt MSS. in the Inner Temple. It is printed by Strype in the Appendix to his *Life of Grindal*, p. 487.

committal in 1560, one called out from the crowd: "The Lord confound or else turn thy heart". Bonner is said to have replied: "The Lord send thee to keep thy breath to cool thy porridge". To another who cried tauntingly, "Good-morrow, bishop *quondam*," he answered, "Farewell, knave *semper* ".[1]

The rest of his history I give from Strype's *Life of Grindal*, in which the reader will easily discern between what is fact and what is merely Strype's surmise or opinion.

"Bonner, late Bishop of London (whose memory is stigmatised for his cruel burnings of so many Protestants under Queen Mary), after he had lived divers years in the King's Bench and Marshalsea, not without often feasting and banqueting there, yielded up the ghost not many days after the beginning of September (1569),[2] having stood excommunicated divers years ; and at this time probably concerned in, or at least privy to, the popish plot against the Queen which broke out in the north this month, since his relations and friends at Bath, with a great sort of popish gentlemen besides . . . were so close in their seditious cabals there, and so free in treasonable speeches. Concerning which the forementioned Churchyard, in his letter to the Secretary, wrote 'that the unbridled braving and talk of Bonner's disciples (there at the Bath) argued some cureless cares[3] too closely crept into their cankered minds, and most of Bonner's blood and kindred dwelt in that town; and that upon colour of coming to the Bath many mad meetings there were '. And of these things the said Churchyard discoursed with the Bishop of Exon, whose hand he got to his letter.

"Bonner was buried in the churchyard of the parish

[1] Wood, *Ath. Oxon.*   [2] He died on the 5th.

[3] "Cuerless corrsij" in original. Lansdown MSS., Burghley papers, n. 11, fol. 126.

wherein the Marshalsea stood. However, he was excommunicated, and so might have been denied burial
either in church or churchyard, but the bishop and some
other of the Commissioners allowed him burial there, but
that it should be late at night, for the preventing any
hubbub among the people. And of this the Bishop of
London sent the Secretary word from Fulham, 9th September, that the truth might be known at Court about it,
which he imagined was apt enough to be misrepresented
in such matters as these . . .

" ' Sir, as I doubt not but ye have hearde of B. Bonner's
death, so think I it good to certifie you of the order of his
burial. The sayd D. Bonner had stand excommunicate
by a sentence in the Arches eight or nine years, and never
desired absolution. Wherefore by the law Christian sepul-
ture might have ben denied him : but we thought not good
to deal so rigorously, and therefore permitted him to be
buried in St. George's churchyard, and the same to be done
not in the day solemnly, but in the night privily : which I
and some other, with whom I conferred, thought requisite
in that person for two causes. One was, I heard that
divers of his Popish cousins and friends in London assembled themselves, intendyng to honour his funeral so
much as they could : of which honour such a persecutor
was not worthy, and specially in these days. Another was,
for that I feared that the people of the city (to whom
Bonner in his life was most odious), if they had seen
flocking of Papists about his coffin, the same being well
decked and covered, &c., they would have been moved
with indignation ; and so some quarrelling or tumult might
have ensued thereupon. By his night burial both the
inconveniences have been avoided, and the same generally
here well liked. What shal be judged of it at the Court, I
cannot tell : it is possible the report of his burial shall not

there be made truly.   But this I write unto you is the very truth.'

" But, however, as it was well observed at that time, concerning Bonner's burial, he was buried among thieves and murderers, carried to the grave with confusion and derision of men and women, and his grave was stamped and trampled upon after he was laid into it ; and that was all the persecution he suffered."[1]

According to the modern taste of writing history like a romance, Mr. Spencer Hall has thus rendered Strype's description of the burial : " Shouts of derision accompanied the bearers.   By the glare of the torches, amid the confusion and the hasty pressure of friends and foes, his body was cast into the Gehenna set apart for thieves and murderers.   Then the crowds rushed together, a wild cry arose, and the corpse of Bonner was trampled down in his grave beneath the pale stars."[2]   This is in rather striking contrast with the official report of Grindal, that by the night burial " all tumult was avoided ".[3]

---

[1] Strype, *Life of Grindal*, pp. 208-210 (1821).

[2] Introduction to the *Documents of Simancas*, p. 13.

[3] Into the controversy as to Bonner's cruelty I have not entered, since in any case it was not the cause of his imprisonment.   His character is given with great fairness by Mr. Gairdner in his biographical notice in Stephen's *Dictionary of National Biography*.

CHAPTER VI.

BISHOPS BOURNE, TURBERVILLE, AND THIRLBY.

GILBERT BOURNE (of Bath and Wells),

Deposed October, 1559 ; died 10th September, 1569.

THE Bishop of Bath and Wells held, at the accession of Elizabeth, the important secular office of President of the Council of Wales. His duties kept him absent from Parliament, and he appointed the Archbishop of York to act as his proxy. In February, 1559, he received a letter from the Queen, saying that she "was informed he had served her well, and done the part of a good justice," and thanking him for his service, but intimating that she had appointed Lord Williams of Thame in his place.[1] This was in execution of her general plan to deprive Catholics of offices of trust. Some hope must have been entertained of his conformity, since he was put in the commission with Tunstall, Poole, and Kitchin, on 9th September, for the consecration of Parker. When it was found that he would not comply, the oath of supremacy was offered to him, and refused, and he was deprived. Special commissioners had been appointed, 18th October, for this purpose.[2]

He was sent to the Tower by the Ecclesiastical Commissioners, 18th June, 1560,[3] and remained there, with five other bishops, until the autumn of 1563,[4] when the plague

[1] *P. R. O., Dom. Elis.*, ii. 49. [2] Rymer, *Fœdera*, xv. 545.
[3] Machyn, p. 238. [4] See *supra*, p. 40.

raging in London caused them to be dispersed among the
Protestant bishops, to the great dismay of the latter, as will
be seen in the notice of Bishop Thirlby.   Dr. Bourne was
quartered upon Nicolas Bullingham, Bishop-intrusive of
Lincoln, and with him he remained until May, 1566.

From the following letter it is probable that, during a few
weeks, he exchanged this confinement for a residence in his
own house.   The Archbishop of Canterbury writes to Sir
W. Cecil :

"SIR,—My Lord of Lincoln desired me to be a suitor to
your honour to obtain licence that his guest, Mr. Bourne,
might be at his own house, which he hath here in London,
for the present time, being sufficiently bound to be quiet
and to return again with him, or otherwise when the said
bishop should repair home, because his own lodging here at
Lambeth is so strait.   If ye think that we by the commission
may do it, we shall not wish it to be moved to the Queen's
Majesty or the Council.   Praying your honour to grant this
desire, and thus. . . .

"This 4th of January, 1565 [*i.e.*, 1566 N.S.]

"Your honour's always,

"MATTH. CANT."[1]

A deed, dated Barton, 31st May, 1566, by which Dr.
Bourne promises to appear when summoned by the Archbishop, shows that he had then been set free from the
restraint of residence in the Bishop of Lincoln's house.[2]

Dodd writes that " he was a prisoner at large under the
inspection of the Bishop of Exeter, but more immediately
of Dr. Cary, the dean.   He died at Silverton, in Devonshire,
10th September, 1569."   I do not know the authority for
this, except that Heylin says he died in the Dean of Exeter's

[1] Lansdowne MSS., viii., fol. 184.
[2] MS. at C. C. C. C., n. cxiv. 137.

house. But neither Dodd nor Heylin makes any mention whatever of Bourne's imprisonment either in the Tower or with the Bishop of Lincoln. Neither Burghley, nor Andrewes, nor Camden had given them the slightest hint of it.

What, now, was the nature of this imprisonment in the house of a Protestant bishop, to which Dr. Bourne was subjected for nearly three years, and Dr. Thirlby and Dr. Watson for a still longer time? Heylin describes it as being "kindly entertained"; Strype speaks of Thirlby "living with much ease"; and others call the prisoners "honoured guests".[1] The word guest is ambiguous. The Catholic bishops were no more truly guests of their Protestant keepers than travellers are guests in a hotel. Their entertainment was paid for. The Council, when sending Dr. Thirlby and Dr. Boxall to the care of Dr. Parker, prescribe the lodging and attendance, and then promise that they will "satisfy his Lordship for the charges of their commons". Andrewes says "they lived free of cost, in plenty, in ease, and with no discomfort"—*gratis sine sumptu, copiore sine defectu, in otio sine molestia omni*. This is a pretty picture, but it rests on no evidence. Indeed, there is a letter of Lord Henry Howard to Burghley, of 26th April, 1572, written from Lambeth, in which he says he would rather have an open imprisonment in the Fleet than the close keeping in the Archbishop's palace.[2] But, supposing Andrewes' picture true as regards the body, what does it imply with regard to the soul? What is the meaning of *otium* under such circumstances? Surely the very bitterest of pains that could be inflicted on a priest zealous for the faith and the Church, as these men undoubtedly were. Even supposing they could forget the souls of which they

---

[1] Rev. J. Cave-Brown, in his *Lambeth Palace*, p. 226. He speaks also of " honourable captivity, if captivity it could be called ".

[2] *P. R. O., Dom. Eliz.*, lxxxvi. 125.

were the legitimate pastors, and from whose care they were
violently torn, what kind of natural activity or of study could
they pursue in the houses of their fanatical hosts? When
the new bishops were issuing injunctions for the utter
destruction of all breviaries (*portuouses*) and other books of
Latin service, is it to be thought they would grant the use of
them within their own houses? We must not think of these
first intruders into the Catholic sees of England as if they
were modern Anglican bishops, gentlemen of refinement
and of enlarged and liberal minds, who, if we could imagine
them in the position of unwilling jailors to Catholic bishops,
would seek by every means to alleviate their lot. The first
Protestant bishops were, almost without exception, the
bitterest of Puritan fanatics, and they were under the
express orders of the Council to seek by every means
to bring their prisoners to conformity. Their unfortunate
"guests"—deprived of mass, of communion, of confession,
of the divine office, of books of Catholic theology—were
continually urged to read their heretical treatises, or to listen
to their wearisome disputations and negations.

However, among the new prelates there was much variety.
Parker of Canterbury must have been a much pleasanter
host than Horn of Winchester; and Horn was in every way
preferable to the foul-mouthed Pilkington of Durham. Of
Dr. Bourne's treatment by Bullingham we must remain in
ignorance.

How little room there was for the least morose of these
gentlemen to grant those indulgences of comfort, plenty, and
liberty imagined by our historians, may be seen from the
code of discipline drawn up by the Council and sent to each
of the custodians.

"That the lodging be in such convenient part of your
house, as he may be both there in sure custody, and also
have no easy access of your household people unto him,

other than such as you shall appoint and know to be settled in religion and honesty, as that they may not be perverted in religion or any otherwise corrupted by him.

"That he be not admitted unto your table, except upon some good occasion to have ministered to him there in that presence, of some that shall happen to resort unto you, such talk whereby the hearers may be confirmed in the truth; but to have his diet by himself alone in his chamber, and that in no superfluity, but after the spare manner of scholars' commons."

None to have access to him except his attendants, none to discuss religion with him except in presence of his custodian.

"That he have ministered unto him such books of learned men and sound writers in Divinity as you are able to lend him, and none other.

"That he have no liberty to walk abroad to take the air, but when yourself is at best leisure to go with him, or accompanied with such as you shall appoint.

"That you do your endeavour by all good persuasions to bring him to the hearing of sermons and other exercises of religion in your house, and the chapel or church which you most commonly frequent."[1]

JAMES TURBERVILLE (of Exeter),

Deposed November, 1559; died 1570.

Bishop Turberville has had the singular fate that his long sufferings for religion have been ignored by almost every writer, Protestant and Catholic. Lord Burghley disposed of him by the one phrase, that he was "an honest gentleman, but a simple bishop, who lived at his own liberty to the end of his life". But as Lord Burghley was one of the Ecclesiastical Commissioners by whom he was imprisoned, we may know

[1] Lansdowne MSS., 155, fol. 198.

what to think of his truthfulness. Camden admits that he was first sent to prison, but adds that "shortly after he was committed to the custody of his friends". Heylin, knowing nothing on the subject, except what he found in Burghley, develops it thus : " He was suffered to retire to what friend he pleased, and being by birth a gentleman of an ancient family, he could not want friends to give him honest entertainment". Strype echoes the words of Lord Burghley. Among Catholics, Dodd gives no hint of imprisonment, nor does Charles Butler, while Dr. M. Brady writes : "He was not imprisoned but lived, according to Godwin, for many years as a private person in full liberty". Let us now compare the legend with ascertained facts.

We have seen that Dr. Turberville was active and zealous throughout the first Parliament of Elizabeth. He went with the rest of his brethren in his votes, and in his refusal of the oath. The date of his deposition can only be gathered from the fact that the spiritualities were seized 16th November, 1559. He was committed to the Tower 18th June, 1560.[1] He remained in the Tower, with five other bishops, until September, 1563.[2] These things are written in a few lines, but when we think what three years and a quarter of "the living death of the Tower" signifies, we shall wonder how the man who inflicted it could dare to extol the *full liberty* of Bishop Turberville simply because he passed the last years of his life out of prison, though, without any doubt, under some limitations and surveillance—in a word, with what in modern language is called "a ticket of leave". He is said by some to have died in 1570, by others in 1559, which is false. I have failed to ascertain the real year of his death.[3]

[1] Machyn, p. 238, who calls him " Docthur Trobullfeld ".

[2] See the documents in proof, *supra*, p. 39.

[3] In Hardy's *Le Neve* it is said that letters of administration were granted in 1567, but his death is put on 1st November, 1559. He was certainly in the Tower in September, 1563.

THOMAS THIRLBY (of Ely),

Deposed 5th July, 1559; died 26th August, 1570.

The Bishop of Ely was absent on an embassy in France at Elizabeth's accession. On 2nd April, 1559, he concluded the treaty of Castle Cambray. He had no sooner returned to England than he joined the other bishops in opposition to the Bill of Royal Supremacy. His name appears in the divisions 17th and 26th April, as well as in opposition to the third reading of the Bill of Common Prayer, 28th April, and that for the Suppression of Religious Houses, 5th May.[1] De Feria tells us that Elizabeth had a personal dislike to Dr. Thirlby, and did not wait for his return to England to depose him from his office of Dean of the Chapel Royal, which he had held under her sister.[2]

He refused the oath and was deposed 5th July, 1559.[3] He was committed to the Tower 3rd June, 1560,[4] and excommunicated 25th February, 1561.[5] He endured the miseries of the Tower in close and separate confinement until September, 1563. During that year the plague raged in London. Stow tells us: " This year, 1563, in September, the Queen's Majesty, lying in her castle of Windsor, there was set up in the market-place of Windsor a new gallows to hang up all such as should come there from London, so that no person, or any kind of wares, might come or be brought from London, to or through . . . upon pain of hanging without any judgment ".[6] Such being the panic at Court, it was but natural that the Protestant bishops should feel

---

[1] *D'Ewes' Journal.*   [2] *Documents of Simancas*, pp. 40, 45.

[3] Machyn, p. 203. Yet the spiritualities were not seized (according to Wharton) until 23rd November.

[4] *Ibid.*, p. 237. See also *supra*, p. 39.   [5] *Ibid.*, p. 249.

[6] His *Notes*, published by Camden Soc., p. 126. Camden says there died of the plague in London, in 1563, 21,130 persons (*Annals*, p. 52).

somewhat uneasy, when the decision of the Council was announced to them that the illustrious prisoners of the Tower should be dispersed among their houses.

Dr. Matthew Parker, the Archbishop of Canterbury, received orders, 15th September, 1563, to admit Dr. Thirlby and Dr. Boxall, Dean of Windsor, "to give them convenient lodging, each of them being allowed one servant man, and to use them as was requisite for men of their sort, and that the Council would satisfy his Lordship for the charges of their commons ".[1] This letter is the sole foundation upon which Andrewes built his description of easy and luxurious living, and Fuller his "sweet chambers, soft beds, warm fires, plentiful and wholesome diet". Dr. Thirlby wrote to the Archbishop, "that he was an unbidden guest, who, according to the proverb, wotteth not where to sit, and that he would bring all his family with him, that is, his man and his boy". He adds: "I doubt what ways we may come without danger of the plague to your Grace, all the places on the way being so sore infected. Yet they say need maketh the old wife to trot. I pray God to bring us well to you, and to preserve your Grace to His pleasure."

The Archbishop replied politely enough: "Sir, an unbidden guest, as you write, knoweth not where to sit, so a guest, bidden or unbidden, being content with that which he shall find, shall deserve to be the better welcome. If you bring with you your man and your chorister too, ye shall not be refused. And if your companion in journey [*i.e.*, Dr. Boxall] can content himself with one man to attend upon him, your lodging shall be the sooner prepared. Your best way were to Maidstone the first night, and the next hither [he was then at Bekesbourne]. I would wish your coming were the sooner afore night, that such as shall come with you, being once discharged of their charge, may return that night

[1] MS., C. C. C. C., cxiv. 27.

to Canterbury, two miles off, to their bed.   And thus God
send you a quiet passage.   20th September, 1563." [1]

Dr. Thirlby's threat of bringing the plague with him, as
well as his man and boy, had thoroughly alarmed Dr.
Parker.

The same day he wrote to Sir W. Cecil: " I understand,
by letters sent to me from Mr. Dr. Thirlby, that the Council
had appointed himself and Mr. Boxall to remain with me in
house, under what conditions he writeth that I shall know
by their letters, which their keeper shall deliver unto me at
their repair hither, which is purposed upon Wednesday next.
Pleaseth it your honour to signify to the honourable Council
that I trust it may stand with their pleasure, if for the fear
that my household is in of them their coming from a con-
tagious air, I do place them in the town not far from my
house here at Bekesbourne, in an house at this present void
of a dweller, till such time as they were better blown with
this fresh air for a fourteen days.   For their provision I
shall see to [it], and for jeopardy of the custody of their
persons I am surely persuaded of the one not to disappoint
your expectations ; as for the other, I know not so well his
nature.   Whereupon, if aught should chance in the meantime till I receive them myself, I trust the Council will
rather bear with me in avoiding the danger of infection, as
may be feared, than for their behoof endanger my whole
family.   I mean not in respect of my own person to repine
at such appointment, nor yet would I be thought slack to
gratify my old acquaintance, so far as my faith to God and
His Word, and my allegiance to my Prince and her Government may bear with it.   Nor I mean not to alledge the
small room of my house already pestured (?), having not
many under a hundred persons uprising and downlying
therein, besides divers of my family which, for straitness of

[1] Printed by Strype from MSS. in C. C. C. C., cxiv. 27.

lodging, be otherwhere abroad.   But if any peril should arise, the country here would make much exclamation, for I see they so wonderfully afeard of all such as come from London. I thought it good, therefore, to signify this much to your honour aforehand, praying the same to be a mean that my doings may be taken to the best.   And thus I leave, wishing you God's favour as to myself, this 20th of September.

"Your honour's assuredly,

"MATTHEW, CANTUAR."[1]

With the Archbishop Dr. Thirlby remained for seven years, when he was released by death.   During the whole of that time he was without confession or holy mass, as well as without occupation.   Yet Strype informs us that "he took more pleasure, as Bishop Godwin assured himself, in this time of his imprisonment than ever heretofore in the midst and fullest stream of his highest honours".   This, of course, is meant rather as a compliment to the liberality of Parker than to the resignation of Thirlby.   Yet it is adding insult to injury.   Godwin assured himself, says Strype, as if Godwin had some special channel of information.   In quoting the words of the Council to Parker, that Dr. Thirlby and Dr. Boxall should have such attendance "as is requisite for men of their sort," Strype omits the words which follow immediately, "foreseeing that there be no other access or conference with them than you think meet, considering for what causes they be restrained from their liberty".[2]   These words would have jarred with the pleasant theory of "honourable guests" and "perfect liberty".   The truth is, the bishops had merely exchanged jail for jail.   They

---

[1] Lansdowne MSS., vi., fol. 178.

[2] The whole is now printed in *Parker's Correspondence* (Parker Soc.), p. 92.

were guarded and watched if they left their rooms, lest they should escape, and their rooms were watched lest any but the authorised servant should see or speak with them.[1]

On the 6th February, 1564, when there was fear of an invasion by the French, Parker wrote to Cecil to ask what were best to be done with Thirlby and Boxall, although, he says, "I judge by their words that they be true Englishmen, not wishing to be subject to the governance of such insolent conquerors".[2]   Dr. Thirlby remained at Bekesbourne till June, 1564, and then went with Dr. Parker to Lambeth. Just before he left, the French ambassador, Monsieur de Gonor, passed through Bekesbourne, and some of his young gentlemen attendants heard of the two illustrious Catholic dignitaries who were in confinement.   Parker writes to Cecil: "I noted unto them the Queen's clemency and mercy for the preservation of them from the plague, and for the distribution of them among their friends.   They seemed to be grieved that they were so stiff not to follow the Prince's religion. . . . They were contented to hear evil of the Pope, and bragged how stout they had been aforetimes against that authority."   If this is true, the young Frenchmen belonged to the then very prevalent party of the Politici, or were infected with the common disease of young men—human respect.   The Archbishop concludes his letter: "I would fain know what is meant or determined concerning my two guests, because I intend, God willing, now shortly to repair to Lambeth.   This country is very dear to dwell in."[3]

[1] Dodd makes a very strange blunder: he says that Thirlby "had the satisfaction of conversing daily with Bishop Tunstall and Secretary Boxall, his fellow prisoners". Tunstall died 1559, four years before Thirlby came to reside with Parker. Whether Thirlby and Boxall were allowed to converse is quite uncertain.

[2] *Parker Corresp.*, p. 203.

[3] Letter of 3rd June, 1564. *P. R. O., Dom. Eliz.*, xxxiv. 26.

Naturally no record has been kept of Dr. Thirlby's long residence with Dr. Parker. There are, however, several papers in which his name occurs in reference to another affair and another personage. The whole have been very amusingly abridged by Mr. Hubert Hall, of the Record Office, in his book called *Society in the Elizabethan Age.* " Amongst the non-conforming prelates who were deprived during Elizabeth's first Parliament by virtue of that Queen's Act of Uniformity was Dr. Thomas Thirlby, the Popish Bishop of Ely. His successor was Richard Cox, a good scholar, and a prominent member of that Protestant party which, during its exile for religion, had, by its feuds and outrages against public decency, cast scandal, not merely upon the cause of the Reformation, but upon that of Christianity itself in many cities of the Continent. By the time that this successor to the Apostles had been duly anointed and installed, and the little matter of commission and tribute arranged to her Highness' satisfaction, it was discovered that a slight oversight had been committed. It was easy enough to depose the former prelate, but it was by no means easy to induce him to lend a finishing hand to the work of emptying out of his own pockets. This, in fact, was the state of affairs. Cox had learnt that money was to be gotten—that it was indirectly owing to him, and the mere thought cast him into a fever of avarice, from which he did not rally for ten years. The Bishopric of Ely had received a Royal endowment of £706 13s. 4d. in the reign of Edward III., as a capital fund or ' Implement '; and this sum was to be accounted for, and handed over by each outgoing bishop to his successor. According to Cox's own account, Henry VIII., of famous memory, bethinking him how that, during the last 42 years of his reign [*sic*], the revenues of that see had fallen into decay, owing, as Cox observes, to the fact that its bishop 'then was, and for

a long time had abode in Rome,' made a grant by Privy
Seal to bring the stock in question up to the old standard,
namely, by an increase of 430 cattle, at 13s. 4d. per head,
and 41 horses for the plough, at 20s. Strict measures were
further taken to ensure the future payment of this capital to
each incoming bishop, who was to stand in the west porch
of his cathedral, before installation, and receive the same
from his predecessor.[1] But, though we may credit Cox with
a readiness to have stood for almost any length of time at
the appointed place to receive a far smaller sum than about
£5000 of our money, it is certain that, in the present
instance, he waited in vain. The new powers that were
could depose Thirlby, and hustle him before the Council,
and 'lay him by the heels' in the Tower, but they could not
coin him into money, and nothing less than money would
satisfy his successor. The Government, therefore, seems to
have given the matter up as a bad job; but not so Cox.
We find him writing a pious letter to Cecil: 'I am so
troubled,' he says, 'with Dr. Thirlby, that I fear I shall be
obliged to trouble the Queen's Majesty at last. For he is so
strong in the Tower that I can get no right at his hands.'"[2]

Mr. Hall then goes on to relate the various efforts made
year after year by Cox to get the money—unsuccessfully.
The bishop had conveyed the remains of his private fortune
to some relatives: Richard Blackwall, citizen of London,
and Margaret, his wife, who administered it for the bishop's
use. "Staunch to the end, he baffled his harsh creditor
by dying intestate." There were thus no executors account-
able for the estate of the deceased, and to all appearance
there was no estate at all. Cox, however, made a last effort,
and commenced a Chancery suit against the Blackwalls.
These admitted the trust, but showed that the whole amount,

---

[1] I suppose from his executors, if the see became vacant by death.
[2] Letter, 2nd Nov., 1561.

small as it was, had been faithfully administered by them to the doctor's own use ; only five marks remaining—that is to say, after his funeral, "who, in August last past at Lambeth, died, and none of his other allies or kinsfolk, being thereunto requested, would meddle with his body ; till Margaret Blackwall, out of charity, caused it to be conveniently laid in the earth at her own charge ".

The concluding of this episode has made me anticipate. On 25th August, 1570, Parker wrote to Cecil : " The cause of my writing is partly of the motion of Master Dr. Thirlby, who (as himself desireth) would wish, in this his great sickness, to be removed from my house to his friends for better cherishing, and in hope of his recovery. I would grant no further, but the choice of three or four large chambers within my house, except you can agree thereto, and for this cause this messenger cometh to your Honour to know the Queen's Majesty's pleasure. . . . I thought by his presence (being both of us much of an age) to learn to forsake the world and die to God [*sic*], and hereto I trust to incline myself what length or shortness of life soever may follow." [1] The choice among three or four rooms came too late. Dr. Thirlby died the very next day, and went, as we may well believe, to that Father's House where there are many mansions, and for whose sake he had renounced ease and liberty, and witnessed a good confession.

To the man who endured these ten long years of imprisonment for his convictions, Burnet could give no better character than the following : " He was a learned and modest man, but of so fickle and cowardly a temper, that he turned always with the stream, in every change that was made, till Queen Elizabeth came to the Crown ; but then,

[1] *Parker Corresp.*, p. 369.

being ashamed of so many turns, he resolved to show he could once be firm to somewhat ".[1]

Dr. Thirlby died on 26th August, 1570, and was buried in the Chancel of St. Mary's, Lambeth, close by Bishop Tunstall. The expenses of his funeral and burial were defrayed, as we have seen, by his faithful friends, the Blackwalls. These good people had, at one period, perhaps between his deposition and imprisonment, entertained Dr. Thirlby in their house, as we learn from a letter of the Recorder of London to the Lord Treasurer : " My good Lord . . . Katharine Carus, the late Justice's wife, my country woman, with all her pride and Popery, is this week gone (as I trust) to God. She died in Bishop Thirlby's chamber, in Mrs. Blackwall's house in the Blackfriars. . . .

" This first Sunday after Michaelmas. At Baem House, in London, 1577.

" Your Lord. most humble,

" W. FLEETWOOD, Recorder."[2]

The register of Dr. Thirlby's burial is as follows :

" 1570, Aug. 28th day, buried Mr. Thomas Thirlby Doctor of the Civil Law, born in Cambridge, a student sometime of Trinity Hall there, and sometime Bishop of Westminster,[3] afterwards Bishop of Norwich, and, in Queen Mary's days, Bishop of Ely, who, in the time of the noble King Edward, professed the truth of the Holy Gospel, and afterwards, in the time of Queen Mary, returned to Papistry, and so continued in the same to his end, and died *the Queen's Majesty's prisoner*, within my Lord Grace's house, at

---

[1] *History of Reform*, book iii., p. 430.

[2] Lansdowne MSS., n. 24, fol. 196.

[3] He was the first and last.

Lambeth ". From this it appears that the theory of honoured guest and full liberty was not yet invented.

The following interesting particulars of the state of Bishop Thirlby's body, two hundred years after his death, are from Ducarel's *History of Lambeth* :[1] "On opening the grave for the interment of Archbishop Cornwallis, in March, 1783, a stout leaden coffin was discovered, 6 feet 6 inches long, 1 foot 8 inches wide, and but 9 inches deep; in which had been deposited the remains of Bishop Thirlby. The coffin was in fashion somewhat like a horse-trough, and had all the appearance of never having been covered with wood; the earth around it being perfectly dry and crumbly. By the ill-judged officiousness of the gravedigger, who had accidentally struck his pickaxe into it, and afterwards enlarged the hole, the discovery became so public, that the Church was crowded before the matter was known to the proper officers, and before such observations could be made as the curiosity of the subject deserved. The principal circumstances that occurred were, that the body, which was wrapped in fine linen was moist, and had evidently been preserved in some species of pickle, which still retained a volatile smell, not unlike that of hartshorn; the flesh was preserved, and had the appearance of a mummy; the face was perfect, and the limbs flexible; the beard of a remarkable length, and beautifully white. The linen and woollen garments were all well preserved. The cap, which was of silk, and adorned with point lace, had probably been black, but the colour was discharged; it was in fashion like that represented in the pictures of Archbishop Juxon. A slouched hat, with strings fastened to it, was under the left arm. There was also a cassock so fastened as to appear like an apron with strings, and several small pieces of the bishop's garments, which had the appearance of a pilgrim's habit. The

[1] Appendix xxii.

above curious particulars were communicated by Mr. Buckmaster to Dr. Vyse, who directed every part to be properly
replaced in the coffin.   Mr. Buckmaster saw the bishop's
head entire ; and the gravedigger put his hand into the
coffin, and said, ' The legs and body were so '.   The remains of Archbishop Cornwallis were afterwards deposited
in an adjoining grave. . . ."

CHAPTER VII.

Nicholas Heath (of York).

Deposed 5th July, 1559; died April, 1579.

THE Archbishop of York survived his deprivation twenty years. He is the pet specimen of Elizabeth's clemency, for the historians have all followed the lead of Lord Burghley. I have given his words in full 'already, but it is necessary now to examine them in detail. He says that at Elizabeth's accession Heath held the two offices of Archbishop and Chancellor, and "continued in both offices, though in religion manifestly differing"; that, later on, he "left willingly both his offices"; that he "was not restrained of his liberty". All this is utterly false, and Lord Burghley knew it was false. Heath did not continue in both offices, for he resigned the Chancellorship on the very day of Elizabeth's accession.[1] He did not resign the archbishopric in any way, but was wrongfully deprived of it, and then excommunicated. He *was* "restrained of his liberty," and that by more than three years of close and painful confinement in the Tower.

I must begin by giving two letters concerning the resignation of the Chancellorship. I give them at length, and in the original spelling, because I do not find them quoted elsewhere. The reason of these letters I do not understand. It would seem as if Lord Burghley had to clear himself from

---

[1] See Lord Campbell's *Lives of the Chancellors.* Bacon, however, was not appointed Lord Keeper for some weeks.

some charge regarding the appointment of Sir Nicholas Bacon to be Keeper of the Great Seal at the beginning of the reign.

"SYR,—For your most gentyll and lovyng letter, I have great cause both to honoure you and thanke you. And concernyng the matter therof, your lordshyp wysely consyderyth as the truthe ys, that for the space of so many yers havyng abandonyed myselfe vtterly from all meadlyng or myndyng of worldye thyngs, and my memorye also beyng very muche decayed, yt ys very hard for me to remember thyngs so many yers past. And beyng yn myne own conscyence very scrupulous to say ony vntrouthe, wyll neverthelesse (as I possyble can) remember myselfe of the matters you wryte of, and by Godd's grace never say but the trouthe as nere as I can. And your lordshyp may be that assured, that yf I shall be examyned of any thyng towchyng of the matter wrytten by you, I wyll answere wythout any corrupt mynde, or any evyl affectyon towards your lordshyp, and nothyng but the very trewthe, as neare as the grace of God and my symple memory can serve me, puttyng away all respect to the world or any worldely person. And further vpon the contents of your letter: I mynde to repayre to London eyther to-morow or on thursday, wheare I may by mouthe make further declaratyon, eyther to anye that your lordshyp shal send, or to any other that shal wyth any authoryte have anye conference wyth me of the matter, for I assure your honorable lordshyp that yt ys a great griefe and a rare thynge for me to wryte ij lynes wyth myne own hand as thys ys. And thus as your lordshyp's poore lovyng ffrend, yf yt be decent for me so to terme myselfe towards your lordshyp (and as one that never could perceave by any your dealyng, ye contrarye yn you towards me, by reason wherof, and by the gracyous favoure of the Queen's Maiestye, through the medyatyon of my synguler good lorde of

Leycester, I have lyved these many years yn greate quyet-
ness of mynde to my syngular cumforth) I commend your
lordshyp to Almyghty God.   From chobbam, thys 22 of
September (1573).

"Your lordeshypps to hys lytyll power,

"NICO. HEYTH."[1]

The old bishop at once set out for London, and on the
26th wrote another letter as follows :

"SYR,—Pervsyng your lordshyp's letter agayn after the
departure of the pursuyvant, and therby perceyvyng that
your lordshyp requyreth to have myne answere in wrytyng
to the matter theryn conteynyd, I have thought yt my
dewtye to certifye what I have or can of myselfe remember
theryn, as foloweth : I doo not remember that I had ever
any talke wyth you touchyng the offyce of Chancellour, but
onely one tyme, which was as I thynke about iii or iiij days
afore the death of Queen Marye, yn myne own house,
whyther you gently came at my desyre.   At whyche tyme,
after a long discourse of dyvers thyngs wherin I was
desyrous to conferre wyth you, both touchyng the Queen's
Maiestie that now ys (whome I beseche Almyghty God
always to preserve), and touchyng the state of the realme,
and also the matter of rellygyon (the particulers wherof I
have cleane forgoten), I doo remember that I dyd erneastly
move you to stande my frend, and to be a meane to the
Queen's Maiestie that now ys, that I myght be vtterly dis-
burdyned of myne offyce, vnto the whych offyce, although I
dyd ever thynke and know myselfe for many respects most
vnmeate, both before I had ytt and when I had ytt, and ever
synce, and for myne own vnmeatnesse was very loth at the

---

[1] *P. R. O., Dom. Elis.*, xcii. 28.   The letter is endorsed 1573.

fyrst to take ytt, and very sone was werye of ytt, and took yt
for a greatt burdon ever after, yet bycause I thought and
partly hard by some that were about Her Grace, that the
Queen's Maiestie that now ys, of her own onely good dis-
posytyon, wythout any cause or meryte on my parte, had a
gracyous and favourabyll mynde towards me, and lyked
better of my servyce and doyngs yn the offyce then I was
worthye, as afterward Her Maiestie (whan I delyveryd vp
the seale yn to her own hands) dyd by her own mowthe
declare yn a great and an honorable presence—for the whych
I am most bound to honour and love Hyr Maiestie perpetu-
ally, and thought my servyce therwyth better rewarded then
yt coulde have ben by any other wordly recompense. Vpon
thys consyderatyon I thought yt good to prevent the matter,
and so craved your frendshyp and ayde that I myght yn any
wyse leave the offyce, whyche my request and earnest desyre
you declaryd yourselfe to myslyke, praysyng and commend-
yng me and my servyce, wheron I conceyvyd that you were
not so ready to set forward my sute as I dyd wysshe. How
be yt I was so erneast wyth you that at length yt came yn
talke betwyxt vs—and as I thynk you demanded of me whom
I could name to be a fytte and a sufficyent man for the office
of whome the Queen's Maiestie myght be advysed [1]—wher-
vnto I answered that, God be thanked, theare was choise
ynough ; but whether I named any particular man or noe I
can not tell, but I rather thinke that I named none, and
because I staggered to name anye, as I remember, you, to
healpe me, sayd, what thynke you of such a man or such a
man, namyng thre or fowre, but, afore God, I remember none
of them but only D. Wotton, and me thinks that I am well
assured yt theare was noe wourd spoken of my Lord Keaper
that now is ; but, for my own point, I thought theim all that
were na [*mutilated*] to be sufficient, for soe my self were ridd

[1] So far in Archbishop Heath's own handwriting.

of the office I nothing doubted but the Queen's Maiestie wold provide noe man for the office but she wold be assured that he shold be sufficient ynough, and, God bee praysed therfore, Her Maiestie had choise ynough of souch at that tyme, and yet hath; and this is all I can remember of that matter. Now, what you did or how you proceded afterward touching the office eyther with the Queen's Maiestie or other wise I am vtterly ignoraunt, for I doe not thinke that ever you or any other talked with me therof afterward. But because the Queen's Maiestie what tyme I delyvered vp the seale sayd that all though Her Maiestie [*mutilated*] toke the seale from me in to her owne custodye for order's sake, yet she wold not vtterly discharge me of the office, I remayned still in feare least I might bee burdened therewith agyne vntill the seale was delyvered to my Lord Keeper yt now is; of whome I heard noe speaking vntill he had the office, but I was very glad that one had yt. Thus I commend your lordshyp to God. Ffrom my house in Southwarke, the xxvjth of September, 1573.

"Your lordshyp's always assured to hys lytyll power,

"NICO. HEYTH."

From the expressions of courtesy and gratitude in these letters the reader would be wrong in concluding that the venerable archbishop owed any very great debt to Sir William Cecil, now become Lord Burghley and Lord Treasurer.

It is unnecessary to repeat what has been previously said of the archbishop's defence of the Church's rights in Parliament and his speech in behalf of the supremacy of the Sovereign Pontiff. He was deposed on his refusal to accept the oath of the Queen's supremacy, 5th July, 1559,[1] committed to the Tower 10th June, 1560, and not released

[1] Machyn, p. 203.

until Septembter, 1563.[1] It is surprising that Mr. Edward Foss, F.S.A., now that the State archives are thrown open, should repeat in our own day what he found in Fox or some old misinformed writer: "The deprived archbishop . . . was allowed after *two or three months'* confinement to retire to his own property";[2] and equally surprising that Lord Campbell, writing the *Lives of the Chancellors*, should have taken no trouble to ascertain the truth. After mentioning the archbishop's deprivation, he writes: "He retired to a small property of his own at Chobham in Surrey, where he devoted the rest of his days to study and devotion".[3] Not one syllable about his three years' imprisonment![4]

After his release from the Tower Dr. Heath was not sent, like Thirlby, and Watson, and Bourne, to reside with any of the Protestant bishops. He was allowed to retire to his own house. Miss Strickland says that this was "one of the houses belonging to his see in Yorkshire".[5] Dr. Lee is more precise: "He was permitted to retire to the manor-house in York, formerly the residence of the Abbot of St Mary's, and subsequently one of the official houses of the See of York".[6] But both of these writers have adopted, as referring to the deposed archbishop, an entry in the *Council Register* of 22nd June, 1565, which probably belongs to some other Nicholas Heath. The entry is as follows: "Letter to the Lord Scrope, in answer to his letters written to Mr. Secretary, with the examination by him taken of Nicholas Heath, whom his Lordship is required to proceed somewhat sharply withal to the end he should declare the full truth, why he wandereth abroad. And if he will not be plain, to use some kind of torture unto him,

---

[1] See *supra*, p. 40.   [2] *The Judges of England*, v. 380.
[3] *Lives of the Chancellors.*
[4] The same remark applies to Drake, the historian of York.
[5] *Lives of the Queens*, vi. 259.   [6] *Church under Elizabeth*, i. 157.

so as it be without any great bodily hurt. And to advertise of his (Lord Scrope's) doings therein, &c., according to the minutes in the Council chest."[1]

From this entry Miss Strickland, followed by Dr. Lee, has dilated on the insignificance of the offence, taking " wandering abroad " to mean a short stroll for exercise into the country, and on the enormity of torturing an old man of eighty. To say nothing of the fifteen years Miss Strickland has added to Dr. Heath's age, there is nothing whatever to identify this Nicholas Heath, not called "late Bishop," or even " Doctor," or " Master," as is the case in nearly all similar entries, with Archbishop Heath. " Wandering abroad " may mean excursions into Scotland, of which the Government was just then very jealous. Besides all this, from the letters given above, it seems very unlikely that either Cecil or the Earl of Leicester had been parties to any torturing of Dr. Heath. Yet their names are signed to the letter in question. Lord Scrope also was at that time warden of the Scottish borders, and would have no jurisdiction or action about York.

Besides this, a rule was invariably followed of restricting the recusants to districts where they had no influence, and excluding them from places where they had formerly lived ; and as I know of no other grounds for supposing Dr. Heath to have resided in Yorkshire after his release from the Tower, I think we may follow the writers who make him retire immediately after his release to Chobham, on the borders of Surrey, and not far from Windsor.[2]

It is true, however, that at the beginning of June, 1565, it was seriously proposed in Council to commit the released

---

[1] From the original, p. 190. Were present on this day, the Lord Keeper, the Marquis of Northampton, the Earl of Leicester, Mr. Secretary, Mr. Cave, Mr. Petre, Mr. Sackville.

[2] This must not be confounded with Cobham, also in Surrey.

bishops once more to prison. This is related by Camden, but I prefer to give the exact words of the consultation, which have been preserved among the State archives.[1] The questions proposed were two: 1. What dangers were likely to arise to England from the marriage of Mary Queen of Scots and Darnley? 2. What remedies should be used? The Councillors thought the marriage would strengthen the hopes of the Papists, and among the remedies one was "that the *quondam* bishops and others which had refused to acknowledge the Queen's Majesty's power over them, according to the law, and now of late dispersed in the plague time to places abroad, where it is known. they cease not to advance their faction, might be returned to the Tower, or some other prison, where they might not have such liberty to seduce and inveigle the Queen's Majesty's subjects as they daily do".

Bishop Watson had been already re-committed to the Tower, but no such measure was taken with regard to Heath or the other surviving bishops. Neither do we know of any molestation at the time of the Northern rising in 1569, or at the publication of the bull of St. Pius V. Heath had purchased from Queen Mary a house and farm that had formerly belonged to the monastery of Chertsey. There was a manor-house surrounded by a moat, and with a chapel attached. There was also a house, garden and orchard, and five hundred acres of land. He lived on this property, as he says in his letter, "in great quietness of mind". Camden writes that in his house "the Queen visited him many times with marvellous kindness". Lord Campbell has rendered this, "she was in the frequent habit of visiting him"; and some authors have multiplied it into "she was accustomed to make him a visit once a year".[2] He had other visitors,

---

[1] *P. R O., Dom. Eliz.*, xxxv., 65.

[2] Brayly and Britton, *History of Surrey*, ii. 160.

as we find from the letter of a spy named Davy Jones. This rascal, who was a Protestant minister, by going to confession to a Catholic priest in the Marshalsea, had got into Catholic secrets. He frequented the houses where mass was said and received communion, and then sent information to his employers what priests said mass and what Catholics received communion or were present. In a letter written on 6th July, 1574, he says: " This shall be to let you understand that I was confessed in the Marshalsea, and twain more with me were confessed. . . . I do give you to understand that there shall be upon Sunday se'nnight a mass at my Lord Bishop Hethe, which was Bishop of York, and he doth dwell within a little way of Windsor, as I heard say, but I will see afore it be long. Also there doth come thither a great sort. . . ." On 20th July he wrote again : " I desire you to send me a word what your pleasure is afore Saturday at three o'clock afternoon, whether I shall go to Doctor Hethe or not, for I will travel all night an if you will ".[1] Whether the venerable archbishop got into any trouble through this spy, or whether he was deprived of the occasional mass, history has not told.

We learn from a return made to the Council that he was still alive on 25th October, 1577. " The certificate of the names of all such persons inhabiting in the County of Surrey, which do refuse to come to the Church, with the just value of their lands and goods. . . . Chobham, Doctor Heath, priest. Other lands or goods to maintain himself withal than Chobham Park we know not."[2] He is supposed to have died in the spring of 1579. Wood quotes from a document in the Prerogative Court of Canterbury that on

---

[1] *P. R. O., Dom. Eliz.*, xcvii. 27-39; given at length by Rev. J. Morris in *The Troubles of our Catholic Forefathers*, 2nd series, pp. 301-303.

[2] *P. R. O., Dom. Eliz.*, cxvii. 14, 1.

5th May, 1579, Thomas Heath had a commission granted to him to administer the goods, debts of Nicholas Heath, S.T.P., sometime Archbishop of York, deceased.[1] He adds that he was buried. in the chancel of the church of Chobham, but that the inscription on the brass plate had in his time been taken away and the stone itself broken. "The picture of the said archbishop I have many times seen," says Wood, "which shows him to have been proper in person, black-haired, pale-faced, thin, and macerated." This picture was in the house of Mr. Ralph Sheldon, near Long-Compton, in Warwickshire.

The account given of Archbishop Heath by Sanders in 1561 is the following: "Being willing neither to crown the Queen, nor to take the oath of supremacy of a woman, and having been left in freedom for a year and a few months after his spoliation, he is now again placed in confinement. But liberty of living where he pleased was offered him, by the authority of the Queen and Council, if only he would promise to be present at the ecclesiastical offices, but he would on no terms accept this offer; 'And why I am unwilling to do so,' he said, 'the Council have often enough heard me say in Parliament, all of which may be summed up thus: Whatever is contrary to the Catholic faith is heresy; whatever is contrary to unity is schism. And when the visitors objected that he should not be required to receive communion, he answered that it is the same thing in reason to act a part of schism as the whole; neither by word or deed of mine (said he) will I approve of what you do, nor would I that ever my back should be seen where scandal might be given, since the heart cannot be read.' He then petitioned the Queen that he might be placed with some friends, for otherwise he should prefer the Tower of London. He added this

[1] From this it appears that he died without making a will.

because they were wont to commit Catholics to the custody of the pseudo-bishops, which custom he could not endure, because there is no agreement between light and darkness, between Christ and Belial. It was peculiar to the bishop that the other bishops regarded him as monks do their abbot." [1]

I think it will be in harmony with the character of these notes if, in the place of any reflections of my own, I conclude with those which were published in 1582, after the death of Archbishop Heath, but before the death of Bishop Watson and Bishop Goldwell, by Cardinal Allen, in his defence of the seminary priests : [2]

" First and foremost for the clergy, it is wholly destained and destroyed, as the world knoweth. The chief prelates, bishops, and others, all spoiled of their dignities and livelihoods, thrust into prisons, forced into banishment, till by manifold and long miseries they be almost all wasted and worn away. These then, so many, so notable, and so worthy, for whom both God, nature, and their place of birth do challenge a part of this so much praised prosperity, feel none of it ; but for mere conscience and confession of the truth, which their holy predecessors laid and left with them *in depositum*, have lost their terrene lot, and either are dead or have passed so many years in misery, as those other good fellows, their intruders, have lived in joy and felicity ; who, indeed, are *filii hominum qui nubunt et nubuntur*, that is, certain fleshly companions, unordered apostates, and contemptible ministers, who, entering into the right and room of others, provided not for them, do think all fair weather in England, and have good cause to like of the luck of these late years, which maketh true men mourn while such thieves be merry."

[1] Vatican MS., fol. 265.
[2] Cardinal Allen, *A Sincere and Modest Defence*, p. 171.

And as Lord Burghley had drawn (as we have seen) an elaborate contrast between the quietness and loyalty of the deposed prelates and the consequent most gentle measure dealt out to them, with the treasons of the Jesuits and seminary priests lately put to death, Cardinal Allen replied :

" All this we put down that no man he abused by the enemy to think that the reverend prelates at the first were less zealous (which he calleth more loyal) or more obedient to the prince in lawful things than we their scholars and offspring be ; or we less loyal than they, and therefore more punishable than they were. Though indeed their perpetual imprisonment and pining away in miserable desolation, their tossing and shifting from one superintendent's house to another, from one keeper to another, from one prison to another, subject to extreme wants and to a thousand daily villainies besides, whereof some of them now have tasted for twenty years together, *is worse than any death in the world.* This, then, is a true persecution indeed, when such men, for such causes, against all reason and laws, be so vexed by such as owe them all reverence, duty, and obedience."

CHAPTER VIII.

THOMAS WATSON, BISHOP OF LINCOLN.

SECTION I.—IN THE REIGN OF HENRY VIII.

I T was the misfortune of Thomas Watson, the subject of this biographical notice, to have lived in the reigns of Henry VIII., Edward, Mary, and Elizabeth. It was his happiness to have learnt wisdom by experience, and to have expiated, by his long sufferings for the Catholic faith, the schism, if not heresy, of his early years.

There exists of him no contemporary biography, [1] and we can only glean the facts of his life from incidental notices in the documents of the time, and can do little more than conjecture his character from the part he played in its varied drama. Yet his heroic constancy during a quarter of a century of imprisonments, and his having been the last of the old Catholic hierarchy who died in England, entitle him to our love and reverence, and make us regret the scantiness of our information.

[1] Pitts has a page or two of little value. Godwin, Burnet, Strype, and the rest have scanty notices, and those often incorrect. Baker has given the principal facts of his life in his *History of the College of St. John the Evangelist, Cambridge*, part i., pp. 137-40 (ed. Mayor, 1869), and Cooper has added a few more details, and given a copious list of references, in his *Athenæ Cantabrigienses* ". These I have consulted, as well as other contemporary works. But it is from the State Papers I have derived the most important and trustworthy information, especially regarding the sufferings of his later life.

The precise date of his birth is not known. In the records of the trial of Gardiner, which took place in June, 1550, and in which Watson appeared as a witness, he is stated in one place to be then " of the age of 33, or there-abouts," and in another to be " 34 or 35 years old ".[1] He was, however, older, for in a letter written by himself in October, 1578, he says he is past 65. He was born, therefore, in 1513. He was of the diocese of Durham, and is said to belong to the family of the Barons of Rockingham. Nothing is known of his early life ; but as he took his degree of B.A. at Cambridge in the year 1533-34, at the age of twenty, he must have been sent at an early age to that University.

The College of St. John the Evangelist, in which he studied, and of which he was elected a fellow immediately after taking his degree, though but recently founded, then, and for some years after, was famous for the group of scholars it contained, and for the lead it took in the revival of letters.

Its foundress was the famous Lady Margaret, Countess of Richmond and Derby, and mother of Henry VII. ; but as she died before her pious intentions were realised, the college really owes its existence to the zeal and labours of her confessor, the Blessed John Fisher, Bishop of Rochester, afterwards cardinal and martyr.[2]

The college had been opened in 1516, and in a decree of Archbishop Warham for its further endowment in 1519 it is said that he gladly co-operates in the work, "considering

---

[1] Foxe, *Acts and Monuments*, vol. vi., pp. 151, 205 (ed. Catley).

[2] See Cooper's *Memoir of Lady Margaret*, edited by Mr. Mayor (1874). Both as a Catholic and as an alumnus of St. John's College, I would express my gratitude to the author and the editor for the noble monument which their patient research has erected to this holy lady.

what great advantages, both private and public, both spiritual and temporal, daily accrue to the Christian faith from
the study of letters.   For by means of them the salvation of
souls is promoted, rising controversies are settled, peace and
tranquillity procured," &c.   At that very moment, however,
a controversy was arising in Germany, from the teaching of
Luther, which was to frustrate the pious hopes of Warham,
of Fisher, and the Lady Margaret, by unsettling the minds
of those whom their liberality was educating.   Before half a
century had passed from its foundation the College of St.
John's was so entirely transformed, that the doctrine of the
Supremacy of the Holy See, for which Fisher laid down his
life, was forbidden to be taught within its walls, and the
Holy Sacrifice, which Lady Margaret loved more than life,
was banished from its desecrated chapel, and impiously re-
pudiated by all its members.   The life of Watson will show
that in his case, at least, the labours of the founders were
not in vain.

When Watson entered St. John's, and for the first three
years of his residence as a fellow, the college was governed
by Dr. Nicholas Metcalf, who had been chaplain to Fisher,
and was master from 1518 to 1537.   His character has
been thus sketched by Roger Ascham, the tutor of the
Princess Elizabeth, and a contemporary of Watson's :   " Dr.
Nicholas Metcalf, that honourable father," he writes, " was
Master of St. John's College when I came thither—a father
to everyone in the college.   There was none so poor, if he
had either will to goodness, or wit to learning, that could
lack, being there, or should depart from thence for any need.
I am certain myself that money many times was brought
into young men's rooms by strangers that they knew not.
In which doing this worthy Nicholas followed the steps of
good old St. Nicholas, that learned bishop.   He was a
Papist, indeed ; but would to God, among all us Protestants,

I might once see but one that would win like praise, in doing like good, for the advancement of learning and virtue. And yet, though he were a Papist, if any young man, given to new learning (as they termed it), went beyond his fellows in wit, labour, and towardness, even the same neither lacked open praise to encourage him, nor private exhibition to maintain him, as worthy Sir J. Cheke, if he were alive, would bear good witness, and so can many more." [1]

Watson was one of those who profited most by the care of this worthy man. He had good talents and a great love of study, so that with the helps he found in his college he became eminent as a classical scholar.

The reader need scarcely be reminded of the struggle that was then going on in England between the old scholastic form of learning and the zeal for polite literature, which we call the Renaissance. Fisher was both a good scholar and an ardent promoter of classical studies, and his influence had drawn many young men of talent to the new foundation.

Sir John Cheke, the famous Greek lecturer, was elected fellow of St. John's in 1529, about the time Watson came into residence, and the youth had the advantage of his public lectures and private instructions. Among his contemporaries and fellow-collegians I may mention the names of Roger Ascham; George Day, afterwards Bishop of Chichester; John Christopherson, afterwards Master of Trinity and Bishop of Chichester; William Bill, who died in 1560, holding the threefold dignities of Master of Trinity, Provost of Eton, and Dean of Westminster; William Cecil, afterwards the famous Lord Burghley; James Pilkington, afterwards Bishop of Durham; Robert Horn, afterwards Bishop of Winchester; John Seton, the logician; Walter Haddon and Dr. Redman, two great revivers of classical learning.

[1] Ascham's *Works*, p. 315.

Roger Ascham writes : " At Cambridge, in St. John's College, in my time, I do know that, not so much the good statutes, as two gentlemen of worthy memory, Sir John Cheke and Dr. Redman, by their only example of excellency in learning, of godliness in living, of diligence in studying, of counsel in exhorting, by good order in all things, did breed up so many learned men in that one College of St. John's, at one time, as I believe the whole University of Louvain in many years was never able to afford ".

In another place he makes honourable mention of Watson : " Cambridge," he says, " at my first coming thither, but not at my going away, committed this fault, in reading the precepts of Aristotle without the example of other authors. But herein, in my time, these men of worthy memory, Mr. Redman, Mr. Cheke, Mr. Smith, Mr. Haddon, Mr. Watson, put so to their helping hands, as that university, and all students there, as long as learning shall last, shall be bound unto them, if that trade in study be truly followed which those men left behind them there." [1]

When Ascham wrote this, in the time of Queen Elizabeth, Watson was in prison for his faith, and it does the author of *The Schoolmaster* no little credit that he was not afraid to declare his esteem and friendship for one now in disgrace, and who differed from him in religion. This is not the only passage in which he is mentioned ; and as we have too little knowledge of the private and personal life of Watson, I am glad to transcribe the few traits recorded by his fellow-student. Ascham and Watson were about the same age ; both took their degrees in arts, and were elected fellows of their college at the same time, and remained together in residence for several years. A great friendship seems to have sprung up between the young men, from similarity in literary

[1] Ascham's *Works*, p. 314.

tastes,[1] though they were already taking different courses in matters of religion.

"When Mr. Watson," says Ascham, "in St. John's College, wrote his excellent tragedy of *Absolon*, Mr. Cheke, he, and I had many pleasant talks together in comparing the precepts of Aristotle and Horace with the examples of Euripides, Sophocles, and Seneca. Few men in writing of tragedies in our days have shot at this mark here in England ; more in France, Germany, and Italy also have written tragedies in our time, of which not one, I am sure, is able to abide the true touch of Aristotle's precepts and Euripides' example, save only two, that ever I saw, Mr. Watson's *Absolon* and Georgius Buchanan's *Jephte*." [2]

Ascham also tells us that Watson was so great a purist in Latin that he would never allow this tragedy to be published, because he himself considered that there was in one or two lines some licence in the metre which the best models did not sanction. It is to be feared that the work has perished.

From another passage it appears that the young classics would have set themselves to mould English verse after the pattern of Greek and Roman metres, "avoiding barbarous rhyming," and attending to "quantity" in the syllables. He gives as a specimen two English hexameter verses of Watson's.[3]

But if Watson's University career was happy and brilliant

[1] Ascham writes: "One of the best scholars that ever St. John's College bred, Mr. Watson, mine old friend, sometime Bishop of Lincoln ". [2] *Ibid.*, p. 320.

[3] Mr. Cole, in his MS. Notes to Baker (in the British Museum) wonders at Ascham's praise of such " doggrel ". He evidently did not notice that the lines were hexameters, though even as such they are only interesting as very early (the earliest ?) attempts in that metre. Among Watson's writings Mr. Cooper mentions a translation into English verse of part of the first book of Homer's *Odyssey*, now lost.

in a literary point of view, it was far otherwise as regards religion.   While he was still an undergraduate those momentous changes began which have severed England from Catholic Christendom.   The minds of several of his fellow-students were infected with the new heresies.   The University was agitated by disputes about the divorce between Henry and Katharine, and the marriage with Anne Boleyn. Cranmer had become Archbishop of Canterbury (consecrated 30th March, 1533), and men were awaiting an open rupture with the Holy See.   In 1534 the schism was consummated, the authority of the Sovereign Pontiff abolished by Act of Parliament, and the Royal supremacy substituted.   In June, 1535, Cardinal Fisher, the venerable founder of St. John's,[1] whom Watson had probably often seen, and whose blessing he may have often received, laid down his life rather than acknowledge that supremacy, and after a few days his example was followed by Sir Thomas More.   Surely a thrill of horror must have gone through the hearts of the fellows and students of his college when they heard that the body of the saintly bishop, stripped naked, had been left to lie all day in the gaze of the people on Tower Hill.   Yet when the oath of supremacy was exacted from them, terror prevailed and none refused.

To the shame of the University it must be said that in May, 1534, a public document had been obtained by the court, signed by the Vice-Chancellor and a great number of the doctors and masters, in which they deny that the Roman Pontiff has by Scripture any greater power or authority in England than any other foreign bishop.[2]   What made this more shameful was the fact that their Chancellor, Fisher, was at that very time in the Tower for his rejection of this

---

[1] Though he would never allow this title, there is no doubt that it rightfully belongs to him after the Lady Margaret.

[2] Cooper, *Annals of Cambridge*, vol. i., p. 367.

heresy. They knew well that their decision was utterly false, and extorted from them by fear. Even if they had forgotten the teaching of all Catholic doctors, they were not ignorant that, only a few years before, the king, in his book against Luther, had proved that (to use his own words) " since the conversion of the world all Churches have been obedient to the See of Rome," and that, " by the unanimous consent of all nations, it is forbidden to change or move the things that have been for a long time immovable " ; and that he had declared that Luther was "void of all charity, not only by perishing himself through fury, but much more by endeavouring to draw all others with him into destruction, by striving to dissuade them from their true obedience to the chief bishop ".

On the 3rd June this same year, 1534, all the scholars of the University took the oath of succession,[1] which for the clergy included that of the king's supremacy, in St. Mary's Church. Cromwell succeeded as Chancellor of the University in the place of Fisher, and in October, 1535, made a visitation.

Among his injunctions were the following:

1. By a writing sealed by the University they were to swear "to obey all statutes made, or to be made, for the extirpation of Papal usurpation ".

2. No more lectures were to be read upon any doctors who had commented the *Master of the Sentences*, nor after the manner of Scotus.

3. No more lectures were to be given in canon law, nor degrees in canon law to be conferred.[2]

Contemporary histories tell us how, after this visitation, the scholastics were cast aside, and Scotus especially condemned to the most ignominious uses.

Watson would not thank me were I to try to excuse him for

---

[1] Cooper, *Annals of Cambridge*, vol. i., p. 368.   [2] *Ibid.*, p. 375.

the part he must have taken in these and other schismatical acts. Still it may be remembered that he was a very young man at this period, and that his studies in theology had not begun, and that by these very injunctions he was cut off from the streams of Catholic tradition in his future studies. Stapleton, a most learned theologian, has made an apology even for men who were older and more learned in ecclesiastical matters than Watson then was. Writing in 1567, he said :

" This matter of the Pope's supremacy and of the Prince's was at the first, even to very learned men, a strange matter, but is now to meanly learned a well-known and beaten matter. Sir Thomas More—whose incomparable virtue and learning all the Christian world hath in high estimation, and who for this quarrel suffered death, for the preservation of the unity of Christ's Church, which was never, nor shall be, preserved but under this one head—as good a man, and as great a clerk, and as blessed a martyr as he was, albeit he ever well thought of this primacy, and that it was at the leastwise instituted by the corps of Christendom for great urgent causes for avoiding of schisms ; yet that this primacy was immediately institute of God (which thing all Catholics now do believe) he did not many years believe. It is the less marvel, therefore, if at the first, for lack of mature and deep consideration, many good and well-learned men otherwise were carried away with ' the volume of this storm and tempest." [1]

Whatever may be the value of this apology for bishops and priests, it seems certainly applicable to young men like Watson, who followed the example of priests and bishops.

In the Parliament which assembled 8th June, 1536, an Act was passed " for extinguishing the authority of the

---

[1] Stapleton's *Counterblast to Mr. Horn's Blast*, pp. 37, 38.

Bishop of Rome". It required every person, promoted to any degree of learning in any University, to make oath that he "from henceforth shall utterly renounce, refuse, relinquish, or forsake the Bishop of Rome . . . and shall accept, report, and take the King's Majesty to be the only supreme head on earth of the Church of England . . . and in case any oath hath been made by him to any person in maintenance, defence, or favour of the Bishop of Rome, he reports the same as vain and annihilate. So help him God, all saints, and the holy Evangelists."

This oath must have been taken by Watson when he received his Master's degree, even if he had not taken it before. If, however, he lived in a state of schism for nearly twenty years (*i.e.*, from 1533 to 1553), he expiated his error by more than twenty years' imprisonment in behalf of the supremacy of the Pope and the unity of the Church. But I am anticipating, and must go back to his earlier years.

He had been elected fellow of St. John's on Ashton's foundation in 1533. In due time he must have taken holy orders. He commenced M.A. in 1537, and was for several years dean of the college and one of its preachers. Dr. Metcalf had resigned his mastership in July, 1537, and was succeeded by Dr. George Day, who governed the college for a year. Both these were staunch Catholics in the rest of their doctrine, however they may have yielded with regard to the supremacy. When Day was elected provost of King's College in June, 1538, he was replaced in St. John's by Dr. John Taylor. The career of this man was very singular, and characteristic of the times. Soon after his election to the mastership he had preached a sermon in London in defence of Transubstantiation. This sermon aroused the zeal of a priest and schoolmaster named Lambert, a disciple of Tyndal's, and he presented Taylor with a paper of reasons against his doctrine. For this paper Lambert was tried for

9

heresy, first by Cranmer, and then on appeal by Henry in person, and condemned to the stake. Taylor, who by making known the paper was one of the causes of Lambert's death, was so touched by his fate or moved by his arguments that he became a convert to the opinions against which he had preached, and was imprisoned for a short time on suspicion of heresy in 1540. But he seems to have retracted, for he was soon restored to his college. He was, however, involved in continual disputes with the fellows, so that the Bishop of Ely had to interfere in 1543, and the disputes still continuing, he resigned in 1546. In Edward's reign he openly professed heresy, and defended the marriage of the clergy, and was one of the compilers of the Common Prayer-book. He was rewarded in 1552 with the Bishopric of Lincoln, of which he was deprived in March, 1554, and died in the following December.

Watson was one of the appellants to the Bishop of Ely against Taylor's government, but it is not necessary to investigate the nature or the merits of these quarrels, which seem to have regarded the government of the college rather than serious questions of religion.

It was complained in the reign of Edward [1] that the University had greatly fallen off in numbers and in learning ; and it is admitted that the continual changes in religion both alienated men from theological studies, and deterred many from an ecclesiastical career. On the band of talented young men at St. John's the effect seems to have been to make them give themselves almost exclusively to classical studies. In these they met on a neutral ground, and by this means kept up a literary friendship. But it was impossible at that time to avoid taking a side, or engaging in

---

[1] Latimer's Sermon, 6th April, 1549. Leaver's Sermon, December, 1550.

theological disputes, and these seem at last to have made Watson glad to leave the University.

Dr. Lingard has truly described the miserable state of things from the time of the schism to the end of the reign of Henry : " The creed of the Church of England depended on the theological caprice of its supreme head. The clergy were divided into two opposite factions, denominated the men of the old and the new learning. The chief of the former was Gardiner, Bishop of Winchester. . . . The latter acknowledged for their leaders Cranmer, Shaxton, Latimer, and Fox. . . . But none of the prelates on either side aspired to the palm of martyrdom. . . . If, on the one hand, Gardiner and his associates, to avoid the Royal displeasure, consented to renounce the Papal supremacy, and to subscribe to every successive innovation in the established creed ; Cranmer and his friends, on the other, submitted with equal weakness to teach doctrines which they disapproved, to practise a worship which they deemed idolatrous or superstitious, and to consign men to the stake for the open profession of tenets which, there is reason to suspect, they themselves inwardly believed. Henry's infallibility continually oscillated between the two parties." [1]

The fellows of St. John's College were divided in sentiment like the prelates. That Watson openly defended the " old learning," that is, the Catholic faith, especially on the sacraments, is certain ; for at the accession of Edward he was looked to as one of the champions of that faith against the novelties of Calvin and Zuinglius. But the greater number seem to have taken the other side.

Cheke was disposed to heresy, and by his fame and position as lecturer had much influence on the younger members of the college. Ascham relates how he himself nearly got into trouble by his audacity, and might have lost his fellow-

[1] *History of England*, vol. v., ch. ii., p. 100 (Ed. 1849).

ship but for the support of Dr. Metcalf. Cecil was there from 1535 to 1541, and, while diligently studying Greek and Latin under Sir John Cheke and Sir Thomas Smith, imbibed that spirit of heresy and hypocrisy which made him in later years so great a persecutor of Catholics, and especially of Watson. John Taylor, William Bill, John Redman, Walter Haddon, James Pilkington, Robert Horne, Thomas Leaver, who were fellows of St. John's during Watson's residence, were all infected with heresy, as their subsequent career proves. On the other hand, George Day, who was master in 1537, and became Bishop of Chichester, courageously resisted the innovations under Edward, and suffered deprivation of his bishopric and imprisonment. John Seton, who was some years older than Watson, seems to have been closely united to him in friendship while they resided as fellows, and, subsequently, when they were both chaplains to Bishop Gardiner; and Seton suffered exile rather than acknowledge the supremacy of Elizabeth.

Another of Watson's friends was Alban Langdale, well known both as a scholar and a theologian, who in Mary's time became Archdeacon of Chichester, and for refusing the oath of supremacy was imprisoned under Elizabeth, and died in exile. ·

Another fellow of St. John's, of about Watson's standing, was John Young, who took the Catholic part in several discussions in Edward's reign, and in that of Mary became Master of Pembroke, Vice-Chancellor of the University, and Regius Professor of Divinity. With Watson he suffered twenty-four years' imprisonment under Elizabeth, and died in Wisbeach Castle in 1580 or 1581, probably assisted by Watson in his last moments.

In the year 1540, after the execution of Cromwell, Stephen Gardiner, Bishop of Winchester, was made Chancellor of the University of Cambridge, and became acquainted with the talents of Watson, and in 1545 appointed him his domestic chaplain, at the same time conferring on him the rectory of Wyke Regis, in Dorsetshire. By the erection of the See of Bristol in 1542, Dorsetshire had been taken from the diocese of Salisbury and transferred to the new see, so that Watson was under the jurisdiction of Paul Bush, its first bishop. "The church of Wyke Regis," wrote Mr. Hutchins [1] in 1779, "is a large structure, very ancient, and one of the best in these parts. It is the mother-church of Weymouth." Indeed, Weymouth at that time had only a small chapel-of-ease, dedicated to St. Nicholas. The patron was the Bishop of Winchester; and Watson succeeded to William Meadow, who was also domestic chaplain to Gardiner. Watson certainly held a second benefice in 1550, as appears from the records of Gardiner's trial, but what it was is not mentioned. He is said to have been presented to the vicarage of Buckminster, in Leicestershire, in the diocese of Lincoln, in 1547. He does not seem to have resided in either of these places, at least not before 1550; and I have not been able to discover any particular which will help to make him known to us as a parish priest.

From several circumstances it is clear that Gardiner had a great esteem for the learning and judgment of his chaplain. He employed him to negotiate with the Lords of the Council about the famous sermon which he was required by them to preach in the beginning of Edward's reign; he took his advice as to the matter of the sermon itself, and Watson is said to have greatly assisted Gardiner in the composition of his answer to Cranmer, called *Confutatio Cavillationum.* A few words about Gardiner and his troubles will be necessary in order to understand the movements of Watson in Edward's reign, though a full account would belong more properly to a biography of Gardiner than of Watson.

[1] *History of Dorsetshire,* vol. i., p. 602.

SECTION II.—IN THE REIGN OF EDWARD VI.

The Protestant party who gathered round the deathbed of Henry both hated and feared Gardiner, and at once began a series of vexations and persecutions, which ended in his imprisonment in the Tower for more than five years. The first pretext found against him was that he had written some warm letters to the Lord Protector Somerset, and to the Archbishop Cranmer, against the introduction of changes during Edward's minority. In consequence, he was summoned before the Council, and required to promise obedience to the Royal injunctions which had just been issued. He replied that should he commit any legal offence he would submit to punishment. But as the object of Cranmer and his party was to keep him out of Parliament during the ensuing session, he was committed to the Fleet prison without crime or trial. Watson had accompanied the bishop to London, to the Council Chamber, and to the Fleet. He was himself committed there soon after.[1]

The cause of Watson's imprisonment appears to have been the complaints laid against him by two preachers named Tonge and Ayre. They had been sent to Winchester to preach by order of the Duke of Somerset, the Lord Protector, and to be instituted canons in that church. The bishop himself deposes that he received them very kindly and hospitably, and in no way disgraced them.[2] They, on the other hand, declared that the bishop said to the people: "I understand there be new preachers sent down ; but I suppose there is none of my flock so mad as to believe them that they never saw before, neither that doctrine that they never heard before". The same Sunday

---

[1] Foxe, vol. vi., p. 151. "Before this deponent was committed to the Fleet." The deponent was Watson.

[2] See the bishop's deposition, Foxe, vol. vi., p. 129.

afternoon Tonge preached, and Ayre on the Tuesday. "And the Sunday after that," so says Ayre, "Watson, the bishop's chaplain, did preach in the said church, and inveighed against the said Dr. Tonge and this deponent, as this deponent heard say;" for which cause this deponent and the said Dr. Tonge did complain to my Lord of Somerset's grace; and this deponent gathered certain articles touching the misordering of the said Dr. Tonge and this deponent by the bishop and his said chaplain, which articles the said deponent delivered, within these three days, to Master Secretary Cecil.[1]

No record appears to exist of Watson's committal, and I can only conjecture that he was made a victim to the indignation of the Protector or the archbishop for the cause I have just mentioned. While in prison, Gardiner indignantly protested against this abuse of power. In a letter to Somerset he writes: "Men be mortal and deeds revive, and methinketh my Lord of Canterbury doth (not) well to entangle thus your Grace with the matter of religion, and to borrow of your authority the Fleet, the Marshalsea, and the King's Bench, with imprisonment in his house, wherewith to cause men to agree to that (which) it pleaseth him to call truth in religion, not stablished by any law of the realm, but contrary to a law. At the least, a law is not yet; and before a law is made, I have not seen such a kind of imprisonment as I sustain."[2]

Watson was kept in separate confinement, for Gardiner complains: "Here I remain . . . without comfort of any of my friends or servants . . . no chaplain to accompany me in prayer"; and in another letter, written towards the end of November, 1547: "I have remained here seven weeks without speaking to any man saving my physician".[3]

---

[1] Foxe, vol. vi., p. 154.   [2] *Ibid.*, p. 48.   [3] *Ibid.*, p. 53.

Mr. Cooper says that Watson remained in the Fleet for two or three years, and was still there when he was brought as a witness in Gardiner's trial in 1550. This is a mistake. A general pardon was granted by the King on 6th January, 1548, and Watson was liberated as well as Gardiner. The bishop, however, was ordered to remain in his own house in Southwark on another frivolous charge, and was not allowed to return to Winchester till Lent. Watson was his constant attendant. From his own evidence we learn that he always kept the bishop's company at table, and waited on him when he went out.[1] It was, however, another chaplain, William Meadow, a man sixty years old, formerly rector of Wyke Regis, and then master of Holy Cross Hospital, who acted as the bishop's confessor.[2] He also had been confined in the Fleet at the same time as Watson and the bishop.[3]

On their return to Farnham, the parish priest of the place told Watson, who was staying at his house, that the people were much exasperated at the changes that had been introduced in the manner of worship by the visitors sent into the diocese by the Government during the bishop's absence in London, and he requested Watson to preach to them and to appease their minds. Watson, however, communicated the matter to the bishop, and the latter undertook the unwelcome duty himself.

The changes indeed had been great. All images had been removed from the churches, the procession at Candlemas had been forbidden, with a number of other acts and ceremonies, all of which had been solemnly approved by the same archbishop a few years before as " most godly, and to be retained". These innovations were trifling compared with those that soon followed—first the mass sung in

[1] Foxe, vol. vi., p. 207.
[2] Deposition of Coppinger. *Ibid.*, p. 192.   [3] *Ibid.*, p. 202.

English, then the abolition of all the guilds and chauntries, the communion in both kinds, the Book of Common Prayer instead of the Missal and other service-books, the freedom for the clergy to marry, and, still more, the repeal of the Statute of the Six Articles, and the consequent leave to preach Lutheran and Calvinistic doctrines. And while preaching was prohibited to all (even to the bishops) who had not a special licence from the King or his visitors, this licence was only given to fanatics of the new opinions. "A set of noisy declaimers," says Mr. Froude, "first to cry reform while reform was in the ascendant, first to fly or to apostatise in time of danger, made the circuit of the towns and parishes."[1] I have not been able to discover how far Watson yielded to any of these measures, or by what means he evaded compliance. A few facts only have come down to us of his conduct in this reign, and these I proceed to give.

Gardiner was not long left in peace. He was again summoned to London in June, 1548, by the Council, and commanded to preach before the young King at Westminster, and to write out his sermon and submit it to the Protector's revision before preaching. This he absolutely refused. He was then commanded to preach on certain topics and to avoid others, and to this he partly yielded. Watson was present at the bishop's house in the Clink when William Cecil was sent, on the part of the Protector, to convey his instructions about the sermon, and next day was the bishop's messenger to Somerset to complain of Cecil's behaviour—a circumstance which Cecil probably did not forget when he had power to revenge himself in the days of Elizabeth. The sermon was preached on St. Peter's day. Watson accompanied the bishop to Westminster, and

[1] *History*, vol. v., p. 97.

during the sermon was present among the throng.[1] The sermon was certainly neither seditious nor dangerous from a Protestant point of view. It inveighed against the supremacy of the Pope; but as it also defended the Real Presence, a point on which Gardiner had been forbidden by Somerset to touch, the bishop was considered contumacious, and the next day was committed to the Tower.

For two years and a half Gardiner remained in prison without trial, and during the whole of that time his chaplains were forbidden any access to him, except that once when he was supposed to be dying, and at Easter his confessor, William Meadow, spent a few hours with him.[2] Watson appears to have returned to Farnham to await events; for in June, 1550, when there was a rumour that the bishop was about to be released, Watson, with the rest of the household at Farnham, took horse at ten o'clock at night, and riding all night, reached London at seven in the morning in hopes to welcome their master.[3] They were however disappointed. In December, 1550, the bishop was brought to trial, and Watson was summoned to give evidence both for the prosecution and the defence. Foxe has preserved the records of this trial. The bishop ably defended himself against the various charges; but by a flagrant abuse of power he was condemned (February, 1551), deprived of his bishopric, and sent back to the Tower, from which he was only released on the accession of Mary, to be restored to his see and become Chancellor of the kingdom.

Meanwhile the lands and revenues of the diocese of Winchester were divided into eight portions, of which one was given to the Crown, and the other seven to the friends of

---

[1] Watson's Evidence. Foxe, vol. vi., pp. 151-53.
[2] Gardiner's Articles. *Ibid.*, p. 72.   [3] *Ibid.*, p. 220.

the Government. The infamous Poynet of Rochester[1] succeeded Gardiner in the See of Winchester, and received various rectories and other lands for his support. With this man's accession Watson's connection with the diocese terminated. The next time we meet with him is in a theological conference held in December, 1551. It is thus related by Strype:[2]

"About this time Cheke, with some others, was engaged in two disputations, or rather friendly conferences, privately with Feckenham (who was afterwards Dean of St. Paul's and Abbot of Westminster), and one or two more of his party, in the great controversy of the Real Presence in the Sacrament. The first was held at Secretary Cecil's house, and the latter at Sir Richard Morison's. The auditors were but six—viz., the Lord Russel, Sir Thomas Wroth, of the Bedchamber; Sir Anthony Cooke, one of the King's instructors; Throgmorton, Chamberlain of the Exchequer; Mr. Knokes, and Mr. Harrington, with whom were joined the Marquis of Northampton and the Earl of Rutland in the second conference. The disputants were Sir John Cheke, and with him Sir William Cecil, Secretary of State; Horn, Dean of Durham; Whitehead, and Grindal, who were against the Real Presence; Feckenham, Young, and, at the second disputation, Watson, who were for it. Some account of these disputations is still extant in Latin, in the MS. library of Bene't College in Cambridge. And to preserve what remainders we can of Cheke's, and likewise to satisfy any that are desirous to look into the Church history of England in those days, I have translated them into English and exemplified them here; only first premising

---

[1] For an account of Poynet, very different from that given by Burnet and others, see an article in the *Saturday Review*, 18th July, 1868.

[2] Strype's *Life of Sir John Cheke*, p. 69 (Ed. 1821).

that I suppose this conference might be occasioned from an appearance of the said Feckenham before Cheke by public order, to be examined by him." Thus far Strype.

I do not think it necessary to transcribe this disputation. It is imperfectly given by Strype as regard's Watson's arguments, since he takes the liberty sometimes to abridge after this fashion : "Watson here cavilled much of I know not what spiritual eating, which yet was proper and without any necessity of suffering " ; or again, " Watson eluded the argument with I know not what logical distinction " ; or, "Watson did endeavour to evade by certain distinctions " ; or, " In which place Watson laboured after a wonderful manner " ; or, finally, "Watson again gainsaid somewhat, I know not what, and the most part rose up that here might be an end ". This is what Strype calls translating into English and exemplifying.

The conference left the disputants convinced of their own opinions as before. It is chiefly interesting as bringing together, under new circumstances, men like Cheke, Cecil, Young, and Watson, who had studied together, perhaps disputed together, at the same college, and were now finally ranged on different sides in the great political and religious struggle of the age.

Whether Watson, after the deprivation of Gardiner, resided at Wyke Regis or at Buckminster, or what were his movements or his acts during the remainder of this reign, I have not been able to discover.[1] The only event mentioned is one without time or place, but as it has been supposed to cast a slur on the character of Watson I cannot pass it over. It is thus narrated by Foxe :[2]

" Moreover, as touching the said Master Rough, this is further to be noted, that he, being in the north country

---

[1] No register exists at Wyke of that period.

[2] *Acts and Monuments*, vol. viii., p. 447.

in the days of King Edward the Sixth, was the mean to save Dr. Watson's life (who in Queen Mary's time was Bishop of Lincoln) for a sermon that he had made there. The said Watson after that, in the said days of Queen Mary, being with Bonner at the examination of the said Master Rough, to requite the good turn in saving his life, detected him there to be a pernicious heretic, who did more hurt in the north parts than a hundred besides of his opinion. Unto whom Master Rough said again, ' Why, sir, is this the reward I have for saving your life when you preached erroneous doctrine in the days of King Edward the Sixth ? ' "

It is not easy to know what to make of this story. No documents are quoted, and we have to rely for its truth first on the veracity of Foxe, and next on that of Rough, a Scotch monk, who had taken a wife and the office of reformer in England. What is to be understood by "erroneous doctrine"? And what doctrine could have endangered Watson's life in that reign ? The only doctrine that was treasonable, and the preaching of which would have subjected its holder to loss of life, was the denial of the King's supremacy. But Watson can scarcely have preached against this, since, in his evidence given in December, 1550, he had admitted the first article proposed in Gardiner's trial, which ran as follows : " That the King's Majesty justly and rightfully is, and by the laws of God ought to be, supreme head in earth of the Church of England, and also of Ireland ; and so is by the clergy of this realm in their Convocation, and by Act of Parliament, justly, and according to the laws of God, recognised ".[1] Moreover, it is not easy to conceive how Rough could have saved Watson's life had he been publicly guilty of treason, or how no record of danger or escape should exist except in

[1] Foxe, vol. vi., p. 151.

this ambiguous boast of Rough. That Watson may have
preached in defence of the Real Presence, or spoken against
the recent innovations, is likely enough ; but to have done
this might have exposed him to fine or imprisonment, not to
the penalty of death. We must, therefore, leave this matter
in its obscurity. But it would be unfair to accuse Watson
of cruelty on such uncertain grounds.

Section III.—In the Reign of Mary.

We must now pass on to the reign of Mary. Edward
expired on 6th July, 1553. Watson was about forty years
old. He had now learnt by experience what was meant by
Royal supremacy, and what were the consequences of casting off that of the successor of St. Peter. He had always
firmly held the Catholic faith except in this particular.
He had been conspicuous for his zeal in defending the
Real Presence. There is no proof that he ever subscribed
to the forty-two articles drawn up by Cranmer, for the
King's command to all clergymen to do so was only issued
shortly before his death. On the other hand, not only had
he seen the communion service substituted for the Holy
Sacrifice of the Mass, but the altars removed from the
churches, and the churches themselves robbed of their
ornaments by Act of Parliament, in virtue of the Royal
supremacy. His eyes were opened to the divine constitu-
tion of the Church, and in future we shall find him, not
only defending with Fisher the sacraments against Luther,
but ready also like Fisher to lay down his life rather than
again renounce his allegiance to the Vicar of Christ.

Mary entered London 31st July, and Watson was so well
known for his attachment to the old faith that three weeks
afterwards he was ordered to preach in her presence. The
matter is thus related by Stow :[1] " The twentieth of August

---

[1] Stow's *Annals of England*, p. 614 (Ed. 1615).

Dr. Watson,[1] chaplain to the Bishop of Winchester, preached at Paul's Cross, by the Queen's appointment ; and for fear of the like tumult as had been the Sunday last past, certain Lords of the Council repaired to the sermon, as the Lord Treasurer, the Lord Privy Seal, the Earl of Bedford, the Earl of Pembroke, the Lord Wentworth, the Lord Rich, and Sir Henry Gernigam, Captain of the Guard, with two hundred of the guard, which stood about the preacher with halberts. Also the Mayor had warned the companies of the city to be present in their liveries, which was well accepted of the Queen's Council, and the sermon was quietly ended."

Mr. Nichols, in his notes to Machyn's *Diary*, has given us the matter of this sermon from a letter, writen in London 22nd August, by William Dalby : " On Sunday last was a sermon at Paul's Cross, made by one Doctor Watson. There was at his sermon the Marquis of Winchester, the Earl of Bedford, the Earl of Pembroke, the Lord Wentworth, the Lord Rich. They did sit where my Lord Mayor and the Aldermen were wont to sit, my Lord Mayor [Marquis ?] sitting uppermost. There was also in the window over the Mayor [*sic*] the old Bishop of London [Bonner, the late bishop], and divers others. There was 120 of the guard, that stood round about the Cross with their halberts, to guard the preacher, and to apprehend them that would stir. His sermon was no more eloquent than edifying—I mean it was neither eloquent or edifying in my opinion, for he meddled not with the gospel, nor epistle, nor no part of Scripture. After he had read his theme, he entered into a by-matter, and so spent his time. Four or five of the chief points of his sermon, that I can remember, I will, as briefly as I can, report unto you, viz.,

[1] He did not take his Doctor's degree until some months after this, but he was doubtless already thus named by courtesy or popular fame.

he required the people not to believe the preachers, but that their faith should be firm and sure, because there is such vanities amongst them ; and if any man doubt of his faith, let him go to the Scriptures, and also to the interpreters of the doctors, and interpret it not after their own brain. He wished the people to have no new faith, nor to build no new temple, but to keep the old faith, and edify the old temple again. He blamed the people, in a manner, for that heretofore they would have nothing that was man's tradition, and now they be contented to have man's tradition, showing that in the reign of the first year of our Sovereign Lord King Edward VI. there was a law established that in the sacrament there was the body and blood of Christ, not really but spiritually; and the next year after they established another law, that there was the body of Christ neither spiritually nor really. These two in themselves are contraries, therefore they cannot be both true. He showed that we should ground our faith upon God's Word, which is Scripture, and Scripture is the Bible, which we have in Hebrew, Greek, and Latin, and now translated into English ; but he doubteth the translation was not true. Also, he said there hath been in his time that he hath seen twenty catechisms, and every one varying from other in some points ; and well, he said, they might be all false, but they could not be all true; and thus persuading the people that they had followed men's tradition, and had gone astray, wishing them to come home again and re-edify the old temple. Thus, with many other persuasions, he spent the time till eleven of the clock, and ended."[1]

No doubt Watson had hastened to London to welcome Gardiner on his release from his long captivity, which hap-

[1] From the Harl MS., 353, f. 141, quoted in note to Machyn's *Diary*, p. 332.

pened on August the 3d; and it was probably by Gardiner's suggestion that he had been chosen to preach this sermon. It was also by Gardiner's authority, as Chancellor of Cambridge, about a month afterwards, on 25th September, he was deputed to proceed to Cambridge to act on his behalf in restoring the old religion, and to make a report on the state of the colleges.

At the same time he was elected Master of St. John's College, and admitted, in the person of Christopher Brown, his proxy, by John Young, Vice-Chancellor, then fellow of Trinity College, at his chamber there, Roger Ascham being present as President of St. John's, with several other fellows of that society. The instrument of his admission is dated 28th September, 1553.[1]

To understand his position we must glance back upon the state of his college since he had left it. The Protestant party had succeeded in getting a new code of statutes in 1545 by the authority of Henry VIII., with whom Cheke was in great favour.[2] Taylor had resigned his mastership at the beginning of the reign of Edward, and had been succeeded by William Bill, recommended for election by the Protector. The fellows, who were enamoured of the new opinions, having now no fear of the terrible penalty which, while Henry lived, attached to all who denied the Real Presence, began openly to profess their heresy. They even went so far as to hold open controversies against the most Holy Sacrament in the chapel. "After they had overthrown the Mass in their disputations," writes Baker, "because the Host was not removed, the pix that hung over the altar was cut down by a private hand, which cost them some apology with the archbishop (Cranmer), to whom Mr. Leaver (one of the leaders in these doings) was sent up to excuse the thing".[3]

<hr/>

[1] Baker's *History of St. John's*, vol. i., p. 137.
[2] *Ibid.*, pp. 118-21. [3] *Ibid.*, p. 125.

They had, however, only anticipated by a few weeks the action of the Government. The college chapel which the martyred Fisher had solemnly consecrated in 1516, and in which he had hoped that the Holy Sacrifice would be daily offered by the fellows of the college, for whose education and maintenance he toiled so much, was now after thirty years to be devoted to the novel rites against which Fisher had so warmly written. "It is a strange thing," he wrote in 1523, "that Luther should have the impudence to lay down new laws for the sacraments, as if he thought that men at the present day were so utterly stupid as to be willing at the bidding of an insignificant friar to depart from the ancient rites observed by the Church."[1] But the age, in its pride of learning, was more spiritually stupid than Fisher believed. Luther's laws, or those of Calvin or of Cranmer, were preferred to those of the saints and doctors, and the Holy Sacrifice was abolished, the vestments sold for profane uses, the liturgical books given to the flames, the altar-stones broken or thrown aside, and the college statutes again reformed "by taking out the venom of Popery and superstition," to use the words of the Protestant historian of the college.[2] At the end of 1551 Bill had been replaced in the mastership by the famous Protestant preacher Thomas Leaver, who continued until the accession of Queen Mary, when he fled into Switzerland to Calvin. It is enough to quote the words of Baker, "that the Reformation nowhere gained more ground, or was more zealously maintained, than it did here under this man's example and the influence of his government".[3]

It was into such an abode of spiritual desolation that Watson now entered. Twenty-four of the fellows had

---

[1] *Assertionis Lutheranæ Confutatio*, fol. lxxv. (Ed. 1523).
[2] Baker's *History of St John's*, vol. i., p. 127.   [3] *Ibid.*, p. 133.

resigned or been deprived,[1] and as it was of course impossible to supply their places at once with men equally skilled
in ancient literature, Ascham, who despised and hated
theology, canon law, and scholastic philosophy, complained
grievously of the ignorance of the new fellows and the
decline of the literary reputation of the college. Had
Watson remained master, he would no doubt have still more
effectually promoted his favourite studies than he had done
when one of the junior fellows. When he first quitted the
college, a copy of Fisher's *Statutes* had been left with him
in trust. These he brought back and enforced, and in other
ways sought to carry out the intentions of the founder.[2]
But at the end of seven months from his election he resigned
his office, probably because he found its duties incompatible
with his other appointment as Dean of Durham.

A few words will be necessary to explain this dignity. In
1540 Hugh Whitehead, the last Prior of Durham, surrendered to Henry; and 12th May, 1541, the King appointed a
dean and twelve prebendaries in the place of the monastic
society, Whitehead himself being the first dean. He had
been succeeded by Robert Horn, one of Watson's contemporaries at St. John's. Under him Protestantism had
triumphed, especially as the bishop, Cuthbert Tunstall, was
imprisoned. The Duke of Northumberland had got bills
through Parliament to suppress the bishopric, and divide it
into two new ones (viz., Durham and Newcastle), hoping,
under the new arrangements, to get into his own hands the
great possessions of the see, when his plans were defeated
by the death of Edward. The Parliament of the 1st of May

---

[1] I am not sure that they were all deprived during Watson's mastership. According to Strype the vacancies were not all made until
October, 1554. Baker speaks hesitatingly (vol. i., p. 141).

[2] See Baker, vol. i., 138, 139.

repealed these Acts.[1]　Although the country was not yet
reconciled with the Holy See, the canon law had been
restored, and by its provisions married priests were at once
removed from their benefices.　Among these was the Dean
of Durham.　The appointment, being in the gift of the
Crown, was, probably by Gardiner's recommendation, conferred on Watson, who was by origin of that diocese.　His
nomination was 18th November, 1553.　In October he had
been one of the proctors of the Convocation, and had
strenuously maintained the Catholic faith against John
Philpot, James Haddon, Richard Cheyney, and other
learned Protestants.[2]　His position as Master of St. John's
exempted him from residence in any of his benefices,[3] yet
he resigned his rectory of Wyke on his appointment to the
deanery.[4]　An Act passed by the first Parliament of Mary
enabled her to make statutes for the cathedrals, and by her
appointment Heath of York, Bonner of London, Tunstall of
Durham, Thirlby of Ely, and William Armistead drew up
those of Durham.　By the 11th chapter of these statutes
the dean was bound to residence, without some reasonable excuse, such as attendance on the King or Queen as
chaplain, business of the Crown or Church, attendance on
Parliament or Convocation, &c.　He might be absent a
hundred days in the year on private affairs.[5]　I am unable
to state the proportions of Watson's residence, or to give

[1] For the detail of all these changes, see Hutchinson's *History of
Durham*, vol. i., p. 430, and vol ii., p. 102.

[2] There is an *ex parte* account of the proceedings in this Convocation published by Foxe.　It is also published in Philpot's *Examinations*,
&c. (Parker Society).

[3] Act of Parliament of 1536.

[4] Thomas Haywood succeeded in 1553 (Hutchin's *Dorsetshire*).

[5] The dean's stipend was £40, and 12s. 5d. each day he was present in choir or lawfully absent.

details of his government of the cathedral.[1] As his zeal for the Blessed Sacrament was so great, it would be very interesting if any records could be discovered of the manner in which he re-established the Catholic worship, and endeavoured to bring back something of the cathedral's ancient splendour.   In December, 1554, the decrees of the Cardinal Legate ratified the erection of dioceses, chapters, and colleges which had been made by Henry VIII.

On the third and fifth Fridays of Lent, 1554, Watson again preached before the Queen two sermons which he afterwards published, one on the Real Presence, the other on the sacrificial character of the Mass.[2] We have a singular testimony to the reputation of Watson as a preacher in an answer that was published in the time of Elizabeth to these two sermons by Robert Crowley, minister of Cripplegate.   He says in his introduction: "Having occasion oftentimes to be in place where such as are not yet persuaded that the Pope's Church can err, have been bold to utter their minds freely, affirming that the doctrine which the Protestants teach is erroneous and false, especially concerning the presence of Christ in the Sacrament of His Body and Blood, and the Sacrifice of the Mass: I have perceived that the same have been chiefly persuaded and stayed by these two sermons made by Dr. Watson in the first year of Queen Mary's reign.   I have therefore wished that some man of like learning would have published in print an answer to those sermons; that thereby such as have been

---

[1] Surtees unfortunately did not live to write the history of the abbey and cathedral.

[2] " Two notable sermons made the 3rd and 5th Fridays in Lent last past before the Queen's Highness, concerning the real presence of Christ's body and blood in the Blessed Sacrament, also the Mass which is the sacrifice of the New Testament." London, 4to and 12mo, 1554.   Printed by J. Cawood.

deceived by the subtlety thereof might, by the plain and simple answer, be brought to the knowledge of the truth.*

And again, in his address to Dr. Watson, he says: "The estimation that you have in the Pope's Church is such, that whatsoever is known to be of your doing is of that sort thought to be so learnedly done that none can be found amongst us able to answer any part thereof".[1] As Watson was in prison when Crowley's book was written, the latter was left to enjoy in peace his imaginary triumph.

In April, 1554, being still Master of St. John's and Dean of Durham, Watson was one of the divines deputed by the University of Cambridge to proceed to Oxford to dispute with Cranmer, Ridley, and Latimer, on which occasion he was incorporated Doctor of Divinity in that University, having already taken his Doctor's degree at Cambridge at the beginning of the year. From the account of these disputes given by Foxe, Watson took no part in the contests with Cranmer or Latimer, and only a slight one in those with Ridley. They all turned on the Real Presence. He was no doubt in London when the Legate, Cardinal Pole, arrived towards the end of November of this year, 1554, and present in Convocation when the clergy were solemnly absolved from all censures and irregularities at the beginning of December.

Cardinal Pole had summoned a National Synod of both Provinces for the restoration of religion. Dr. Watson was present; and it is a clear proof of the estimation in which he was held for his character, learning, and eloquence, that when the Council assembled, 21st January, 1555-56, in the

---

[1] "A setting open of the subtyle sophistrie of Thomas Watson, &c., written by Robert Crawley, Clearke." Printed by Henry Denham, 1569. Ridley also made annotations on Watson's sermons, which he sent to Bradford. In his letter he calls Watson "a man of acute parts". See Bradford's *Writings*, vol. ii., p. 207 (Parker Society).

Archbishop's Chapel in Lambeth, to hear the promulgation of the legatine constitutions, Dr. Watson was the orator selected to deliver the sermon in Latin, in presence of the Cardinal Legate, the bishops and clergy, "and a great multitude of people ".[1]

This is the place to say something of the work by which Watson is now best known, his Sermons on the Seven Sacraments, for though the volume did not appear until the summer of 1558, it was begun in consequence of the Synod.

Printed sermons are of two sorts. They are either intended to preserve the memory of a discourse which the author has already made, or they are written that they may be preached by others. Watson's sermons on the sacra· ments belong to the latter class. Their place in Catholic literature will be better understood if I draw up a list of the principal sermons that had been previously published in English, after the invention of printing. It will not be very long.

The sermons by John Myrc, called the *Liber Festivalis* had been translated and were printed by Caxton in 1483, and were frequently reprinted by Wynkyn de Worde, Pynson, and others. The Blessed John Fisher, Bishop of Rochester, had preached on the Penitential Psalms, as well as against the heresies of Luther, and funeral sermons at the death of Henry VII., and of the Lady Margaret, Countess of Richmond and mother of Henry VII. His sermons on the Psalms had passed through at least six editions during his lifetime. Cuthbert Tunstall published the sermon which he preached in 1518, in praise of marriage, at the espousals of Mary, daughter of Henry VIII. with Francis I. (Pynson) ; and another when he was Bishop of Durham in 1539 (published by Berthelet). John Longland, Bishop of

---

[1] Wilkins, *Concilia*, vol. iv., p. 132.

Lincoln, published in 1531 three sermons preached at Westminster : one against Luther, one when the Legates à Latere began their visitation, and a third at the foundation of Westminster College. These were printed by Pynson. Petit in 1538 printed a fourth sermon preached by the same prelate at Greenwich.

Latimer's first printed sermon seems to have appeared in 1537, and in due time several others. The first book of Protestant Homilies was printed in 1547 by Grafton. Other Protestant sermons by Hooper, Leaver, and Ponet, were printed in the reign of Edward VI.

The only other Catholic sermons with which I am acquainted are :

Three godly and notable sermons of the most honorable and blessed sacrament of the altar, by William Peryn (printed in 1546 both by Hill and by Herforde). Five Homilies by Leonard Pollard, Prebendary of Worcester, printed by Jugge in 1556. These were corrected and edited by Bonner. Bonner's Homilies, printed by Cawood in 1555. Sermons preached at S. Paul's Cross, by Brookes in 1554, by Hugh Glasier in 1555, by John Harpsfield in 1556. (Printed by Robert Caley.) A Sermon by Feckenham, Abbot of Westminster, on the death of Joan, Queen of Spain, in 1555, and two Homilies by the same preacher on the first, second, and third Articles of the Creed (Caley). Sermons by Roger Edgeworth, Canon of Salisbury, printed in 1557. These are on the seven gifts of the Holy Ghost, on the articles of Christian faith, on ceremonies, and of man's law, and an exposition of the first Epistle of St. Peter (printed by Caley). Lastly, Two Sermons on the Real Presence, by Dr. Watson, preached before Queen Mary in 1554.

It will be seen from this list how very scanty was the help afforded to a priest anxious to announce the Word of

God to his people. He had neither discourses prepared for his use, nor models to direct him in composing. Most of the sermons of the above list were too ambitious for his flights ; they were preached by great dignitaries of the Church on solemn occasions. Old John Myrc's *Liber Festivalis* was out of date. Not only was its English antiquated, but it was unsuited to a people whose minds were agitated by theological discussions, and prejudiced by the sarcasms and invectives of the Reformers.

On the other hand, the Catholic clergy were not yet well prepared for instructing and exhorting the people by their own efforts and from their own stock of learning. More than twenty years had passed since the schism. Theological studies had been thrown into utter confusion in the Universities. The controversies that raged, while they tended to produce a few champions of the faith, such as Watson, only perplexed ordinary minds, or disgusted them, and turned them from the study of truth. Many priests simply floated with the stream, and were carried round in its eddies at the bidding of men in power. When Cardinal Pole, therefore, assembled a Council to remedy all these evils, its attention was at once directed to the subject of preaching and the instruction of the people. Among other measures taken one was that homilies should be prepared, to be used by rectors and vicars unable to compose instruction themselves.[1] The *Institution of a Christian Man*, which had been composed in the time of Henry VIII., was brought up for examination. It was divided into three parts, and some of the lower house of Convocation were chosen to make homilies from it. This was in December, 1555. They

---

[1] " Ubi defuerint concionandi periti rectores aut vicarii, homilias ex hujus synodi mandato conscriptas, dominicis et aliis festis diebus legere tenebuntur " (Wilkins' *Concilia*, vol. iv., p. 123).

also ordered a translation of the New Testament to be prepared, and a treatise on the seven sacraments.

The Council was prorogued from time to time, and never reassembled. But in the Convocation of January to March, 1558, the subject was again treated.[1] It was ordered that four books of sermons should be made :

1st. On the eucharist, on penance, confession, and the other sacraments ; on free will, justification, and good works ; on the Church and its authority, unity, and ministers.

2nd. On the articles of the faith, the Lord's Prayer, angelic salutation, decalogue and sacraments.

3rd. Sermons for the Sundays of the year and for saints' days.

4th. On ceremonies, on virtues and vices, and on the last judgment.

The death of Mary prevented the full carrying out of these measures. Yet something was done. Bonner's *Book of Homilies* was published. But as no one was more capable of supplying the want, so no one more zealously undertook to do so than Dr. Watson. Hence his book, called *Wholesome and Catholic Doctrine concerning the Seven Sacraments of Christ's Church*, " expedient to be known of all men, set forth in manner of short sermons to be made to the people ".[2]

Being intended for general preaching, or rather public reading, these sermons are, of course, unimpassioned and colourless. We cannot judge from them of Bishop Watson's own style of preaching. We cannot gather from them, as from the sermons of Latimer and Leaver, pictures of the manners and passions of the times. They scarcely even reflect Watson's personal character, except by the very

[1] Wilkins, vol. iv., p. 156.

[2] These sermons were reprinted by the present writer in 1876.

absence of invective, and the simple dignity which distinguishes them.   As specimens of old English before the great Elizabethan era they are interesting to students of our language, especially as being the work of one of the best classical scholars of the day.

From this digression we may now return to the story of Watson's life.

We may suppose that the greater part of the years 1555 and 1556 was spent by him in Durham.   On 7th December, 1556, the Queen issued a licence for filling up the See of Lincoln, and Watson was elected to that bishopric.   On the 24th of the same month he had a grant of the temporalities, with all the profits accruing since the vacancy. His bull of confirmation by the Pope is dated 24th March, 1557, but he was not consecrated till August.

Lincoln had formerly been one of the richest, as it was the largest, diocese in England.   But during the episcopate of John Longland (1521-47) Henry VIII. had carried off all the treasures of the cathedral, 2621 ounces of gold, 4285 ounces of silver, and an immense number of pearls, diamonds, and other precious stones.[1]   Longland's successor, Henry Holbeach, surrendered in one day to the Crown all the episcopal estates,[2] and reduced the see to utter poverty.   He also abandoned the episcopal palace in London.   During his time the church was again plundered of the few ornaments that remained.

Holbeach died in 1551, and was followed by John Taylor, whose acquaintance we have already made as Master of St. John's.   Taylor was deprived on the accession of Mary, and John White elected 1st April, 1554.   The translation of White to the See of Winchester caused the vacancy which

---

[1] A complete list is given by Dugdale, vol. viii., pp. 1279-86.

[2] Rymer, vol. xv., p. 66.

was filled by the election of Dr. Watson. Owing to the
poverty of the see, Cardinal Pole (29th May, 1557)
empowered him to hold the deanery of Durham *pro tempore
in commendam* with his bishopric. He did so till his consecration. He succeeded in recovering many rich vestments, articles of plate, and other furniture, of which his
church had been despoiled ; and, 9th November, 1557,
obtained, by letters patent, a re-grant of certain of the estates
which had been alienated by Holbeach, and also the
patronage of certain benefices in his diocese which had
belonged to the dissolved religious houses. But his
Protestant successors did not much profit by his zeal, since
Nicholas Bullingham, who usurped his place in January,
1560, " surrendered all that his predecessors had obtained,"
says the historian of Lincoln ; " and when he had stripped
the see of its recent wealth, he procured himself to be translated to a richer one, Worcester, leaving to his successor the
pious opportunity of conforming himself more strictly to the
apostolical example of contentment with little ". [1]

I have not been able to discover any documents throwing
light on Dr. Watson's spiritual government of his diocese,
and must be content to give, in chronological order, the few
scattered notices of him which occur in the last two years of
his freedom.

Shortly after his election to Lincoln he was named by
Cardinal Pole as one of his delegates to visit the University
of Cambridge, of which the Cardinal had been elected
Chancellor after the death of Gardiner. The incidents of
this visitation have been recorded day by day, and almost
hour by hour, by an eye-witness, John Mere, the Esquire
Bedell, and with more than usually blasphemous com-

---

[1] *History of County of Lincoln*, by Allen, vol. i., p. 151. Willis,
in his *Survey of Cathedrals*, enumerates the benefices (about 150 in
number), all in the diocese of Lincoln (vol. iii., p. 65).

mentary by Foxe.[1] The account·of the inspection of the
various colleges has no general interest. The event that has
made this visitation memorable was the burning of the
bodies of Bucer and Fagius. Martin Bucer and Paul
Fagius, two foreign heretics, had been invited to Cambridge
in 1549, and appointed professors of Divinity and of
Hebrew. Their stay was not very long, for Fagius had died
the November after his arrival, and Bucer in February,
1551. They had both had public funerals given to them
by the University, and Fagius was buried in St. Michael's,
Bucer in St. Mary's Church. Cardinal Pole considered that
the University ought to make a solemn act of reparation for
this apostasy from the Church, and had given instructions
for the reversal of all the honours paid to the foreign
reformers. They were consequently accused and tried as
heretics,, then exhumed, and their coffins and bones burnt
in the market-place with heretical books. This act will
probably appear barbarous ; but at least it was more
humane than the burning of living heretics ; and it would
seem to have been the wish of Pole, as well as of the
visitors, to spare the living, while vindicating the faith. It
is, however, probable that the effect was misjudged, and that
the burning of these dead bodies caused greater disgust and
indignation than the burning of one or two obstinate disputants would have done. The latter course would have
been defended as necessary severity; the former was
generally condemned as a needless outrage.

Watson, however, was not the principal visitor. He was
accompanied by Scott, Bishop of Chester, and Christopherson, Bishop of Chichester, and by Nicolas Ormaneto,

---

[1] Mere's Diary was published in 1838 by Dr. Lamb, in his *Collection
of Letters, &c., illustrative of the History of the University of Cambridge.* A very full account, taken from Lamb and Foxe, is also given
by Cooper in his *Annals of Cambridge.*

an Italian prelate who had accompanied the Cardinal into England, and who is commonly called in the records by his title of Datary. He seems to have guided the English theologians in their proceedings.

I need merely add that Foxe gives a summary of a sermon preached on Candlemas Day, 1557, during the visitation, by Dr. Watson, which anyone who has read his published sermons will at once see to be utterly untrustworthy. Dr. Watson also preached in St. Mary's Church while the bodies of the reformers were being burned in the market-place, "setting forth Bucer's wickedness and heretical doctrine," says Mere. Foxe has also given an abridgment of this sermon, but as he himself was then on the Continent, and only knew what some sympathising friend of Bucer's chose to report, it would be useless to reproduce it here. The day after the Church of St. Mary's, which had been interdicted as regards the Mass, was reconciled, the Blessed Sacrament was brought to it in solemn procession, and Mass was celebrated, the Bishop of Chester preaching. On the 17th February the Bishop (elect) of Lincoln returned to London.

Of his stay in the capital we have the following notices in the diary of the worthy citizen Machyn :

" The 17th March, preached afore the Queen, the new Bishop of Lincoln, Dr. Watson."[1]

" The 3rd day of April, did preach Dr. Watson, Bishop of Lincoln, at All Hallows the More, at afternoon, where was great audience of people."[2]

" The 22nd of April, did preach at St. Mark's, Spital, Dr. Watson, new chosen Bishop of Lincoln, a godly sermon."[3]

He was consecrated on the Feast of the Assumption 15th August, 1557), at Chiswick, by Nicholas Heath, Arch-

---

[1] Machyn's *Diary*, p. 128.   [2] *Ibid.*, p. 131.   [3] *Ibid.*, p. 132.

bishop of York, acting under a commission from Cardinal Pole, assisted by Thomas Thirlby, Bishop of Ely, and William Glynn, Bishop of Bangor.[1]

His duties in Parliament and in Convocation often required his presence in London, and it was probably on such an occasion that he preached another sermon thus noticed in Machyn's *Diary* : " The 20th day of February (1558), did preach at Paul's Cross, Dr. Watson, Bishop of Lincoln, and made a godly sermon, for there were present ten bishops, beside my Lord Mayor, and the aldermen and judges, and men of the law, and great audience there was".[2]

But we have now to turn to very different scenes.

SECTION IV.—IN THE REIGN OF ELIZABETH.

On the 17th November, 1558, Queen Mary died, and a few hours later Cardinal Pole. Though Elizabeth's plans were already formed for the establishment of Protestantism, yet she acted cautiously at first, hoping to gain over the bishops. The Protestant exiles at Strasburg, Frankfort, and Zurich, as soon as they heard of Mary's death, came back into England ; and Elizabeth, with the advice of her Council, appointed a solemn conference to be held between them and the bishops, professedly to prepare the minds of the nobility and legistators for the questions regarding public worship which were about to come before them in the Parliament then being held. The conference having been resolved on, the disputants on the Catholic side were the Bishops of Winchester (White), Lichfield (Bayne), Chester (Scott), and Lincoln (Watson) ; and theologians, Drs. Cole, Harpsfield, Langdale, and Chedsey. On the Protestant side were Scory, Coxe, Whitehead, Grindal, Horn, Guest, Elmer, and Jewel. The place was West-

---

[1] Stubbs, *Registrum Sacrum Anglicanum*, p. 82.
[2] Machyn's *Diary*, p. 166.

minster Abbey, where a table was set for the bishops and Catholics on one side of the choir, and for their opponents on the other, the Lords of the Council being seated at a cross table. The nobility and members of Parliament were to be present.

The points to be urged against the bishops were these :

1. That it is against the Word of God and the customs of the ancient Church to use a tongue unknown to the people in common prayer, and in the administration of the sacraments.

2. That every Church hath authority to appoint, take away, and change ceremonies and rites, so the same be to edification.

3. That it cannot be proved by the Word of God that there is in the Mass offered up a sacrifice propitiatory for the living and the dead.[1]

Of what happened in these conferences we have only a one-sided statement, all to the disadvantage of the bishops. The third Article never came into discussion, and there was no orderly disputation regarding the others. It had of course been intended that the bishops should be worsted or declared so. Hayward concludes his account by these words: "Then the Assembly was dissolved, the expectations frustrated, the purpose defeated". The contrary would be the truth. "It is very probable," continues Hayward, "that the bishops could either not be provided in so short a time, their minds being somewhat clogged with former pleasures and present cares ; or else that they discovered such an inclination against them that all their hopes did plainly vanish. And being men no more able to endure

---

[1] Letter of Jewel to Peter Martyr (20th March, 1559), *Zurich Letters*, ii. Also Hayward's *Annals of Queen Elizabeth* (Camden Society), p. 20.

adversity than they had been to moderate prosperity, they weakly yielded, and abandoning both their credit and their cause, gave full way to their own ruin." So far the annalist. Whether Watson's mind was clogged by pleasure the reader knows, and whether he was not able to endure adversity the rest of his life will declare. " Afterwards," says Hayward, " the Bishops of Winchester and Lincoln, who behaved themselves—especially Lincoln—more indiscreetly than others, were for this contempt committed to the Tower."

Camden has given another, and in some respects fairer, account of these proceedings.[1] He says the bishops complained that Bacon, the Lord Keeper, was appointed judge in such matters, of which he knew nothing, and that no good ever came of such disputations which do always bend that way that the sceptre inclines.

But Camden adds, that the Bishops of Winchester and Lincoln threatened the Queen with excommunication, and this statement has been since copied by a multitude of writers. It is intrinsically improbable, for the excommunication of the Queen would not belong to a simple bishop ; nor is it in harmony with anything we know of Watson's character, to suppose him thus hastily uttering such a threat. Besides this, Camden's statement rests on no previous and contemporary authority, nor is it borne out by other historians who lived nearer to the events. Hayward has nothing of it, nor has Holinshed,[2] who, however, copied his account from a statement published soon after the conference by authority of the Queen. The original memorandum, signed by Bacon, the Chancellor, the Earls of Bedford, Shrewsbury, Pembroke, by Cecil and others, is still in existence,[3] and has not a word about excommunica-

---

[1] *History of Elizabeth*, book i.
[2] Holinshed, vol. iii., p. 1183 (Ed. 1586).
[3] *P. R. O.*, *Dom. Elis.*, vol. iii., n. 52.

tion. This paper says: " Afterwards, for the contempt so notoriously made, the Bishops of Winchester and Lincoln, having most obstinately both disobeyed common authority and varied manifestly from their own order, and especially Lincoln, who showed more folly than the other, were condignly committed to the Tower of London ".

If it be said that the Council would not make public so great an outrage on the Queen as a threat of excommunication, I reply that most certainly the eye-witnesses of the conference, who wrote an account of it in private letters at the very time, could not have passed over such a matter. Now Cox and Jewel, two of the disputants, each wrote independent accounts of what took place within a few days of the events, and yet neither of them, while dilating on the contempt and contumacy of the Bishops of Lincoln and Winchester, mentions any threats against the Queen. Yet Jewel gloats over their punishment. " White and Watson," he writes to Peter Martyr, "were committed to the Tower. There they are now employed in castrametation." [1]

For some months the Bishop of Lincoln had been suffering from a severe attack of ague. The report of his death had reached Strasburg in January.[2] This will explain why his name does not occur in the journals of the House of Lords in the debates in which the other bishops nobly defended the Catholic faith. He had not yet entirely recovered, as appears by the letter of the Council to the Lieutenant of the Tower for his committal, dated 3rd April, 1559:

" He is willed to keep in sure and several ward the two bishops, suffering them nevertheless to have each of them

---

[1] Letter, 6th April, 1559, in *Zurich Letters*, i., p. 13. Cox's letter to Weidner is dated 20th May, 1559. *Ibid.*, i., p. 28.

[2] Letter of Jewel, written from Strasburg, 26th January, 1559. *Zurich Letters*, i. 6.

one of their own men to attend upon them and their own
stuff for their bedding and other necessary furniture, and to
appoint them to some convenient lodgings meet for persons
of their sort using them also otherwise well, specially the
Bishop of Lincoln, for that he is sick, for which respect also
and because this is his sick night, the said lieutenant is
willed to have the rather regard unto him, and to spare him
some of his own lodging and stuff for this night, and also
to suffer his surgeon and such other as shall be needful for
his health to have access unto him from time to time.

"My Lords of the Council did this day appoint Sir
Ambrose Cave and Sir Richard Sackville to repair to the
houses of the said Bishops of Winchester and Lincoln here
in London, and both to peruse their studies and writings,
and also to take order with their officers for the surety and
stay of their goods." [1]

Another letter written on the 27th of April gives instruction
to the lieutenant " to suffer the Bishop of Lincoln to come,
at such times as he by his discretion shall think meet, to
his table for the better relief of his quartan ague ; and also
to have that liberty of the house, as prisoners heretofore
having the liberty of the Tower hath used, the ordering
whereof is referred to his discretion ".[2]

On the 26th June the Queen deprived the two bishops
of their sees. For this purpose they were brought, says
Machyn, " to Master Hawse, the King's Sheriff, in Mincing
Lane, and the Bishop of Winchester to the Tower again,
and the Bishop of Lincoln delivered away ".[3] If this means
that he was set at liberty, whither he then repaired I can

---

[1] *Council Register*, vol. i., A 1558-1559. *Mary, Elizabeth*, p. 263.
Machyn notes in his *Diary* that the two bishops were sent to the
Tower by the guard by water, to the Old Swan, and to Billings-
gate after (*Diary,* p. 192).

[2] *Ibid.,* p. 278.   [3] *Diary*, p. 201.

only conjecture. It was probably to his brother's house in London. This brother is mentioned in 1556 in Mere's Diary as having come to Cambridge during the visitation.[1] His name was John. It was probably to him that a lease was granted, when Dr. Watson was Master of St. John's, of a tenement belonging to the college, mentioned in the college registers.[2] He is then called "John Watson, of London, gentleman," and he has permission to alienate the lease to William Roper, of Lincoln's Inn, probably the son-in-law of Sir Thomas More. In the State papers of 1578 there is a list given by an informer of the names and addresses of certain Papists in London, with particulars of those who keep chaplains, attend mass, &c. Among these is mentioned Watson, of Great St. Helen's, attorney of Guildhall.[3] This is all the information I can glean about this brother, unless he is the same John Watson who is mentioned in 1579 as laying complaints before the Privy Council against the Protestant Bishop of Lincoln, and who is said to be *non compos mentis*.[4] But to return to the year 1559.

Sanders, writing to Cardinal Morone in 1561, gave the following account : " Watson, Bishop of Lincoln, surpasses all the rest in learning. Being offered his liberty if he would attend the services, he refused, saying that if his conscience permitted him to assent thus far, it would allow him both to preach and communicate. Being required by the visitors to give his reasons, he answered that experience had not taught him, nor was he prepared to dispute on religion without first knowing who was to be his judge."[5]

---

[1] Lamb's *Collection*, p. 207.

[2] See Cooper's Notes to Baker's *History of St. John's*, vol. i., p. 374, n. 163, 165, and p. 377, n. 182.

[3] *P. R. O., Dom. Eliz.*, Addenda, vol. xxv., n. 118.

[4] *Privy Council Register*, 16th October, 1579, p. 641.

[5] Vatican MS., fol. 266.

If in truth he was left in liberty, after his release from the Tower on 25th June, 1559, he was once more sent to the Tower on 20th May, 1560.[1] Strype tells us[2] that he was committed thither by the Archbishop of Canterbury (Parker) and other Ecclesiastical Commissioners. There were at the, same time five other bishops, the Abbot of Westminster, and Dr. Boxall, who had been secretary to the late Queen, as well as Dean of Peterborough and of Windsor.

A letter from the Privy Council to the Archbishop, 4th Sept., 1560, allowed them to come together for their meals if he approved of it; the Archbishop of York (Heath), the Bishop of Worcester (Pate), the Abbot of Westminster (Feckenham), and Dr. Boxall, at one table; the Bishop of Ely (Thirlby), the Bishop of Bath (Bourne), the Bishop of Exeter (Turberville), and the Bishop of Lincoln, at another table. Strype adds, that "after a while they were all committed to easier restraint, and some restored to their perfect liberty". This is incorrect, as we have seen. As to Dr. Watson, he is returned by the Lieutenant of the Tower[3] a year afterwards, 26th May, 1561, as still under his charge; and so far from the restraint becoming easier, in June, 1562, the lieutenant writes to "put their Lordships of the Privy Council in remembrance that the late bishops, with Mr. Feckenham and Mr. Boxall, being all' eight in number, be close and severally kept, for the which they continually call upon him to make in their names humble suit to have more liberty," and he informs their Lordships that "it is very troublesome to serve so many persons so long together".[4] What result this application may have had I cannot say. The Bishop

[1] Machyn's *Diary*, p. 235.

[2] *Annals of the Reformation*, vol. i., part i., p. 211.

[3] *P. R. O., Dom. Eliz.*, vol. xvii., n. 13.

[4] *Ibid.*, vol. xxiii., n. 40.

of Lincoln was still in the Tower on September 5, 1562.[1]
In March, 1563, an Act was passed[2] enabling the Protestant
bishops to require the oath of the Queen's supremacy from
any who had ever held office in the Church during the last
three reigns, or who should say or hear a private mass, &c.
The refusal to take this oath when tendered the first time
subjected the refuser to perpetual imprisonment; a second
refusal subjected him to death, as in cases of high treason.
The Queen, however, secretly warned the bishops not to
proceed to tender the oath a second time without her leave.
Had this not been the case, Watson would be now ranked
among the martyrs instead of the confessors.

In the autumn of 1563 Watson was given into the custody
of Edmund Grindal, Bishop of London, one whom he had
known at Cambridge, and whom he had met more than once
in disputation since.[3]   But if he had been ready to discuss
with him when they met on equal terms, he wisely refused to
renew the encounter with one who was his jailor.   This we
learn from the following letter of Grindal to Cecil (15th October, 1563): "I thank you that . . . ye remembered to ease
me of one guest . . .   My Lord of Ely received him on
Sunday last past, and writeth that he is welcome for their
sakes that send him, otherwise not.   I signified to Dr.
Watson that, if he had tarried, I was willing to have conferred
with him in divers points, but he answereth that he will not
enter in conference with no man.   The reason is, he will
not incur penalties of laws.   I said only one law was penal,[4]
that might be forborne; but he persisted in his opinion.   I
here said, 'Mr. Feckenham is not so precise, but could be

---

[1] *P. R. O., Dom. Elis.*, vol. xxiv, 39, I.

[2] See Lingard, vol. vi., p. 83.

[3] *E.g.*, at Sir Richard Morison's in 1551, at the Convocation of
1553, and at the Westminster Conference in 1559.

[4] Denying the Queen's supremacy, by statute 1 Eliz., c. 1.

contented to confer'.   The Bishop of Winton,[1] when he was with me, said that if he should have any, he could best deal with Feckenham, for in King Edward's days he travailed with Feckenham in the Tower, and brought him to subscribe to all things, saving the Presence, and one or two more articles.   Ye might do very well (in my opinion) to ease the poor Dean of Westminster,[2] and send the other also " (*i.e.*, Feckenham) "to some other bishop, as Sarum or Chichester, &c.   It is more'reason that we bishops should be troubled with them than the poor dean." [3]

It appears from the above letter that Watson, after being about a month in the custody of the Bishop of London, had been transferred in October, 1563, to that of Coxe, Bishop of Ely.   With him he remained rather more than a year, for by a letter from the Privy Council,[4] dated 9th January (apparently of the year 1564-5), the Bishop of Ely is ordered to send him to the Tower again, while at the same time the Lieutenant of the Tower is instructed " to keep him in safe ward, without having conference with any ".

This is an indication of what we shall see explicitly stated by the Government on another occasion, that Watson both had and exerted great influence in keeping Catholics faithful to God and His Holy Church, in spite of persecution.

Five years after his recommittal, a return of the prisoners in the Tower, made April, 1570, shows him to have been still confined in the State prison.[5]   Baker says that, on the

---

[1] Horn.

[2] Goodman, in whose custody Feckenham then was.

[3] Grindal's *Remains*, p. 281 (Parker Society).   Feckenham was sent to Horn, who was not so successful as he had hoped.   For an account of the controversy between Horn and Feckenham see Stapleton's *Counterblast*.

[4] *Privy Council Register, Eliz.*, vol. i., p. 143.

[5] *P. R. O., Dom. Eliz.*, vol. lxvii., n. 93.

publication of the bull of excommunication against the
Queen by St. Pius V. in February, 1570, Bishop Watson was
interrogated, together with Feckenham, Cole, and Harpsfield, concerning the bull, and that his answers (given under
his hand) were very temperate, and with due regard to his
allegiance to the Queen.[1]

Baker refers to Goldast, a German, who wrote in Latin.
I have consulted Goldast and find the following declaration
attributed to Watson :

"Respondeo me eam rem non aliter quam ex auditu
compertam habere.　Neque enim Bullam præfatam aut legi
unquam aut vidi.　Confiteor reginam nostram Elizabetham,
non obstante Pontificis Romani bullâ, aut declaratione quacunque, veram nostram esse et legitimam Angliæ et Hiber-
niæ Reginam, eique ut Reginæ ab omnibus suis subditis
obedientiam debere præstari.　Confiteor me, non obstante
bullâ præfata, vel quacunque alia jam facta aut deinceps
facienda, Reginæ Elizabethæ, ut subditum legitimæ principi
suæ, obedientiam et fidelitatem debere."[2]

I have taken much trouble to investigate this matter, but
with only partial success.　Dr. Lingard, in a Tract[3] published in 1812, and Mr. Charles Butler, in his *Historical
Memoirs of English Catholics,*[4] quote Caron's *Remonstrantia
Hibernorum* for the fact of the above declaration.　Lingard
adds that to the same questions similar answers were given
by the deposed bishops, Heath, Pool, Tunstall, White,
Ogelthorpe, and Thirlby, referring in a note to Lord
Burghley's *Execution of Justice in England.*　But as Tunstall, White, and Ogelthorpe died ten years before the bull

---

[1] *History of St. John's,* p. 140.

[2] Goldast, *Monarch,* tom. iii., p. 66 (Ed. Francof., 1613).

[3] Reprint of 1826, p. 275.

[4] Vol. i. 422.

of St. Pius V., and before any question whatever arose on the subject of allegiance, there is here evidently some confusion. On reference to Caron, who wrote in 1665, I find that Lingard has copied from him both his assertions, and that Caron refers to Burghley for the second, although his authority for both is really an *Apology of the Catholics of England*, presented to King James I., and printed at Douai in 1604.[1]

A book printed in Tournai in 1623, called *The Image of Both Churches*, by P. D. M. [Pattinson], is more explicit than Caron. " I will show you the opinion of the bishops and prelates of Queen Mary's time. The new devised six articles (composed by D. Hammon) were proposed to all priests as the touchstone of their loyalty. 1. Whether the bull of Pius V. were a sentence to be obeyed? 2. Whether Queen Elizabeth were a lawful queen, notwithstanding the bull? 3. Whether the Pope had power to give authority to her subjects to rebel and depose her, &c. Upon these questions Bishop Watson, Abbot Feckenham, D. John Harpsfield, D. Nicolas Harpsfield, and others were curiously examined. Some of them answered they never see [*sic*] the bull, but all of them professed their obedience notwithstanding the bull, *ei ut veræ reginæ obediendum.* And fully Nicolas Harpsfield resolved them : *ego regalem ejus auctoritatem in omnibus rebus causisque civilibus et temporalibus agnosco,* the which Goldastus (tom. iii., *de Monarchia S. Imperii Rom.*) doth report."[2]

Here again there is confusion. " The six articles pro-

---

[1] The words of Lord Burghley may be seen at p. 2. They are general, and refer to contemporaries. Though he goes on to commend the peaceable behaviour of the bishops who were dead, he does not say they made any profession of resisting the Pope. This mistake has been too often repeated.

[2] *The Image of Both Churches*, p. 347.

posed by D. Hammon " are referred to, and then only three questions are given.   Dr. John Hammond was one of the Queen's Commissioners who presided at the trials of the Blessed Everard Hanse, the Blessed Edmund Campion, and others who were executed in 1581 and 1582.   The Government published in 1582 an account of the six questions proposed and of the answers given by these holy martyrs, to show that all who were executed were guilty of treason, and that such as answered satisfactorily were pardoned.[1]   Now, the questions, as drawn up by Dr. John Hammond in 1581, could not have been proposed to Archdeacon Nicolas Harpsfield, who died in 1575, nor to his brother John, who died in 1578, nor to Dean Cole, who died in 1580.   And on referring to Pattinson's authority, Goldast, I find that the date he gives for the questioning of the deposed priests is 1570, at least this date is placed in the margin.   The first edition of Goldast's book appeared in 1611.   He was a laborious compiler, but all was fish that came to his net.   It is clear that he got his informa- mation from an Englishman, or from an English book ; but we have no guarantee of its authenticity.   He gives three questions and distinct answers by each of the five prisoners, viz., Watson, the two Harpsfields, Feckenham, and Cole. Watson answers as follows : " 1. I reply that I only know the matter by hearsay ; I have never read or seen the bull. 2. I confess that our Queen Elizabeth, notwithstanding the bull of the Roman Pontiff, or any declaration whatever, is the true and lawful Queen of England and Ireland, and to her as to the Queen obedience should be paid by her subjects.   3. I confess that, in spite of the foresaid bull, or

---

[1] The greater part of this Government manifesto has been reprinted by Charles Butler in his *Historical Memoirs*, vol. i., pp. 208-235. The questions and answers may also be found in 'Bridgewater's *Con- certatio.*

any other already made or to be made hereafter, I owe obedience and fidelity to Queen Elizabeth, as a subject to his lawful prince." [1]

I do not venture to deny the authenticity of this document ; yet I would make the following observations : The declaration is not found in any of the Calendars of State Papers, nor in the reports of the Historical Manuscripts Commission. It is not alluded to in the manifesto of the Council in 1582. They give the answers of the " traitors," adding that " two of them only now acknowledge their true duty of allegiance, though in points of religion not reconciled, as also one other named Edward Rishton that did before openly at the bar, at the time of his arraignment, acknowledge his said duty and allegiance to Her Majesty. Towards whom Her Majesty doth mean to extend her grace and mercy." The two not named were James Bosgrave and Henry Orton. It would have suited the purpose of the Council to allege the declaration of the more dignified confessors in prison; yet they do not. Nor did Lord Burghley in his *Defence of the Execution of Justice in England*, published in 1583, except in very general terms. [2] That some priests as well as laymen made a declaration similar to that attributed to Watson is clear. The words of Bosgrave and Orton were published at the time ; and in the Record Office is still to be seen the profession of Dr. Oxenbridge, one of Watson's fellow-prisoners in Wisbeach at a later period. It runs as follows :

" 14 *Maii*, 1583, at Wisbiche Castell.

I, Andrewe Oxenbridge, doctor of the lawes, doe francklie

---

[1] Goldastus, *Monarchia*, tom, iii., p. 66 (Ed. Francof., 1613). From a copy in the Bodleian, the third volume not being in the British Museum. I have given the Latin above.

[2] See p. 2.

and from my harte acknow*ledge and*[1] avowe the moste
gratious Ladie Elizabeth, nowe Queene of England, to be'
most rightfull and Lawfull Queene thereof, de jure, as
Whereof shee is most justelie possessed *from the* first daie of
hir Raigne till nowe. And to hir ma^tie alone, as to my
most juste and sole soveraigne magistrate I owe all my
Lyoelltie, service and wholle dutie of subjection next under
God. And even soe will I repute hir ma^tie duringe Liffe,
against the Bull (if anie be) of Pius 5, Gregorie or anye
other Pope heartofore or hearafter. Ffurthermore, if any
man pretendinge Catholike Romaine religion *be of* minde that
the Pope for one cause or other may depose her or dispence
with her subjects othe of Loialltie, I hould it a Trayterous
article *such as doe* beleve. But contrarilie am redie and
vowe to spend my Liffe and goodes *for the* Peace and quiet
of Queene Elizabethe and this present state againste *every*
invador, disturbor, or undemyner, by what authoritie, Bull
or Direction he shall doe yt, of Prince or prest, or Potentate
or prelate, namelie of *the pope* himselfe, by what jurisdiction,
power or name be yt soever he comaunde."[2]

It is not pretended that the Bishop of Lincoln wrote so
strongly as Dr. Oxenbridge, but if he wrote the words
reported by Goldast (which I consider uncertain), I will
neither venture to commend him with Lingard and Butler,
nor am I so bold as to condemn him. Dr. William
Bishop (as Charles Butler remarks) used much stronger
language, notwithstanding which he was appointed Vicar
Apostolic by the Pope, without any retractation being required
from him. The power of the Sovereign Pontiff over Christian princes, whether direct or indirect, was not an article of

---

[1] The words in *italics* are altogether or nearly illegible from the
mutilation of the paper.

[2] *P. R. O., Dom. Eliz.*, vol. clx., n. 44.

Catholic faith, and in judging of men's conduct at a particular crisis it behoves a modern writer to be very reserved, especially when he has to judge between a pope who is a canonised saint and a bishop who proved his fidelity to the Catholic Church, and especially to the Sovereign Pontiff, by twenty-five years of imprisonment. I repeat, however, that, for anything we know to the contrary, the declarations of Watson and the rest may be a forgery framed on the paper of Oxenbridge.[1]

But to return to the record of the bishop's imprisonments, I may here insert a letter written about this time by Grindal, Bishop of London, to Cecil, on February 3, 1569-70 :

" SIR,—I pray you most instantly to be a mean that I be not troubled with the Bishop of Ross.[2] He is a man of such quality as I like nothing at all. If needs I must have a guest, I had rather keep Mr. Hare[3] still. If it please you to know mine opinion *in genere*, surely I think it were good that such as deserve to be committed should be sent *ad custodias publicas*. Experience declareth that none of those

---

[1] Dr. Milner has treated the subject in his Sixth Letter to a Prebendary. He takes for granted the protestation of allegiance of Bishop Watson, of which he approves, and defends his loyalty to St. Pius V., by the remark that that pope " did not require the English Catholics to receive or observe his bull," and that " he never published or signified it to them ". But this is beside the question. It was one *de jure*, not *de facto*, and of any future possible bull, not of the existence or publication of that of 1569. That " Gregory XIII., his successor, explicitly declared that the bull did not regard the consciences of English Catholics," as Milner says, is both incorrect and not to the point. Gregory did not deny the binding force of the bull of Pius, but suspended it as regards English Catholics. But according to the supposed declarations, no such suspension was needed.

[2] John Leslie.

[3] Michael Hare, Esq., a Catholic gentleman.

are reformed which are sent to me and others, and by securing of them the punishment lighteth upon us."[1]

Whether in consequence of this remonstrance, or for other reasons, Watson, as I have said, was kept in the Tower. An anonymous letter, dated 2nd August, 1570, shows the bitter zeal with which some opposed the least relaxation of his sufferings : " There was one died lately in the Tower of the plague, as it is suggested, whereby is some hope of deliverance, or, at least, great suit. There be some in the Tower,[2] to whose cases I would otherwise turn it, that their men come no more abroad to fetch the plague, nor themselves go too far abroad to carry a worse plague. Close prison is best for all sides."[3] This cruel plan of incarcerating innocent men, without law or trial, while the weary years rolled on, and in the hope of their more speedy death by prison plague, lest the sight of them should encourage any heart to fidelity to England's religion of a thousand years, was being constantly urged by the Protestant bishops. If there was any relaxation, it never came from their proposal, nor met with their approval.

So years passed on with Bishop Watson. In July, 1574, we find him in the Marshalsea. I have not been able to discover the time of his removal thither from the Tower. At that date the Privy Council[4] sent " a letter to the Bishop of Canterbury in the behalf of Dr. Watson, prisoner in the Marshalsea, that upon sufficient sureties and bonds taken to the Queen's Majesty's use, that the said doctor shall not by speech, writing, or other means, induce or entice any person to any opinion or act to be done contrary to the laws esta-

[1] Grindal's *Remains*, p. 320.
[2] On the margin is here written *Episcopi quondam.*
[3] *P. R. O., Dom. Eliz.*, Addenda, xix. 1.
[4] *Privy Council Register, Eliz.*, vol. ii., p. 246.

blished in the realm for causes of religion, to give order that he may be delivered to his brother, John Watson, to remain with him at his house, and not to depart from thence at any time, without the licence of the lords of the Council; nor that any person shall resort to the said doctor Watson any time, other than such as shall have occasion to resort to the said John Watson ".

These various imprisonments have taken but a few pages to relate, but they had extended over fifteen years. When the bishop was sent to the Tower at the close of the Westminster Conference, he was scarcely forty-five years old ; he is now sixty-one. We know that at his first committal he was suffering from a severe attack of ague ; he can scarcely have escaped relapses in such places as the Tower and the Marshalsea. In a letter of Grindal's, written 15th August, 1569, he says : "The prison sickness reigns usually at this time of the year. Milerus, the Irishman, in my custody, is very sick of an ague." Nothing can be more piteous than the description which Richard Creagh, Catholic Archbishop of Armagh, who was confined there at the same time as the Bishop of Lincoln, gives of his various infirmities brought on by bad air, bad food, and confinement.[1] From a letter of Watson's, to be quoted presently, we find that during his imprisonment in the Marshalsea, he lost the sight of one eye and became lame with acute sciatica. We have no other details of the nature of his imprisonment, of the books allowed him, or persons who could resort to him. In those days prisoners sometimes purchased the connivance of their jailors and managed to say or hear Mass ; and priests found their way to them in disguise and heard their confessions and gave them Holy Communion. Whether and how far the

---

[1] Published by the Bishop of Ossory in his *Spicilegium Ossoriense*, from the State Papers.

Bishop of Lincoln gained any such consolations can only
be a matter of conjecture.   We can, however, easily imagine
the joy of the venerable confessor when in the security of
his brother's house he might once more offer the holy sacrifice, recite his breviary, study and converse with Catholics.
He could not, indeed, go out, and visitors were forbidden
under penalties to communicate with him.   Dodd writes as
if he " administered confirmation and gave advice on matters
regarding government and discipline " to the afflicted
Catholics, now without a bishop to direct them, and with
only fugitive priests to instruct or feed them with the sacraments.   But Dodd is here clearly writing from conjecture.[1]
He says also in his short biographical notice: " While
Bishop Watson lived, he was consulted and regarded as the
chief Superior of the English Catholic clergy, and, as far as
his confinement would permit, exercised the functions of his
character ".[2]   This is vague, yet it is somewhat borne out
by the documents I am about to produce.   After the bishop
had remained three years with his brother, viz., in July,
1577, the following letter was sent by Walsingham to the
Bishop of London :

" After my very hearty commendations unto your Lordship, the inconvenience and mischief being daily found to
increase, not only to the danger of Her Majesty's person,
but to the disturbance of the common quiet of this realm ;
and the lenity that hath been showed to such persons as
obstinately refuse to come to the Church in the time of
sermons and common prayer.   It is resolved, therefore,
that for the redress thereof, there shall be some consultation
and thereupon some general order to be set down, which
shall not be changed.   And because it is intended that your

---

[1] Dodd's *Church History*, vol. iii., p. 45 (dE. Tierney).

[2] *Ibid.*, part iii., book ii., art. 3 (original edition).

Lordship shall be present at the said consultation, I am for
that purpose also appointed by my lords to require you to
be there upon Thursday, and to bring with you Mr. Doctor
Hamon, your Chancellor, and such as you shall think meet.
And forasmuch as the special point of the said consultation
will stand upon the order that may be taken generally with
all them that refuse to come to the Church, and in particular
what is meetest to be done with Watson, Feckenham,
Harpsfield, and others of that kind that are thought to be
the leaders and the pillars of the consciences of great numbers of such as be carried with these errors, whether it be not
fit they be disputed with, all in some private sort, and after
disputation had with them, and they thereby not reduced
to conformity, then whether it shall be better to banish them
the realm, or to keep them here together in some strait sort,
as they may be kept from all conference to the further
maintenance of this corruption. . . . I have thought meet
to give you of the same these short remembrances, that by
thinking thereupon, and of some such other things as may
further this good intention, your Lordship may come the
better prepared to the furtherance of so good a purpose.
And so I bid your Lordship most heartily farewell." [1]

Enclosed with this letter were the following memo-
randa : [2]

*How such as are backward and corrupt in Religion may be
reduced to conformity, and others stayed from like corruption.*

"For the reducing to conformity of such as are corrupt in
religion, and refuse to yield obedience to the laws of the
realm provided in that behalf, and the staying of others

---

[1] *P. R. O., Dom. Eliz.*, vol. xlv., n. 21.   [2] *Ibid.*, n. 10.

from falling into like corruption, three things principally are to be put in execution.

" 1. The first in taking order generally with such as are recusants, as that they may be brought to obey the laws.

" 2. The second in providing, either by banishment or restraint, that Watson, Feckenham, and the rest upon whose advice and consciences the said recusants depend, may do no harm.

.   .   .   .

"Touching the second point for the restraining or banishing of Watson and the rest: if banishment be not thought meet, then it is to be considered how they may be restrained in such sort as there may be no access had unto them, which may be performed by putting these things following in execution :

" First, in making choice of some apt place for the keeping of them.

"Secondarily, in appointing some man of trust to take charge of them.

" Lastly, in taxing upon the bishops and clergy such as are non-residents, and have pluralities, some yearly contribution for the finding of them, and a convenient stipend to be given to their keeper."   .

The result of all these deliberations was that the following letter was addressed by the Council to those into whose charge the poor Catholics were committed : [1]

"After our right hearty commendations unto your Lordship, whereas Her Majesty heretofore, after the restraining of Feckenham, Watson, and others, very backward and obstinate in religion, upon persuasion and some opinion conceived that by granting them liberty they might be drawn in time to yield themselves conformable unto Her Highness'

[1] *P. R. O., Dom. Elis.*, vol. cxiv., n. 69.

laws, she was contented to have them enlarged, and bonds taken of them for their good behaviours, as that they should refrain all manner of conference, secret practices, or persuasions to seduce her said subjects by withdrawing of them from the religion presently received within this realm, and their dutiful obedience towards Her Highness and her laws : forasmuch as it is informed that Feckenham, Watson, and the rest, contrary to their bonds, promise, and hope conceived of their amendment, have and do daily and manifestly abuse the liberty granted unto them, whereby many of Her Highness' said subjects are by their secret persuasions lately fallen and withdrawn from their due obedience, refusing to come unto the church, and to perform that part of their duties which heretofore they have been dutifully contented to yield.   Upon consideration whereof Her Majesty foreseeing of what consequence the effects of these lewd persuasions and practices may be, if in time they shall not conveniently be met withal, hath thought it convenient again to restrain them of their liberties, and to make choice of some of your calling, unto whom they might be committed, and carefully looked unto, and, namely, hath appointed the person of A. B. unto your Lordship's custody, to be straitly kept and dealt withal, according to a form which we send your Lordship herewith in writing, requiring you in Her Majesty's name, at such time as the said A. B. shall be sent unto you to receive him, and in all points to do your endeavour strictly to follow the said form for the usage of him during the time he shall remain with you, unless upon some good report made by you of hope of his conformity, it shall be by Her Majesty or us ordered, that he shall be more favourably dealt withal."

" Wherein not doubting but you will thoroughly perform the expectation had of your care in this behalf, we bid your Lordship right heartily."

A form to be observed by my Lords the Bishops in the ordering
of such as were committed to their custody for Popery.

" 1. That his lodging be in such a convenient part of
your house as he may both be there in safe custody and
also have no easy access of your household people unto
him other than such as you shall appoint, and know to be
settled in religion and honesty, as that they may not be
perverted in religion or any otherwise corrupted by him.

" 2. That he be not admitted unto your own table except
upon some good occasion to have ministered to him there,
in the presence of some that shall happen to resort unto you,
such talk whereby the hearers may be confirmed in the
truth ; but to have his diet by himself alone in his chamber,
and that in no superfluity, but after the spare manner of
scholars' commons.

" 3. That you suffer none, unless some one to attend
upon him, to have access unto him ; but such as you shall
know to be persons well confirmed in true religion, and are
[not] likely to be weakened in the profession of the said
religion by any conference they shall have with him.

" 4. That you permit him not at any time and place while
he is with you to enter into any disputation of matters of
religion, or to reason thereof otherwise than upon such
occasion as shall be by you, or in your presence with your
good liking by some other, ministered unto him.

" 5. That he have ministered unto him such books of
learned men and sound writers in divinity as you are able to
lend him, and none other.

" 6. That he have no liberty to walk abroad to take the
air, but when yourself is at best leisure to go with him, or
accompanied with such as you shall appoint.

" 7. That you do your endeavour by all good persuasions
to bring him to the hearing of sermons and other exercise of

religion in your house and the chapel or church which you most commonly frequent."

I do not think that it is a rash conjecture that Watson's old antagonist Grindal was at the bottom of these severe measures. In 1570 he had been promoted from the See of London to that of York, and in the beginning of 1576 to that of Canterbury. We have seen him express his opinion that the recusants should be confined in the public prisons rather than in the bishops' houses. When he was Archbishop of York (on November 13, 1574) he did not disguise his vexation, in a letter to Lord Burghley, at the news which had reached him of the greater measure of freedom lately granted to Dr. Watson. I give a long extract from this letter, because it contains some interesting details regarding one of Watson's old companions at Cambridge, Thomas Vavasor, a physician :

" MY VERY GOOD LORD,—We of the Ecclesiastical Commission have here sent a certificate to my Lords of the Council of our proceedings this term. Only five persons have been committed for their obstinacy or papistical religion. For the number of that sect (thanks be to God!) daily diminisheth, in this diocese especially. None of note was committed, save only your old acquaintance, Doctor Vavasor, who hath been tolerated in his own house in York almost three-quarters of a year. In his answer, made in open judgment, he showed himself the same man which you have known him to be in his younger years: which was sophistical, disdainful, and eluding arguments with derision when he was not able to solute the same by learning. His great anchor-hold was in urging the literal sense of *hoc est corpus meum*, thereby to prove transubstantiation, which to deny, saith he, is as great an heresy as to deny consubstantiation,[1] defined in the Nicene Council. The diversity was

---

[1] The consubstantiality of the Son with the Father.

sufficiently declared unto him by testimonies of the fathers. *Sed ipse sibi plaudit.* My Lord President and I, knowing his disposition to talk, thought it not good to commit the said Dr. Vavasor to the castle of York, where some other like affected remain prisoners ; but rather to a solitary prison in the Queen's Majesty's castle at Hull, where he shall only talk to walls.

" The imprisoned for religion in these parts of late made supplication to be enlarged, seeming, as it were,'to require it of right, by the example of enlarging Feckenham, Watson, and other papists above (*i.e.*, in London). We here are to think that all things done above are done upon great causes, though the same be to us unknown. But certainly my Lord President and I join in opinion that if such a general jubilee should be put in use in these parts, a great relapse would follow soon after." [1]

We may, then, well suppose that when Grindal became Archbishop of Canterbury, he should have looked with a jealous eye on the liberty enjoyed by Dr. Watson, however restricted it was, and should have used his influence to destroy it.

There was, however, another whose malice has been left on record. This was Aylmer, appointed to be Bishop of London in March, 1577. Strype quotes a letter from him to the Lord Treasurer, written in June, 1577, urging him " to use more severity than hitherto hath been used, or else we shall smart for it. For as sure as God liveth they look for an invasion, or else they would not fall away as they do." Strype remarks that at this time—which, it must be observed, was at the very beginning of the preaching of the first missionaries sent from Douai—many who had outwardly complied now withdrew from Church, many refused the

---

[1] Grindal's *Remains*, p. 350.

oath of supremacy, and many converts were being made from among the Protestants. Aylmer, therefore, suggested that the "chief captains" should be placed in close prison, among whom he mentions Sir Thomas Fitz-Herbert and Townely, and Watson, Feckenham, and Young. He proposed that they should be again quartered on the bishops, such as Winchester, Lincoln, Chichester, or Ely; and that, for his part, if he were out of his first fruits, he could be content to have one of them.[1]

In July, 1577, then, Bishop Watson was given over to the custody of Dr. Horn, Bishop of Winchester, with the instructions given above.[2] At the same time Young was sent to the Dean of Canterbury, Harpsfield to the Protestant Bishop of Lincoln, and Feckenham to the Bishop of Ely.

Robert Horn, who was now Bishop of Winchester, has been already mentioned as one of the fellows of St. John's, contemporary with Watson. He had been one of the leaders of the Protestant movement, and had been made Dean of Durham during the reign of Edward. He had been deprived because of his marriage and heresy, and had been succeeded by Watson. He would naturally, therefore, not look very favourably on his theological opponent and ecclesiastical rival. Mr. Cooper thus gives his character: "Bishop Horn was no doubt a man of considerable learning and ability, although he appears to have had an imperfect control over a somewhat unhappy temper. His memory is obnoxious for his furious zeal in defacing the monuments of the piety of a former age."[3] Horn had also brought an action against the Bishop of Lincoln for some goods and books which he said had been unjustly taken

---

[1] Strype's *Aylmer*, p. 24 (Ed. 1821).

[2] *Privy Council Register, Elis.*, vol. iv., p. 1.

[3] Cooper's *Athenæ Cantabrigienses.*

from him wheh he was deprived of his deanery of Durham. This was in February, 1560, after Watson himself had been deposed from his bishopric.[1] It seems, then, quite natural that he should not have relished the company of Watson, any more than Watson his guardianship.

In August the Council wrote to the Bishop of Winchester : "That whereas Dr. Watson hath been a suitor unto their lordships to have a man of his own to attend upon him during his being in the custody of the said bishop, whereof, although their lordships made difficulty, for that his man is of his religion, they are notwithstanding upon consideration that it is less danger to let one already corrupted than a sound person to attend upon him, he is required to permit his said man to attend upon him so he shall be contented to repair unto the church ; and withal his lordship to take heed that in using the company of his men, none of them do receive infection from him ".[2]

Bishop Watson remained under Horn's custody, principally at Farnham, for eighteen months. I can here, fortunately, give two letters not hitherto printed, from the Cecil Papers, in the possession of the Marquis of Salisbury.[3] They were written, by mutual agreement, by Watson and Horn. Watson's letter, which is dated October 6th, 1578, is as follows.' It is addressed to Lord Burghley :

"RIGHT HONOURABLE AND MY SINGULAR GOOD LORD,—In all my distresses, I thank God, which I have sustained these many years, I have had no refuge to find relief but at your honour's hand and good means. For the which I render most humble thanks, and do not fail but to be your daily

---

[1] See Letter of Horn to Cecil, *P. R. O., Dom. Eliz.*, vol. xi., n. 16.

[2] *Council Register, Eliz.*, vol. iv., p. 10.

[3] They are given in abridgment in the Report of the Historical MS. Commission, 1888. *Cal. of MS. of Marquis of Salisbury*, part ii., n. 621 and 624.

orator to Almighty God, that hath prepared your heart to be always a succour to me in my necessities. And now two special infirmities drive me to run again and crave your honour's succour and aid, which be blindness and lameness. For before four years ago, in the Marshalsea, I lost one of my eyes, and though afterwards I found remedy to have the deformity (*diffusio albiginis*, to be taken away) yet the use and sight thereof is now gone. And the other eye also is so dimmed with suffusions that I can scarcely see my meat upon the table but with great light, and fear daily to lose it also.

"My other infirmity of lameness cometh by means of sciatica in both my thighs, which, though I mitigate it with warm sheets in the night and with furs and other warm clothes in the day, yet if I sit any little while I halt when I rise. And in riding I can neither get on nor off my horse but with great help of other and pain of myself. (I beseech your honour to pardon my rudeness in expressing mine infirmities after this sort; 'need,' they say, 'thinketh no shame'.) And besides that I came hither to my good Lord of Winchester's custody being sick, and was also this last summer in his house sick of an ague, my strait keeping in divers prisons these twenty years together heretofore hath wrought in me great weakness and decay, both in memory and mind, senses and body, especially being aged of three-score and five years already past, and age, they say, is a sickness itself, though no other cause or occasion be added.

"The effect of my most humble suit to your honour is now, that by your honour's good help, I may be released from the custody of my good Lord of Winchester, who hath dealt with me this whole year and quarter as if I had been his natural brother, and be committed again to the custody of my brother, John Watson, to remain at his house at London, or (if the sickness be near unto him) at his house in the country four miles off, where I may have such attending and keeping as mine age and weakness requireth. He and I will gladly undergo and keep such bonds and conditions as your honour shall appoint; only craving most humbly that I may once a week with my brother take the open air in the field, without which, they say, my sight will be altogether soon gone. As for matters of religion already established within this realm, as I have not meddled in them with any person when I was before in his house, so also will I promise and be bounden to do hereafter. And as for resort of any persons to me, I shall admit none, only craving that the barber, tailor, physician, and other artificers be not accompted for resorters.

"My good Lord of Winchester, I hope, will report well of my quiet behaviour in his house, which kind of life I intend to keep to my life's end, and daily meditate how I may end it well. Good my lord, I most humbly beseech your honour that, among all your good and charitable deeds, this your relieving of me in my necessities at this time may be one, and I shall accompt myself most bounden to pray for your honour to my life's end to Almighty God, Who ever preserve to His good will. Amen.

"Written at Farnham this 6th day of October, 1578, by your honour's most humble and daily orator,

"THOM. WATSON."

The letter of Dr. Horn was as follows:

"IMMANUEL.

"*Gr. et pa. in Xo.*—

"RIGHT HONOURABLE,—I am to trouble your honour with a double suit, partly for myself, partly for D. Watson, who remaineth with me by th' order of the most honourable Council. I am very desirous to be delivered of the charge for many respects, but chiefly for that I am myself shortly to be brought to London if the plague cease, or

if not, yet must I needs be there to consult and to deal
with some physicians, whereby to be eased of such griefs as
I am much vexed and tormented withal, if it shall please the
Almighty to send me some ease of my pains. I think it not
meet to have such a charge when I myself cannot see thereto
—your wisdom can conceive what may follow. As to Mr.
Watson himself, my humble suit is, that your honour will be
a mean that he may be returned to his brother's keeping
upon good bonds, if it shall so seem good to the honourable
Council. Surely his griefs are no less than he writeth himself unto your Lordship; so that he is very troublesome to me
and mine, and no less to himself. I think he will not be a
meddler with any in disorderly sort, for he hath seemed to
have much mislike of Feckenham, whom he calleth abbot,
and D. Young for the unwise usages of themselves. He is
old, impotent, and was of mine old acquaintance in St.
John's College, as your honour knoweth. I wish well to his
soul, which is sore infected with an incurable disease; yet
would I have his body to descend into the grave in peace,
and so to leave him to God's merciful judgment. Thus your
honour hath my suit; I humbly beseech you to help me
therein, and I shall not cease, God willing, to make my
hearty prayers to God, as I do daily, for you, that you may
continue long time among us, in health and welfare, to God's
glory, the good of the land, and the comfort of yourself and
all yours.

"At Farnham Castle, 7th Oct., 1578. Your honourable
Lordship to command in Xto., "ROB. WINTON."[1]

The plague continued to rage in London, and the suffering old man remained three months longer at Farnham, and

[1] Both the above letters are addressed to Lord Burghley. It may
be remarked that Horn spells the name Burleigh, and Watson, Burlee.
—*Cecil Papers*, 161/69.

at the end of that time was not given to his brother's charge, but delivered to another Episcopal jailor. There is an entry in the *Privy Council Register* (16th January, 1579) that a letter should be written to the Bishop of Winchester :

"That whereas he desireth to be discharged of the custody of Dr. Watson, in respect that his Lordship intendeth for recovery of his health to repair to London, his Lordship is required to bring the said Watson thither with him, who for like infirmity desireth to go thither; and further orders shall be taken for his custody ".[1]

Their lordships resolved to transfer him to the custody of the Bishop of Rochester, John Young, who had been appointed to that see in 1578. They accordingly wrote to him (on 19th February, 1578-9) :

"That whereas Dr. Watson, committed to the keeping of the Bishop of Winton, is, by occasion of sickness of the bishop, to be removed, and is ordered to remain with the said Bishop of Rochester ; his Lordship is required to take him into his charge, to use all good means to bring him to conformity, and to have regard that he have no such conference nor repair as he may corrupt others.

"To Bishop of Winton to give him notice what is done, and to require him to give order that the said Watson may be safely delivered into the custody and charge of the Bishop of Rochester." [2]

It would be interesting to know in which of the houses of this bishop he resided. It is not likely that in any place he would forget the example left him by the Blessed Cardinal Fisher, whom he had known in his youth.

The only incident on record connected with Dr. Watson's imprisonment under this official is, that a certain Portuguese,

---

[1] *Council Register, Eliz.*, vol iv., p. 376.

[2] *Ibid.*, vol. iv., p. 403. Also Strype's *Annals*, vol. ii., part ii., app., p. 660.

named Antonio Fogaça, induced the Bishop of Lincoln, then in London, and the Archbishop of Armagh, who was imprisoned in the Tower, to sign two letters, one to the King of Portugal, the other to His Majesty's Confessor. These were intercepted. Antonio, on being interrogated, declared that he himself indited the two letters in Spanish, and gave money to Dr. Watson's servant to obtain his master's hand to the letters.[1]

This was in April 1580. The bishop's servant was also interrogated, and as his answers contain some interesting particulars I will transcribe them. I omit the questions for brevity's sake, as the answers will speak for themselves.

The answer of William Whiting, unto such interrogatories as were ministered unto him the 17th of March, 1579-80.

"To the first interrogatory he saith, that he knoweth Fogaça if he see him, and hath only known him but since one month before Christmas, and never saw him before that time, nor ever since but once, meeting him by chance in the streets; and saith that at the first time of his acquaintance with the said Fogaça he came unto him in the streets, but where about in the streets he cannot remember, at which time the said Fogaça demanded of him if he were not Dr. Watson's servant, and this examinate answering 'yea,' the said Fogaça desired him to carry two letters from him to his master, and to procure him to sign them; which at the first he refused, for that (as he saith) his master had forbidden him to bring him any letters, but afterward (at the earnest instance of the said Fogaça, declaring unto him that the contents of the letters were only to signify what good deeds he had done here to good men, and that the commendation thereof confirmed by Dr. Watson would do him much good),

[1] *P. R. O., Dom. Eliz.*, vol. cxxxvii., n. 647, 649.

he was contented, and did thereupon carry them unto his said master.

"To the second he saith, that he knoweth no Catholic prisoner by name, but only some few in the Marshalsea—Wood, Bilson, Pound, Bluet, Webster, with whom he came acquainted, being himself prisoner in the Marshalsea by the space of one-half year, committed upon suspicion to be a priest. And to these men he hath sundry times repaired since his enlargement as of himself, but never carried or received anything to or fro between his master and them.

"To the third he saith, he hath had recourse unto his master since the time of his commitment unto the Bishop of Rochester, at the least every week once, but never carried any letters or writing unto his master from any man ; neither ever brought any letters or writings from his master to any other person.

"To the fourth he saith, that he knoweth not any man from whom his master hath ever received any exhibition or relief, but only from John Watson, his brother ; but what he hath had from him, this examinate knoweth not.

"To the fifth he saith, that he never delivered any other letters, writings, or papers unto his master than the two letters he received from Fogaça, unto whom he restored them after his master had subscribed them, within one day, at his house in Mark Lane, where (as he saith) he never was before, but had notice of the place of Fogaça's dwelling at the time when he received the letters of him ; of whom he had a crown in money at the bringing of the letters unto him : and no speeches he had with Fogaça, but was asked of him how his master did, and he answered him that he was well, and no more.

"To the sixth he saith as in the first, that the letters contained only matters of Fogaça, his commendation.

" To the seventh he saith, that he knoweth not by whom the letters were penned, nor whose handwriting they were, and were received by him and delivered as is above said.

"Signed by me,

WM. WHITING."[1]

When the Archbishop of Armagh was interrogated why he signed these letters, he replied that "he was persuaded that thereby there should grow some relief unto such as are in prison for religion".[2]   Hugh Kenrick, a Sheriff's Protonotary, who had helped to convey the letters, being questioned, "confessed that one William Whiting, servant to Dr. Watson, did bring unto him, a little before Christmas, a letter, written in a Roman hand, directed unto the King of Portugal . . . and touching the reading of the said letters, he saith he never read them, for that he conceived that being subscribed by Watson, they did contain no undutiful matter ".

There are other papers on this matter, which may be truly described as "much ado about nothing ".   The incident is interesting, as bringing together two great confessors of the faith, and in proving the truth of the long imprisonment in the Tower of the Archbishop of Armagh, which Mr. Froude has recklessly denied.

There exists, among the State Papers, a memorandum, in Lord Burghley's handwriting, seemingly made in July, 1580. It runs as follows :

" Things to be considered—That all the deposed ecclesiastical Papists be collected together, and sent to divers castles, as to Wisbeach [or] Banbury.   That all the Papistical laymen, being manifest recusants, remaining upon bonds, may be sent for by the Commissioners, and be bestowed into some convenient places near London, under sure guard.

---

[1] *P. R. O., Dom. Eliz.,* vol. cxxxvi., n. 62.   [2] *Ibid.,* n. 54.

" That their armour be seized.

" That generally all such others as will not come to the Church may be fined and imprisoned by virtue of the Ecclesiastical Commission." [1]

The result of the Council's deliberations was the choice of Wisbeach Castle, in Cambridgeshire, as a fit receptacle for the unfortunate priests, and thither in consequence Bishop Watson was committed, in August or September.

Strype says that " when certain Roman emissaries came into the realm, and began to disturb the Church, Watson (being too conversant with them) was committed to Wisbeach Castle a close prisoner ".[2]

These " Roman emissaries " were the seminary priests from Douay and the Jesuits. Into the history of this movement I must not enter. It is being illustrated by better hands than mine. I will merely say that the epoch of Catholic martyrdoms had now begun. " Cuthbert Maine had led the way in 1577, the first of the glorious holocaust of Douay priests. In 1578, one priest had been martyred, John Nelson ; and one layman, Thomas Sherwood, a Douay student. Four priests suffered in 1581, Campion's year ; and in 1582 no less than eleven." [3]

Baker says : " Upon the alarm given by the coming over of Parsons and Campion, Jesuits, Watson and others were committed to Wisbeach, where they lived in a collegiate and friendly manner, no one assuming authority over the rest till after the Jesuits coming among them ".[4]

He also tells us that Bishop Watson " greatly disliked the violent proceedings of the Jesuits ". This is also repeated

[1] *P. R. O., Dom. Eliz.*, Addenda, vol. xxvii., n. 21.

[2] *Annals of the Reformation*, vol. i., part i., p. 214.

[3] *The Troubles of our Catholic Forefathers*, by Father Morris (2nd series, 1875), p. 13.

[4] *History of St. John's*, vol. i., p. 140.

by Mr. Cooper.   A few words must be said in explanation
of these statements, which are likely to be misunderstood.
By "violent proceedings" is meant the method of acting of
the Jesuit missionaries, adopted generally in England.   By
"assumption of superiority," reference is made to an unhappy dispute which arose among the prisoners at Wisbeach.
Though these two matters are perfectly distinct, yet they
were confounded and worked up together in some passionate
pamphlets published in the years 1601-3, and it will be
necessary at least to disentangle the truth regarding Dr.
Watson, though I have no intention of reviving the memory
of former quarrels.   I begin then with some extracts from a
pamphlet, printed in 1601, called *Important Considerations
by the Secular Priests*, which gives a review of the policy of
the government, and of the treatment of Catholics, from the
schism until the death of Bishop Watson.

"It cannot be denied," say these writers, "but that for
the first ten years of Her Majesty's reign the state of
Catholics in England was tolerable, and after a sort in
some good quietness.   Such as for their consciences were
imprisoned in the beginning of her coming to the Crown
were very kindly and mercifully used, the state of things
then considered.   Some of them were appointed to remain
with such of their friends as they themselves made choice of.
Others were placed, some with bishops, some with deans,
and had their diet at their tables, with such convenient
lodgings and walks for their recreation as did well content
them.   They that were in the ordinary prisons, had such
liberty and other commodities, as the places would afford,
not inconvenient for men that were in their cases.

"The Catholics here continued in sort, as before you
have heard, till the said Rebellion broke forth in the North,
1569, a little before Christmas ; and that it was known that
the Pope had excommunicated the Queen, and thereby

13

freed her subjects (as the bull importeth) from their sub-jection. And then there followed a great restraint of the said prisoners.

"Their [the Jesuits] first repair hither was Anno 1580, when the realm of Ireland was in great combustion, and then they entered (viz., Mr. Campion, the subject, and Mr. Parsons, the provincial) like a tempest, with sundry such great brags and challenges, as divers of the gravest clergy then living in England (Dr. Watson, Bishop of Lincoln, and others) did greatly dislike them, and plainly foretold that (as things then stood) their proceedings after that fashion would certainly urge the State to make some sharper laws, which should not only touch them, but likewise all others, both priests and Catholics.

"Besides, to the further honour of Her Majesty, we may not omit that the States of the whole realm assembled in Parliament, Anno 1576, were pleased to pass us over, and made no laws at that time against us. The ancient pri-soners that had been restrained more narrowly in the year 1570, were (notwithstanding the said enterprises in Ireland) again restored to their former liberty, to continue with their friends as they had done before.

"But when the Jesuits were come, and that the state had notice of the said excommunication, there was then within a while a great alteration . . . thence was a greater restraint of Catholics than at any time before. Many, both priests and gentlemen, were sent into the Isle of Ely, and other places, there to be more safely kept and looked unto. . . .

"The same month [January, 1581] also a Parliament ensued, wherein a law was made agreeable in effect to the said proclamation, but with a more severe punishment annexed; for it was a penalty of death for any Jesuit or seminary priest to repair into England, and for any to receive and entertain them, which fell out according to Bishop

Watson's former speeches or prediction, what mischief the Jesuits would bring upon us.

"Such of us as remained in prison at Wisbeach (and were committed thither 1580, and others not long after committed also thither, to the number of about thirty-three or thirty-four), continued still in the several times of all the said most wicked designments, as we were before ; and were never brought into any trouble for them, but lived there, college-like, without any want, and in good reputation with our neighbours that were Catholics about us." [1]

On these extracts I would observe that it is certainly true that the persecution of Catholics in the latter part of Elizabeth's reign was more severe than in the first twenty years, and that the change was produced in part by the action of the Sovereign Pontiff, of the seminary priests, and of the Jesuits. But this is easily explained without blaming any for "violent proceedings". At the beginning of Elizabeth's reign, those who remained faithful to the Church waited to see what would happen. They had been accustomed to changes in the reigns of Henry, Edward, and Mary. Elizabeth might marry a Catholic, or she might die, and another change occur in favour of the Catholics. But as years rolled on, it became clear that the whole policy of the Government was to bring about external conformity at least to the State religion, and that no toleration would be granted to nonconformity. The priests, therefore, who by the efforts of Cardinal Allen and others were educated with a view to this new state of things, came into England with the clear purpose of resisting this absorption of the Catholics into the national schism and heresy with all their power. In this work the Jesuits zealously co-operated. Their policy was exactly the same as that of the seminary priests, of Cardinal Allen,

[1] *Important Considerations by the Secular Priests*, A.D. 1601. From a Reprint : London, 1688. Pp. 34-49.

and of the Holy See.   It would perhaps be rash to assert
that Dr. Watson never let fall any expression of fear as to
the results of Father Campion's public challenge, which was
afterwards distorted by the enemies of the Society into a
dislike for their general policy.   But to say that he really
blamed the boldness, the zeal, and self-sacrifice with which
the new race of priests sought to arouse the faith and constancy of the Catholics, as well as to bring back heretics,
would be absurd.   He had himself suffered in that cause for
twenty years.   He is mentioned in State documents as one
of the most active in persuading Catholics to refuse any
compromise, and in winning back those who had yielded.
In 1577 he was called by Walsingham one of "the leaders
and pillars of the consciences of great numbers"; while
Strype tells us that the very reason why he was committed
to Wisbeach was that he was too conversant with the new
" Roman emissaries ".

   I conclude therefore that, in the heat of subsequent disputes, the little party of secular priests, who resisted the
archpriest, and complained of the rigour of the persecution,
willing to strengthen their cause by an appeal to great names,
exaggerated some casual expression of Dr. Watson, or
wrested it from its meaning, just as they in the same way,
after Cardinal Allen's death, reported that he too had made
use of some expression in conversation derogatory to the
illustrious Society of which he had been always the warmest
friend.   These appeals to the unwritten *obiter dicta* of great
and holy men *after their decease* are very uncertain grounds
on which to base historical conclusions.

   As it is evident that the writers of the pamphlet highly
over-estimated the small amount of liberty or comfort
granted to Bishop Watson and the others in their long
imprisonments, for the sake of contrasting with it the fierce-
ness of the subsequent persecution which they laid to the

charge of the Jesuits; so would they exaggerate the quiet endurance of the holy bishop into a condemnation of the aggressive activity of the younger men who came into England at his death. The truth, however, is, as we shall see directly, that in many respects the imprisonment which the bishop endured at Wisbeach was far more severe than that of which these writers speak. Some time after his death a good deal of freedom was granted to the prisoners and even facilities for public worship, but I find no trace of this during his lifetime.

In 1582 Father Parsons wrote an account of the persecution, which he published. In this he describes the treatment that the Bishop of Lincoln and his companions were then enduring at Wisbeach—that they were deprived of all their books, and not allowed any intercourse one with another, except at table.[1] Whether even that degree of freedom was granted at first I should doubt from the following letter,[2] written 16th October, 1580, by the keepers of Wisbeach to the Privy Council:

" All duty and obedience unto your honourable Lordships —We crave pardon in that we have not so shortly observed your honours' direction in advertising the state of the recusants in Wisbeach Castle as was set down. The greatest reason for our excuse is to crave more time than the allowance of one month for certifying the state of our proceedings therein; for else, by not searching into the particular conditions of the parties, we might inform more for order than for matter, and so in vain. Let it therefore please your honours to understand that the recusants here now imprisoned are eight in number, namely, Watson, Feckenham, Young, Windham, Oxenbridge, Metham, Wood, and Bluet.

[1] *De Persecutione Anglicana Libellus*, p. 60 (Ed. 1582).

[2] *P. R. O.*, *Dom. Eliz.*, vol. cxliii., n. 17; given by Father Morris in his *Life of Weston*, p. 226.

And we, according to your lordships' letters and articles to the same adjoined, have (as duty have charged) performed carefully what was enjoined, as well to the Bishop [of Ely], Gray the keeper, as the prisoners themselves. Advertising further that the lord bishop hath appointed a preacher unto the recusants, a man of holy life, learned, and able to give account of his doctrine strongly. The men restrained before us both, and others have been called divers times, and as often required to hear the preacher, and abide the prayer; but they all with one voice generally, and after that every man particularly answering for himself, denied to allow either, saying that they are not of our Church, or, they will neither hear, pray, nor yet confer with us of any matters concerning religion. Yet, as touching conference, we must confess that Oxenbridge, Metham, and Bluet (being privately dealt with) were contented to abide some conference with the learned; but when the place and time was appointed for disputation upon their own questions, the first of them that spoke made his protestation that, for obedience' sake and our pleasings, they were content to dispute before us, upon divers causes between their Church and ours now in question; nevertheless, with such minds, as what and whatsoever could be said against them, they meant not to be reformed. The disputation held by the space of two hours, the Lord be thanked! to the great profit of us and such as stood by, though to them a hardening.

"We have also, according to the article, with the preacher perused their books and writings, of which we restrained all, saving the canonical Scriptures and the allowed writers, which to forego (together with their Romish notes upon the same) was a great grief unto their hearts, alleging that the Book of God simply carrieth not such force and comfort to their consciences as when the same is unfolded by the Councils and Church of Rome.

"It may further please your honours that divers of the recusants have their servants to attend upon them, and yet for them to be allowed is not warranted. We have suffered them (as restrained only within the walls) to attend their masters till we know your further pleasure, and in the meantime we find that their repairing together and not so abridged as their masters, is in manner all one as if their masters might as well confer as eat together, which conferring, as it is restrained, so we wish their eating together were. For if they be such offenders as in your honours' letters appear, ordinary meeting at meals doth not only strengthen them in error, but also layeth a persuasion before them that this late earnest restraint, with such favour added, will end with restoring of their former liberty. But it were too much boldness for us to show any further our opinions before your wisdoms, what we think meet for such obstinates, without further understanding of your honourable minds herein.

"Even thus, therefore, beseeching the Lord our God to endue your honours with all knowledge, judgment, and obedience, of and to His will in this behalf, and that even upon these monsters somewhat may be wrought by your authority that may yield to His glory and the godly peace of this part of His church, in the preservation of the life and continuance of the prosperous government of her most excellent Majesty, with increase of all grace, we most humbly take our leaves. From Wisbeach Castle the 16th of October, 1580.—Your honours most humbly in the Lord at commandment,

> "GEORGE CARLETON,
> "HUMPHREY MICHELL."

The Castle of Wisbeach was an old, dilapidated palace of the Bishops of Ely, surrounded by a moat, and being situated in the fens was a most unwholesome residence for an old man (Dr. Watson was now sixty-seven years old) subject to ague.

It is no wonder that he did not survive more than four years.

But few events connected with these four years have been recorded. Not long after the arrival of the prisoners at Wisbeach, Dr. William Fulke, a busy and disputatious Puritan, was sent by order of the Privy Council, for the purpose of conferring with them, and persuading them to resort to church. They had had enough of these unprofitable discussions, and refused to gratify this man's vanity. Parsons, in the book above referred to, charged him with thrusting himself upon them without authority in order to get the credit with his party of disputing *cum magnatibus*, and with having put out a foolish and false account of the occurrence. An account, indeed, had been published, but if we may believe Fulke, without his knowledge. The matter is of no importance.[1]

If we may give credit to a letter,[2] written in 1581, in Latin, by a Catholic prisoner in the Tower, the venerable bishop had to bear worse insults than the intrusion of Dr. Fulke. "Not many days since," says this letter, "an infamous woman, the tool of some ruffians, was introduced into the chamber of the Bishop of Lincoln (who remains still in prison at Wisbeach), and dared in the most shameless way to solicit to sin that holy man, worn out as he is with cruel treatment. When the old · man with all his might endeavoured to drive the impure beast from his cell, her evil instigators, who awaited the result, even threatened him with blows." This history seems almost incredible, but unfortunately it is not without parallel in the records of those days.

One more paper existing in the public records[3] throws

---

[1] Fulke's version is in Strype's *Annals of the Reformation*, ii. 243.

[2] *P. R. O., Dom. Elis.*, vol. cxlix., n. 61.

[3] *Ibid.*, vol. clxviii., n. 1.

some light on the character of the bishop's jailors. It is anonymous, but from internal evidence seems to have been written by the Bishop of Ely, and to be addressed to Lord Burghley.

"My right honourable Lord, I am in some conscience moved to write, but yet this world liketh me so ill, that I have no hope of good success therein. The recusants of Wisbeach Castle are the men of whom all the rest do depend. They are sworn against Christ, and His Church here. I see how it fareth amongst our grave Reformers. I like them so well that I will not trust them in so good a service. Therefore upon your Lordship and the rest of my Lords, and upon the consciences of you all, do I lay this burden. The former letters from the Lords to me directed, was to lay upon the recusants a learned preacher, to offer them conference and disputation, and withal to bring them to the service of our Church. They refuse all, they obey nothing, they regard not what ye enjoin.

"If my boldness might not be disliked, I would make my suit thus : The care shall be mine, much charge shall be mine, and the danger shall be mine. Let the Lords then make Gray's number of the recusants to be twenty. They and their lodgings shall be all enclosed within a brick wall : they shall eat and speak together : they shall conspire and do what they list. I and mine, my lands and goods shall answer for all. For I mean if walls, locks, and doors will separate them from out practice, they shall not want a sufficient provision of such. Now let it not be thought, and as some bishops have reported, that I have, or ever mind to make trade or gain by overruling such wretches. Only Thomas Gray is faithful in his calling ; to him, therefore, let that belong. I have obtained of him a consent, if his number might be twenty, certain and special, to give out of his commodity rising from them, unto two preachers, fourscore pounds by year. For the considerations before, and my care therein, let me then have the favour of naming the preachers, upon which point all hope of doing good and winning glory to God doth consist ; for your honour must know that formality and goodly words of consent to all traditions whatsoever screeneth not the reins [?] of an obstinate mind. But it must come from them, that by holy life and deep judgments are able to set down God's anger and wrath to come.

"May it, therefore, please your Lords to be a mean that of these four here named two of them may be preferred to preach, confer, and dispute within—viz., Lancelot Andrewes, of Pembroke Hall ; Lawrence Dewse, of St. John's College ; Bartholomew Dod, of Jesus' College ; and William Flood. The assembly shall be in Wisbeach Castle hall. The recusants shall be conveyed thither by a secret way without seeing any ; they shall have a secret place for themselves to be in, to hear and not be seen.

"The Lords must give me authority to see all this performed, and what else they shall think good and meet to be done. This is the holy ordinance of God. He will bless His own ways. Other courses have not prospered with them. If it please God to move your hearts to consider hereof, you shall try the success. And as I have thus boldly presumed upon your Lordships, so have I done the like with Mr. the right honourable Secretary. Thus most humbly I take my leave, this first of February, 1583 " [*i.e.,* 1584].

Whether the suggestions contained in this letter were acted on I cannot say. To force money out of poor Catholic prisoners, in order to pay preachers to annoy them, was a device worthy of the Reformers. But to say, "This is the holy ordinance of God, He will bless His own ways," was a consummation of impudence that must have startled even the Privy Councillors of Elizabeth.

The other question touched on in the pamphlets already alluded to is the demeanour of Bishop Watson to his fellow-prisoners. Happily I can extract what they have said of him without concerning myself with the purpose for which they brought it forward.

A book published in 1600 asserted that the fear of incurring a *præmunire* "made the late reverend Bishop of Lincoln to refuse all external jurisdiction offered him over his fellow-prisoners". In answer to this, another book called *A Brief Apology* accused the writer of misstatement. In 1603 a reply was published to this Apology, and the statement is reiterated on the authority (alleged) "of those who were priests and fellow-prisoners with Bishop Watson, and who were present at the offer and his refusal, and are ear-witnesses thereof ".[1]

We are, however, left in the dark as to the nature of this jurisdiction. If it were episcopal, he still had it by right in his own diocese, but how could priests offer it to him in the diocese of Ely? If, as it seems more likely, they merely asked him, being a bishop, to rule them as a community, it seems far-fetched to connect his refusal with fears of *præmunire*.

However this may be, I am glad to extract the following account of Dr. Watson from the ugly controversy in which it is related—a controversy which began long after the bishop's death, and in which he is in no way concerned.

"In the year 1580," says an anonymous writer,[2] " Doctor Watson, Bishop of Lincoln, Doctor Feckenham, Abbot of Westminster, Doctor Young, Master Metham, Doctor Oxenbridge, and Master Bluet, were sent to remain as prisoners in the Castle of Wisbeach, where they lived in great unity and brotherly kindness; every man intermeddling only with his

---

[1] A Reply to a notorious Libel intituled *A Brief Apology*, p. 127.
[2] Christopher Bagshaw, according to Dodd.

own affairs and private meditations. They were all in
commons with the keeper, and for their recreation had a
garden there to walk in, and to solace themselves as they
thought good. Such money as was sent to any particular
man he had himself the disposition of it, as he thought it
convenient; that which came for the common use was by
all their consents delivered still to Master Bluet, who
divided the same to every man alike. There was then
no affectation of superiority, but every man yielded of his
own accord that duty and precedency which to everyone
was due, the keeper having the commandment over them
all. Afterwards, within about three years, eight or nine
gentlemen were likewise sent to remain there as prisoners,
upon certain speeches that the Duke of Guise had some
intendment against England, whereby the number of the
prisoners increased, without any disturbance at all to the
foresaid unity. These gentlemen lived at their own
charges, and as most dutiful children, demeaned themselves
towards their fellow-prisoners and spiritual fathers. If at
any time some little indiscretion happened in any, a word
(especially of his ghostly father) was more than sufficient to
reform it: or if upon such like an occasion Bishop Watson
were moved to reprove this or that, his answer was: ' What,
are we not fellow-prisoners? Are we not at the commandment of another? Shall I add affliction to one that is
afflicted? Are we men who profess ourselves to be examples to others in suffering for our consciences, and shall
we not be thought then able, without controllers, to govern
ourselves? Be content; I will not take upon me to reprove
my fellow-prisoners.' And indeed this was the course that
every man held, so as by submitting themselves one to
another every man had a commanding power one over
another; such was the most Christian and brotherly affection
amongst them. In this sort they lived till all were either

dead or gone, but Master Metham and Master Bluet, which
was for the space of about six or seven years." [1]

We have now exhausted our information regarding Bishop
Watson. We know nothing of the length or nature of the
disease of which he died. We do not know who assisted
him, though it is probable that one or other of the priests
then in Wisbeach was not denied access to him in his last
moments. It is related of Bishop Gardiner that " when he
was lying on his death-bed, he caused the Passion of Christ
to be read unto him, and when he heard it read that Peter,
after the denying of his Master, went out and wept bitterly,
he, causing the reader to stay, wept himself full bitterly,
and said, ' *Ego exivi sed nondum flevi amare* ': ' I have gone
out, but as yet I have not wept bitterly ' ".[2] Gardiner died
in the possession of dignity and wealth ; his chaplain, Dr.
Watson, was more happy. The sincerity of his repent-
ance for the schism of his early years, of his love to
the Church, and fidelity to the Holy See, had been
proved by twenty-five years of suffering. He died on
27th September, 1584, at the age of seventy-one. He was
the last survivor of the Catholic bishops in England, and
with the death of Thomas Goldwell, Bishop of St. Asaph's,
in the year following, the ancient hierarchy of England
ceased to exist. He was buried in the parish church of
Wisbeach. The register, still in existence, contains simply
the entry " 1584, 27th September : John [3] Watson, Doctor,
sepultus ". No memorial was ever erected,[4] owing to the

---

[1] *A True Relation of the Faction begun at Wisbeach*, printed in
1601 (pp. 1-3).

[2] Stapleton, *Counterblast*, p. 368.

[3] By mistake for Thomas. He may have died that day or the day
before.

[4] Cole, the antiquarian, searched for one in vain in 1748. See
Cole's MS., vol. xvii., p. 90 (British Museum).

circumstances of the times; but I will venture to express a
hope that before many years each diocese of our restored
hierarchy will commemorate by some fitting monument its
confesssors and martyrs; and that Hexham in which Watson
was born, and was dean, Nottingham which contains his See,
and Northampton which contains his university, as well as his
prison and his grave, may each inscribe on its list the name
of Thomas Watson.   I have sought in vain for any portrait,
nor am I aware of any description of his personal appearance.
His character may be gathered from his life and writings.
Strype calls him " altogether a sour and morose man,"[1] probably for no other reason than his refusal to sully his priesthood by a sacrilegious marriage, like some of his fellow
collegians, or to preserve the honours and revenues of his
episcopate by apostasy.   On the other hand, Thomas Nash
bears testimony, not merely to his merit and scholarship,
but to his wit and good humour.   There is a calmness and
absence of invective in his sermons very unusual in those
days; and in the various disputations in which he was engaged you will seek in vain for a word of bitterness against
an opponent.   Even Foxe, who rails incessantly at all the
Catholic champions, makes no charge of unfairness or
overbearing temper against Watson.   The only apparent
exceptions that I have met with are his treatment of Rough,

---

[1] *Annals of the Reformation*, vol. i., p. 214.   He has merely copied
Godwin in this, and Burnet and others repeat the same thing on the
same authority.   Mr. Cooper says that the reflection on Watson's
temper is not only entirely unwarranted by facts, but the very
reverse of the truth.   The first author of this description was Lord
Burghley, who in his book called *Execution of Justice in England*,
published in 1583, thus calumniated the man whose constancy he had
vainly endeavoured to break during four-and-twenty years.   From
him Camden borrowed, saying that Watson was " *spinosa Theologia
eruditus sed austera gravitate morosus*".   Godwin goes still further:
" a very austere, or, rather, a sour and churlish man ".

which I have discussed already, and his resistance in the
Westminster Conference. But even then he is not charged
with pride towards the disputants, but with contumacy
towards those who had power to commit him to prison, and
"his folly and violence," as they are called, were merely the
bold vindication of the dignity of his office and the rights of
the Church. He was a man who, by his learning, his
talents, and his energy, would in all probability, had God
allowed him to govern the church of Lincoln longer, have
left a name in that see as famous as that of Robert Grosteste.
But in the prime of his age and beginning of his career God
permitted him to be torn from his flock, and, as men might
say, to waste his mature years in inactivity. But though his
pen was wrested from his hand and his tongue was silenced,
he glorified God and edified the Church by patient suffering
and invincible constancy as the opponent of heresy and
schism, and his name will ever be in benediction in the
Catholic Church in England, as the last and not degenerate
successor of St. Hugh.

CHAPTER IX.

(By the late Rev. Thomas F. Knox.)

Thomas Goldwell, Bishop of St. Asaph.

AT the beginning of the sixteenth century Europe was still one vast Christian land, whose inhabitants, though divided in race, nationality, language, manners, and form of government, were knit together in the unity of the one faith under the spiritual rule of the one Roman Pontiff. Everywhere, throughout the whole length and breadth of the Continent, men worshipped at the same altars, according to the same rite, the same Incarnate God. No other pretended form of Christianity was even tolerated. Its divergence from the one traditional faith and ecclesiastical organisation would have alone sufficed to brand it in the eyes of all, whether governors or governed, as an imposture, and therefore as a pestilence. Nor did this unity of belief manifest itself only in matters of religion. The supernatural truths of faith interpenetrated and influenced the whole fabric of political and social life, ruling over philosophical speculation, leavening literature, and consecrating art.

Such was the state of Europe at the birth and during the early youth of Thomas Goldwell, sometime Bishop of St. Asaph, the last survivor of the ancient English hierarchy. Born when that period, which has been truly termed the age of faith, was about to close, he saw Europe one. And he also saw the coming in of a new era, of which the unlooked-for and almost instantaneous break-up of Europe's religious unity was at once the herald and the cause. On a sudden, at Luther's fiery exhortations to spiritual rebellion (1517), a wild lust of independence in belief, thought, and action seized upon the multitudes, spreading far and wide like a conflagration. Kings and nobles took advantage of it to lay their hands upon the Church's property which their forefathers had consecrated to God. And they saw their way by the ruin of the spiritual polity to concentrate in themselves all authority, spiritual as well as temporal. Thenceforth, freed from the check which Christ's Vicar had till then placed upon their passions, they would bow to no will but their own. Thus it came to pass that nation after nation fell away or was torn violently from the centre of unity, until in a few years only southern and part of central Europe remained true to the ancient faith, while the scattered few who elsewhere clung to the religion of their ancestors were despoiled of their goods, driven into exile, or persecuted to death.

Thomas Goldwell was a witness of all this; and he beheld, too, that revival of fervour among the faithful—that new spiritual life which God breathed so abundantly into His Church, and which followed close upon and characterised this period of widespread apostasy. He saw saint after saint arise and grow to perfection ; among whom not a few became the founders of new religious orders and congregations, destined not only to labour among the faithful, but to bring back numerous wanderers to the fold. Moreover, it was during his lifetime that the Ecumenical Council of Trent bestowed permanence on the work of reform and reconstruction within the Church, by adapting the ecclesiastical laws to the needs of the new epoch, and giving to the dogmas which Protestantism had denied a more definite and complete expression.

But Goldwell was not merely a witness of the events of

14

this momentous period. He was an actor in them; busily engaged throughout the greater part of his long life of eighty-four years in the very thick of the contest. Nor was he, like so many of his countrymen, an uncertain waverer between God's Church and God's enemies; but he' was always, from first to last, on the right side, heedless whether it might bring him honour or dishonour, high position in this world or martyrdom.

The life of such a man must be interesting, even though the few facts about him which have come down to us furnish matter for an outline rather than a picture. And yet scanty as these facts are, one whole portion of them has entirely escaped the notice of English writers, whether Catholic or Protestant, ancient or modern. No one apparently was aware of Goldwell having been a Theatine, much less of his having lived, though a bishop, the life of a religious among his Theatine brethren, during the many years of his banishment from England at Queen Mary's death. Nor, again, has the work he did at Rome as vicar of St. John Lateran, and as suffragan to the Pope, been put into due prominence even by writers who were acquainted with the facts. In the following pages an attempt has been made to supply from foreign sources, especially from the chronicles of the Theatine Order, this gap in Bishop Goldwell's history; and, so far at least, this biographical notice may claim to be a real addition to our knowledge of a man whose memory deserves to be cherished with veneration by all English Catholics.

Thomas Goldwell was born in or about the year 1500. He was of ancient and gentle lineage. His family had lived for several centuries in the parish of Great Chart in Kent, on their manor of Goldwell, from which they derived their name. One of his ancestors was Sir John Goldwell, Knight, a commander of considerable note in the reign of King John. Dr. James Goldwell, principal Secretary to

King Edward the Fourth, Ambassador from that monarch to the Pope, and Bishop of Norwich from 1472 to 1498, was his great-grandfather's brother.[1] In 1520 Thomas Goldwell was admitted a scholar of All Souls College, Oxford, of which his kinsman, the Bishop of Norwich, had been formerly a scholar and a considerable benefactor, as the list of benefactors, on which his name stands first, testifies.[2] In 1527 he took the degree of B.A., in 1531 that of M.A., and in 1533 that of B.D.[3] During this period he appears to have applied himself with considerable success to the study of astronomy and other branches of mathematics, since the memory of his acquirements in this department of learning lingered as a tradition at Oxford long after he had left the University.[4] We do not know the year in which he

[1] Halsted's *Kent*, iii. 246 ; Blomefield's *Norwich*, iii. 252, 540.

[2] Wood's *Oxford*, continued by Gutch, 262.

[3] Wood's *Fasti*. Edit. Bliss., 76, 87, 96.

[4] Wood's *Athen*. Edit. Bliss., ii. 823 ; Dodd, i. 507. Compare the following passage from a contemporary Protestant writer, which, in spite of several absurd errors of fact, bears testimony to Goldwell's acquaintance with mathematics ; for the science which deals with geometrical figures and calculations is evidently meant by "the black art ". " Oxford hath Oxfordshire onlie, a verie young jurisdiction, erected by King Henrie the Eighth, and where in the time of Queene Marie, one Goldwell was bishop, who (as I remember) was a Jesuit, dwelling in Rome, and more conversant (as the constant fame went) in the blacke art than skilfull in the Scriptures, and yet he was of great countenance amongst the Roman monarchs. It is said that, observing the canons of his order, he regarded not the temporalities of that see ; but I have heard since that he wist well enough what became of those commodities, for by one meane and other he found the sweetness of 354 pounds, sixteen shillings, threepence halfe penie yearelie growing to him, which was even inough (if not too much) for the maintenance of a frier toward the drawing out of circles, characters, and lineaments of imagerie, wherein he was passing skilfull, as the fame then went in Rome, and not unheard of in Oxford " (The Description of England by William Harrison, booke ii., ch. ii., prefixed to Holinshed's *Chronicles*).

resigned his scholarship, though the registers of All Souls College may supply the date. At any rate, he must have left Oxford before the middle of 1535, since his name does not occur in an official list of the warden and scholars of All Souls made about that time.[1] It is possible that in 1531 he was presented to the rectory of Cheriton, near Folkestone, in the diocese of Canterbury; for one Thomas Goldwell, M.A., was certainly admitted to that church on March 11, 1531, as appears from Archbishop Warham's register;[2] but the mere identity of name, unsupported by other evidence, hardly warrants the conclusion that the rector of Cheriton and the future Bishop of St. Asaph were the same person. Thomas Goldwell was still "the parson of Cheriton" at the beginning of 1535.[3]

Hitherto the false doctrines of the Reformation had been unable to penetrate into England. King and people were Catholic in faith, and obedient sons of the Apostolic See. But a storm had been gathering for some years past. A time of trial and sifting was at hand, in which it would be seen who were ready "to render to Cæsar the things which are Cæsar's, and to God the things which are God's". On March 30, 1534, the Royal assent was given to the Bill by which the kingdom was formally severed from the communion of Rome, and during the following summer the

[1] "*Valor Ecclesiasticus*, or the returns of a survey instituted to ascertain the amount of the first-fruits and tenths of all the English 'dignities, benefices, and promotions spiritual,' given to Henry VIII. by an Act of Parliament passed on January 15, 1535. The survey was made by sworn commissioners, and it appears to have been executed by them chiefly between January and June, 1535" (Note in the Catalogue of the Library of the London Institution, vol. ii., p. 237).

[2] Registr. Warham, quoted in a note to Wood's *Athenæ*. Edit. Bliss, ii. 824.

[3] *Valor Eccles.*, vol. ii., pp. 51, 95.

King's commissioners were occupied throughout the length and breadth of England in extorting from the reluctant "clergy and clerical bodies, and from the monks, friars, and nuns in their several abbeys and convents," a declaration and subscription under oath, "that the Bishop of Rome had no more authority within the realm than any other foreign bishop, and a recognition, under the same oath, that the King was the supreme head of the Church of England, without the addition of the qualifying clause—as far as the law of Christ will allow—which had been in the first instance (May, 1531) admitted ".[1] There were not many who had the courage to refuse this oath ; for to do so entailed the pains and penalties of high treason. Fisher, More, many of the Carthusians, the Franciscans of the Observance, and some others, chose rather to die on the scaffold or in prison than to take it. Reginald Pole, that he might have no share in these transactions, had retired to the north of Italy. Goldwell seems to have left England on the same account ; for in December, 1538, we find him, and several other servants of Cardinal Pole, included by name in the same Act of attainder with their master, "for casting off their duty to the King, and submitting themselves to the Bishop of Rome ".[2] Goldwell was now an exile for the faith, and, with the exception of the brief interval of Mary's reign, he spent in banishment from home and country the remaining fifty years of his life.

There was at this time in Rome, in the Via di Monserrato, an hospital for the reception of English pilgrims and travellers which had been founded about the year 1362, under the patronage of the Blessed Trinity and St. Thomas, by John Shepherd, a London merchant. This hospital, to

[1] Lingard, *History of England*, v. 33.
[2] Strpye, *Mem.*, vol. i., pt. i., p. 477.

which another similar institution in Trastevere had been united in 1464, began to decline during the dispute between Henry the Eighth and the Holy See. As the schism advanced, its resources gradually failed, and the supplies which it had hitherto received from England ceased. In 1538, almost all the resident members were dead. In that year, Pope Paul the Third, anxious to preserve the hospital for the English nation, ordered the vacant places to be filled up, and committed the superintendence of it to Cardinal Pole.[1] Thomas Goldwell was at the same time appointed warden, Hilliard, another of Pole's followers, who had been attainted with him, being named rector.[2]

For the next ten years we have no particulars of Goldwell's history; but as we know that he was for several years Reginald Pole's chaplain,[3] it could only have been during this period that he filled that office. In after times he used to relate that "when the Cardinal was abroad in any place of retirement, at Caprancia or the like, he would order Mass to be said, and then serve the priest as acolyth, and help him to vest and unvest, leaving it only to one of his servants to hold the napkin".[4]

Thus far we have beheld in Goldwell the man of letters, the priest, and the confessor for the faith. But a new and higher vocation now opens out before him. The readiness with which he forsook country, kindred, and temporal prospects found its reward in the further call to give up all things for Christ by entering religion. The order which attracted him was that of the Clerks Regular, or Theatines, founded in 1524 by St. Cajetan and Caraffa, Archbishop of

---

[1] Tierney's *Dodd*, ii. 169, note.
[2] Strype, *Mem.*, vol. i., pt. ii., p. 481.
[3] Beccatelli's *Life of Pole*. Pye's trans., 160.
[4] *Ibid.*

Chieti, afterwards Paul the Fourth, and still in the full fervour of primitive observance. It was the first in time of many similar orders of Clerks Regular, which, under the names of Barnabites, Somaschi, Jesuits, Clerks Minor, Ministers of the Sick, Clerks of the Mother of God, and Clerks of the Pious Schools, sought to combine the strict discipline of the regular with the apostolic life of the secular clergy. The aim of the Theatines was the reformation of the secular clergy and the sanctification of the faithful. While maintaining the most rigorous poverty within their houses, they strove to honour the Divine Majesty by the splendour of their churches and the regularity of their cere- monial observance. Men of birth and position seem to have been especially drawn to them, and several cardinals and not a few holy and zealous bishops were taken from their ranks. An unworldly spirit was in the popular mind so associated with the order that devout seculars were com- monly nicknamed Chietini, or Theatines.[1]

On 7th August, 1547, St. Catejan died at Naples in the Theatine house of St. Paul, of which he was the founder and superior. The following year, on 23rd November, 1548, Thomas Goldwell began his novitiate in the same house,[2] the Blessed John Marinoni[3] being then its rector. It was no light or easy undertaking for a man of forty-seven, already a priest, and accustomed to have the charge of others, to become, as it were, a child again and to recast his

---

[1] Moroni, *Dizionario Ecclesiastico*, vol. lxxiii., p. 124.

[2] *Vita del S. P. Paolo IV. Fondatore della Religione dei Chieric, Regolari, e Memorie d'altri cinquanta Padri, che in essa fiorirono il secolo passato M.D. Raccolte dal P. D. Gio. Battista Castaldo dell' istessa religione*, p. 240. Roma, 1615 ; *Historia Clericorum Regularium. Auctore Josepho Silos, Clerico Regulari*, i. 302. Romæ, 1650.

[3] Pope Clement the Thirteenth authorised his *cultus* in 1762. Moroni, *Dizion. Eccles.*, vol. xxxi., p. 40.

whole life in the mould of religion. It needed great graces, and great faithfulness to these graces. The high esteem in which Goldwell was held in his order, and the offices of trust subsequently confided to him, are a proof that neither of these were wanting to him, but that he fully acquired the spirit and perfection of a true religious.

The first year of his novitiate was not quite completed when an event occurred which obliged him to return for a short time to the world which he had forsaken. On 10th November, 1549, Pope Paul the Third died, and Cardinal Pole at once applied to Goldwell's superiors that his former chaplain and friend might be allowed to attend upon him at the approaching Conclave.[1] This request, so honourable to Goldwell, was granted, and during the time the Conclave lasted, from 29th November, 1549, to 7th February, 1550, he remained in waiting on the cardinal. At length the election of Julius the Third set him free to return from the excitement and intrigues of the Conclave to the quiet of the novitiate at Naples, where he was admitted to make his solemn profession, 28th October, 1550.[2]

In England, the prospects of the Church were as yet no brighter. During the short reign of Edward the Sixth, though Catholics were not persecuted with the same virulence as under Henry the Eighth, the ancient faith was still proscribed. In 1553, an Act of Parliament was passed, granting a general pardon to offenders, but from it were specially

[1] Silos, i. 305.

[2] Castaldo, 240. It appears, from a letter of St. Andrew Avellino, that it was not the custom in the early days of the Order to give a postulant the habit until many months after his entry (Bonaglia, *Vita del B. Cardinale d'Arezzo*, p. 174. Roma, 1772). This may account for the long time which elapsed between Goldwell's entry and profession. The interruption of his novitiate by the Conclave would be a further reason.

excepted by name Cardinal Pole, Goldwell, and others.[1] Queen Mary's accession, 6th July, 1553, was the dawn of better things for England. On 5th August, 1553, Pope Julius the Third held a Consistory, in which he appointed Cardinal Pole his legate to Queen Mary. In accepting this arduous legation, it was natural that the cardinal's thoughts should turn to his old and trusted servant, Father Goldwell, and he at once obtained an express precept from His Holiness requiring Goldwell to accompany him to England.[2] Father Tufo, the chronicler of the Order, who knew Goldwell personally, says that he possessed peculiar qualifications for this work. To a more than average knowledge of philosophy he added a familiar acquaintance with theology, the doctrine of the Fathers, and Holy Scripture. His reputation stood high in the Order, and even at Rome, as an excellent religious. He was, moreover, gifted with singular goodness and zeal for God's glory and the salvation of souls ; while at the same time he was naturally a man of great prudence and remarkable dexterity in the management of affairs.[3] The Theatine Order acquiesced in his appointment with satisfaction, and, as a testimony to his merit, conferred on him, at the General Chapter which was held that year at Venice, the right of voting at the capitular assemblies of the Order.[4]

In September, 1553, Goldwell joined Cardinal Pole at the Benedictine monastery of Maguzzano on the Lake of Garda, where he had been living for some time past in retirement, and at the end of the month set out with him towards the

---

[1] 7th Edward VI., ch. 14 ; *Statutes of the Realm*, iv. 193.

[2] Silos, i. 315.

[3] *Historia della Religione de' Padri Chiereci Regolari. Raccolta da Gio. Battista del Tufo, vescovo dell' Acerra, dell' istessa Religione,* p. 43. Roma, 1609.

[4] Silos, i. 315.

Low Countries, on his way to England. At the instance of the Emperor Charles the Fifth, who feared that the cardinal's presence in England might interfere with the proposed marriage of his son, Philip the Second of Spain, with Queen Mary, Pole was stopped at Dillingen. Thence he despatched Goldwell to England, with full written instructions, the substance of which he was to communicate by word of mouth to the Queen.[1] Goldwell reached Calais on 30th November, but as he stated on examination that he came from Cardinal Pole, and had been in his service, the governor, Lord William Howard, refused him permission to cross over, and sent to the Queen's Council for directions how to act.[2] The reply of the Council being favourable, Goldwell was allowed to continue his journey to England, and, after fulfilling his commission to the Queen, rejoined the cardinal in Germany, and proceeded with him to Brussels. From this city he wrote, on 16th June, 1554, apparently by the legate's direction, a severe but affectionate letter of reprimand to Dr. Richard Thorndon,[3] suffragan Bishop of Dover, whose reconciliation and absolution he had obtained, though not without difficulty, from Cardinal Pole. It is as follows :

" RICHT REVEREND AND MY GOOD LORD,—After my hearty thanks for your good cheer at my last being with your Lordship, this shall be to certify you that as soon as I arrived with my Lord's grace [Cardinal Pole], I gave him your letter :

---

[1] British Museum, Cotton MSS., " Titus," B. ii. 170.

[2] *P. R. Foreign, Mary*, 1553, Dec. 1.

[3] Strype, *Mem.*, vol. iii., pt. i., p. 211. " Richard Thorndon was a Benedictine monk of Christ Church in Canterbury, and educated in Canterbury College, Oxford, of which he was warden about 1528. He was in great esteem for his profound knowledge in divinity, in which faculty he proceeded doctor, 10th October, 1531. He died. suffragan Bishop of Dover, in the year 1577 " (Dodd, i. 483).

but I had much work to obtain anything of him for you. For there have been given very evil informations of you, and it hath been said that you have concurred with all manner of evil proceedings, the which hath these years past been in England, as well against the holy Sacrament of the Altar and against the supreme authority of Christ's Vicar on earth, as with the use of the abominable late communion and with the marriage of priests, as well religious as secular ; and that you have given orders to (I cannot tell how many) base, unlearned, and evil disposed people, by reason of the which they have taken upon them to preach and do much hurt in Kent. So that men think that yet, if any new mutation (the which God forbid) should chance, you would be as ready to change as any other. And indeed it maketh me to fear the same, by reason that notwithstanding it hath pleased Almighty God to provide that absolution was sent unto you (not looking, I dare say, for any such thing) of all manner of matters past, yet your Lordship (more regarding the vanity of the world than the offence of God, the which He only knoweth how much it grieves me, for the due love I bear unto you) presumed to sing Mass *in pontificalibus* the holy-days immediately following ; and also to ministrate to children the Sacrament of Confirmation, because that one (being a member of the devil) did somewhat comfort you so to do.

"O my Lord, what honour should it have been both to God and to yourself, and also edification to all good people (though all worldly men and heretics would therefore have laughed you to scorn), if you, considering your great offences towards God, and His goodness again toward you, would, like as you have offended in the face of the world to the damnation of many, likewise have showed yourself penitent in the face of the world to the edification of many, and not only not to have celebrated for vanity *pontificaliter*, but also for a time to have abstained for reverence *totaliter* from the altar according to the old custom of the Church ; the which I have also observed of some honest men, not being thereto enjoined of any man : but that which is past cannot be called again.   And I thought it not my part to leave your Lordship, mine old friend and master, in the mire.   Wherefore I ceased not to solicit your cause with my Lord's grace, till at last I obtained of his grace for your Lordship all the faculties of the which I send you a copy here inclosed partly for your own consolation, and partly for others, desiring your Lordship so to use them to the honour of God, that there come to me therefore no rebuke ; not publishing them to any person, but to such as you know will gladly receive them ; for hitherto there is never a bishop in England who hath granted to him so great authority concerning those which be under his cure.   Only Master Archdeacon [Harpsfield[1]] hath the like, and in one thing more great than be these your Lordship's.   Wherefore your Lordship shall do well to remit unto him all such priests as have cure of souls, whether they be beneficed men or parish priests. For he hath not only authority to absolve them, as you have, but also to give them authority to absolve such as be underneath their cures.   And thus I commit your Lordship to the protection of Almighty God.   .

   " Written at Brussels, the 16th of June, 1554.

" Your Lordship's bead-man,

"THOMAS GOLDWELL."[2]

It was not until the middle of November, 1554, that matters were so far arranged as to permit the cardinal

---

[1] Dr. Nicholas Harpsfield, fellow of New College, Oxford, in 1536, was distinguished for his knowledge of civil law.   He was made Archdeacon of Canterbury in 1554.

[2] Fox's *Acts and Monuments*, vol. vii., p. 297 (Ed. Townsend).

legate to enter England.   Goldwell doubtless accompanied
him thither, and was present at that touching ceremony on
St. Andrew's Day, when the cardinal, as the Pope's legate,
appeared in Parliament and solemnly absolved the realm
from all heresy and schism, and restored it once more to
the unity of the Catholic Church.   Soon after this Goldwell was nominated by the Queen to the vacant bishopric
of St. Asaph, and the customary writ was issued in her name
on February 12, 1555, by which the temporalities of this
see were intrusted to his custody and granted to his use, as
"the now nominated and elected bishop of the aforesaid
Cathedral Church of St. Asaph," from "the time of the
vacancy of the see by the translation of the last bishop, and
so long as the see should be without a bishop, and until we
or our heirs shall set free and restore the temporalities of
the bishopric to Thomas Goldwell, now elected to the
same".[1]   The sovereign may nominate to a bishopric and
consign the temporal possessions of the see to the person
nominated, but only the Pope, as Christ's Vicar on earth,
can give the necessary jurisdiction, or spiritual authority, by
which a bishop has power to govern the sheep of Christ's
flock who live within his bishopric.   Hence the next step
was for the Queen to write to the Sovereign Pontiff, praying
His Holiness to make Goldwell Bishop of St. Asaph.   We
do not possess a copy of this letter ; but it was probably the
same in form as the following one, which was addressed by
Henry the Eighth on a similar occasion to Pope Leo the
Tenth.

" *To our most holy and clement Lord, the Pope.*

"Most blessed Father, after most humble commendation
and most devout kisses of the blessed feet,—When it was

---

[1] Rymer, *Fœdera*, vol. vi., pt. iv., p. 38.

announced to us that the Cathedral Church of St. Asaph, in our principality of Wales, had become vacant by the death of the Rev. Father in Christ, Edmund, the last bishop, and is now without its pastor, we, thinking to make provision for it, have deemed the venerable and religious man, Henry Standysh, of the Order of Friars Minor conventuals, professor of sacred theology, and not unknown as a preacher of the Divine Word, dear to us, moreover, through his eminent learning, modesty, probity, circumspection, and integrity of life and morals, to be worthy of having the care and burden of the said Church entrusted to him. Wherefore we earnestly commend him to your Blessedness, and pray you, as a special favour to us, to deign to set over the same Church the aforesaid Henry, and to constitute him its bishop and pastor, which, as we hope it will prove to the honour and profit of the said Church, so will it also be very pleasing to us. May your Holiness enjoy all happiness, and may the Almighty God grant you a long life.

"From our palace at Woodstock, 28th April, 1518.

"Your Holiness' most devoted and most obedient son, by the grace of God King of England and France and Lord of Ireland,

"HENRY."[1]

Early in the summer of 1555, Father Goldwell was in Rome. He had gone thither on business of Cardinal Pole, who, having only consented at the Queen's request to accept the archbishopric of Canterbury, on condition that the Pope would allow him to remain in England and reside in his

---

[1] Theiner, *Monumenta Hibernorum et Scotorum*, n. 931. Romæ, 1864. It may be remarked, by way of contrast, that in the Protestant Established Church of England, the nomination to bishoprics, virtual election, and spiritual jurisdiction all proceed from the sovereign as supreme governor of the Church of England.

diocese, had sent Goldwell to Rome to negotiate this and other matters for him.[1]   In the preceding February, Queen Mary had despatched to Rome as her ambassadors the Bishop of Ely, Viscount Montague, and Sir Edward Carne, representing the three orders of the kingdom, to tender to the Sovereign Pontiff the obedience of the whole nation. They were still on their road when the death of Julius the Third occurred, March 23.   Then followed the three weeks' pontificate of Marcellus the Second; so that they did not arrive at Rome until after the election (May 23) of Cardinal Caraffa, who took the name of Paul the Fourth.   The new, Pope received them in solemn Consistory on June 21, and, after accepting the submission of the kingdom which they offered to him, provided with bishops the Sees of York, Norwich, Bristol, Ely, Exeter, and Bangor., He also confirmed the appointment to the See of Coventry and Lichfield, which had been made by Cardinal Pole in virtue of his faculties as legate.[2] Father Goldwell must have been preconised Bishop of St. Asaph at one of the next Consistories which occurred, as his episcopal consecration took place in the summer of that year.[3]   When he returned to England, Paul the Fourth gave him two letters for the Queen, which he presented to her on reaching London in the month of December.   We do not know their contents; but Goldwell, in a letter to Cardinal Scotti, of the Theatine Order, speaks of the pleasure they caused to the Queen, and he adds that, considering the difficulties she had to contend with in re-

---

[1] Beccatelli, *Life of Pole*, p. 137.

[2] Raynaldus, *Annales*, 1555, pp. 25, 26.

[3] Tufo, *Supplim.*, 94; Silos, i. 335; Godwin, *De præsul. Angl.*, 642. Godwin calls the Bishop of St. Asaph a Benedictine monk, evidently confusing him with his namesake, Thomas Goldwell, Prior of Christchurch, Canterbury, at the suppression and for twenty-three years previously.

storing the ancient religion, it would be advisable for the Pope to write to her occasionally and encourage her to persevere courageously in the good work which she had undertaken.[1]

Bishop Goldwell arrived in time to be present at the national synod which Cardinal Pole was then holding as legate. A month after his return, he obtained the restitution of the temporalities of his see. The Queen's writ, dated January 22, 1556, was to the following effect: " Inasmuch as the Supreme Pontiff, on the late vacancy of the Cathedral Church of St. Asaph by the translation of the last Bishop of that Church, has by apostolic authority provided the person of our beloved Thomas Goldwell, bachelor of sacred theology, elect of the same Church, for the Church of St. Asaph aforesaid, and has set him over it as bishop and pastor ; all which appears from the bulls of the Supreme Pontiff directed to us; we . . . desiring to deal graciously with the said Thomas, have received his homage, and restored to him according to custom the temporalities of the said bishopric of St. Asaph ".[2] The temporal possessions of the See of St. Asaph, thus made over to Bishop Goldwell, were of small value ; for the revenues of the bishopric, which were never large, had been greatly reduced by the prodigality of the late Bishop, Warton, who, to raise the money he required for his sumptuous style of living, had leased the episcopal lands at a low rent for a very long term of years.[3] The see was considered so poor that four years later Queen Elizabeth authorised the first Protestant bishop, Davys, to hold at the same time with the bishopric several other benefices *in commendam*, as the revenues of St. Asaph did not exceed £187 11s. 6d. per annum.[4]

In the spring of this year Bishop Goldwell was called upon to be present at the consecration of Cardinal Pole, who had been appointed Archbishop of Canterbury by Pope Paul the

[1] Silos, i. 335.   [2] Rymer, vol. vi., pt. iv., p. 40.
[3] Godwin, *De. præsul. Angl.*, 642.   [4] Rymer, vol. vi., pt. iv., p. 91.

Fourth in a Consistory held December 11, 1555., The ceremony was performed on Passion Sunday, March 22, 1556, in the Church of the Observantine Friars Minor at Greenwich, by Nicholas Heath, Archbishop of York, with the assistance of six bishops, among whom was the Bishop of St. Asaph.[1] The thoughts of Bishop Goldwell would now naturally turn to the diocese committed to his charge. A series of injunctions for the better ordering of the clergy and laity of St. Asaph, which he issued in .the year 1556, are a testimony to his pastoral solicitude.[2] He was zealous in promoting pilgrimages to St. Winefrid's Well in Flintshire, and obtained from the Pope a renewal of the indulgences granted to those who visited it.[3] The only other thing we find recorded about his occupations in his diocese is that, on September 27, 1556, "John Griffith was instituted Dean of St. Asaph by Bishop Goldwell, at Denbigh, where he lived".[4] It is not surprising that our information on this head is so scanty, since none of the registers of the diocese before the Reformation have been preserved.[5]

[1] Strype, *Mem.*, vol. iii., pt. i., p. 473.

[2] Wilkins, *Concilia*, iv. 145.

[3] Wood's *Athen.*, vol. ii., p. 823.

[4] Brown Willis, *Survey of the Cathedral Church of St. Asaph*, p. 102. London, 1720.

[5] "As to the old registers before the Reformation, there is a tradition that Bishop Goldwell carried them to Rome; though I see not the least grounds for that tradition, there scarcely appearing to have been any care taken about keeping registers by reason of the bishops' non-residence before Bishop David Owen's time (1629-1651), since the conflagration of this church in 1402, when it seems they were all destroyed except one called Côch Asaph" (Brown Willis, *Survey of St. Asaph*, p. 123). Bishop Humphreys, who states as an unquestioned fact the charge against Bishop Goldwell which Brown Willis sees not the least grounds for believing, adds that "Côch Asaph was also lost in the late wicked times of rebellion against King Charles the Martyr" (Hearne's *Otterbourne et Wethamstede*, 727).

Bishop Goldwell's merits and services were not unappreciated by the Queen. In October, 1558, she nominated him, though without his knowledge or consent, to the vacant See of Oxford, and by a writ of November 9, granted him the custody of the temporalities of this diocese, the custody of those of St. Asaph having been conferred four days before on Thomas Wood, nominated to that see in Goldwell's place.[1] Queen Mary's death, eight days later, and the change of religion in England which ensued under Elizabeth, prevented the translation from being carried out. A still further proof of the high confidence Queen Mary placed in Bishop Goldwell may be seen in his appointment as her ambassador to the Sovereign Pontiff, in place of Sir Edward Carne, who had prayed to be relieved of that office. The letter of credence to Paul the Fourth, which the bishop was to take with him, dated St. James', October 31, 1558, still exists.[2] The only thing wanting is the Queen's signature, which death prevented her from affixing to it. An order of Council had been already made "for allowance of five marks per diem for dyet and five hundred pounds in prest for the Bishop of St. Asaph to be sent the Queen's Embassadour to Rome ".[3]

Queen Mary died November 17, 1559. Cardinal Pole survived her only twenty-two hours.[4] The Bishop of St. Asaph was in constant attendance upon his ancient master and friend. " He gave him Extreme Unction, and was always in the room with him. An hour before the cardinal expired, he asked if the book of recommendatory prayers to be used at the soul's departure was ready; which, when the

[1] Rymer, vol. vi., pt. iv., pp. 65, 64.

[2] British Museum, Lansdowne MSS., 116, n. 2.

[3] British Museum, Lansdowne MSS., Kennett's Collections, vol. xlvii., p. 165. Extract from Council-book—Philip and Mary.

[4] [Only twelve hours. T. E. B.]

bishop showed him, he looked upon it and said, 'Now then is the time to use it,' and with these words he expired."[1] Beccatelli heard this from Goldwell's own lips. Afterwards the Bishop of St. Asaph, together with Bishop Pate of Worcester, attended Cardinal Pole's funeral by Queen Elizabeth's express command, she having at the instance of Signor Prioli, the Cardinal's devoted friend and executor, signified to them through the Lords of the Council that such was her desire.[2]

On the accession of Elizabeth all hope of England's permanent restoration to Catholic unity soon disappeared. The measures which she took to root out the ancient faith are too well known to require mention. Her first Parliament was convoked for January 23, 1559, the writs of summons to the Peers bearing date December 5 of the preceding year. In this month Bishop Goldwell wrote as follows to Secretary Cecil : [3]

"RIGHT HONORABLE MR. SECRETARY,—I would gladly have come unto you myself at this present, but that I am informed that, by reason of your continual occupation in the affairs of the Queen's Highness, I should not have commodity to speak unto you. Wherefore I am so bold as by writing to desire you to show me so much favour that by your help I may gain licence to depart hence, considering my poverty and that I am not by the Queen's Highness' writ called to be present at the Parliament ; for the which I am nothing sorry, though indeed it seemeth somewhat strange unto me, for I am still Bishop of St. Asaph, the which bishopric I never did nor could resign. And as Bishop of St. Asaph I was present and gave my voice in the

---

[1] Beccatelli, p. 130.

[2] British Museum, Lansdowne MSS., Kennett's Collection, vol. xlvii., p. 163. Extract from Council-book—1 Elizabeth.

[3] P. R., *Domestic, Elizabeth*, 1558, vol. i., n. 52.

last Parliament, though before my coming to London, without mine other knowledge or consent, I was named to Oxford, the which bishopric, if I may otherwise have the Queen's Highness' favour, I do never intend to accept : for I, longing not for heaven in this world, am very well contented with my little benefice. Truth it is that the Queen's Highness that dead is, God have her soul, having consideration of my poverty and certain other respects, gave me the vacancy of Oxford, the which I trust that the Queen's Highness, by yours and other good friends' favour, will of her goodness suffer me to enjoy. And if it be your pleasure to speak with me, I will be ready at any time that you will appoint me. And thus fare you well.

"Yours to my little power,

"THOMAS, ASAPHENS.

"To the Right Honourable Sir William Cecil,
Secretary to the Queen's Highness."

From this letter it is clear that Bishop Goldwell was not summoned to Queen Elizabeth's first Parliament, probably on the pretext that by his nomination to Oxford he had ceased to be Bishop of St. Asaph, but had not as yet done homage for the temporalities of Oxford. His enforced absence from Parliament will explain why his name does not appear in the protests which the bishops, who were present, made against the various Acts which were passed in this Parliament subversive of the Catholic faith in England.

On May 15, 1559, seven days after the Parliament had been dissolved, fourteen bishops, among whom was the Bishop of St. Asaph, were "called together by the Queen, and she told them that they should take into their serious consideration the affairs of the Church, and expulse out of it all schisms and the superstitious worship of the Church of Rome ".[1] Three days later, May 18, "the Council met upon the bishops' business, and advised the Queen to tender them the oath of supremacy and allegiance, and they refusing were all expulsed from their bishoprics ".[2] Queen Elizabeth, however, did not use threats only to obtain her end ; she made great offers to Goldwell, promising him a rich bishopric if he would take the oath acknowledging her as the "chief governor of the English Church ".[3]

It was now plain to the Bishop of St. Asaph that he could no longer remain in England and exercise there the functions of a Catholic bishop. In the deposition which he made at Rome in 1570, before the judge appointed by St. Pius the Fifth to investigate judicially the misdeeds of Queen Elizabeth, we have in his own words a statement of the reasons which moved him to abandon his diocese and return once more into exile. "Being asked why he left England and came to Rome, the Bishop of St. Asaph made answer : I quitted England because I was no longer able to perform a bishop's office, of which all the bishops that then were had been despoiled by the Queen of England. Wherefore, though I was Bishop of St. Asaph, which is a bishopric in the realm, as I was unable to celebrate Mass, minister the sacraments and preach, and was unwilling to give security as other bishops not to leave the kingdom, I thought it best to betake myself to Rome."[4]

---

[1] Strype, *Annals*, vol. i., pt. i., p. 206. [These statements about the summons to the bishops on May 15 and 18 are founded on documents forged by Robert Ware, as I have shown in the *Tablet* for May 25, 1889.—T. E. B.]

[2] *Ibid.*, 209. Goldwell was deprived of his see July 15, 1559 (Tierney's *Dodd*, vol. ii., p. 138, note).

[3] Tufo, 45.

[4] Laderkius, *Annales*, 1570, xxv.

But it was no easy matter for one so well known as Bishop Goldwell to leave England undiscovered. We learn from documents in the Record Office the following circumstances of his escape : Sunday night, June 25, 1559, the bishop with four of his servants lay at St. Albans, the shrine of the protomartyr of England. The next day, Monday, he came to London, where he dismissed his servants, telling them to go with a letter from him to his brother Stephen, at Great Chart in Kent. But he took one servant with him until he came to the bank which leads to Lambeth ferry, and there he bade his man return and leave him alone. He then proceeded in disguise to the sea-coast, and crossed over to the Continent without being recognised.

Meanwhile the servants journeyed on horseback to Stephen Goldwell's house, which they reached on Tuesday night, bearing the bishop's letter, and they said that they knew not where their master was. This letter, which was dated St. Albans, June 26, and addressed on the outside, "To my loving brother, Mr. Stephen Goldwell, in the parsonage. In great haste," ran as follows :

"BROTHER,—After hearty commendations this shall be to certify to you that I am determined to leave my bishopric. Wherefore, I being now no longer able to retain my poor servants that came to London with me, am so bold as to send four of them to your house, desiring that they may continue with you till you may provide them with masters. And where I am in debt to the Queen's Highness about three hundred pounds, part in full payment of a subsidy due the 25th of March, 1558, and part for a whole subsidy due at October last past, and was not nor yet am able to pay this money out of hand, I wrote in Easter term last past to my Lord Treasurer and to Sir Edward Rogers, desiring them to obtain me licence to put in sureties for this money to be paid at reasonable days, specially seeing that I had spent a great part of it in the service of the realm as it was then pretended; nevertheless, I could not be heard. I am, therefore, now compelled to desire you to travel into Wales as soon as you may conveniently, and to sell such goods as I have there left behind me, and to pay my said debt out of hand. For I would be loath that any man, much more that the Queen's Highness, should be defrauded of anything through me. And if peradventure my said goods will not amount to so much as my debt is (as indeed I fear that they will not), then I desire you to supply the rest, and to see my said debt satisfied, and if I live and be able I will thoroughly recompense you again. And as touching the tenth due at Christmas last past, and the subsidy due 25th of March last past, they remain as yet ungathered, partly that by reason of the death of your bed-fellow I could not well have you to take the pains, and partly because that I could not tell whether the Queen's Highness would have the whole tenth or the half, and by that means was ignorant what to demand for the foresaid subsidy. And thus fare you well, as well as I would myself, and commend me to my brother Goldwell and his wife, to my sister Alice, and all the rest of my friends. And if it had been my fortune to continue in Wales, I would have wished you a good wife there. But now I pray God send you a good one in your own country.

"At St. Albans, the 26th of June.

"Your brother,

"THOMAS, ASAPHENS."

Stephen Goldwell, on receiving this letter, in evident alarm lest he should be held responsible by the Queen as privy to the bishop's intended escape, went at once to his brother, John Goldwell, to consult with him how he ought

to act.   By his advice, and furnished with a letter from him
to the Lord Keeper Nicholas Bacon, Stephen started for
London the next day, taking with him two of the bishop's
servants and leaving the other two in sure custody, and on
his arrival laid the whole matter, together with the bishop's
letter, before the Lord Keeper.   On the same afternoon,
June 29, Bacon wrote an account of what had happened to
Secretary Cecil, enclosing the bishop's and John Goldwell's
letters, and adding that he had issued orders to those who
had charge of the ports to be "well ware what men they
suffer to pass ".[1]   But these precautions were too late.   The
Bishop of St. Asaph was already safe from his pursuers
beyond the sea.

On reaching the Continent, Bishop Goldwell set off at
once for Rome, but, falling ill on the way, was obliged to
return to Louvain, where he spent the next winter.   In
February, 1560, he visited Antwerp to provide necessaries
for his journey to Rome, for which place, as we learn from
Sir John Legh's letter to Queen Elizabeth,[2] he had already
started on March 8.[3]   The report at Antwerp was that he
would be made cardinal on his arrival.

But Bishop Goldwell's thoughts were fixed on something
very different from dignities.   After a short stay at Rome,
he pursued his journey to Naples, where he returned once
more to the Theatine house of St. Paul's, in which he had
been formerly professed, and resumed, though a bishop, the
manner of life and exercises of a simple religious.[4]   Still, his
heart never ceased to yearn towards his native country, and

---

[1] *P. R., Domestic, Elizabeth*, 1559, vol. iv., n. 71, with two in-
closures ; Silos, i. 301.

[2] *P. R., Foreign, Elizabeth*, 1560, 838.

[3] Dodd, vol. i., p. 513, adds that he travelled thither with Dr. Maurice
Clenock.

[4] Silos, i. 382.

he refused at different times rich bishoprics which were offered him in Italy, that he might be more free, as opportunities should arise, to labour for his countrymen.[1] Often in conversation he would give vent to his burning desire for the conversion of England to the Catholic faith, and he used to say to Father Tufo, when talking familiarly with him, that "he could never have brought himself to return to Italy and leave those unhappy souls, especially those of his own diocese, a prey to the heretics, like sheep to wolves, if he had entertained any hope of being able to help them, even by shedding his blood for them, as so many others of his countrymen had done.   But that when he saw every way of saving these souls from the devil's hands intercepted, he had determined to return to his Order."[2]

Bishop Goldwell had not been many months at St. Paul's when the General Chapter of the Order, which met at Rome, January, 1561, appointed him Superior of that house.[3] There were then living at St. Paul's, Blessed Paul of Arezzo, afterwards Cardinal and Archbishop of Naples, whom Goldwell succeeded in the office of Superior; Blessed John Marinoni, who was Superior after him; and St. Andrew of Avellino, who filled the post of Master of Novices.   To be chosen Superior with such men for subjects shows the extraordinary opinion which the General Chapter must have entertained of Goldwell's virtue and capacity.   "He exercised this office," Father Tufo writes, "in a paternal manner, with great charity and prudence, and to the entire satisfaction of his fathers and brothers."[4]

But Bishop Goldwell was not destined to remain long in

---

[1] Tufo, 46.

[2] Tufo, 45.   Father Tufo was received into the Theatine Order in 1568 (Silos, i. 493).

[3] Tufo, 45; Silos, i. 446.

[4] Tufo, 45.

this position; for in the month of March or April he was sent for to Rome by Pope Pius the Fourth, at the petition of the English Catholics, on some matter of grave importance to the interests of the Church in England, though what its nature was has not been left on record. When this affair was ended, he at once prepared to return to Naples; but was prevented from doing so by an order from the Pope to attend the Ecumenical Council, which had been summoned to resume its sittings at Trent on Easter Day, 1561. Before, however, he set out for Trent, he was appointed Master of the English Hospital at Rome, in succession to the last master, Sir Edward Carne.[1] On Sunday, June 15, the Bishop of St. Asaph arrived at Trent, and on Wednesday, the 25th of the same month, being the vigil of St. Vigilius, the Protector and Advocate of Trent, he officiated at Vespers in the presence of the Legates and all the Fathers of the Council.[2] " His arrival," Pallavicino says, " was regarded as a matter of honour and joy; but it was a cause of no less indignation to the Queen of England, as implying contempt and non-recognition of her as head of the Anglican Church."[3] Secretary Cecil was duly informed by his agent, Guido Giannetti, in a letter dated Venice, March 14, 1562, that besides bishops from Italy and other countries there was then at Trent, " I will not say from England, but rather from the Roman Court, Thomas Goldwell, called Bishop of St. Asaph".[4] Queen Elizabeth's annoyance at the presence of an English bishop at Trent is evident from a letter which she wrote to Mundt, her envoy in Germany, March 21, 1562. "As to the first matter," she says, "we think it may be

---

[1] Tierney's *Dodd*, ii. 169, note.
[2] Acta Conc. Trid. Massarello, i. 668. Edit. Theiner.
[3] Pallavicino, l. iv., ck. xi., n. 4.
[4] *P. R., Foreign, Elisabeth*, 1562, 935.

that one Goldwell, a very simple and fond man, having in our late sister's time been named to a small bishopric in Wales called St. Asaph, though never thereto admitted, flying out of the realm upon our sister's death, is gone to Rome as a renegade, and there using the name of a bishop, without order or title, is perhaps gone in the train of some cardinal to Trent, and so it is likely the speech hath arisen of a bishop of England being there."[1] The Queen would not have told such a palpable falsehood to her envoy, if Goldwell's presence at the Council had been a matter of indifference to her.

On the part of Bishop Goldwell, however, there was no reluctance to serve the Queen at Trent, if she had been willing to give him the opportunity of doing so. On May 4, 1562, he wrote as follows to Cecil:

"RIGHT HONOURABLE MR. SECRETARY,—I, seeing so many ambassadors and prelates sent hither from other princes, and none to be here in the name of our Queen, thought it my duty to advertise you how things go here; not that I seek thereby, God is my witness, any profit, but only to do Her Highness and my country service, if it is in my power. We here of late keep congregations almost every day, the holidays except. In the which hitherto we have entreated nothing but such as pertains to the reformation of the Church: so that though much matter be meetly well digested, yet there is nothing decreed; for that we do only in the sessions, of the which we have hitherto kept but two. The first was only the opening of the Council. In the second was granted that there should be safe-conduct given to all men that would require it to come hither of what faith soever they were. And in this session were admitted the ambassadors of the

---

[1] *P. R., Foreign, Elizabeth,* 948.

Emperor, and of the King of Portugal, and other. The third session shall be kept the 14th day of this month; in the which the ambassadors of Venice and other shall be admitted. But I think that the decrees shall be deferred eight days longer at the instance of Mgr. Lansac, who desireth, if he can, then to be present. The number and names of the prelates and ambassadors here you shall perceive by the bill inclosed. If you be disposed to write unto me, wrap your letters in a piece of paper and make the superscription, Al Mag^co. M. Bap^ta. Burdono, m^ro delle poste in Trento, and cause your letters to be directed to the master of the post in Antwerp, and they shall come as safely to my hand as if you sent a post for that purpose. So that without expenses, rumour, or knowledge of any man we may entreat anything that shall seem good to the Queen's Highness. And thus fare you well.

"At Trent, the 4th of May.

"Yours to my power,

"THOMAS, ASAPHENS."[1]

The letter was directed to Sir William Cecil. It bears an endorsement by Cecil's secretary: "4 May, 1562. Goldwell to my master, from Trent, with the names of those that were present at the Council." No answer seems to have been sent to this communication; probably the writer expected none.

We may now turn to the Bishop of St. Asaph's occupations at the Council.

The correction of the Roman Breviary and Missal had been long recognised by the Sovereign Pontiff as an urgent

---

[1] *P. R., Foreign, Elizabeth*, vol. xxxvii., p. 14.

necessity. But a work of such grave importance required much time and labour before it could be brought to completion. Already, in 1529, Pope Clement the Seventh had encouraged the Theatines to make this matter the object of their special study, and he even permitted them to put to a practical test the result of their labours, by giving them leave to recite the Divine Office and celebrate Mass, for the space of one year, with such changes and corrections as they might judge to be expedient. Paul the Fourth, who when a Theatine had paid great attention to the subject, on becoming Pope granted permission to adopt certain minor alterations, but he did not consider that the matter had been as yet discussed with sufficient completeness to admit of his imposing any of these corrections on the Universal Church. When the Council of Trent met anew under Pope Pius the Fourth, His Holiness referred the whole question to the Fathers of the Council; and he sent them at their request the annotations made by Paul the Fourth and preserved in the Theatine archives. The Council entrusted the work of revision to a Commission, of which the Bishop of St. Asaph, as a Theatine, was naturally appointed a member. There is a letter written by him in this capacity to the Theatine, Bernardino Scotti, Cardinal of Trani, who had been long occupied with the subject of liturgical reform. It is as follows :

" To the most Illustrious and Reverend Lord Cardinal of Trani.

"Your most illustrious lordship's very courteous letter of the 5th inst., and the information it contains, have given no small consolation to these most reverend prelates, who by commission of the Council have been charged with collect-

ing the abuses regarding the holy Mass, and who, knowing
that our Lord [the Pope] has intrusted to your most illustrious Lordship the care of correcting the Breviary, and aware
that the emendation of the Missal is connected with that of
the Breviary, hope that in the reform both of the one and
the other you will surpass our expectations, so that they will
not have to give themselves any more trouble about the
Missal, but will only have to make some canons concerning the abuses.   We are labouring hard here in preparing
things for the coming session.   Last week we buried
the most reverend Monsignor elect of Turli.   The other
prelates, by God's grace, are very well.   The most
illustrious legates, Monsignor Seripando and Monsignor
of Ermeland, salute your most illustrious Lordship.   The
most reverend Monsignor Cerenda and I most humbly
kiss your hand.

"At Trent, 24th August, 1562.

"Your most illustrious and reverend Lordship's most
humble servant,

> "DON THOMAS, Bishop of St. Asaph."[1]

The Council of Trent had not time to bring this important
work of reformation to a conclusion.   It was obliged in its
last session to refer the matter back again to the Sovereign
Pontiff, praying him to do by his own authority whatever
he might judge necessary.[2]   Accordingly, Pope Pius the
Fourth appointed a special Congregation at Rome, of
which the Bishop of St. Asaph was a member, to con-

---

[1] Tufo, *Supplim.*, 13; Silos, i. 94-98, 448. The Theatines, as
Regular Clerks, retained at first for a time the title of Don, which was
usually borne by the secular clergy.

[2] Conc. Trid. Sessio xxv. *De indice librorum et catechismo, breviario
et missali.*

tinue the work of revision.   St. Pius the Fifth added
to this Congregation other learned men, and was able
at length (July 9, 1568) to bring the labours of so
many years to a conclusion, by giving to the Universal
Church the Roman Breviary and Missal in their present
amended form.[1]

The Bishop of St. Asaph took an active part in another
question of importance which was at one time agitated in
the Council.   In June, 1563, there was much debate among
the Fathers as to whether it would not be advisable for the
Council to pronounce a solemn sentence of excommunication
against Queen Elizabeth of England.   For two days the
matter was greatly discussed, and at length it was resolved
to refer the decision of it to the Sovereign Pontiff.   Bishop
Goldwell did his best to induce the Council to excommunicate the Queen, and he also wrote to the Cardinal
of Trani, begging him to use all his influence with the
Pope for the same object.   Pius the Fourth was personally in favour of what had been proposed ; in de-
ference, however, to the express wishes of the Emperor
Maximilian the Second, he judged it more prudent to let
the matter drop.[2]

Bishop Goldwell remained at Trent until the end
of the Council.   During the whole of his stay there
he was treated, as he mentions in a letter to the
Cardinal of Trani, with singular kindness by the Cardinal Legate, Hosius, Bishop of Ermeland, who even
obliged him, in spite of his reluctance, to live with him
as his guest.[3]

On December 4, 1563, the Bishop of St. Asaph was

---

[1] Merati, tom. iii., p. 15.   Edit. Venet.
[2] Silos, i. 447.
[3] *Ibid.*

present at the concluding Session of the Council, and signed the decrees. He was now free to leave Trent. But a work of great difficulty and importance was awaiting him. St. Charles Borromeo was anxious to introduce without delay into his vast and long-neglected diocese of Milan the reforms of Trent. But it was impossible for him to do this in person, since he could not leave Rome, where, as cardinal-nephew to Pope Pius the Fourth, he had to bear no small portion of the solicitude of the Universal Church. He needed, therefore, some one of zeal and spirit like his own to represent him at Milan; and finding no one better suited for this work than the Bishop of St. Asaph, he appointed him his Vicar-General.[1]

Scarcely, however, had Bishop Goldwell entered upon his new office, when he was obliged to leave it, owing to the Pope having sent him a command to go into Flanders, with the view of crossing thence into England. There is an allusion to this in a letter from St. Charles to the Blessed Paul of Arezzo, at that time Superior of St. Paul's at Naples It is interesting as showing once more how greatly the Theatines valued Goldwell. The Blessed Paul, having been compelled by express precept of the Pope to accept the office of Ambassador from the city of Naples to Philip the Second of Spain on a matter of very great importance to the city, wrote to St. Charles to entreat that the Bishop of St. Asaph might be sent to take his place as Superior of St. Paul's during his absence. St. Charles replied (May 27, 1564): "As to the Bishop of St. Asaph, His Holiness has thought of sending him into Flanders, where he will be able to render some service to his Church, though not altogether as much as would be needful. Have patience, then, if he

---

[1] Silos, i. 469.

cannot go to Naples in your place."[1] On leaving Milan, Bishop Goldwell went to Rome to receive the Pope's instructions relative to his mission to England. While there he became acquainted with Richard Creagh, a young Irish priest, who had been sent thither by the Nuncio in Ireland as a fit person to fill one or other of the vacant sees of Armagh and Cashel. Creagh's own desire was to become a Theatine, but instead of obtaining permission to carry out this wish, for which he had petitioned the Pope, he received a command from His Holiness, under pain of excommunication, to accept the archbishopric of Armagh. He was accordingly consecrated bishop on Easter Day, 1564, and set out on his return to Ireland in the month of July following. Being taken prisoner and sent to England next year, he was examined on February 22, by Sir William Cecil, and in reply to the question, How many English or Irish he was acquainted with in Rome? he answered: "I saw and spake some time with . . . the Master of the English Hospital, called there the Bishop of St. Asse, and others dwelling in the said hospital". Again, in the report of another examination to which he was subjected in the Tower of London, March 17, it is recorded that "he saith that Goldwell and he dined and talked together divers times, and at one time this examinate heard that a Frenchman of the Pope's palace should report that Frenchmen had entered and invaded England, the which talk Goldwell doubted to be true, and thereupon they sent to the palace to inquire the certainty, and then after the Frenchman denied it, and so they found it untrue ".[2]

---

[1] Tufo, 93; *Supplimento*, 94.

[2] The original examinations are given in Shirley's *Letters and Papers illustrative of the History of the Church of Ireland*, 1851.

The news of Bishop Goldwell's intended journey to England seems to have preceded him. For it was in vain that he and those who accompanied him tried to cross from Flanders. They found that the English coasts were watched, that portraits of the bishop had been sent to the different seaports, and a reward offered for his arrest. Nothing remained but to abandon the attempt and return to Italy.

The Bishop of St. Asaph seems to have stopped for a short time at Milan on his way back to Rome, for on June 25, 1565, we find him addressing the following letter of congratulation to his friend the Archbishop of Armagh, on the occasion of the latter's miraculous escape from the Tower of London:

"MOST ILLUSTRIOUS AND REVEREND LORD,—As I grieved much on hearing that your Grace, after reaching Ireland, had been treacherously seized and taken to the Tower of London, so I rejoiced exceedingly when I heard that you had escaped thence, as it seems, miraculously, and had gone to Louvain, where you are the guest of your friend and mine, good Master Michael, who I doubt not rejoiced as much at your arrival as I was glad at your escape. And when your Lordship has leisure, you would do me a very great pleasure if you would kindly write to me the particulars of your deliverance. For when I first heard of it, the thing appeared to me so stupendous, that it seemed like St. Peter's vision when the angel led him forth from prison. But however it happened, praise be to God for having been pleased to take care of His servant; and to His divine protection I commend your Grace, and myself to your prayers. And as it is reported here that your Lordship was accompanied to Ireland by an English Father of the Society of Jesus, some of those who are here desire much to know what has become of him. There lives in this city a very worthy Irish Jesuit, named Maurice, who was exceedingly rejoiced at hearing of your escape. May it please your Lordship to salute in my name the reverend Master Michael, your host.

"At Milan, 20th June, 1565.

"Your most illustrious Lordship's unworthy brother and servant,

"THOMAS GOLDWELL, Bishop of St. Asaph."[1]

It was in the second half of 1565 that Bishop Goldwell returned to Rome, and took up his abode at the Theatine house of St. Sylvester on Monte Cavallo.[2] Here he lived a life of the strictest retirement, avoiding the courts, punctual in every religious observance, and only distinguished from his brethren by his episcopal insignia.[3] Outside the house he was occupied in works of charity, and he especially devoted himself to the service of the English exiles, who, after abandoning their kindred and possessions for the

---

[1] *Analecta Sacra, nova et mira de rebus Catholicorum in Hibernia,* pt. iii., p. 17. Coloniæ, 1617. By David Rooth, or Rothe, Bishop of Ossory. Archbishop Creagh was subsequently recaptured in Ireland and recommitted to the Tower of London, where he died of poison, October 16, 1585, after a captivity for the faith of eighteen years. See a sketch of his life in the *Rambler,* vol. xi., p. 366, 1853.

[2] The House and Church of St. Sylvester continued in the possession of the Theatine Order until 1801, when for a compensation of four or five thousand scudi, they were transferred by Pius the Seventh to Father Paccanari and his companions. In 1814, at the dissolution of Father Paccanari's society, they were given by Pius the Seventh to the Congregation of the Mission, or Vincentians (Moroni, *Dizionario,* vol. lxxiii., p. 131).

[3] Silos, i., 477; Castaldo, 241.

faith, flocked for aid and consolation to the common centre of Christendom. The mastership of the English Hospital, which he continued to hold until 1567, gave him greater opportunities of exercising his charity in their regard. An incidental proof of his kindness towards his countrymen may be found in a letter of Arthur Hall to Cecil, dated Venice, August 7, 1568, in which the writer says that at Rome "he found divers Englishmen. Mr. Goldwell, late Bishop of St. Asaph, used him courteously, but the rest being about fourteen or sixteen, the most being in a hospital there, reported him a heretic."[1]

On February 1, 1566, Bishop Goldwell consecrated the Theatine Church of St. Sylvester, attached to the convent of this name, in which he lived, and also the high altar of the same church. Seventeen years later, September 14, 1583, on the occasion of the enlargement of the sanctuary of the church, he consecrated anew the high altar, as an inscription in the case of relics testifies.[2] In the spring of 1566 the bishop presided over the General Chapter of his Order, which was held at Venice. He had been appointed to this office by the General Chapter of the preceding year. Under his presidency it was resolved to urge the Superiors of the different houses to tighten the reins of discipline, lest the great increase of the Order which had taken place should lead to laxity of religious observance.[3] On two other occasions, namely, in 1567 and in 1572, Bishop Goldwell presided over the General Chapter of the Theatines.[4]

[1] *P. R., Foreign, Eliz.*, 1568, 2404.
[2] Tufo, 51.
[3] Silos, i. 483.
[4] *Ibid.*, 485, 511.

But the Bishop of St. Asaph was not long suffered to live in retirement at St. Sylvester's. The office of Vicar, or representative of the Cardinal Archpriest, in the Lateran Church had lately fallen vacant, and St. Pius the Fifth, knowing no one more fit than Bishop Goldwell to watch over the conduct of the clergy and the due performance of divine worship in the Basilica, appointed him about the year 1567 to this responsible post. Goldwell fulfilled the duties of his charge to the complete satisfaction of St. Pius the Fifth and of the succeeding Pope, Gregory the Thirteenth, who confirmed him in the appointment. At length, however, perceiving that the canons of the Basilica bore with difficulty the strictness of his govern- ment, he resigned the office, and retired once more to St. Sylvester's, where he resumed the life of re- ligious observance and sacred study which was so dear to him.[1]

On August 1, 1568, we find him taking part as assistant bishop in the consecration of one of his religious brethren, the Blessed Paul of Arezzo, the Superior of St. Sylvester's, whom St. Pius the Fifth had compelled, under a precept of obedience and the pain of mortal sin, to accept the bishopric of Piacenza.[2]

In 1570, St. Pius the Fifth, before publishing to the whole Church the sentence of excommunication and deposition which he had pronounced against Queen Elizabeth, ordered a judicial process to be formed, in which evidence of her guilt was taken according to the strict forms of law before the delegated judge, Alexander Riario, general auditor of the Apostolic Camera. Twelve witnesses were interrogated regarding eighteen articles.

[1] Tufo, 45 ; Silos, i. 492.
[2] Tufo, 105 ; Silos, i. 491.

Bishop Goldwell was cited to give evidence, and his deposition, which was received on February 6, 1570, may still be seen, transcribed from the original process, in Laderkius' *Annals*.[1]

About the year 1572, Bishop Goldwell addressed the following letter to Laurence Vaux, warden of the Collegiate Church of Manchester in Queen Mary's reign, and an exile for religion under Elizabeth. Father Vaux, after joining the Regular Canons of St. Augustine at Louvain, in 1572, returned as a missionary to England in 1580, where he was soon afterwaids apprehended, ,and condemned to death for the faith in 1585. He died the same year, in prison, of hunger and privations.

"DEAREST FATHER LAURENCE,—I am very glad to hear that you have not only left dignities and possessions for the Catholic faith in England, but have also lately entered the Order of Regular Canons. This Order of yours has existed since the times of the Apostles, before St. Augustine, who reformed it. And it was held in such high esteem, that eight members of this Religious Order were successively elected Sovereign Pontiffs, one of whom was Adrian the Fourth, an Englishman, our countryman. For five years under Pius the Fifth I presided over the Church of St. John Lateran, which, being the mother and first church of the whole world, was formerly in your Religious Order. I found there many ancient monuments in praise of your Order, and many privileges granted to your Order."[2]

[1] Laderkius, *Annales*, 1570, xxv.

[2] Molanus, *Historiæ Lovaniensium*, lib. v., cap. 32. See a life of Vaux in the *Rambler*, N.S., vol. iii., p. 399, 1857. Pope Boniface the Eighth, in 1295, substituted Secular Canons for the Regular Canons of St. Augustine at St. John Lateran, which, from being the first in dignity of the five Roman Basilicas, is termed the mother and first church of Rome and of the whole world.

The Bishop of St. Asaph's merit was too well known in Rome to allow of his long remaining unemployed. In 1574, James, Cardinal Savelli, the Cardinal Vicar, a prelate most exact in sacred and ecclesiastical ceremonies, appointed him his suffragan, or, as it would now be termed, Vicegerent.[1] As the Cardinal Vicar's office is to represent and replace the Pope in those duties and functions which belong to him, not as Pope, but as Bishop of the diocese of Rome ; so it is the Vicegerent's place to act as a kind of vicar-general in *pontificalibus* to the Cardinal Vicar. Hence the office of Vicegerent involves great labour and responsibility. Bishop Goldwell, however, in spite of his advanced age, performed the duties of his new post with marvellous diligence and alacrity. Among the various functions which belonged to him as Vicegerent, he was very frequently called upon to administer the Sacrament of Holy Orders ; and since many persons from different nations came to Rome for ordination, priests ordained by him were to be found in all parts of Christendom. This gave occasion to Dr. Robert Turner, Rector of the University of Ingolstadt, when writing to him, to say : "God willed that England should reject thee as bishop, in order that the whole world might honour thee as bishop. It is a thing too evident to need mention that there are scattered abroad throughout Italy, England, France, and Spain, priests anointed by thy hand, and called into

---

[1] Tufo, 45 ; Silos, i. 527. Before 1558 the Pope's Vicar for the City of Rome was sometimes a cardinal and sometimes a bishop, but in 1558 Paul the Fourth united the office to the Sacred College of Cardinals. The office of Vicegerent began with the vicariate of Cardinal Savelli, who was made Vicar in 1560. Until 1717 the Vicegerent was named by the Cardinal Vicar, with the Pope's approval ; since then the appointment is made by the Pope himself (Moroni, *Dizion. Eccles.*, vol. xcix., pp. 64, 163).

being by the power that is in thee."[1] Bishop Goldwell, when exercising the functions of office, never seemed to be fatigued.   In performing ecclesiastical ceremonies it was his custom to say the prayers by heart, instead of from a book, and he went through everything very expeditiously.   The pontifical which he was in the habit of using was full of corrections and notes in his handwriting.   After his death the Fathers of the Congregation of Rites begged earnestly to have this book, and they made great use of it in the correction of the old Roman Pontifical, and many emendations were adopted in conformity with the bishop's sentiments. Subsequently this book passed into the hands of the Cardinal of Monte Reale, who gave it back to the Theatines. When Father Silos wrote his Chronicle of the Order, it was still preserved as a precious treasure in the sacristy of St. Sylvester's.[2]

, The English College of St. Thomas of Canterbury, at Rome, which was founded by Pope Gregory the Thirteenth in 1578, and endowed by him on 24th December, 1580, with the possessions of the English Hospital, must necessarily have been an object of great interest to the Bishop of St. Asaph.   The aged bishop testified on all occasions the

---

[1] Tufo, 48. Anthony Munday, "a rambling stage-player, and, according to his own account, an apostate Seminarist of the Roman College, in a scurrilous piece called *The English Romayne Life*" (Tierney's *Dodd*, vol. iii., p. 16, note), printed in 1582, and reprinted in the *Harleian Miscellany*, vol. vii., p. 150, alludes to Bishop Goldwell's office of Vicegerent, where he says that Goldwell, Bishop of St. Asaph, "maketh all the English priests in the College, and liveth there among the Theatines very pontifically". Mr. Brewer, who quotes this passage in a note to his edition of Fuller's *Church History*, vol. iv., p. 279, has, without remark, substituted Florentines for Theatines, not knowing apparently what to make of the latter word as it stands in the original.

[2] Silos, i. 527.

warmest affection for the students who were preparing there
for the toils and dangers of the English mission.   It was
also partly due to him that the College was placed under
the care of the Jesuit Fathers, for he was one of those
who petitioned the Holy Father to intrust it to that
Order.[1]

But Bishop Goldwell was not satisfied with labouring
in Rome for the salvation of his countrymen.   He was
ready, nay eager, though in his eightieth year, to encounter the perils to which the Catholic missioner in
England was then exposed.   And an occasion arose
at this time in which he gave proof of his readiness.
In 1580 there were only two bishops surviving of the
ancient English hierarchy: Goldwell, Bishop of St. Asaph,
who lived at Rome, and Watson, Bishop of Lincoln,
who had been long confined in various prisons.   The
want of a bishop in England was therefore keenly felt
by the English Catholics.   There was no one in the
country to administer the Sacrament of Confirmation,
and there was no ecclesiastical superior to give unity and
direction to the affairs of the mission.   For these reasons
the English Catholics petitioned the Pope to send them a
bishop.   His Holiness, however, after due consultation
thought it unadvisable to comply with their request, for
he feared to expose to certain and immediate danger
one whose dignity as a bishop would mark him out
as an object of special persecution to the enemies of
the faith.   When the Bishop of St. Asaph heard of this,
he went at once to the Pope, and earnestly besought
His Holiness' leave and blessing to undertake this
dangerous mission ; and with great difficulty, on account
of his advanced age and the high esteem in which he

[1] Silos, i. 598.

was held, at last obtained, or rather wrung, from the
Pope the permission which he craved.[1] A number of
priests were at that time about to leave Rome for
England ; some of them were old or Marian priests, as
they were termed, others had been educated and ordained
in the newly-founded seminaries on the Continent; and,
last not least, were Fathers Campion and Persons of the
Society of Jesus, which had just then decided to send its
members on the English mission. It was arranged that
Bishop Goldwell should be the leader of this little company to the scene, as he fondly hoped, of his future
labours. An intercepted letter, dated Rome, 18th April,
1580, from Robert Owen to Dr. Humphry Ely, at
Rheims, tells us " how that my lord of St. Asaph and
Mr. Dr. Morton are gone hence, some say to Venice,
some to Flanders, and so further ; which, if it be true,
you shall know sooner than we here. God send them
well to do whithersoever they go, and specially if they
be gone to the harvest. The sale that Mr. Dr. Morton
made of all his things, maketh many think *quod non
habet animam revertendi.*"[2] The letter goes on to say that
the rest of the company, " with good Father Campion," had
started from Rome on foot that very day. Their first des-
tination was Rheims, to which the College for English priests
which Dr., afterwards Cardinal, Allen had founded at Douay
had been temporarily transferred. The story of their proceedings will best be told in the following entries extracted
from the *Douay Diary*, and made day by day as the events

[1] Bridgewater's *Concertatio*, pt. i., p. 69, verso ; Simpson's *Campion*, p. 105 ; Tufo, *Suppl.*, 94 ; Silos, i. 597.

[2] *P. R., Domestic, Elizabeth*, vol. cxxxvii., n. 38. " Dr. N. Morton
was a prebendary of York in Queen Mary's reign, who leaving England for conscience' sake in the beginning of Queen Elizabeth, resided
for the most part in Rome " (Dodd, ii. 114).

occurred.[1] "May 24, there came to us from Rome the Reverend Father in Christ, the Bishop of St. Asaph, and Doctor Morton, with only one servant attending them ; who did not disdain to go to table with us in our common refectory, but desired to give us daily the consolation of their presence, until the Reverend Father Bishop was prevented by sickness from coming to the refectory." It may be observed by the way that Father Campion, Persons, and the rest reached the College on 31st May, and left for England 7th June. "On the same day [June 11], immediately after Vespers in the President's [Dr. Allen] room, the Lord Bishop of St. Asaph fortified with the Sacrament of Confirmation in the constant profession of the Christian warfare, Hubert, gentleman, and Hauseworth, also gentleman, Johnson, Sherson, Jodocadoe, wife of our steward, and her little son, Vavasor, Sherwold, William Powell, Philippa Coffin." "On 14th June there started for Paris the Lord Bishop of St. Asaph, with Dr. Morton, and Edward, the Bishop's servant. They had for conductor on their journey Henry Brown, the President's servant." "On the same day [June 19] there returned from Paris the Lord Bishop of St. Asaph, Dr. Morton, and the Bishop's servant Edward." "On July 27 there came from Paris Mr. Greene . . . whose arrival is said to have displeased the Governor [of Rheims], because of the plague raging at Paris." "On July 28 were confirmed in the President's room Mr. Leie, Mr. Daniel, the boy Eydon, and two of our steward's children." "On August 7 there were confirmed in St. Stephen's Church, by the Lord Bishop of St. Asaph, Mr. Grimston, Mr. Catheriacke, Mr.

---

[1] The *Douay Diary* is written in Latin. The volume of it from which the Rev. John Morris, S.J., kindly made the above quoted extracts, is in the Archivium of the Archbishop of Westminster. [It was afterwards edited by Father Knox.—T. E. B.]

Coniers, Mr. Clibborne, Pibushe." "On August 8 departed the Reverend Father in Christ, the Lord Bishop of St. Asaph, and Dr. Morton, with Edward the Bishop's servant."

Thus ended, according to the narrative of the *Douay Diary*, Bishop Goldwell's attempt to return to England. As might have been expected considering his great age, the fatigues of the journey had broken down his health, and a continual cough from which he suffered made it clear that he had no longer sufficient strength for a missionary life in England. Besides this, his intention of returning to England had become known there, and special measures had been taken to prevent his entering the country or to seize him on his first arrival. Prudence, therefore, obliged him to make the sacrifice of his cherished desires, and while his companions, as we have seen, proceeded on their journey to England, he wrote on 13th July as follows to the Pope, placing himself at His Holiness' disposition.

"MOST BLESSED FATHER,—If I could have crossed into England before my coming had been known there, as I had hoped to do, I think that my going thither would have been a consolation to the Catholics and a satisfaction to your Holiness, whereas now I fear the contrary, since there are so many spies in this kingdom, and my long stay here has made my going to England so well known there, that I doubt now it will be difficult for me to enter the kingdom without some danger. Nevertheless, if your Holiness is of a different opinion, I will make the attempt, even though it should cost me my life. Still it would be impossible for me alone to supply the needs of all those Catholics, who are many thousand more than I had thought, and in almost every part of the kingdom. The most, I think, I possibly could do would be to supply for the City of London and some miles round it. And therefore in my ignorance I cannot but wonder that, when God has given your Holiness the grace to plant, as it were, anew and to maintain the Catholic faith in that kingdom, you make such great difficulty about creating there three or four titular bishops to preserve and propagate it, although this might be done at as little cost as your Holiness pleases; since God has so inclined the minds of those priests to spend their lives in helping to bring back that kingdom to the Catholic faith, that, if they were made bishops, they would be content to live as poorly as they do now, just as the bishops of the primitive Church did. May God inspire your Holiness to do whatever shall be most for his honour, and prosper you many years. I humbly kiss your feet.

"From Rheims, 13th July, 1580.

"Your Holiness' most devoted servant,

"THE BISHOP OF ST. ASAPH."[1]

On the same day Bishop Goldwell wrote the following letter to the Cardinal of Como[2] on behalf of one of the English exiles who had been deprived of his pension from the King of Spain!

"Most illustrious and reverend Lord, my most respected

---

[1] Theiner, *Annales*, vol. iii., p. 700.

[2] Tolomeo Galli, born in 1525, was raised to the Cardinalate by Pius the Fourth in 1565. He was called the Cardinal of Como from the city to which his family belonged. Among other important offices he held that of Secretary of State to Gregory the Thirteenth. He died Bishop of Ostia and Dean of the Sacred College, in 1607.

master,—Owing to the King of Spain having withdrawn all the pensions which His Majesty has hitherto given in Flanders, there are many persons there suffering great poverty, among whom the most illustrious Charles Neville, Earl of Westmoreland,[1] has been forced on this account to have recourse to His Majesty. Although he is not known to your most illustrious Lordship, he kisses your hand as the Protector of our nation. And seeing that he is not only a Catholic, but is also ruined in his estate and property, and banished from his country for the Catholic faith, he beseeches your most illustrious Lordship to be pleased to be his protector, and to obtain from our Lord [the Pope] that His Holiness will deign to write on his behalf to His Catholic Majesty: which if your most illustrious Lordship will do, it will oblige him to be always at your command. In truth, most illustrious Lord, he is worthy to obtain this favour from His Holiness through your most illustrious Lordship's means because, besides being a Catholic and suffering for the faith, he belongs to a most illustrious house, of great power and following, and he is connected in blood with almost all the old nobility of England, and especially with the most illustrious Cardinal Pole, of good memory; and, more than this, he has served with honour His Catholic Majesty in these his wars in Flanders, as is well known to the Duke of Alva and the Prince of Parma; and since Mr. Maurice

---

[1] " Charles Nevil, Earl of Westmoreland, was a zealous maintainer of the old religion and ready to support its interest upon any occasion. On the 15th of November, 1569, he joined in an insurrection with Thomas Piercy, Earl of Northumberland, whose forces being routed and dispersed, he fled into Scotland. From thence he transported himself into Flanders, where he obtained a pension and a regiment under the King of Spain " (Dodd, vol. ii., p. 38).

[Clenock [1]] can fully inform your most illustrious Lordship concerning him, I will say no more. As to myself, I know not what to write to your most illustrious Lordship. For a month past, through God's grace, I have been free from the fever, and yet I am not well either in body or mind. I am waiting for His Holiness' decision; and I pray your Lordship to do me the favour of letting me receive it as soon as possible. I humbly kiss your hand.

"From Rheims, July 13, 1580.

"Your most illustrious Lordship's servant,

"THE BISHOP OF ASAPH."[2]

The Pope's decision, which the bishop was so anxiously expecting, soon arrived; and in accordance with it on 8th August he set out,[3] as we have seen, with a heavy heart for Rome, after first bidding farewell to Ralph Sherwin, who

[1] Dr. Maurice Clenock, a native of Wales, was Professor of Canon Law (B.C.L., 1548) and Doctor of Divinity at Oxford. In Queen Mary's reign he was a prebendary of York, almoner and secretary to Cardinal Pole, and Chancellor of the Prerogative Court of Canterbury. Shortly before the Queen's death, in 1558, he was nominated to the bishopric of Bangor, but never consecrated. He left England at Queen Elizabeth's accession, and went to Rome, where he was made Master of the English Hospital in 1578. At the foundation of the English College he was appointed by Gregory the Thirteenth its first Superior; but he only held the office for a short time, until the College was transferred to the care of the Jesuits (Dodd, vol. i., p. 513).

[2] Theiner, *Annales*, vol. iii., p. 701. Bishop Goldwell was himself in receipt of a pension from the King of Spain, if we may trust a list of pensioners in the Public Record Office. *P. R., Domestic, Elizabeth*, vol. cxlvi., n. 18.

[3] Dodd, vol. i., p. 507.

had stayed behind to wait on him when ill at Rheims, and who was soon afterwards to die a martyr's death in London.[1]

The Bishop of St. Asaph on reaching Rome went back again to St. Sylvester's, and resumed once more his functions of Vicegerent. We will group together here the few remaining incidents of his life. If some of them seem hardly worth recording, they will at least help us to picture him to ourselves in his everyday occupations.[2] "On the 7th [March, 1579]," Mr. Haddock writes from Rome, "there was a Solemn Mass sung at the Minerva by my Lord of St. Asaph's, before thirty-three Cardinals, upon St. Thomas' Day."[3] In 1583, on the Feast of the Purification, Bishop Goldwell tonsured St. Camillus of Lellis, and on the following Sunday, being the feast of St. Matthias, gave him Minor Orders in the sacristy of St. Sylvester's. In 1584 he conferred upon the same saint the subdiaconate on an ember day in Lent, the diaconate on *Sitientes* Saturday, and the priesthood at Pentecost.[4] In 1584 he consecrated several altars in the Basilica of St. Cæcilia across the Tiber.[5] He led Matthew Cudner, a young English confessor for the faith, to enter the

---

[1] *Concertatio*, pt. i., p. 70.

[2] Cole, in a note to Wood's *Athenæ*, Edit. Bliss., says that in 1569 Goldwell was executor to Sir Robert Peckham, who died at Rome. Laderkius mentions that he had seen Bishop Goldwell's name on the tomb of Robert Peckham in St. Cecilia's Church at Rome (*Annales*, vol. iii., p. 212). Peckham was a member of the Privy Council in Queen Mary's reign, and died in exile on account of the faith (Dodd, vol. ii., p. 56).

[3] Richard Haddock's letter to Dr. Allen from Rome, 9th March, 1579; Tierney's *Dodd*, vol. ii., p. ccclix.

[4] *Vita di S. Camillo*, p. 32. Roma, 1837.

[5] Laderkius, *Annales*, vol. iii., p. 212.

Theatine Order, in which he lived and died holily.[1] He was consulted by Dr. Allen, afterwards cardinal, upon everything of moment, as appears from a letter of the bishop to Allen, which Dodd has printed, " in which he gives Allen his opinion concerning the Apology he was publishing for the seminaries, and other writings of that doctor ".   The letter is as follows :

" *To our very loving and assured friend Dr. Allen, at Rheims.*

" RIGHT REVEREND MR. PRESIDENT,—By the last post, save this, I received your letters common to Father Rector and me ; and we both together did what we could with my Lord Cardinal Como.   But of him we could get no great hope.   Me thinketh that our cause doth scant penetrate into these men.   We also delivered your letters, and a copy of the proclamation, to my Lord Cardinal Sti. Sixti.   But with him, according to your counsel, we intreated your need but superficially, who gave us gentle audience and good words. Thus, because the Pope was at his villa, it seemed good to Father Rector to send a copy of your common letter to the Master of the Chamber, who did both present it and read it to His Holiness ; and of this and of what has followed, I doubt not but Father Rector has certified you at length.   Upon the 14th of this month, after Evensong, I received your letters of the 14th of the last month ; but not the part of your apology, because the Father gave it to be translated as soon as he had read your letter.   Wherefore, the next day, as soon as I had said Mass, I went to the College and in-formed Father Rector that out of England you had been prayed to use no words and terms towards the Queen but honourable : for fear lest it should turn to the poor Catholics

---

1 Castaldo, 244 ; Silos, i. 612.

more trouble at home. I ordered also that in the title
should be written: 'Authore Gulielmo Alano, Præsidente
Collegii Rhemensis'; and that the colleges should be called
the Pope's Colleges, with such other things which yourself
ordained in your letters. If you have written any other
letters to me, I have not had them; nor Mr. Baily's letter
of the receipt and distribution of His Holiness' alms ever
came to my hands. Insomuch that at this present, if Mr.
Martin had not written to me a courteous letter of the receipt
of his part, I had not to this hour known that Mr. Baily had
received it. At which I have sometimes so much marvelled
that I was half determined never to entangle myself any
more in that matter. For it is no small danger for me to
stand here bound to be countable for it. Wherefore, I pray
you, desire Mr. Baily to think by what way he sent me that
letter; that I may either have it, or that he will be content
to take the pains to write me another of that matter for my
discharge. I pray you commend me to Mr. Martin, and
thank him for his long letter. It doth hurt me to write
much, and therefore I trust he will be content that I write
not particularly to him. You know that I am old and not
very lusty. But this notwithstanding, I will advertise you of
such things in your book, *De Eucharistia*, which do not
please all men, although peradventure you will be able to
defend them. As in the third chapter of the first book,
where you do intreat the difference between this sacrament
and the others, you say in this very well: 'Quod forma
hujus sacramenti applicatur ad materiam, et non dicitur
super recipientem, ut in cæteris, ubi dicitur applicando
materiam ad personam: Ego te abluo,' &c., more had
bettered by it, if you, using the common words of the
Church, had said: 'Ego te baptizo'. In the eleventh
chapter, where you write, 'De vino congelato,' you have
almost all here against you, because they follow the common

Doctors : Sylvester, verbo *Eucharistia*, viz., prope finem: 'Si vinum in calice congeletur, sacerdos illud ante consecrationem resolvat ; ut habeat rationem actualem potus. Si tamen non resolvat, adhuc conficit, quia vinum congelatum a non congelato specie non differt, sed solum accidentali qualitate.' Io de Lapide, cap. vii., art. 4, in fine : 'Sacerdos curam adhibere debet ut vinum congelatum resolvatur, vel per applicationem prunarum, vel alio modo, ut recipiat rationem actualem potus. Si tamen non resolveretur, nihilominus posset confici, quia per congelationem natura vini non est corrupta.' Armilla, verbo *Missa*, n. 24: 'Si vinum congeletur in calice ante consecrationem, debet liquefieri, si potest, et sic consecrari, ut sit actu potabile. Si autem congelatum consecretur, erit consecratum, quia non differt ab alio non congelato specie, sed tantum qualitate.' Io de Lapide, cap. vii., art. 5, n. 4 : 'Quid agendum, si cum sumi debet sanguis, species vini sit congelata? Solutio. Fiat resolutio.' The whole leaf of the thirty-first chapter does almost wholly displease them. When in the thirty-first chapter you say : 'Quod Papa solemniter celebrante, cardinales etiam assistentes et ministri communicent'. This is not true. But if you would peradventure have said : 'Quod cardinalis diaconus et subdiaconus communicent de eadem hostia quam de calice ; et sic de utraque specie,' you should have said truth. Thus fare you well, as I should myself. .

"At Rome, the 17th of April, 1581.

"Yours,

"THOMAS, ASAPHENS."[1]

Lastly, as the Sovereign Pontiffs and the Council of Trent

---

[1] Dodd, vol. i., p. 507 ; vol. ii., p. 224.

had at an earlier period employed Bishop Goldwell in the correction of the Roman Breviary and Missal, so towards the close of his life, in 1582, he was appointed by Gregory the Thirteenth a member of the Congregation for the revision of the Roman Martyrology.[1]

The Bishop of St. Asaph's life was now drawing very near its close. The death of Watson, Bishop of Lincoln, in Wisbeach Castle on 27th September, 1584, had left him the sole survivor of the English hierarchy. But he was not long to outlive his brethren. The following year, 3rd April, 1585,[2] he died at St. Sylvester's, fortified with the last Sacraments, in his eighty-fifth year. On his deathbed he predicted that the Sovereign Pontiff, Gregory the Thirteenth, would die within a few days; and though the Pope was at that time well enough to be able to hold a Consistory on the following Monday, two days later, namely, on Wednesday, which was the seventh day after Godwell's death, he expired.[3] The Bishop of St. Asaph was buried in the cemetery of St. Sylvester's and his funeral was attended by the principal English gentlemen at Rome, who bewailed in him one who had been to them a refuge in their exile, and whom they loved and venerated as a father. He was also tenderly lamented by his fathers and brothers in religion, to whom he had endeared himself by many years of loving intimacy. And as the purity and sincerity of his heart, says Father Tufo, shone in his face, so did he ever bear himself with a gay and cheerful demeanour towards all men, but especially towards

---

[1] Tufo, 47; Silos, i. 638.

[2] Tufo, 47; Castaldo, 243; Silos, i. 637. Wood, whom other English writers follow, gives the date incorrectly. Strype is correct as to the year. He says: "Anno 1559. Goldwell . . . went privately away beyond the sea. . . . [He] lived afterwards at Rome twenty-six years, and there died" (*Annals*, vol. i., pt. i., p. 215).

[3] Silos, i. 639.

his brothers in religion, with whom he was very courteous and affable in his manners. He was very strict in following all the regular observances of the community, and until his last illness, though he had been a bishop thirty years, he always went to the common refectory, nor would he allow anything additional to be set before him. It was with great difficulty that the fathers prevailed upon him to add to his morning meal two eggs, which they thought his advanced age rendered absolutely indispensable. In like manner he was most regular in attending the choir, and, up to the end of his life, he used to rise every night with the fathers to say Matins. He had a particular devotion to the Most Holy Sacrament, and made a practice of saying the first Mass at St. Sylvester's, every morning, winter and summer.[1] He would never accept any privilege or dispensation from the rule on account of his episcopal dignity; and he was not only most exact himself in regular observance, but, when Superior, he insisted on no less exactness in others, alleging as a reason that the religious state is an hospital for souls not bodies, and that our chief solicitude should be about the former, not the latter. He gave a remarkable proof of this in the illness of which he died; for though repeatedly pressed to do so, he never would show the slightest wish for anything but what the infirmarian had got ready for him, and he would say to the brother, "Prepare what God inspires you with, and I will eat as much of it as I am able".[2] Cardinal Baronius, in his notes on the Roman Martyrology, published in 1586, has left the following testimony to the high esteem in which he held Bishop Goldwell. After referring to the accounts older writers have given of the miracles worked at St. Winifred's Well, he adds: "But I have heard greater things than these from a most faithful eyewitness, the most

---

[1] Tufo, 47. [2] Castaldo, 243.

reverend Thomas, Bishop of St. Asaph, suffragan of the Roman Pontiff for the performance of episcopal functions, a man conspicuous for holiness of life, the confession of the faith, and learning, who lately died at Rome, to the sorrow of all good persons." [1] Nicholas Sanders, or rather Sanders' continuator, Rishton, when reckoning up the bishops who had been deprived of their sees by Queen Elizabeth at the beginning of her reign, says : " Thomas Goldwell, Bishop of St. Asaph, lived for twenty-six years full of piety and days at Rome, and not long since died most happily and holily in the Lord ".[2] At the beginning of the last century there was a portrait of Goldwell still existing in the Theatine Convent at Ravénna. It bore this inscription : " R.D. Thomas Gould-wellus, Ep. Asaph. Trident. Concilio contra hæreticos et in Anglia contra Elizabeth Fidei confessor conspicuus ".[3] There is another portrait of him in the English College at Rome.

Thus lived and died Thomas Goldwell, the last Bishop of St. Asaph, in whom ended that long line of bishops who for nearly one thousand years, from St. Augustine downwards, had ruled and fed Christ's flock in England. This ancient hierarchy has passed away with that England which knew but one Christian faith and one spiritual Sovereign. Since then, a new hierarchy has taken its place, the creation of the same hand which called its predecessor into being. Pius the

---

[1] Baronius, *Martyrologium Romanum*, November 3. St. Philip Neri must have been well acquainted with Bishop Goldwell, since, according to a Theatine writer, the Saint " used often to come to our house of St. Sylvester " (*Vita di Orsola Benicasa*, p. 75. By Bagatta, Clerico Regolare. Venetia, 1671).

[2] Sanders, *De Schismate Angl.*, lib. iii. Sanders mentions that he was himself ordained priest by Bishop Goldwell (*De visib. Monarch.*, p. 662).

[3] Addison's *Travels through Italy and Switzerland in the years* 1701, 1702, 1703. Mavor's Collection, vol. xiv., p. 55.

Ninth has done in our day what St. Gregory the Great did in his. But the memory of the saints, martyrs, and saintly men who once filled those elder sees has not passed away. Their deeds and sufferings are still as household words among us. And therefore it is pleasant to reflect that, when England's ancient hierarchy came to an end, its last survivor was one whose life had proved him not unworthy of such ancestry.

THE END.

SELECTION

BURNS AND OATES' CATALOGUE
OF PUBLICATIONS.

—➤➤➤✦ ✦◀◀◀—

ALLIES, T. W. (K.C.S.G.)

See of St. Peter.	. . . . . .	£0	4	6
Formation of Christendom. Vols. I., II., III. . each		0	12	0
Church and State as seen in the Formation of Christendom, 8vo, pp. 472, cloth		0	14	0
The Throne of the Fisherman, built by the Carpenter's Son, the Root, the Bond, and the Crown of Christendom. Demy 8vo		0	10	0

"It would be quite superfluous at this hour of the day to recommend Mr. Allies' writings to English Catholics. Those of our readers who remember the article on his writings in the *Katholik*, know that he is esteemed in Germany as one of our foremost writers."—*Dublin Review.*

ALLIES, MARY.

Leaves from St. John Chrysostom, With introduction by T. W. Allies, K.C.S.G. Crown 8vo, cloth .	0	6	0

" Miss Allies 'Leaves' are delightful reading; the English is remarkably pure and graceful; page after page reads as if it were original. No commentator, Catholic or Protestant, has ever surpassed St. John Chrysostom in the knowledge of Holy Scripture, and his learning was of a kind which is of service now as it was at the time when the inhabitants of a great city hung on his words."—*Tablet.*

ALLNATT, O. F. B.

Cathedra Petri. Third and Enlarged Edition. Paper.	0	5	0

"Invaluable to the controversialist and the theologian, and most useful for educated men inquiring after truth or anxious to know the positive testimony of Christian antiquity in favour of Papal claims."—*Month.*

Which is the True Church? New Edition . .	0	1	4
The Church and the Sects	0	1	0

ANNUS SANCTUS:

Hymns of the Church for the Ecclesiastical Year. Translated from the Sacred Offices by various Authors, with Modern, Original, and other Hymns, and an Appendix of Earlier Versions. Selected and Arranged by ORBY SHIPLEY, M.A.

Popular edition, in two parts . each	0	1	0
In stiff boards	0	3	6
Plain Cloth, lettered . .	0	5	0
Edition de luxe . . .	0	10	6

ANSWERS TO ATHEISTS: OR NOTES ON

Ingersoll. By the Rev. A Lambert, (over 100,000 copies
sold in America). Ninth edition. Paper. . . . £0 0 6
    Cloth 0 1 0

B. N.

The Jesuits: their Foundation and History. 2 vols.
crown 8vo, cloth, red edges 0 15 0
"The book is just what it professes to be—*a popular history*,
drawn from well-known sources," &c.—*Month.*

BACQUEZ, L'ABBE.

The "Divine Office": From the French of l'Abbé
Bacquez, of the Seminary of St. Sulpice, Paris. Edi-
ted by the Rev. Father Taunton, of the Congregation
of the Oblates of St. Charles. Cloth . . . 0 6 0
"The translation of this most edifying work from the walls of St.
Sulpice, the source of so much sacerdotal perfection, comes to us most
opportunely, and we heartily commend it to the use of the clergy and
of the faithful." THE CARDINAL·ARCHBISHOP OF WESTMINSTER.
"A very complete manual, learned, wholesome, and devout."—
Saturday Review.

BORROMEO, LIFE OF ST. CHARLES.

From the Italian of Peter Guissano. 2 vols. . . 0 15 0
"A standard work, which has stood the test of succeeding ages; it
is certainly the finest work on St. Charles in an English dress."—
Tablet.

BOWDEN, REV. H. S. (of the Oratory) Edited by

Dante's Divina Commedia: Its scope and value.
From the German of FRANCIS HETTINGER, D.D.
With an engraving of Dante. Crown 8vo . . . 0 10 6

"All that Venturi attempted to do has been now approached with
far greater power and learning by Dr. Hettinger, who, as the author
of the 'Apologie des Christenthums,' and as a great Catholic theologian, is eminently well qualified for the task he has undertaken."—
The Saturday Review.

BRIDGETT, REV. T. E. (C.SS.R.).

Discipline of Drink 0 3 6
"The historical information with which the book abounds gives
evidence of deep research and patient study, and imparts a permanent interest to the volume, which will elevate it to a position
of authority and importance enjoyed by few of its compeers."—*The
Arrow.*

Our Lady's Dowry ; how England Won and Lost that
Title. Popular Edition 0 5 0
"This book is the ablest vindication of Catholic devotion to Our
Lady, drawn from tradition, that we know of in the English lan-
guage."—*Tablet.*
Ritual of the New Testament. An essay on the prin-
ciples and origin of Catholic Ritual in reference to
the New Testament. Third edition . . . 0 5 0
The Life of the Blessed John Fisher. With a repro-
duction of the famous portrait of Blessed JOHN
FISHER by HOLBEIN, and other Illustrations. Cloth 0 7 6

BRIDGETT, REV. T. E. (C.SS.R.), Edited by.

Souls Departed. By CARDINAL ALLEN. First published in 1565, now edited in modern spelling by the
Rev. T. E. Bridgett £0 6 0

CASWALL, FATHER.

Catholic Latin Instructor in the Principal Church
Offices and Devotions, for the Use of Choirs, Con-
vents, and Mission Schools, and for Self-Teaching.
1 vol., complete 0 3 6
Or Part I., containing Benediction, Mass, Serving at
Mass, and various Latin Prayers in ordinary use . 0 1 6
May Pageant : A Tale of Tintern. (A Poem) Second
edition 0 2 0
Poems 0 5 0
Lyra Catholica, containing all the Breviary and Missal
Hymns, with others from various sources. 32mo,
cloth, red edges 0 2 6

CATHOLIC BELIEF: OR, A SHORT AND

Simple Exposition of Catholic Doctrine. By the
Very Rev. Joseph Faà di Bruno, D.D. Seventh
edition . . . . . Price 6d.; post free, 0 0 8½
Cloth, lettered, ... 0 0 10
Also an edition on better paper and bound in cloth, with
gilt lettering and steel frontispiece 0 2 0

CHALLONER, BISHOP.

Meditations for every day in the year. New edition.
Revised and edited by the Right Rev. John Virtue,
D.D., Bishop of Portsmouth. 8vo. 5th edition . 0 3 0
And in other bindings.

COLERIDGE, REV. H. J. (S.J.)

(See Quarterly Series.)

DEHARBE, FATHER JOSEPH, (S.J.)

A History of Religion, or the Evidences of the
Divinity of the Christian Religion, as furnished by
its History from the Creation of the World to
our own Times. Designed as a Help to Catechetical Instruction in Schools and Churches.
Pp. 628. . . . . net 0 8 6

DEVAS, C. S.

Studies of Family Life : a contribution to Social
Science. Crown 8vo 0 5 0

"We recommend these pages and the remarkable evidence brought
together in them to the careful attention of all who are interested in
the well-being of our common humanity."—*Guardian.*
" Both thoughtful and stimulating."—*Saturday Review.*

DRANE, AUGUSTA THEODOSIA.

History of St. Catherine of Siena and her Companions.
A new edition in two vols. £0 12 6

It has been reserved for the author of the present work to give us
a complete biography of St. Catherine. . . . Perhaps the greatest
success of the writer is the way in which she has contrived to make
the Saint herself live in the pages of the book."—*Tablet.*

ENGLISH CATHOLIC NON-JURORS OF 1715.

Being a Summary of the Register of their Estates, with
Genealogical and other Notes, and an Appendix of
Unpublished Documents in the Public Record Office.
Edited by the late Very Rev. E. E. Estcourt, M.A.,
F.S.A., Canon of St. Chad's, Birmingham, and
John Orlebar Payne, M.A. 1 vol., demy 8vo. . 1 1 0

"This handsomely printed volume lies before us. Every student
of the history of our nation, or of families which compose it, cannot
but be grateful for a catalogue such as we have here."—*Dublin
Review.*
"Most carefully and creditably brought out. . . . From first to last
full of social interest, and it contains biographical details for which
we may search in vain elsewhere."—*Antiquarian Magazine.*

EYRE, MOST REV. CHARLES, (Abp. of Glasgow).

The History of St. Cuthbert : or, An Account of his
Life, Decease, and Miracles. Third edition. Illustrated with maps, charts, &c., and handsomely
bound in cloth. Royal 8vo 0 14 0

"A handsome, well appointed volume, in every way worthy of its
illustrious subject. . . . The chief impression of the whole is the
picture of a great and good man drawn by a sympathetic hand."—
Spectator.

FABER, REV. FREDERICK WILLIAM, (D.D.)

All for Jesus	0	5	0
Bethlehem	0	7	0
Blessed Sacrament	0	7	6
Creator and Creature	0	6	0
Ethel's Book of the Angels.	0	5	0
Foot of the Cross	0	6	0
Growth in Holiness	0	6	0
Hymns	0	6	0
Notes on Doctrinal and Spiritual Subjects, 2 vols. each	0	5	0
Poems	0	5	0
Precious Blood	0	5	0
Sir Lancelot	0	5	0
Spiritual Conferences	0	6	0
Life and Letters of Frederick William Faber, D.D., Priest of the Oratory of St. Philip Neri. By John Edward Bowden of the same Congregation . .	0	6	0

FOLEY, REV. HENRY (S.J.)

Records of the English Province of the Society of
Jesus. Vol. I., Series I. . . . . net £1 6 0
Vol. II., Series II., III., IV. . . . net 1 6 0
Vol. III., Series V., VI., VII., VIII. . . net 1 10 0
Vol. IV. Series IX., X., XI. . . . net 1 6 0
Vol. V., Series XII. with nine Photographs of
Martyrs. . . . . net 1 10 0
Vol. VI., Diary and Pilgrim-Book of the English Col-
lege, Rome. The Diary from 1579 to 1773, with
Biographical and Historical Notes. The Pilgrim-
Book of the Ancient English Hospice attached to
the College from 1580 to 1656, with Historical
Notes . . . . net 1 6 0
Vol. VII. Part the First : General Statistics of the Pro-
vince ; and Collectanea, giving Biographical Notices
of its Members and of many Irish and Scotch Jesuits.
With 20 Photographs . . . . . net 1 6 0
Vol. VII. Part the Second : Collectanea, Completed ;
With Appendices. Catalogues of Assumed and Real
Names : Annual Letters ; Biographies and Miscel-
lanea. . . . . net 1 6 0

"As a biographical dictionary of English Jesuits, it deserves a
place in every well-selected library, and, as a collection of marvellous occurrences, persecutions, martyrdoms, and evidences of the
results of faith, amongst the books of all who belong to the Catholic
Church."—*Genealogist.*

FORMBY, REV. HENRY.

Monotheism : in the main derived from the Hebrew
nation and the Law of Moses. The Primitive Religion of the City of Rome. An historical Investiga-
tion. Demy 8vo. 0 5 0

FRANCIS DE SALES, ST. : THE WORKS OF.

Translated into the English Language by the Rev.
H. B. Mackey, O.S.B., under the direction of the
Right Rev. Bishop Hedley, O.S.B. . . .
Vol. I. Letters to Persons in the World. Cloth . 0 6 0

"The letters must be read in order to comprehend the charm and
sweetness of their style."—*Tablet.*

Vol. II.—The Treatise on the Love of God. Father
Carr's translation of 1630 has been taken as a basis,
but it has been modernized and thoroughly revised
and corrected. 0 9 0

"To those who are seeking perfection by the path of contemplation
this volume will be an armoury of help."—*Saturday Review.*

Vol. III. The Catholic Controversy. . . . 0 6 0

"No one who has not read it can conceive how clear, how convinc-
ing, and how well adapted to our present needs are these controversial
'leaves.'"—*Tablet.*

FRANCIS DE SALES, ST.: WORKS OF.—*continued.*

Vol. IV. Letters to Persons in Religion, with introduction by Bishop Hedley on "St. Francis de Sales
and the Religious State." £0 6 0

"The sincere piety and goodness, the grave wisdom, the knowledge
of human nature, the tenderness for its weakness, and the desire for
its perfection that pervade the letters, make them pregnant of instruction for all serious persons. The translation and editing have
been admirably done."—*Scotsman.*

*** Other vols. in preparation.

GALLWEY, REV. PETER (S.J.)

Precious Pearl of Hope in the Mercy of God, The.
Translated from the Italian. With Preface by the
Rev. Father Gallwey. Cloth. 0 4 6

Lectures on Ritualism and on the Anglican Orders. 0 8 0
2 vols.
Or may be had separately.

GIBSON, REV. H.

Catechism Made Easy. Being an Explanation of the
Christian Doctrine. Fourth edition. 2 vols., cloth 0 7 6

"This work must be of priceless worth to any who are engaged in
any form of catechetical instruction. It is the best book of the kind
that we have seen in English."—*Irish Monthly.*

GILLOW, JOSEPH.

Literary and Biographical History, or, Bibliographical
Dictionary of the English Catholics. From the
Breach with Rome, in 1534, to the Present Time.
Vols. I., II. and III. cloth, demy 8vo . . *each.* 0 15 0

*** Other vols. in preparation.

"The patient research of Mr. Gillow, his conscientious record of
minute particulars, and especially his exhaustive bibliographical information in connection with each name, are beyond praise."—*British
Quarterly Review.*

"No such important or novel contribution has been made to English
bibliography for a long time."—*Scotsman.*

The Haydock Papers. Illustrated. Demy 8vo. . 0 7 6

HEDLEY, BISHOP.

Our Divine Saviour, and other Discourses. Crown
8vo. 0 6 0

"A distinct and noteworthy feature of these sermons is, we certainly think, their freshness—freshness of thought, treatment, and
style; nowhere do we meet pulpit commonplace or hackneyed phrase
—everywhere, on the contrary, it is the heart of the preacher pouring
out to his flock his own deep convictions, enforcing them from the
'Treasures, old and new,' of a cultivated mind."—*Dublin Review.*

HUMPHREY, REV. W. (S.J.)

Suarez on the Religious State: A Digest of the Doctrine contained in his Treatise, "De Statû Religionis."
3 vols., pp. 1200. Cloth, roy. 8vo. . . . 1 10 0

"This laborious and skilfully executed work is a distinct addition
to English theological literature. Father Humphrey's style is quiet,
methodical, precise, and as clear as the subject admits. Every one
will be struck with the air of legal exposition which pervades the
book. He takes a grip of his author, under which the text yield
up every atom of its meaning and force."—*Dublin Review.*

LEE, REV. F. G., D.D. (of All Saints, Lambeth.)

Edward the Sixth : Supreme Head. Second edition. Crown 8vo £0 6 0

"In vivid interest and in literary power, no less than in solid historical value, Dr. Lee's present work comes fully up to the standard of its predecessors ; and to say that is to bestow high praise. The book evinces Dr. Lee's customary diligence of research in amassing facts, and his rare artistic power in welding them into a harmonious and effective whole."—*John Bull.*

LIFE OF FATHER CHAMPAGNAT

Founder of the Society of the Little Brothers of Mary. Containing a portrait of Fr. CHAMPAGNAT, and four full page illustrations. Demy 8vo 0 8 0

"A work of great practical utility, and one eminently suited to these times."—*Tablet.*

"A serious and able essay on the science and art of the Christian education of children, exemplified in the career of one who gave his life to it."—*Dublin Review.*

LIGUORI, ST. ALPHONSUS.

New and Improved Translation of the Complete Works of St. Alphonsus, edited by the late Bishop Coffin :—
Vol. I. The Christian Virtues, and the Means for Obtaining them. Cloth elegant 0 4 0
Or separately :—
1. The Love of our Lord Jesus Christ . . . 0 1 4
2. Treatise on Prayer. *(In the ordinary editions a great part of this work is omitted)* . . . 0 1 4
3. A Christian's rule of Life 0 1 0
Vol. II. The Mysteries of the Faith—The Incarnation ; containing Meditations and Devotions on the Birth and Infancy of Jesus Christ, &c., suited for Advent and Christmas. 0 3 6
Cheap edition 0 2 0
Vol. III. The Mysteries of the Faith—The Blessed Sacrament 0 3 6
Cheap edition 0 2 0
Vol. IV. Eternal Truths—Preparation for Death . 0 3 6
Cheap edition 0 2 0
Vol. V. Treatises on the Passion, containing "Jesus hath loved us," &c. 0 3 0
Cheap edition 0 2 0
Vol. VI. Glories of Mary. New edition . . . 0 3 6
With Frontispiece, cloth 0 4 6
Also in better bindings.

LIVIUS, REV. T. (M.A.,C.SS.R.)

St. Peter, Bishop of Rome ; or, the Roman Episcopate of the Prince of the Apostles, proved from the Fathers, History and Chronology, and illustrated by arguments from other sources. Dedicated to his Eminence Cardinal Newman. Demy 8vo, cloth . 0 12 0

LIVIUS, REV. T. (M.A., C.SS.R.)—*continued*.

Explanation of the Psalms and Canticles in the Divine
Office. By ST. ALPHONSUS LIGUORI. Translated
from the Italian by THOMAS LIVIUS, C.SS.R.
With a Preface by his Eminence Cardinal MANNING.
Crown 8vo, cloth £0   7   6

MANNING CARDINAL.

Blessed Sacrament the Centre of Immutable Truth. Second edition	o	1	o
Confidence in God. Fourth edition	o	1	o
England and Christendom	o	10	6
Eternal Priesthood. Seventh Edition . . .	o	2	6
Four Great Evils of the Day. Fifth Edition. Paper	o	2	6
Cloth	o	3	6
Fourfold Sovereignty of God. Third edition Paper	o	2	6
Cloth	o	3	6
Glories of the Sacred Heart. Fourth edition. .	o	6	o
Grounds of Faith. Seventh edition. . . .	o	1	6
Holy Gospel of our Lord Jesus Christ according to St. John. With a Preface by His Eminence. . ;	o	1	o
Religio Viatoris. Third Edition. Wrapper. .	o	1	o
Cloth. :	o	2	o
Independence of the Holy See. Second Edition. .	o	5	o
Internal Mission of the Holy Ghost. Fourth edition .	o	8	6
Love of Jesus to Penitents. Seventh edition . .	o	1	6
Miscellanies. 3 vols. . . . . each	o	6	o
Office of the Holy Ghost under the Gospel . . .	o	1	o
Petri Privilegium	o	10	6
Praise, A Sermon on ; with an Indulgenced Devotion.	o	1	o
Sermons on Ecclesiastical Subjects. Vols. I. II. and III. . . . . each	o	6	o
Sin and its Consequences. Sixth edition . . .	o	6	o
Temporal Mission of the Holy Ghost. Third edition .	o	8	6
Temporal Power of the Pope. Third edition . .	o	5	o
The Office of the Church in Higher Education . .	o	o	6
True Story of the Vatican Council. Second Edition .	o	5	o

MANNING, CARDINAL, Edited by.

Life of the Curé of Ars.   New edition, enlarged.   o   4   o

MIVART, PROF. ST. GEORGE (M.D., F.R.S.)

Nature and Thought.   Second edition . . .   o   4   o

"The complete command of the subject, the wide grasp, the
subtlety, the readiness of illustration, the grace of style, contrive
to render this one of the most admirable books of its class."—
British Quarterly Review.

A Philosophical Catechism.   Fifth edition .   o   1   o

"It should become the *vade mecum* of Catholic students."—*Tablet.*

MONTGOMERY, HON. MRS.

Approved by the Most Rev. George Porter, Archbishop of Bombay.

The Divine Sequence: A Treatise on Creation and Redemption. Cloth	£0	3	6
The Eternal Years. With an Introduction by the Most Rev. George Porter, Archbishop of Bombay. Cloth	0	3	6
The Divine Ideal. Cloth	0	3	6

"A work of original thought carefully developed and expressed in lucid and richly imaged style."—*Tablet.*

"The writing of a pious, thoughtful, earnest woman."—*Church Review.*

"Full of truth, and sound reason, and confidence."—*American Catholic Book News.*

MORRIS, REV. JOHN (S.J.)

Letter Books of Sir Amias Poulet, keeper of Mary Queen of Scots. Demy 8vo	0	10	6
Troubles of our Catholic Forefathers, related by themselves. Second Series. 8vo, cloth.	0	14	0
Third Series	0	14	0
The Life of Father John Gerard, S.J. Third edition, rewritten and enlarged	0	14	0
The Life and Martyrdom of St. Thomas Becket. Second and enlarged edition. In one volume, large post 8vo, cloth, pp. xxxvi., 632,	0	12	6
or bound in two parts, cloth	0	13	0

MURPHY, J. N.

Chair of Peter. Third edition, with the statistics, &c., brought down to the present day. 720 pages. Crown 8vo	0	6	0

"In a series of clearly written chapters, precise in statement, excellently temperate in tone, the author deals with just those questions regarding the power, claims, and history of the Roman Pontiff which are at the present time of most actual interest."—*Dublin Review.*

NEWMAN, CARDINAL.

Annotated Translation of Athanasius. 2 vols. each	0	7	6
Apologia pro Vitâ suâ	0	6	0
Arians of the Fourth Century, The	0	6	0
Callista. An Historical Tale.	0	5	6
Difficulties of Anglicans. Two volumes—			
Vol. I. Twelve Lectures.	0	7	6
Vol. II. Letter to Dr. Pusey and to the Duke of Norfolk	0	5	6
Discussions and Arguments	0	6	0
Doctrine of Justification	0	5	0
Dream of Gerontius	0	0	6
Essay on Assent	0	7	6
Essay on the Development of Christian Doctrine	0	6	0

NEWMAN, CARDINAL—*continued.*

	£	s	d
Essays Critical and Historical. Two volumes, with Notes . . . . . . each	0	6	0
Essays on Miracles, Two. 1. Of Scripture. 2. Of Ecclesiastical History	0	6	0
Historical Sketches. Three volumes . . . each	0	6	0
Idea of a University. Lectures and Essays . .	0	7	0
Loss and Gain. Ninth Edition	0	5	6
Occasional Sermons	0	6	0
Parochial and Plain-Sermons. Eight volumes. . each	0	5	0
Present Position of Catholics in England. . .	0	7	0
Sermons on Subjects of the Day. . . .	0	5	0
Sermons to Mixed Congregations . . .	0	6	0
Theological Tracts	0	8	0
University Sermons	0	5	0
Verses on Various Occasions.	0	5	6
Via Media. Two volumes, with Notes . . each	0	6	0

NORTHCOTE, VERY REV. J. S. (D.D.)

Roma Sotterranea; or, An Account of the Roman Catacombs. New edition. Re-written and greatly enlarged. This work is in three volumes, which may at present be had separately—

	£	s	d
Vol. I. History	1	4	0
Vol. II. Christian Art.	1	4	0
Vol. III. Epitaphs of the Catacombs .	0	10	0
The Second and Third Volumes may also be had bound together in cloth	1	12	0
Visit to the Roman Catacombs: Being a popular abridgment of the larger work. . . .	0	4	0
Mary in the Gospels	0	3	6

POPE, THOMAS ALDER, M.A. (of the Oratory.)

	£	s	d
Life of St. Philip Neri, Apostle of Rome. From the Italian of Alfonso Capecelatro. 2 vols . . .	0	15	0

"No former life has given us so full a knowledge of the surround-ings of St. Philip. . . . To those who have not read the original we can say, with the greatest confidence, that they will find in these two well-edited volumes a very large store of holy reading and of in-teresting history,"—*Dublin Review.*

QUARTERLY SERIES (Edited by the Rev. H. J. Coleridge, S.J.)

	£	s	d
Baptism of the King: Considerations on the Sacred Passion. By the Rev. H. J. Coleridge, S.J. . .	0	7	6
Christian Reformed in mind and Manners, The. By Benedict Rogacci, of the Society of Jesus. The Translation edited by the Rev. H. J. Coleridge, S.J.	0	7	6
Chronicles of St. Antony of Padua, the "Eldest Son of St. Francis." Edited by the Rev. H. J. Cole-ridge, S.J.	0	3	6
Colombière, Life of the Ven. Claude de la . . .	0	5	0

QUARTERLY SERIES—*continued.*

Dialogues of St. Gregory the Great : an Old English
Version. Edited by the Rev. H. J. Coleridge, S. J. £0 6 0
During the Persecution. Autobiography of Father
John Gerard, S.J. Translated from the original
Latin by the Rev. G. R. Kingdon, S.J. . . . 0 5 0
English Carmelite, An. The Life of Catherine Burton,
Mother Mary Xaveria of the Angels, of the English
Teresian Convent at Antwerp. Collected from
her own Writings, and other sources, by Father
Thomas Hunter, S.J. 0 6 0
Gaston de Ségur. A Biography. Condensed from
the French Memoir by the Marquis de Ségur, by
F. J. M. A. Partridge 0 3 6
Gracious Life, A (1566--1618); being the Life of
Madame Acarie (Blessed Mary of the Incarnation),
of the Reformed Order of our Blessed Lady of
Mount Carmel. By Emily Bowles. . . . 0 6 0
History of the Sacred Passion. By Father Luis de la
Palma, of the Society of Jesus. Translated from
the Spanish. With Preface by the Rev. H. J.
Coleridge, S.J. Third edition . . . 0 5 0
Holy Infancy Series. By the Rev. H. J. Coleridge, S.J.
Vol. I. Preparation of the Incarnation . . 0 7 6
,, II. The Nine Months. Life of our Lord in
the Womb 0 7 6
,, III. The Thirty Years. Our Lord's Infancy
and Hidden Life 0 7 6
Hours of the Passion. Taken from the Life of Christ
by Ludolph the Saxon 0 7 6
Life and Teaching of Jesus Christ, in Meditations for
every Day in the Year. By P.N. Avancino, S. J. 2 vols. 0 10 6
Life and Letters of St. Francis Xavier. By the Rev.
H. J. Coleridge, S.J. 2 vols. 0 10 6
Life of Anne Catherine Emmerich. By Helen Ram.
With Preface by the Rev. H. J. Coleridge, S.J. 0 5 0
Life of Christopher Columbus. By the Rev. A. G.
Knight, S.J. 0 6 0
Life of Henrietta d'Osseville (in Religion, Mother Ste.
Marie), Foundress. of the Institute of the Faithful
Virgin. Arranged and edited by the Rev. John
George M'Leod, S.J. 0 5 6
Life of Margaret Mostyn (Mother Margaret of Jesus),
Religious of the Reformed Order of our Blessed Lady
of Mount Carmel (1625-1679). By the Very Rev.
Edmund Bedingfield. Edited from the Manuscripts
preserved at Darlington, by the Rev. H. J. Cole-
ridge, S.J 0 6 0
Life of our Life : The Harmony of the Gospel, arranged
with Introductory and Explanatory Chapters, Notes
and Indices. By the Rev. H. J. Coleridge, S.J.
2 vols. (out of print) 0 15 0

QUARTERLY SERIES—*continued.*

Life of the Blessed John Berchmans. Third edition.
By the Rev. F. Goldie, S.J. £0 6 0

Life of the Blessed Peter Favre, First Companion of
St. Ignatius Loyola. From the Italian of Father
Boero. (Out of print). 0 6 6

Life of King Alfred the Great. By Rev. A. G. Knight,
S.J. Book I. Early Promise; II. Adversity; III.
Prosperity; IV. Close of Life. . . . 0 6 0

Life of Mother Mary Teresa Ball. By Rev. H. J.
Coleridge, S.J. With Portrait 0 6 6

Life of St. Jane Frances Fremyot de Chantal. By Emily
Bowles. Third Edition 0 5 0

Life of St. Bridget of Sweden. By the late F. J. M.
A. Partridge . . . . 0 . 6 0

Life and Letters of St. Teresa. 3 vols. By Rev. H.
J. Coleridge, S.J. . . . . . each 0 7 6

Life of Mary Ward. By Mary Catherine Elizabeth
Chambers, of the Institute of the Blessed Virgin.
Edited by the Rev. H. J. Coleridge, S.J. 2 vols.,
each 0 7 6

Life of Jane Dormer, Duchess of Feria. By Henry
Clifford. Transcribed from the Ancient Manuscript
in the possession of the Lord Dormer, by the late
Canon E. E. Estcourt, and edited by the Rev.
Joseph Stevenson, S.J. 0 5 0

Mother of the King, The. By the Rev. H. J. Coleridge, S.J. 0 7 6

Mother of the Church. "Sequel to Mother of the King." 0 6 0

Of Adoration in Spirit and Truth. By the Rev. J. E.
Nieremberg. S.J. Old English translation. With a
Preface by the Rev. P. Gallwey, S.J. A New
Edition 0 6 6

Pious Affections towards God and the Saints. Meditations for every Day in the Year, and for the
Principal Festivals. From the Latin of the Ven.
Nicholas Lancicius, S.J. With Preface by Archbishop George Porter, S.J. 0 7 6

Prisoners of the King, a book of thoughts on the doctrine of Purgatory. By the Rev. H. J. Coleridge,
S.J. New Edition. 0 5 0

Public Life of our Lord Jesus Christ. By the Rev.
H. J. Coleridge, S.J. vols 1 to 9 . . . each 0 6 6
Vols 10 and 11 . . . . . . each 0 6 0

Return of the King. Discourses on the Latter Days.
By the Rev. H. J. Coleridge, S.J. . . . 0 7 6

St. Mary's Convent, Micklegate Bar, York. A
History of the Convent. Edited by the Rev. H.J.
Coleridge, S.J. 0 7 6

Story of St. Stanislaus Kostka. With Preface by the
Rev. H. J. Coleridge, S.J. 0 3 6

QUARTERLY SERIES—*continued.*

Story of the Gospels, harmonised for meditation. By the Rev. H. J. Coleridge, S.J. £0 7 6

Works and Words of our Saviour, gathered from the Four Gospels. By the Rev. H. J. Coleridge, S.J. . o 7 6

Sufferings of the Church in Brittany during the Great Revolution. By Edward Healy Thompson, M.A. o 6 6

Suppression of the Society of Jesus in the Portuguese Dominions. From Documents hitherto unpublished. By the Rev. Alfred Weld, S.J. . . . . o 7 6
[This volume forms the First Part of the General History of the Suppression of the Society.]

Teaching and Counsels of St. Francis Xavier. Gathered from his letters. Edited by the Rev. H. J. Coleridge, S.J. . . . . o 5 o

Three Catholic Reformers of the fifteenth Century. By Mary H. Allies. . . . . . o 6 o

Thomas of Hereford, Life of St. By Fr. Lestrange . o 6 o

Tribunal of Conscience, The. By Father Gasper Druzbicki, S.J. . . . . o 3 6

RAWES, THE LATE REV. Fr., Edited by.

The Library of the Holy Ghost:—
Vol. I. St. Thomas Aquinas on the Adorable Sacrament of the Altar. With Prayers and Thanksgivings for Holy Communion. Red cloth . . . o 5 o
Little Books of the Holy Ghost:—(List on application.)

RICHARDS, REV. WALTER J. B. (D.D.)

Manual of Scripture History. Being an Analysis of the Historical Books of the Old Testament. By the Rev. W. J. B. Richards, D.D., Oblate of St. Charles ; Inspector of Schools in the Diocese of Westminster. Cloth . . . . o 4 o
"Happy indeed will those children and young persons be who acquire in their early days the inestimably precious knowledge which these books impart."—*Tablet.*

RYDER, REV. H. I. D. (of the Oratory.)

Catholic Controversy: A Reply to Dr. Littledale's "Plain Reasons." Sixth edition . . . o 2 6
"Father Ryder of the Birmingham Oratory, has now furnished in a small volume a masterly reply to this assailant from without. The lighter charms of a brilliant and graceful style are added to the solid merits of this handbook of contemporary controversy."—*Irish Monthly.*

SOULIER, REV. P.

Life of St. Philip Benizi, of the Order of the Servants of Mary. Crown 8vo . . . . . o 8 o
"A clear and interesting account of the life and labours of this eminent Servant of Mary."—*American Catholic Quarterly.*
"Very scholar-like, devout and complete."—*Dublin Review.*

STANTON, REV. R. (of the Oratory.)

A Menology of England and Wales ; or, Brief Memorials of the British and English Saints, arranged according to the Calendar. Together with the Martyrs of the 16th and 17th centuries. Compiled by order of the Cardinal Archbishop and the Bishops of the Province of Westminster.   Demy 8vo, cloth   £0 14 0

THOMPSON, EDWARD HEALY, (M.A.)

The Life of Jean-Jacques Olier, Founder of the Seminary of St. Sulpice. New and Enlarged Edition. Post 8vo, cloth, pp. xxxvi. 628   .   .   .   .   0 15 0

" It provides us with just what we most need, a model to look up to and imitate ; one whose circumstances and surroundings were sufficiently like our own to admit of an easy and direct application to our own personal duties and daily occupations."—*Dublin Review.*

The Life and Glories of St. Joseph, Husband of Mary, Foster-Father of Jesus, and Patron of the Universal Church. Grounded on the Dissertations of Canon Antonio Vitalis, Father José Moreno, and other writers. Crown 8vo, cloth, pp. xxvi., 488,   .   .   0 6 0

ULLATHORNE, BISHOP.

Endowments of Man, &c. Popular edition.   0 7 0
Groundwork of the Christian Virtues : do.   0 7 0
Christian Patience,   .   . do. do.   0 7 0
Ecclesiastical Discourses 0 6 0
Memoir of Bishop Willson.   .   .   .   0 2 6

WARD, WILFRID.

The Clothes of Religion. A reply to popular Positivism   0 3 6
"Very witty and interesting."—*Spectator.*
"Really models of what such essays should be."—*Church Quarterly Review.*

WATERWORTH, REV. J.

The Canons and Decrees of the Sacred and Œcumenical Council of Trent, celebrated under the Sovereign Pontiffs, Paul III., Julius III., and Pius IV., translated by the Rev. J. WATERWORTH. To which are prefixed Essays on the External and Internal History of the Council. A new edition. Demy, 8vo, cloth 0 10 6

WISEMAN, CARDINAL.

Fabiola. A Tale of the Catacombs. . . 3s. 6d. and   0 4 0
Also a new and splendid edition printed on large quarto paper, embellished with thirty-one full-page illustrations, and a coloured portrait of St. Agnes. Handsomely bound. 1 1 0